7.
Lin

HEATHEN VALLEY

Heathen Valley

a Novel

ROMULUS LINNEY

SHOEMAKER & HOARD

Washington, D.C.

Library of Congress Cataloging-in-Publication Data
Linney, Romulus, 1930–
Heathen Valley : a novel / Romulus Linney.— 1st Shoemaker & Hoard ed.
p. cm.
ISBN 1-59376-012-4
1. Valle Crucis Region (N.C.)—Fiction. 2. North Carolina—Fiction.
3. Mountain life—Fiction. 4. Missionaries—Fiction.
5. Evangelists—Fiction. 6. Bishops—Fiction. I. Title.
PS3562.I55 H35 2004
813'.54—dc22
2003025206

Book design by Mark McGarry, Texas Type & Book Works
Set in Dante

Printed in the United States of America

Shoemaker & Hoard
A Division of Avalon Publishing Group Inc.
Distributed by Publishers Group West

10 9 8 7 6 5 4 3 2 1

Contents

Prologue

ALL JOIN HANDS

THE DEW leans heavy on the grass, pressing it down. Mary's Peak has vanished in the night and the mist is on the slopes, leaving only the tops of my hickories moonlit now. Past them, down there in that scooped-out, blackdirt valley, I can see the broken stones, wet and slick from the rain. They are reflecting the moon that just came out, that peers down through the mist like a delicate lady trying to find somebody in a crowd.

It was hot this morning. I was in the field, sweating and thirsting. I was wishing for a night like this one, heavy, final, soaked through by afternoon rains, cool and silent. It has eased me somewhat. My eyes don't hurt me like they did. Like they did this morning when it was so hot, when I looked up and saw them all again, where they walked and chatted and squabbled and knelt years ago.

I was bending over to cut a brown cabbage leaf when it came about. The sweat off my face rolled down my chin and I raised up too quick. There was a buzzing somewhere at the back of my head. My legs shook and I went down on one knee and there they were, walking toward me and smiling.

I blinked at them, and some blinks the men wore work jeans and linseys, some blinks the long frock coats from the city, some blinks the black cassocks with the dangling rope belts, while behind them, at the mission house, bonnet-headed women waved their fans from the porch.

Then the sweat ran in my eyes and stung. I was standing in timothy grass with the wind all in it, so I watched that for a while, then looked again and they were gone. The valley was empty again, just me and nobody else.

I dried off my face and blew my nose. Blew it too hard maybe, I don't know, anyhow I got dizzy all over again and saw them trudging along once more, cheerful as the day. I saw the Bishop slap Starns on the shoulder, call him "Nestor"; saw Juba giving Tate Benson a mouthful and him shaking his head at her, mad; saw Cora with her legs apart like a man standing across Two Rivers; and then, down in the far hollow, Harlan plowing for wheat with little Jean on his shoulders, her thin whiteblond hair blown out behind them by the wind.

I had to let my cabbages be, go home in the morning, and lie down.

The rain dripped off the leaves all afternoon, and the wind spattered its drops on the steps of my porch. I sat there and thought about them. I got up once and went in the cabin to go down into the cedar chest. I burrowed down past the coverlid Cora gave me once, past the mothragged blue uniform I wore in the war, down the years my shaking hands fumbled until they touched the bottom of the chest, where they found what they were after. A cigar box, and in it a sheet of yellowed paper, folded twice, and slipped inside it a strip of dry leather with a tarnished belt buckle clipped onto one end. I took them back out on the porch, rocked in my chair and studied them.

The yellow paper was his first official note to the mission, the first of many. At the top was his title and office: "Right Reverend Nahum Immanuel Ames, S.T.D., LL.D., Bishop." Then his first list, written out in the elaborate script of his time. I read it again.

1. By oral catechism, teach the fundamentals of our Christian faith.
2. Conduct three services daily. Upon arising, before the noon meal, before the evening meal. Prayers before sleep.
3. Teach the fundamentals of grammar and simple calculation.
4. To those who are able to receive them, teach the classical subjects.
5. Search out the human material from which a native mountain ministry may be formed.

6. Devote two full hours each day to the physical improvement of the mission, that is, to hard manual labor.

7. One evening each week if they desire it, though I do not think they will, the boys may visit their homes.

Then, underneath, his greetings and best wishes and this note:

Marcus, if you can do it, try to get at least one barn up and whatever sheds are needed and one springhouse. In the spring I will be with you. We will plant then and see to the orchards, livestock, and so on. I am sending a man up to help you in April, but I won't tell you who he is except that it will be a surprise. But I have no doubts he will work hard, as we all must work hard, to make this mission an independent colony, worthy of the task it has taken up for the glory of God.

Then his warm wishes again and signature, sweeping across the page.

"In the spring I will be with you," he wrote. On my rain-spotted porch, looking down on the empty valley, I counted the spring winds that have come and gone since he left us forever, and I thought, That's what you get when you speak in Christlike phrases.

I folded the yellow paper up again and set it down by the rocker, holding on to the scrap of leather. It was dry and crumbling at the edges, the buckle was thick with green tarnish, but both silver buckle and tough leather were still there, useful even now if need be. They lay together by Starns's hand the night he died. I pulled at the leather. Weak as I am, I knew it was still good, could be used as a patch or something, that a stronger pull would not tear it.

I got up and put them back in the cigar box, laid it on the bottom of the cedar chest, pausing a minute to finger the heavy quilt Cora brought me when I was sick. I think she told me it was the one belonged to Harlan's first wife, Margaret, who wove it on her own loom, something Cora could never learn to do. The fabric was sound and thick, embroidered with little trees that dangled tiny apples of scarlet thread. I closed the chest.

In the evening I sat on my porch, feeling sorry for myself. Once I thought I heard the foot organ going, and I let my mouth fall open in a big grin, thinking it was Rachael playing again in the afternoon, me pumping it for her. But the sound passed away, changed and came back again, and I knew it was only the noise of Carson's Fall, the waters swollen from the rain, pouring down Sand Mountain. I drank whisky, felt sorry for myself, smoked some and drank some more and thought that I was no good at last, weak in my head, that I just couldn't go on keeping the land up any longer. Good for nothing, I said.

But the night objected to that, wouldn't let me say so without a second thought. And through the dusk the mighty valley itself leaned down on my porch, saying, Reconsider, old man, reconsider, Billy Cobb. You're good for something, all right, you are good for me. Soon now you will come back into me and make grow what I want to grow. Out of you I will send up dandelions and laurel, which I like better than your cabbages, which I will have of you when your fields grow them no more, when you see your loved ones here no longer.

I didn't answer, because I didn't care to think about it that way. The sun went down and I was too tired to do a thing, too tired to fix my supper, even. I sat and watched the mist and I drank and smoked.

I saw them one more time. I had dozed off in my chair and when I opened my eyes I saw one of them standing in the yard. Then the rest walked up the slope to the cabin, one by one, looking at me and saying not a word. There was some I had forgotten about, or thought I had, John Barco, Clayton Gaines and the like, men I hardly knew at all. They came through the mist and stopped and waved to me from the yard. Cora was there, Grandpa Jacob calling her snarly bitch, Harlan with Jean on his shoulders, Tate and Juba and their two boys, Marcus Sales looking at his black hands, and then the Bishop himself, the gray mist crawling up and down his arms and the back of his dark frock coat like smoke.

And finally Starns, who spoke to me. I didn't hear him at first. I leaned forward in my chair and said: "What was that, Starns?"

And he said: "I'm sorry to bother you, but I'm looking for my own. They live around here somewhere. Can you tell me where?"

And into the night I said: "You know I can't tell you that, Starns. I wish I could."

And he said: "I'm sorry to trouble you," and then he went into the mist, and we all watched him go.

Now they all look at me and I know it is time for me to come down from my porch and join them. But I will sit here for just a little while, remembering everything, watching them in the mist and the gray rain.

Part One

HEATHEN

1

STARNS

FOR HIS BIRTH the bed was pushed closer to the fireplace, its warmth helped him into the world. He was the seventh child of his mother, the second to live. There was an older brother named Henry, he was William, later there was a sister, whose name he never knew.

The chimney of the cabin was made of sticks, daubed inside and out with clay. When a fire burned in the fireplace, the clay went soft and warm, and from the time he learned to crawl and to know what firelight was, a favorite path led across the dirt floor to the chimney. There, with a grubby forefinger, he would gouge out a lump of clay and put it in his mouth.

"Clay-eating already," said his mother the first time she caught him at it. She looked at the father, then at their meal of ground corn and coffee, and said nothing more. In the cold night, sometimes, she went to the fireplace herself.

The cabin measured fourteen by fifteen feet. Its walls were unhewn logs, warped and twisted. They had been cut from timber still dripping with sap and thrown up at once. They had warped immediately. Now the wind raced through the walls without stopping. The cabin floor, dirt packed down, was a littered battleground of filth reaching out the door, always left open, and scattering itself on the surrounding land. There was one bed for them all.

His father had run away from fighting, that is the reason they were

there. He had come to the mountains with his young wife, childless
then, to hide out where no one would bother them. He left behind him
a murdered uncle, a crippled brother he had grown up running with, a
first wife and child shot to pieces, in the arms and legs first, the head
later, an Indian trick done with rifles then instead of knives.

Around the cabin the mountain slopes rose imperious and steep.
Lonely blackbirds, ravens sometimes, played on the updrafts. Faraway
gunshots, when heard at all, sounded like the snapping of twigs. They
stayed, grateful for a silence that made up for many lost things.

One morning his brother Henry ran away. He was not in the cabin
anymore. Nothing was said. William did not think about it much at
first, but in a few days he asked about his brother, who had been good
to him, and he was told: "Don't fret."

When he was older, he left the cabin, too, taking its lessons with
him. Already his thin face was bland and set. No longer childish, though
he was only twelve, it masked a passion common to mountain children.
He took it from his father: a scorn and deep loathing for those who run
and sweat and pick and haul to avert for a few years the certainties of
death and dissolution.

Now his mother worked all day and very hard, in both the cabin and
the field. This was right. A woman was made to yield, not to a man, but
to the clouded vision of one more day's food, clothing. But his father,
his clear-eyed father, was not so easily fooled. He negligently farmed a
few slanting acres of stump corn, kept five or six razorback hogs, two
mules. He wanted nothing more, so William thought, and when they
would come home after a visit to the store in the hollow William felt his
father's scorn for those with whom they had traded, and cherished it.

A man did not scurry when the crop-blasting storms came, the hell
with them. He did not fool himself into the fool's belief that tomorrow's bounty changed anything. He did not fearfully spin or furrow,
only to have such labor's gain ripped from his hands the day after
tomorrow. He did not scramble for the land's begrudged handouts of
corn and wheat and fruit. To William, his father's eyes were bold and
clear, free from the frightening looks he saw on those trips, in the desperate eyes of the industrious.

He watched his father throw seed at the ground and turn his back on it. For this he loved and respected his father. He never once questioned the taste of the clay.

He was thirteen when the circuit rider came by. The man rode his horse into the cabin yard, yelled: "Praise to Christ!" and fell out of the saddle, drunk. He had a high fever, diseased lungs and a crumbling set of vital organs eaten away by harsh whisky. William's mother insisted on tending to the man. She fed him corn mush and boneset tea, and he repaid them by reading the Bible. William would sit by him while he read, fascinated by the picture in the book of the man in the long white dress, with curly golden hair that touched his shoulders. So when the circuit rider was well enough to leave, he asked to take the boy with him.

It was a swift thing, but the boy saw it. His mother wanted him to go, his father wanted him to stay. He waited while they looked at each other.

Then his father pursed his lips and said: "Well, maybe he'd be glad to go. William?"

That was enough. "Yessir," he said. Then, to the circuit rider: "I don't want to cause no trouble."

"Proud to have ye," said the circuit rider. "Only thing, ye'll have to ride something of ye own. My mare's too old for the both of us."

With his father he made a makeshift harness for one of the mules. They patched it together from scraps of rope and bits of leather. When it was done, the father considered it a moment, then unsnapped the silver buckle of the belt he always wore, the shining silver buckle William had watched as he grew up beside his father. He cut a strip of leather from the belt and laced it onto the bit, making a noseband for the mule. The bridle would have been fine without it, it wasn't needed. William's heart sank as he watched his father take such pains with the thing, slipping it carefully over the mule's nose, tightening it twice. Only then did he realize that his father was actually giving him one of the mules. He was amazed, and hurt. When he tried to thank him, he got no answer, and when it was time to go, his father just went into the cabin and shut the door that was always left open.

William did not exactly want to go, he just did, mostly because his father had said he might want to; anyway, he went, carrying over his shoulder a hemp bag that held a pair of shoes given proudly by his mother, who cautioned him to wear them only when he walked in a door. Then take them off, son, when ye come out. That's what the bag's for. He had one shirt, a loose homespun coat, baggy patched trousers and two eyes burning with a pure and deadly sense of fatality.

They hadn't gone two miles before the circuit rider tried to steal the mule. William had been expecting it, had cut himself a thick hemlock stick. He laid it across the preacher's chest, knocked him down, then helped him up again. They went on together, repeating the ritual several times as the days became weeks, as the mountains fell into hills and then long, gentle mounds, untenanted and brush-choked: the middle of the Carolinas in the 1830's.

The preacher had suddenly bolted his mare ahead, gone up to the top of a hillock, where he stood up in his stirrups and looked around. Now he was back with William again, the mare breathing hard, the preacher's eyes shining.

"Hold up right here," he said. "I mean it, now, don't ye move. And lend me that big stick of yours. Naw, by the Holy Ghost, I won't betray ye with it. All right, thank ye. Stay here, now, I'll be back directly."

He slipped the hemlock rod down his left leg into the stirrup, kicked the mare again and bounced away, going over the mound out of sight. William scratched his head, frowned, then drew up his legs and stood on the bare back of the mule. He still couldn't see where the preacher had gone. "C'mon!" he said. His legs flew out and kicked the mule as he slipped down on its back again, and he rode up to where he could see over.

The preacher was sitting his mare with a big smile on his face, one leg slung casually over the frayed saddle horn. He was holding his big Bible in one hand and waving it as he talked. A few feet away from him was a traveler on a big reddish-brown roan, stopped to hear him. The man had a thick beard, looked pretty old. The roan was a vigorous, handsome horse, restless at the meeting, shying sideways and back. William couldn't hear what they were saying, but after a minute the preacher had his Bible open, pointing in it with one finger. The traveler then reached into a saddlebag and pulled out a Bible of his own. He opened it and turned the pages, holding them down with his palm in the wind.

The traveler read some, then shook his head. The preacher nodded sharply and pointed in his Bible again. The traveler caught his reins up short around the roan's neck and walked him next to the preacher, who held out his Bible. The traveler looked into it.

The hemlock stick whirred in the air. William saw it hit, a second later heard the soft thud of its impact on the traveler's neck.

"C'mon!" His legs flew out and slammed against the mule, his arms jerked the bridle around. In a minute he was back behind the hill, waiting, his face bland and set. The preacher took a few minutes, but soon came riding fast. He was on the big roan, wearing a glossy new coat, black and about four sizes too big for him.

"All right, here's your stick, boy. I thank ye, I shore do. Now, come on with me, we got the Lord's work to do now. Things to do and a place to go, that's right."

William took the stick, wiped blood and hair off it against the sweaty flanks of the mule. He stared at it a minute, then followed the galloping roan, the preacher on it singing a hymn.

He thought it must be all the people in the world, all come together. They came in buggies and wagons, by horse and mule and on foot. Some brought food and spread picnics, but most just stood around and eyed each other curiously, with looks that were hungry and shy. All around the sides of the great open field were small tents, set up this way and that for the night. It was still early in the afternoon when William followed the preacher into the campground, trying to remember what the preacher had told him to do.

They rode up to a log structure in the center of the field, with two graceful oaks left standing beside it. William couldn't understand what the thing was for, he had never seen anything like it. It was a big box with half its front cut out, made of smooth, scored logs, with a roof, a long bench inside, a railing across the cut opening with a flat plank running its length and another bench outside. William couldn't make much out of it, it looked like a big animal trap of some kind. On the ground facing it, still more benches. On them sat the hungry-eyed people, glancing at each other, then the ground.

The preacher hopped off the roan and mounted the platform. He stood at the cut opening and raised both hands high.

The people got up from their benches.

"Praise be to Jesus Christ Almighty," he called, and they said, "Amen," but doubtfully.

Then, in slow, measured words, drenched in the rhythms of mourning, he told them that their good brother who was to preach to them, oh, he was mortally ill. From his canopied deathbed he had sent the preacher to preach to them, to carry on the undying work of the Saviour. With his hands still raised in the air, he led the people in a short prayer for the soul of the fallen minister who could not be with them.

Then he slapped the big Bible down on the flat plank in front of him and began to preach.

In an hour the benches were filled, in two the people were standing around the log structure in a great, close-packed circle. Two men with banjos and one with a battered horn mounted the platform, now a Negro with a homemade drum joined them, all ready to strike up the hymns as the preacher called for them. They sang several, each one louder and a little faster than the other. After the third hymn the preacher, mopping his face and watching the crowd closely, motioned to William with a flip of his hand.

William remembered he was to stand off to one side then, outside the circle. He slithered through the crowd and took up his position and waited.

"Behold!" said the preacher, finding his text. "Behold their sitting down, and their rising up; I am their musick!" He slapped the Bible, and his imagination roamed, carrying him from condemnation to condemnation, returning from the chaos of his ideas to slap the Bible again and summarize: "Behold their sitting down, and their rising up; I am their musick!"

William felt that all the people were breathing together, faster. He could not see why.

The preacher's voice changed, took on a high-pitched wail, punctuated at rhythmic intervals with spat shrieks. The crowd, as one person, moved when he shrieked that way, twitched their arms and hands and dug their feet into the ground. In the front row a woman tore off her bonnet and began to sway, then jump from side to side, her clumsy, work-stiffened body held straight, but her arms and head swinging.

The preacher pointed at her. "Yes, ma'am, for Jesus!" he called. "Now jerk out that devil!" he yelled, and they did, all of them.

"Now TREE THE DEVIL!!" screamed the preacher, and like dogs they began to pant, then sniff and howl.

Terror rooted itself in William's stomach, but he stood where the preacher told him to, while the people, hungry-eyed no longer, broke their circle and moved about him like leaves in the wind.

The preacher grabbed a battered horn and blew it. Then he pointed at William.

"There! Looky there! You folks, get away and looky there!"

They cleared a place where the boy could be seen, and the preacher said, "Oh, there's a little boy, mighty young and pretty, ah. But you know it and I know it, he's rotten, ah. With sin and with death he's rotten, ah, like all sinners. Fair on the outside, mighty pretty and young, ah, but death inside him, ah. See him, see yeselves! The devil's in him, like he's in us, ah! Get him out, ah, tree that devil!"

The swaying crowd drew away from the boy, shrank back into itself and glared at him, snorting and wailing. William put a hand over his eyes and stepped backward a few steps. His fingers were wet with tears of fright that washed out their faces, blurred them into a noisy, swimming mass of bodies. He tried to say something, but they glared at him,

hating themselves in him, and the preacher said, "TREE! TREE THAT
DEVIL!"

Livid, all the faces of the people barked at him.

Desperately William blinked his eyes. His sight came clear again and
he saw them milling about him, all the people in the world, he thought,
blown about by this unknown wind, with the preacher standing above
them, his arms outstretched, his face now calm and in strange repose,
looking up, saying, "Behold! Behold their sitting down, and their rising
up; I am their musick!"

He cried, wanting to see something else. He blinked his eyes again
and then he saw it. It was a ragged man swishing a stick, his careless
father, saying to him, The hell with all that, son, the hell with it.

William's foot was on a rock. He picked it up. "Behold," said the
preacher, and William threw with all his might. The rock hit the
preacher on the cheek, tore it open.

Blood spurted. The crowd howled. William ran.

"What's your name, son?" said the man.

"William."

"William what?"

He wouldn't say. He kept his mind on the weakness in his arms, the
weakness that had driven him to the farmhouse to ask for food. He
could not bear the weakness, so he begged. It was the begging kept him
from saying his name.

"William what? You better answer me, boy."

He looked at a poker the man held in one fist. He thought: Iron. He
said: "Arn."

"Starns? Is that it?"

He nodded.

"All right, William Starns, come on in the house here and have yourself something to eat. Then we'll think about something for you to do.
That your mule?"

"Yes."

"You have feelings against that mule working, too?"

"No."

"Come in, then."

He entered slowly, hushed and awed. The house was a cabin, made of logs like his father's, but it was bigger than any building he had ever seen. The long timbers of the walls and floor were straight and dry and unwarped. Between them the clay was packed tight, hard as rock. Slowly he realized he was in a new world, man-made, a world not subject to wind or rain, sun or snow. There were rugs on the floor. He wondered what they were for.

A silent woman with dull eyes and pink cheeks gave him supper, setting before him a plate heavy with food. Ham, greens and eggs; from a pitcher came fresh milk. He ate carefully, delicately, but could not keep from feeling sick when he had finished.

A ladder to the loft was pulled down and he climbed it, up to the room above the cabin, smelling of straw and old leather. He was alone there, lying for the first time all by himself in a bed. Long after the trapdoor closed, leaving him in darkness, his eyes stared upward, his fingers shot straight out from his palms. He lay awake for a long time until sleep came like night, unnoticed until half upon him. He sighed, hands and body went limp, eyelids fluttered, his shoulders sagged and he slept.

In the middle of the night he woke up hearing voices quarreling. His eyes came open and in the blackness he heard them yelling at each other below his bed. Why do they yell, he thought, living in a fine cabin like this here? Something got smashed downstairs, shrill laughter pierced the darkness. He knew at once it had been a great mistake to climb to the loft, a greater one to beg in the first place.

The trapdoor was raised. Yellow light shot up and gleamed dully on the timbers of the roof. A man stumbled up the ladder, sprawled out on the floor, pulled his legs up after him and closed the trap. He sat there for a while, giggling to himself, cursing, coughing and snorting. He fumbled about and a light flared up as he lit a cotton thread sunk in a saucer of bear oil. The man smelled of whisky. William was used to that, but when the light came, he saw it did not strengthen the man as it used to strengthen his father. The stranger saw him, stared vacantly and then laughed very loud. William thought of a raven he had seen once, its feathers ruffled, one wing crushed, its beak wide open, screaming. The man held up the light, giggling, and William saw a bright red sore on his forehead.

"Hey. Who're you?" said the stranger.

"William. William Starns."

"Well, William, move over."

He did. The stranger fell into the bed without touching his clothes and lay still. William tried to sleep again and he was drowsing off when a hairy arm was thrown over his chest and yes he felt himself pulled against the man's body. He shivered as the man's thighs pressed against him, once, twice, three times, then he was violently pushed away.

"God dammit, boy, aw, boy, god dammit." Then the man began to pray. "O Lord, I wish you would do something for me. I have done wrong, but still, O Lord. But I have done wrong, I know it, still..."

William waited until the man fell asleep, slobbering, then he crept over the inert body, lifted the trapdoor and was gone. On his mule again under a clear, starry night sky, he went his way. It was very cold and he shivered, but mostly thinking about the farmhouse and his escape from something dreadful. The clean, cold air of the night welcomed him.

What's your name, sonny?

William Starns.

Can you swing this ax before you eat?

Yes.

What's your name, son?

William Starns.

Can you use this pick? Really use it, I mean?

Yes.

What's your name?

Will Starns.

Can you clear this land? So it'll stay cleared?

Yes. Handle this plow? Yes. A lathe? A frow? A harrow? A six-team wagon? A scythe? A bottle? A woman? A gun?

Yes.

Painfully, he learned. He learned that a tree must be girdled and left to die before it makes good cabin timber; that rawhide must be treated with oak or hemlock tannin or it will rot; that cedar shingles, split with the grain, make the best roofing; that every single stone must be picked from the field before swinging the razor-bladed scythe; that most corn whisky is swallowed quickly or not at all; that it is best to drink some before handling a woman.

He got no further than his eighteenth year before he killed a man. Swung on him in a rage, caught the side of the man's head with the flat of a plowshare. He had just picked the plow up and swung, both hands gripping the split handle. He stood over the man, his rage subsiding, and the last thing he thought about it was that the man's head looked like a turtle shell he had seen once, cracked open.

What's your name?

William Starns.

In the prison he would lie on his straw bed, remembering the mountains, dimly. Some far-off country he had never seen, only heard about. A place he wanted to visit someday. His father lived there, why shouldn't he?

Prisons in those days weren't much. A new governor was elected, state officialdom reshuffled itself like a gambler's deck of cards. The prison was moved to a farm somebody sold for a killing, and on the move over, ten or more prisoners saw a clear path and walked it, Starns among them. The records got lost, nobody chased them. Starns thought it was natural. Imprisonment, like anything else, can come to a quick end for no other reason than carelessness, chance. All you do is move when the time comes.

What's your name?

William Starns.

Can you boss these men? Bunch of bastards.

Yes.

Honey, what's your name?

William.

William, honey, do you love me? Show me how much.

Yes.

This son of a bitch is out to get me, Starns. Can you stop him?

Yes.

Through the settlements, the small towns, the work camps. In the taverns, the gambling shacks, the brothels, the kitchens and the ditches. And when he had worked and was paid, or not paid, he would go on to the same somewhere else. In small towns he would stand around and watch the carriages, the lumbering wagons, the decked-out surreys. He would listen to the chattering and stare at the sweeping hems of the women's dresses. Around him, as he walked along or stood leaning, busy leather snapped and axles creaked, men and women called to each other, complained to each other. He walked through them, past them, his eyes burned no longer, loathing was not in him anymore, only a vast aloofness, like the topmost branches of a tall poplar in the wind.

On a raw December Sunday in the year 1849 Starns stood on top of a mound of dirt thrown up from a newly dug ditch and gazed across a quarter mile of open land. Beyond that he saw the outskirts of the state capital. Thick gray clouds, pushed and tumbled by the wind, held the sky, now and then allowing some sunlight, cold and white, to fall on the rooftops of the city. Some of the rooftops, not all, were painted. Starns watched their pale colors brighten a little as the sunlight passed over them.

His boots sank down into the loose dirt of the diggings. He felt a damp chill from the wet earth pass through thin leather and begin to climb up his legs.

Starns was in his late twenties then, but his face looked like a dry and withered seed. Already the skin was coarse and cracked, already there was the beginning of a curve reaching down his spine from the back of his neck. He put his empty hands under his armpits and watched the cold sunlight touch the roofs.

A man could freeze, he said to himself.

The buildings of the city began at the far edge of the quarter mile of freshly cleared, gullied land. The ditches and uprooted stumps told that the city was a lively one, that it was expanding, reaching out for more fields for its uses. Behind a broken line of flimsy outskirt shacks rose the rooftops. At places Starns could see some of the walls that held them up. He admired the ruddy color of sturdy bricks, red in the cold sunlight. Broad rooftops spread downward like the wings of hovering birds, and from one rooftop a white wooden dome stuck up in the air. He cocked his head to one side, wondering at it. Then he heard the sound of a bell, carried along on the damp December wind, and knew the building was a church. He shivered and pressed his arms tight to his body.

His teeth began to chatter, cold sweat came out of the pores of his skin. He looked at the ditches and the tall buildings, felt the chill of the loose dirt he stood in.

I don't know where to go now, he said to himself, or what to do. I tell myself, get a move on, but that don't seem to do it no more. A man could just freeze.

A wagon rattled by, then slowed down. A farmer in a shapeless wool hat called out to him.

"Going to town?"

"Yes, I reckon. Thanks."

He got off as soon as they had passed the first of the shacks. The farmer wanted to talk, he told Starns that the city part was on ahead anyhow, but Starns said no, he'd walk the rest, thank you kindly. He got down from the wagon and stood there until the man hefted his reins and the horses jolted the wagon forward. Starns waited until the wagon and the wool hat passed out of sight. He began to walk into the city, like a man climbing a steep hill on an empty stomach.

He went up a wide dirt street, almost deserted on Sunday afternoon. People were inside, sleeping after dinner, chatting by smoldering iron stoves, considering themselves at week's end. He did not think about them. He looked at the storefronts, and when he came to some that were painted he would stop and gaze at the colors and the crude ornaments on their wooden faces.

He walked on, moving forward in a shambling, heavy gait. At the corner of one small street, whose store buildings ran into shacks fifty yards down, he came upon a wide hole dug into the ground. It was only three or four feet deep but several yards across the middle. In the hole, partially covered with dirt, Starns saw charred, smoking remains of timbers and clapboard. Some parts of it were still burning, throwing up a crackling row of strong, wind-swept flames.

Cold man, he thought, get warm.

Eagerly he moved to the edge of the hole. He felt dry waves of heat come up to his body and was grateful for them. He held out his hands and slapped them together.

What I need now, he thought, is a drink.

He pulled out his shirt at the neck, hooked it over his chin and blew his breath down his bare chest. He moved the toes of his feet inside his damp leather boots. Slowly the taut muscles in his neck and shoulders came undone.

Across the hole, through a stream of vapor coming from the fire, Starns saw a man in a black frock coat standing still and watching him. He was in middle age, his skin was smooth and soft, pink and healthy-looking. The coat he wore was big, it reached down almost to his feet.

Well, he won't have no drink, not one he'd show, anyhow, thought Starns. That's certain.

The man was a clergyman. He wore a high, gleaming collar that emerged neatly from the thick lapels of his black coat. He stared at Starns, who looked into the hole for a while and then stared back. The clergyman was a handsome, nervous man. Across his clean-shaven face, as he stared at Starns, rippled a stream of small but violent expressions, noticeable but transient as disturbances on water. He chewed at his inner lip and stared. Starns felt like moving on, but the heat from the fire had not yet warmed him through, so he slapped his hands and stayed where he was.

"Well, sir," said the clergyman, speaking across the smoking tangle of burning wood, "they didn't fool around, did they?"

"Who didn't?" asked Starns.

The clergyman waved a graceful hand at the fire. "The men who did this, whoever they are." Then he began walking around the edge of the hole, peering down at the charred sticks with curiosity and regret. He stopped a few feet from Starns, who shifted his weight and took a step backward.

"Did what?" said Starns, looking at his hands.

"Burned this church. No, sir, they didn't fool around at all. Burned it and then half buried it, whoever they are." He kicked a black stick into the hole.

"Was it your church?" Starns asked politely.

The clergyman looked away quickly, fingering the lapel of his coat. He blinked, answered very rapidly. "No! No, indeed, hardly. It was a Catholic church."

"Oh?" said Starns softly. "What's that?" He did not mean to startle anyone.

"A different kind of church, that's all. I am an Episcopalian, sir. What is your faith?"

"Don't know," said Starns. He slapped his hands one more time, regretting the loss of the fire, and turned away. "Nice to have talked to you."

He walked away, but did not go far. The buildings ahead had no sun on them, and the damp wind hurt his skin the fire had softened. He stopped, turned again and saw the man looking after him, still staring but smiling, too. He'd been friendly, after all. Starns shrugged and went back to the fire.

They stood there awhile.

"I don't mean to pry," said Starns, feeling he should say something to justify his return, "but ain't you a preacher?"

"Well, yes, in a way I am."

"Then why ain't you at church? It's Sunday, ain't it?"

The clergyman smiled. "It's Sunday, all right, but sometimes I can't worship with everybody else."

"Why not?"

"Because I am Bishop of the churches around here and, contrary to what most people say, Bishops can't always do what they want on Sundays."

"Well," said Starns, "I reckon. Well, so long, Bishop."

"Wait a minute, I'll walk with you."

They went up the street together until the Bishop stopped beside a surrey. A sleek, fat, reddish-brown bay was harnessed to it and hitched to a street rail.

"Want a ride?" said the Bishop. "Climb in."

"No, I'll walk, thank you kindly. I don't want to be no trouble."

"Nonsense, get in. A man might as well ride when he can. And I have walked it far enough in my time to know the truth of that, sir."

The Bishop's smile was easy, his manner open, affable and straightforward. His features were sharp and refined, almost feminine, but the eyes were large and dark and intelligent, and there was a deep cleft in the center of a strong, firm chin.

"Well. I thank you."

The surrey, new and shiny with bright paint, rocked gracefully as the two men mounted it. Starns wanted to touch the smooth wood with its layer of bright blue paint, but he didn't. He held his hands in his lap, folded. The seats were padded with thick cushions of heavy leather. Starns sat up stiffly and did not look back.

They rode into the city. The buildings became taller and closer together. More and more people walked the streets. A few waved to the Bishop, who nodded and smiled at them.

Bishop Ames made the ride last a long time. He drove through sections of the city he had never seen before, took small, winding streets that went nowhere and then doubled back again. He kept riding so that from time to time he could steal another look at the drifter he had picked up, the man who sat quietly looking ahead and did not speak.

There seemed to be no life in him. This was what made the physical resemblance so astonishing. The Bishop saw no spark in him, no bit of life driven deep down into the man by years of drudgery and shiftlessness, the kind of thing the Bishop prided himself on seeing in anyone who had it. No, there was only that aloofness, that dignified, nerveless unconcern of a corpse that moved its arms and legs now and then.

But the man was nevertheless the image of the Bishop's high-strung, impassioned father, dead thirty years.

Slowly, as they rode, the astonishment faded. The man did look like his father, yes, there was the wrinkled, coarse skin of the face and hands and neck, skin like river clay split open and baked into cross-cracks by the sun, there were the large hands like roots, the stoop and the slightly askew cast of the head and bony shoulders. All those were of his father, yes, but there was more, much more. Something his father had had and then lost, something he only dimly remembered, something driven from his memory by what happened later, at the end.

He has his energy inside, thought the Bishop. Something humming there, so quiet I didn't get it at first, but still it's there. What was it, now, that she said? Oh, yes.

He remembered his mother speaking of his father when they had married, telling him that to her he was then a big lamp with the wick turned down low. And that something—who was to say what?—had turned it up too high.

What would he do, thought the Bishop about Starns, if he got excited, or mad, or drunk, even? That would bring it out, that would tell me why he is so much like him.

The surrey slid through a part of the city the Bishop had never seen before, and didn't see then. The wheels bumped over rocks jutting out of the street dirt, and the sleek bay changed his smooth gait now and then to avoid holes and scattered pieces of plank and refuse.

Would this calm leave him then? If the wick was turned up high, would the calm go? Not just go, either, but shatter, and then the wild-ness. Then screaming and raving and then the ditch, thought the Bishop.

At that moment Starns cleared his throat and spat over the side of the surrey into the street. He crossed his arms and settled back against the leather seat cushions, tranquil and relaxed, it seemed. He said noth-ing about the length of the trip.

Like a mother going somewhere with a sleeping child, thought the Bishop. Or a father.

Thinking about that, Bishop Nahum Immanuel Ames remembered a frosty morning in New England and a wagon he had ridden with his father, the two of them out to hunt for the day. He remembered the patience and ease of his father that morning as he fingered the reins and talked to the horses and laughed at his son.

I have come upon him again, thought the Bishop. When he was still a whole man, in his innocence, free from his cross. Before he fell into the ditch, my father. I am riding along with him and he is as he was then, he is sane.

At a standstill, the handsome bay tossed his head and twitched the skin of his flanks under the harnessing. Bishop Ames held the reins loosely and looked at his passenger. Starns looked back at him.

"That's where I live," said the Bishop, pointing.

Starns saw a large frame house with an inclined, well-kept front yard. A willow grew near the house, its languid arms reaching almost to the ground. A maple and two big oaks stood in the yard, and their leafless branches waved and creaked a little in the December wind.

"Do you need a job?"

Starns didn't answer.

"Well, I know you need one. What I mean is, do you want one?"

Starns nodded his head. He looked at the tall house beyond the trees. There were four small columns on the porch, painted white. Against one of them he saw a boy's sled set up on its side. It had bright crimson streaks painted down its back.

"Yes, I want a job."

"Good. Now, do you mind if I ask you some questions?"

"No."

"Are you a drinker?"

"I drink whisky, yes."

"I mean, does it make you cause trouble?"

"It did once. No, twice."

"I see," said the Bishop gently. "Have you ever been married?"

"No."

"What are some of the jobs you've handled before?"

Starns told him.

"You've done a lot of different things. How old are you?"

"I don't rightly know, not exactly, I mean. I think about twenty-eight or twenty-nine, maybe thirty, something like that."

Bishop Ames stared at him. "You look a lot older than that, Mister."

"I know it," said Starns quietly.

"Well," said the Bishop, "I'm the kind of man who sees things in people, and what I see in you I like. Now, one of the churches in this city can use a man, uh, as janitor. Not much pay, but you get a room of your own that will be clean and dry anyway. And some meals, too, I think, but I'm not sure about that. The work is steady and I think you'd be the man for it, unless maybe you have something against Episcopalians."

Starns smiled and shook his head. "Don't know whether I do or not. What's an Episcopalian?"

"Never mind," said the Bishop, grinning. "They'll tell you soon enough. Well, now, can you do things like this, scrub floors and do the fires and polish things and so on? Some men call it woman's work, I have to tell you that. It's beneath them these days."

"Yes, I can do those things."

"Good. Now, there is one more thing. There's no need to mention where we happened to meet. If anybody asks you about it, tell them, but don't bring it up yourself. All right?"

"All right."

"Fine. By the way, can you handle a forge?"

"Yes, I can handle a forge." Yes, I can pick and haul and push and hammer and scrub and clean. Why not? What else is there to do, except die? I can kill a man, too.

"We're agreed, then?"

"Yes."

The Bishop handed Starns the reins to the surrey and jumped down nimbly. "Take it around to the back of the house and put up the horse for me. His name is Henry, by the way, and he answers to it. There's a shed there, and he'll know where to go anyway, he's hungry. When you're done, come on in the house and my wife will give you some supper. Then we'll go down to the church. I have to speak there tonight, so it's no trouble."

Starns held the reins of the bright surrey and looked down at the Bishop gravely, unsmiling.

"All right," he said. "But I don't know how long I'll be staying. I ought to have told you that before."

"Well, we'll see," said the Bishop. "By the way, what's your full name again?"

"William Starns."

The church was large and stately, the oldest in the city. It was a towering frame building with a high dome and a bell, set back from the street in a yard barren of trees.

The day after he arrived Starns faced his first problem. Two stained-glass windows were shipped in from New York, carefully boxed and crated. With two hired carpenters he pried open the boxes and unwrapped the glass. He saw at once that both sheets were about three feet wider than the windows for which they were intended. The Bishop had already announced their dedication for the following Sunday, they had to be up that morning. Starns tried to listen while the carpenters speculated hesitantly about possible ways of melting or cutting the precious glass, but it was no good. He lost his temper, told them to clear out, tore down both windows of the church itself and rebuilt the frames.

He swore as he worked, sweating and stamping his foot now and then in anger. An astonished minister, who had strolled out to chat, retreated quickly.

God-damned foolishness, Starns muttered to himself, painting glass thisaway. All this fuss. Great God Almighty.

But Saturday night the windows were in their places, firm as the wall. Sunday morning he did not attend the service. He walked out of the church when the first worshiper arrived. Only later, in the afternoon, did he return. The sanctuary was empty then, and he liked that, felt at home in its imperious calm. He sat stiffly on a cushioned seat and looked scornfully at the windows he had sweated over.

As he looked, they brightened suddenly, transforming a wash of harsh, cold sunlight into rich, rainbow-spectrumed streams of falling colors. He stared, seeing vermilion and gray, grass green and violet, pink and corn yellow. In the dome the church bell struck, its voice deep and strong and proud.

Well, now, he thought, maybe I might stay here awhile.

2

STARNS AND THE BISHOP

THE FIRST WEEKS after that, Starns did his work quietly and well. The minister of the church, Reverend Marcus Sales, did not like him at all, but he couldn't quarrel with the silent, thorough labor. "Does nothing but follow his nose," Sales said to his wife. "Too dumb to cheat." "Well, that's fine, then," said his wife, and Sales, who also knew that for some reason utterly beyond him Bishop Ames was partial to the man, agreed. So when he spoke to Starns he was scrupulously affable, and the church stayed in very good order all that time.

The trouble came in the third month. A quiet defiance that never left Starns led to the inevitable, embarrassing pauses, mortifying for the more outgoing members of the congregation when they tried to talk with him. They began to watch him on Sunday mornings, when he might hand out pamphlets or hang up greatcoats but, the instant the service began, leave the church with measured strides. It upset a few people.

In the late afternoons, when the slanting, mellow rays of the sun washed the stark wall of the church, the stained-glass window colors were at their best. It became his habit to sit alone in the sanctuary then, his hands folded in his lap, watching the creeping courses of the rich colors as they draped themselves over the backs of the pews and climbed up into the pulpit. There, at the end of the third month, three elderly ladies of the church, trim frigates in full sail under breezes of joy and innocence, moored themselves around Starns and attempted his conversion.

"Mister Starns," said one, a stately vessel in harbor water, "it is but a step into the arms of the Lord."

"Do come and take that step with us this coming Sabbath," said another, her bonnet tilted to one side.

"You cannot defy the Heavenly Father," intoned the third lady, cannon-voiced. "He is terrible in his judgment."

Starns looked at them floating before him. His gaze was withering, deadly. He was filled with sudden loathing of himself for seeking this sanctuary, for living so long in this place of comfort and warmth where now he must suffer the foolish demands of presumptuous women who thought they reigned over it, and over him.

"I scrub floors here. That's all. You old bitches can go to hell."

And he threw a duster at them.

Instantly the ladies reversed their tack. Forgoing the breezes of innocence and joy, they set sail toward the Reverend of the church under black winds of indignation. Sales was overwhelmed, and had been looking for just such an excuse anyway. He informed Starns that such an attitude, heathen and insulting, would not be tolerated. He cast Starns from the Temple and hired another janitor.

Then he let two careful days slip by before telling the Bishop.

"Starns is no longer with us at St. Mark's," said Marcus Sales with quiet authority, standing in the Bishop's study, before the desk. "Now, he was a good worker, let me be the first to say so. And he has obviously led a hard life. I was deeply sorry to let him go. Yet it was necessary for the peace of my parish. I had to do it. He is a disturbed and unstable man. From what I heard, and saw myself, for that matter, it is possible the fellow is losing his mind."

Only then did Bishop Ames look up at Reverend Sales, ice in his eyes. He was thinking: That must be the way they talked about my father while he was running to the ditch. He remembered that his father, to please his mother, had applied to their New England church for a vestryman's position, and that the elders of that church had deliberated, uneasy about him. While they discussed his suitability, the Bishop recalled, his father found his ditch, there to cancel all his applications. So when Bishop Ames finally looked up at Reverend Sales, his icy gaze stripped the priest's authority from him.

"I see. Where is he now?"

"Starns? Well, I don't know."

"Well, you are going to find out. Before dark. Starns will be back in that church by tomorrow morning,"

"Bishop, that's quite out of the question."

Bishop Ames was not afraid of ecclesiastical discord. "It had better not be," he said quietly, then looked down at some papers in his hand.

Offended, frightened, Marcus Sales returned to his church. There he was dismayed to find that nobody, not even the new janitor, knew anything about Starns. He had just gone, saying nothing. In his room in the church basement his work clothes were found hanging from a peg. On a rickety table stood a shaving mug, a comb and a razor, and a few more clothes were found under his bed. That was all.

Reverend Sales was a refined man, considered elegant by the ladies of his church. It pained him to do what he knew he had to do, but he did it—hired a sheriff's man on the sly to search the city for William Starns. He didn't hope to have Starns back by the next morning, so he went and said so to the Bishop, obedient and cowed but angry, too. Bishop Ames said: "All right. Do it any way you have to. Just so he's found. The diocese will pay for your expenses."

After a four-day scouring of the city the sheriff's man found William Starns. He said, "Move." Starns didn't. He laid hands on Starns and got one of his arms broken. Snapped, the way you split a green stick. The sheriff's man ran howling up the street. While his arm was being set, the sheriff sent a boy running to Marcus Sales with a note telling where Starns had been found. Sales went immediately to the Bishop and together they reached Starns's hideout, only seconds before a large group of men on horseback, led by an angry sheriff. The Bishop's bright surrey, behind the handsome bay, skimmed across their path as they came riding, its two front lanterns lit brightly. It was well into a warm April night.

"He's in there?" asked the Bishop, blocking their way.

"That's right," said the sheriff, dismounting. He walked to the surrey. "We'll handle him for you, Bishop."

Bishop Ames hopped nimbly out of the surrey. He said: "Church business. I'll do it, thank you."

The Bishop of North Carolina stood in the sticky warmth of the late spring night, facing a rotting, dirt-floored shack left tenantless to molder and decay. He stared at it a moment, then suddenly bent his head and walked in the doorless opening. The stench of the place brought a wave of nausea sliding up his throat. He put out a hand and touched a crumbling wall thick with old yellow newspaper and cardboard. Under his feet the sandy, pulverized, dark dirt sank unevenly. He could not see if anyone was there or not.

"Starns?" he said. "Is that you, William?"

The sheriff handed in a kerosene lantern, then backed out the doorway when Bishop Ames held it up. The swaying light lurched across the shack, passing over the figure that seemed to materialize out of the darkness and the dirt floor. He was sprawled in one corner, staring blindly with frightened eyes, like an animal dazzled by torchlight. Starns had thrashed and kicked his legs out, digging himself a two-foot-deep hole he half lay in. His lips and chin were streaked with dirt and vomit. A jug of raw whisky lay upturned by his hand. He lay stinking like a dying goat.

The Bishop walked up to him slowly and squatted down on his haunches, looking at the ground. He waited. Then he said: "Well, Starns, what happened?"

"I ain't going to be treated like that," mumbled the man on the ground. "Not by nobody."

"Now, Starns, wait a minute."

"Not by nobody. Not by God Almighty hisself, whatever kind of bastard he is. And shorely not by that preacher, or them damn women. I push and haul and scrub just because I feel like it. Listen here. I will lie on the ground just because I feel like it. That's all."

He despises himself, thought Bishop Ames, for loving that church. I saw the work he did on its old body. He loved it. Yet this passion against it, set off by clumsy women, it's awful. He hates and loves all at once. He must hate and love God all at once.

Squatting in the dirt, Bishop Ames remembered his own father, gone to earth like this, and wondered how similar were the horrors that chased them both. He resolved that he would not leave until Starns came with him, walking.

Starns choked and coughed, slobbered and was sick again. He pressed his bearded cheek against the dirt and remembered with shame and fury the stature of his mountain father, the proud, dirty man who one day, with his son watching, stood by a stump, scornfully slapping a tassel of dry, spindly corn with one hand, saying, "Grow if ye feel like it, or don't, who gives a damn."

"Need any help?" said the sheriff, sticking his head in the doorway. This time, at his shoulder, gleamed the appalled face of Marcus Sales, his pale complexion shining in the lantern light like a yellow moon. The Bishop stood up, turned around slowly and walked out of the shack, pushing them before him.

"Sales, what did you say to him?"

"Nothing out of the ordinary," insisted Reverend Sales. "I dismissed him, that was all."

"You must have said something. Think."

"Well, I did say . . . I did call him heathen."

"Fine," said the Bishop. "Congratulations. What else?"

"Well, now, he was violent. He had just attacked three ladies in the sanctuary. I told you he was losing his mind." Marcus Sales shivered, looking about at the desolate shacks.

"What do you mean, attacked?" continued the Bishop.

"He cursed them and threw things at them."

"Why?"

Sales began to whisper, as if the man in the shack, or perhaps the shacks themselves, might overhear him. "No reason whatsoever. They had just invited him to join the church, that's all."

"Who were they?"

Sales told him.

"I see. What did he throw at them?"

"I don't recall."

"Try. A chair, a rock, what?"

Marcus Sales looked at the ground, stared at his Bishop's feet and told the truth. "A duster," he said.

In the shack Bishop Ames could hear the rasping sounds of pawing, digging. Starns's boots thrashing at the dirt. A duster, he thought.

"Gentlemen," he said to the men on horseback, "there is no reason for you to stay out any longer. Thank you for coming."

"Now, hold on," said the sheriff. "That feller broke a man's arm. I'm going to arrest him."

"If it suits you, Sheriff," said the Bishop coldly, "I will take him into custody. And I will be responsible for him."

The sheriff was a burly man and a good officer, but he was not eager to cross the Episcopal Bishop of the state. He nodded and got on his horse. "Well," he said, "you're responsible, then." The men began to turn their horses.

"Should I leave?" said Marcus Sales softly.

"Yes!" snapped the Bishop, turning his back.

By the crumbling shanty he waited like a black statue until the sounds of their horses fell away into silence. Then he began to poke about the place, kicking at rubbish with his foot. He found an old cracker box, its front bashed in but with three good sides. He carried it into the shack, put it down next to Starns and sat on it.

"Go on, Starns," he said. "Talk if you want to." He set the lantern on the ground between them and turned the wick down low.

Starns's eyes were wet and red. He stared at the Bishop. His legs kicked at the dirt like those of a rabbit pinned down in a trap.

"All right, then, I'll talk," said the Bishop. "And you listen. Kick all you want to, but listen."

His voice was taut, thin but strong, like a piece of tight, vibrating wire. He spoke the words you can find in his sermons, in the long polemics reprinted in New York magazines and sold between the leather covers of published books. He had never talked religion to

Starns before, but he did then, with the full authority of his Christian office. He spoke clearly, simply, definitely, sure of the human soul and the agony of its earthly searching. Bishop Ames pleaded, cajoled, argued and explained, burning his words into the consciousness of the fallen drifter. "Go on, then," he said as he finished, "go on, lie down in a ditch and cover yourself up. Take the breath out of your body, try it. The only thing you can kill is that body, nothing else. You know that, and it shames you, doesn't it? You can't end everything, you can't kill yourself, no man can do that. You will go on living whether you want to or not, Starns, whether you kill yourself or not, and that's your shame. Sooner or later you have to face up to it. And then there is only one thing to do, one place to go."

Starns lay listening in the dirt. He waited until the Bishop stopped talking.

"You through?" he whispered hoarsely.

"Yes."

Starns laid back his dirt-caked head and howled, splitting the silence of the night. He rolled over and over in the hole, like a man in a fit. Then he got still again, breathing hard, licking his lips.

"Run to Jesus Christ," he whispered. "The long-haired man in that white dress, that's what you mean. Well, who's he? Did you ever see him, you lying son of a bitch?"

The Bishop unclenched his fists slowly. The childish question had been asked by a man, after all. He pushed back his anger and said: "No, I have never seen him. But he is there."

"You mean to tell me you believe what you preach about? Believe it all day long, and at night, too? If you do, you're a liar, that's all. Nobody believes nothing all the time."

No, he's not crazy, thought the Bishop, not crazy. He looked at Starns and answered truthfully.

"No, Starns, I don't believe always," he said. "Most of the time. And especially at night. But not always."

Starns considered it. "Well," he said, "then neither of us has seen Jesus Christ. But I seen plenty else. You want to know some of the things I seen in my life?"

"Yes."

"Well, I killed a man once. Knocked in his god-damned head. I didn't care then and still don't. I just might do it again, too." He lashed out with one foot. His boot thudded against the flimsy wall of the shack, shaking the whole thing violently.

"Would you?" said the Bishop calmly. "I don't think so."

"You're right," said Starns, quiet again. "I wouldn't. Once was enough. But look here, why not? Why shouldn't I? What difference would it make? And don't talk no more about sinners and good people up in heaven, neither. It ain't none of it true."

"How do you know that?"

"I know it, all right, don't you worry. Here, if there's any more whisky in this thing, I'll tell you."

He fumbled with the jug, holding it up over his face. A few reeking drops fell on his lips and cheeks. He swore and threw the jug skidding across the dirt. "It's all gone!" he howled, and his powerful legs began to thrash and kick the dirt again.

A hundred catechisms, a hundred catchwords to lure in a soul, a hundred things to say in the night, they all passed shapeless and soft through the Bishop's mind. None of that will do right now, he thought, none of it. But he opened his mouth to say something, anything, because he had to, though he did not know what it could possibly be. He opened his mouth to speak, but finally did not speak, finally was silent. In the fetid air of the shack, watching Starns writhing in the hole his feet had dug for him, Bishop Ames lost his strength, felt it go from him like water pouring from a split barrel and vanishing into the ground.

For Starns had changed. To the Bishop he was no longer Starns. Nahum Ames was looking again at his father, seeing once more those flashing, insane eyes the day before he died thrashing about in the New England farm ditch, the day he took his son walking and with a shaking hand on his shoulder said, "Sonny, I am like a man caught in the world the way a man gets caught on top of a runaway horse sometimes, everything goes by me in different directions, the horse has that bit in his teeth, sonny, it all goes by me like that and I can't do nothing but close my eyes and wait to fall."

From the shack the sounds of two men breathing deeply whispered out into the night. The bay stirred restlessly, neighed and shook his handsome head. The wheels of the surrey went backward, then forward an inch.

After a while the Bishop spoke again. His voice was relaxed, loose, free. "Starns," he said, "I have a bottle of whisky at the house. Come on with me and you can have it. Maybe it will help you, because I don't think I can right now. I'm sorry."

Starns blinked at him, surprised. He looked out the doorway, saw moonlight on scattered piles of rotting wood. The bay stamped a foreleg on the damp ground.

"Is that Henry out there?"

"Yes, that's Henry. He's hungry and wants the barn. You haven't been around to feed him, and I forget it sometimes."

Starns blinked a few more times. He said: "All right. I'm willing."

He got to his knees, and the Bishop helped him stand up. They made their way out of the shack and into the surrey without Starns falling. The Bishop gathered the reins and snapped them, and they bumped down the road, leaving the crumbling shack with the cracker box inside it by the ditch.

The bottle of whisky stood unopened on the Bishop's kitchen table; Starns had not wanted it. He ate from a dish of spoon bread the Bishop's wife, Rachael, put down for him, ate with his hands, sopping the soft, milky bread into his mouth with shaking fingers. Bishop Ames sat across the table, talking about nothing, smoothly, easily. After a while he became aware that Starns was talking, too. Mumbling, as if answering questions the Bishop had not asked. Pieces of the bread fell from his lips onto the table, and he was still in the chair, spent, and talking.

Rachael Ames stood by her stove, watching a pan of apples bubble and steam. In any crisis, large or small, she cooked apples as soon as she could because the sound and odor soothed her. In her right hand she held a long wooden spoon, carved for her when she was a child in upper

New York State, a thing she always carried now that she had a kitchen of her own. From time to time she stirred the apples with it, lifting the lid, stirring, then putting the lid back and turning to look at her husband and the wretched creature he had brought into their home.

Outside, the warm wind rose and slid through the trees, slithering over the new leaves like snakes in soft grass. A barking dog began to yelp and then whine, finally giving up his reproaches to the moon.

"I wasn't doing nothing in them days nohow," mumbled Starns. "Just wandering about, hiring out to whoever would use me. I got a job working for a man near Wilmington, I think it was, and he had a pretty big farm. Two silos and a barn with eight stalls and a loft. Even a cabin for the help, though he didn't keep no slaves, as I recall."

He stopped abruptly, as if listening for something, then began to chew again in silence. Rachael Ames started to say something, but her husband put up his hand an inch off the kitchen table where he sat across from Starns, and they waited. Starns pushed more bread into his mouth, chewed, then began again.

"This man, he had two young'uns, half growed. They took to following me about. There was a boy and then a girl, half growed. That's right. She must be a fine woman now, somewhere."

He doesn't say a word for three months, thought Bishop Ames. Now he wants to dictate his memoirs. He looked at Starns's face, wrinkled, weather-beaten, dirty in the kitchen lamplight, and he thought, Well, let him. He said: "Yes, Starns?"

"One day in the winter," Starns continued, "that man brung home to them young'uns a fine litter of pups. Eight or nine, it was a smart litter. We all watched them crawling over each other and the bitch nursing them, flopping around, stepping in each other's faces and all that. Watched them right in that kitchen there. Them young'uns went wild over it, and the girl, she stood by me and she said, Well, Starns, we must take good care of them. They have to be fed every day and kept warm, you know. I said, Yes, they do, you're right, and the chief, he said, Starns, I hereby make you number-one dog man. And everybody laughed. Then later on he told me to do that truly, to see that them young'uns learned to care for them pups, to show them how and not let them forget. I said I would, and when I told the girl she looked at me smartly and said we would do it together, that she'd be the one would see I didn't forget."

Rachel Ames tapped her wooden spoon against the sides of the hot black stove. How long, she thought, am I supposed to listen to this? A wandering vagrant with all his sense worked out of him. What's the matter with Nahum, doing this to me tonight?

Starns cocked his head to one side. In the light his face looked suddenly eager and soft, childlike as he remembered. "I mainly recall them pups as beagles, but that couldn't be, they growed up big as hounds. I don't know, but anyhow they come along fine. I put up a kennels for them, and in the early mornings and at suppertime them young'uns and me would set out their food and the girl would always stand around with me to watch them gobble it up."

Bishop Ames rested his chin on his palm, thinking, That's right. That's the way to teach children the care of living beings. He looked at his wife, then away.

"Yessir," mumbled Starns. "Them dogs did fine for a year. And that year was the longest I ever stayed in one place, too. Because of her. I was waiting for her to grow up, too, you see. Now, it was that next winter, in January, I think it was, that them dogs commenced to drag about and whine. And the morning after that they took to dying. By night ever last one was stretched out dead in that kennels, lying thisaway and that. The man told me we would have to get rid of them the next morning."

He rubbed his coarse, filthy hands together and began to blow on them as he talked, as if he had just come inside out of the cold.

"I got up early, met the man. He was talking about distemper, but it wasn't that killed them dogs. I didn't know what it was, don't know now. Nobody does, I reckon. Anyhow, he said, Quick, let's us get them out of here before the young'uns come down on us. So I hitched up the wagon and brought it by. Them dogs had froze during the night, they was lying ever which way, frost on their hides, their coats all ragged, legs and heads all froze stiff the way they had laid down. We had commenced to lift the first one when the young'uns stuck their heads out of a window, commencing to yell. The chief, he got mad, saying, Starns, you go, I don't want to. You see to them."

His eyes were vacant, as if gazing over water. He rubbed a forefinger on the table by the dish of spoon bread.

"Now, the boy had run a splinter in his hand off the windowsill. That's what he was yelling about. I reached up and squeezed and got the splinter out. He sucked it and seemed all right. So I told them to never mind now, but to go get their breakfast, and the boy, he went, but not the girl. No, she stayed there in the window, looking at me funny, that girl I had fancied so. She wouldn't take her eyes off me. Just kept looking, and I didn't know what to say to her. Then she did look towards the kennels and she grabbed me by the arm and pointed and said, Oh, Starns, what's he doing to them now? She had come to care a lot, to care a lot for them dogs, you see."

Rachael Ames turned back to her apples on the stove, her hand against the soft flesh of her stomach. She listened, as did the Bishop, both caught up in the tale Starns was telling, the words coming faster now, loud and determined, rising like a flooding creek.

"It was hazy all along the ground and so cold. There was frost on my boots, the laces were stiff, and when I breathed deep, it hurt, it was that cold. I looked where she was pointing and I seen that the man had got mad with it, tired of it all. There was a pitchfork in the wagon bed. He pulled it out and then commenced hauling them dogs to the wagon that way. He was working hard at it, pushing hisself, and when he throwed he throwed hard, and one dog turned up in the air, head all twisted and legs stuck out funny, and landed in the wagon bed with a bad noise. He yelled at me to come on now, and I had to go. He throwed that pitchfork to me and so I had to commence. I stuck the prongs down through the ribs of one dog and lifted and hauled him to the wagon and throwed him in. She commenced to scream at the window, and I commenced to perish right there for her and for me and for them dogs, too, but I had to go on with it."

Bishop Ames leaned forward, his face in the yellow lantern light, thinking, This is how my father thought, this is what hurt him so, this was his torment. He said: "Starns, Starns, this is why I am a priest, Starns."

Gazing through the kitchen wall, wandering in the barren landscapes of his youth, Starns did not hear him. He thought he was moving, riding somewhere in a wagon whose bed was piled up with a stack of dead dogs, passing by a long double row of angry people, all yelling at him to do this, do that, push here and build there, while he was trying all the time to see over their heads or between their arms, stretching his neck to look for that one figure who denied them all, that one lean, ragged man, the only one who ever made any sense to him at all, his father, saying, "The hell with all that, son, the hell with it."

Rachael's hand went limp, her spoon dropped clattering on the floor and lay at Starns's feet. She did not move to pick it up. She stood silently, thinking of her two stillborn children, lost in agony. Somewhere in Starns's tangled story of freezing dogs and crying children the memory of it had come heavy upon her.

"That girl," said Starns, "she wouldn't have nothing to do with me after that. Not a look, not one. I didn't blame her. No, not a bit. And, you see, all I can do is just wish it was somebody else used that pitchfork, or seen her face then, or piled up them dogs in that wagon that way, or done most of the things I done in my life. Then maybe it would be me yelling about Jesus Christ and them saying, shut up, shut up."

"That's enough!" said Rachael Ames. "Please, Mr. Starns, that's enough." She bent over quickly and got her spoon, turned back to the sizzling apples, stirred them without washing it, leaning over to feel the hot steam on her face, to smell the bubbling juices.

Starns looked around the kitchen as if he only then realized where he was. He got up slowly and stood as best he could, jerking his head like a horse looking at a ditch he knows he must jump.

"It is time for me to go," he said. "I am sorry to put you to this trouble," he said.

The Bishop stood up with him, thinking, He can't say it, he can't say help me. That's all that's wrong with him, he isn't insane, no more than my father was, and they are stupid and cruel who say so. Merciful God, use me, let me show it is not madness to cry for help in this world.

He said: "Starns, hold on. You can't go anywhere now."

Starns tried to find out where the voice was coming from, but couldn't. He looked around him, lifting his chin, saying, "Oh, yes. Oh, yes, I can." He took one step and fell sprawling, rocking the kitchen table, sending the spoon bread dish spinning to the floor, where it cracked apart. He got up on his knees and tried with clumsy, dirty hands to pick up the pieces, then slashed the heel of his palm on the broken dish. He made a noise deep in his throat and collapsed. The Bishop and his wife jumped to help him.

Starns woke up lying in a large feather bed. The first thing he saw, through a red haze, was the gray canopy above him. He lifted himself up on one elbow, his head throbbing, and saw a walnut-faced Negro woman, with a red bandanna swishing at flies from her hand, rocking in a chair. When she saw he was awake, she pulled herself up and wobbled out of the room. Starns watched the chair rock on, empty. The muscles of his stomach tightened, sending a cramping pain up his side, and he felt the beats of his heart like hammers in his head. He lay back in the bed, closed his eyes and waited.

Soon he heard a rustling noise that he thought sounded like dried-out corn husks trailing across a floor. He opened his eyes again and saw the soft, round face of Rachael Ames hovering above the bed, vague and blurred. He tried to focus his eyes, blinking them hard, until he could see clearly the black hair parted in the middle, the two starched collars at her throat, the thin black shawl draped over her shoulders. She was smiling at him, smelling of soap and sweet lavender, behind the smile a hurt, puzzled expression.

"You are going to be all right, Mr. Starns," she said.

He tried to get up, but his heart beat in his head again. "I don't mean to put you out none."

She made a quick face, saying: "Mr. Starns, if you say that one more time, I am not only going to be put out, I am going to be downright insulted. Like it or not, you are going to rest here and have some soup in a minute. I'll tell you when I am put to more trouble than I can handle."

"Yessum," he said meekly.

When the Negro brought her the soup he was asleep again, his face lined and contorted, barklike against the white pillow linen. Rachael decided not to wake him and sent the soup back downstairs. Then she sat for a while in the rocker, resting and wondering what kind of man he was, lying filthy dirty between her clean guest-bed sheets, wondering what was between such a man and her husband.

In his study, his forehead perspiring and gleaming in lamplight, his head bent forward almost under the curve of the rolled-up desktop, Bishop Ames studied a pile of large maps. Some were surveyor's maps, some army cavalry and infantry reports, and some the cartooned sheets of trappers and hunters, men who could hardly read or write. He had been collecting them since September of the previous year, since the day his friend, the botanist Asa Gray, had slapped the first one down on his desk. That particular map was now tacked onto a flat board that hung on the wall by his desk. He was checking the other maps against it, doing it carefully, patiently.

The botanist's map was a reminder of the botanist's story, one Bishop Ames did not like much. It was a neat, capably drawn map, made by Asa Gray on a summer field trip in July of 1848. Gray was a young but already well-known scientist whom the Bishop had first met in England at the home of a distinguished elder of the Church. So when he had come with his map and his story, the Bishop had accepted it and told Asa Gray he would certainly investigate the situation. Since that day, late into the night, Bishop Ames had compared it with the other maps as he found them, seeking to disprove the original, as if by discovering a misnamed river he would do away with the stories told along its banks, whispered there into the ears of the botanist Asa Gray.

He sat back in his swivel chair, brought down from his old study in New York, and rubbed his eyes. He listened to the clatter of a wagon passing the house, heard the faint whistling of a banjo tune come floating in his window through the clopping of hoofs and the creaking of old wood held together by rusted iron. He took up the gay tune himself, whistling softly, looking up at the ceiling that was the floor of Starns's room above, thinking about Starns in his dead sleep. The Bishop looked at the map on the wall, thought of Starns's panic and his invisible injuries, thought of his own father's violent death. He whistled the banjo tune and heard the voice speak over it: *I am come not for the righteous, but the damned,* it said. *Not the righteous,* said the slightly hoarse voice that was Christ's in the Bishop's imagination. As a child he had always thought Christ's voice surely was hoarse from all his sermons, and one of his favorite boyhood reveries was a scene in which he handed the Saviour cool water in an earthen cup, then faded back and sat down with the crowd to listen. *But the damned,* the voice said, and it cracked. The boy jumped forward with the earthen cup.

The Bishop often thought of this scene when he was in his pulpit, when his own throat went feather dry and splintered his voice into hoarseness. It was one of the few childhood fantasies he remembered without embarrassment or fright.

He whistled until the wagon creaked into silence, then he stopped and rubbed his eyes again. Across the room was a large, split-bottomed rocking chair. Bishop Ames stared at it, remembering the botanist sitting there, telling his story while the Bishop looked over the map. He had rocked in the chair that night, smoking a pipe, telling stories of trees deciduous and plants uncatalogued, of the wild conglomeration of life growing tangled and untrampled from the soil of the heaving western mountains. The Bishop recalled the botanist's tale of the dead seagull, somehow blown inland from the Atlantic or from Chesapeake Bay, whose exhausted white corpse he had found on the tiny pebbled beach of a mountain creek. The bird must have seen it, dived to it from the troubled, stormy air, thinking it was the sea again with its wide, warm beaches waiting. It was soon after that, the Bishop remembered,

that Asa Gray came upon and named the place marked on the hanging
map: Heathen, a valley that forgot God.

In the split-bottomed rocker Gray told Bishop Ames that he had
come upon a high, upland valley, boxed in by vicious spurs and ridges. It
was isolated and desolate and romantic, choked with plants of species
he had not seen before except in books of Oriental botany. He knew
that his two predecessors, the Frenchman Michaux and Elisha Mitchell,
had not mentioned it, never chanced to see it as he did under its floating
gray mist, a valley you could barely see from the top of a peak bordering the gap called Mary's Pass. He made his way to it and found a
botanist's paradise. He spent two full weeks there, gathering and collecting and cataloguing. Also watching and listening.

He told the Bishop of the people who lived there, forsaken and isolated, slipping back into savagery as the memories of the eastern
seaboard, of Pennsylvania and New England, of towns and houses and
churches and meetings left them. A people the botanist vividly charac-
terized as haunted by hallucinations and night spirits, obsessed by
lunacy and death, hungry and violent, celebrating their passions and
fears in wild, amoral sprees, wandering barefoot with ancient homemade long rifles that sometimes blew up in their faces, brandishing
old, stone-sharpened barlow knives, and speaking a curt, blunt language occasionally obscured by forgotten words unknown to him.
They killed and they starved, the botanist said, they lived like goats and
dogs and monkeys, inbreeding, not only close kin but direct descen-
dants, father and daughter, mother and son, sister and brother, so that
one old man told the botanist, laughing, that he was his own grandfather, and proud of it. He told the Bishop of wan, hollow-cheeked faces
peering from dark, smoky doorways of dirt-floored shacks, huts so
rickety at times that they were no more than lean-tos propped up
against an outcropping boulder, the fourth wall the wet, living rock.
He said he saw a man who had been kicked in the face and chest by a
mule, saw him die without hope, to be thrown into the ground an
hour later by his family, without ceremony. He told of wild-haired
women running amazed out of their shacks to stare at him as he

passed, children whose stomachs were distended with hunger and disease, men with long, scraggly hair matted like a spaniel's ear, standing aloof, watching him go by as they might watch a snake slide over a rock at their feet.

And after two hours of such description he told Bishop Ames about Sand Mountain, one of the staggered ridges that shut the valley in, where at Christmas unspeakable riots took place. It was their last, sad remembrance of their religion, the botanist said, that something should happen December 25 or thereabouts, and so they celebrated the nativity in loathsome savagery.

The Bishop listened, not with alarm or shock or even interest, but with weariness. He had finished, two years before, a long and agonizing crusade for slave churches on the plantations of eastern Carolina. The crusade had lasted several years, in that time he had given hundreds of speeches, traveled several thousands of miles and built exactly three churches, for which act no Negro had ever thanked him. So the botanist and his story filled him with the weariness that comes only from a bone-deep sense of futility, futility and waste, time and means sinfully squandered by idealism, weak and openhanded, always wrong, always.

But he did not doubt or rationalize the botanist's story, he accepted it. As the year went on, it grew in his consciousness. It appeared in the daily things he saw and did. Plaster falling from the ceiling reminded him of it. A beggar in the street brought him up short and sent his mind to the mountains. Then one night he dreamed of a great mountain splitting down the middle, making a ditch, and in it was the Bishop's father, blood streaming from his head down the front of his denims, shrieking.

He began to collect maps.

Starns, then, was the final, needed shock. For Bishop Ames, William Starns was the pitiful creation wriggling like his father half mad in the dirt. He was wild ignorance, unleashed self-destruction. Starns was the incarnation both of his father and of the forsaken mountain pagans, in that same agony because their bleak cabins remained unvisited by Christ, by sanity and order and hope. Starns was the father he had not been old enough to save, the damned, not the righteous, the work to be done, Christ's work, whether a disillusioned Bishop liked it or not.

The wagon, creaking desperately, its driver whistling the same banjo tune, lumbered past the house again, bouncing even more violently, empty of its load. The Bishop set his maps in order. As he stacked them, he whistled along with the faceless man going by in the night. He felt giddy, relieved, expectant. Boyishly he slammed down the rolltop of his desk and thought that Christ's voice had broken again, too hoarse it was to carry over the high mountains, yet strong enough to make him, Christ's Bishop, forget his fantasies of earthen cups and cool water, forgo reality again in His name, march into the still-shadowed wilderness and seek out the heathen who waited there, fearful and dying in the dark, bloody ditches.

He went to bed whistling, laughed violently at a new white nightcap Rachael wore, and dreamed about nothing at all.

Rachael Ames insisted that Starns stay in bed all the next day. He lay helpless, blushing between the clean linen sheets, eating food in bed for the first time in his life. A bed's where you sleep or die, he puzzled, what's all this? When the Bishop visited him that night, pulling up a chair by the bed, Starns regained his dignity with a desperate effort and sat up against the bank of white pillows like a giant crow, nodding his head soberly while the Bishop talked, telling him the story of Heathen valley. Bishop Ames made a performance of it, using his orator's gifts to paint pictures even more wretched than had the botanist.

When he was through, Starns pursed his lips and considered it. Then he said: "Poor folks has poor ways," several times. That was all.

The Bishop handed over the botanist's map, sliding it across Starns's knees that humped up the bedspread. He put his finger on name places and said them aloud for Starns, who kept on nodding. "Well," he said, "do you recognize any of them?"

"Yessir, I do," said Starns. He remembered many of the names, and he saw how they fitted together on the map, making up the country where he was born. Dagman's Gorge he remembered, and Stand Around Gap, Watauga River, Grandfather Mountain. "Yessir, I been through some of them places, all right."

"How about this?" said the Bishop, and he read the inscription Gray had written at the top of the map: "Heathen, a valley that forgot God."

"Well, I don't know nothing about that. But if this here is the Watauga River I crossed many a time, and if that is Boone town, and if that is the Grandfather, I'd say you got a pretty good map. So I reckon the valley is where the map says it is, all right."

The Bishop read the inscription to him again, emphasizing the words *forgot God*.

"I don't know nothing about that at all," said Starns. "Poor folks just has poor ways, though, Bishop."

Folding the map, the Bishop said: "Starns, in a week or two I'll be taking a trip. I want to see that valley and what's there. How would you like to come along? I'll need your help anyway, and you might find some answers about yourself there, some I can't give you. How about it?"

Starns hesitated. "You'd be preaching a lot on the way?"

"Yes," said the Bishop.

Gently Starns asked: "Do I have to listen to you preach, Bishop? Or like what you say?"

"No, Starns," said the Bishop. "No, you don't."

"Then I would like to come. Yessir, I'd like that."

"Good. By the way, the church is in a mess. That new janitor was a loafer and he's on his way already. How about that, too?"

"Well, how about Preacher Sales? That man don't care for me much."

"I have already spoken to Reverend Sales," said the Bishop. "He is anxious that you help him at St. Mark's as soon as you can."

"He said that?"

"Yes. And I told him I would tell you personally."

"Well," said Starns, "I do feel some better." He pushed at the covers nervously with his huge hands. "If I go, can I go now? Get out of this bed and go right now?"

The Bishop laughed and nodded.

Starns swung his long legs out from under the covers and onto the floor. Then he paused, thought a minute and said: "Oh. Just one more thing. No more bitches, is that right?"

"That's right," agreed the Bishop solemnly, "no bitches."

The next afternoon, launched against their will by an adamant Bishop, the three frigates, sails drooping, glided silently to the church. At anchor, the offending Christians apologized.

Starns nodded and went on with his work.

3

ADVENT

GELDER'S KNOB is a steep mountain spur rising up out of foothills to face the blue peaks of Appalachia. It is bald, its grassy summit free from trees or brush—a high meadow some say the wind keeps clear, some say the ghosts of banished Indians tend. It is below timberline, in savage mountain country, nevertheless the grass grows free and gentle there, like a slightly neglected lawn. Some are puzzled by it, some delighted, but when Starns rode up on Gelder's Knob and looked at the waving grass, he only thought, Oh, yes, a bald. I had almost forgotten that.

The Bishop's party waded the grass on horseback, riding to the rock-lined drop, to look out and check their maps. They dismounted by a big projecting boulder: Starns, the Bishop, Marcus Sales, who had been asked along because Bishop Ames felt he had been too hard on him lately, and a thin, redheaded boy of fifteen with skinny arms and a fair face, a student in the Raleigh Episcopal School for Boys, named Billy Cobb. They stepped cautiously along the rocky spine of the boulder until they could see off, then checked what they saw against their maps, turned and stepped cautiously back and made rest camp. Bishop Ames unfolded a campstool and sat on it, wiping his neck with a red kerchief, and began to chat theology with Billy Cobb, who poured him some water from a canteen. Marcus Sales spread his blankets and napped, a white handkerchief over his face to keep away the gnats. It was hot June in the mountains, sticky and overcast, and the winds around the spur were damp.

Starns tethered the horses, which were anxious to graze the mountaintop meadow. He stood by each one, rubbing the wet circles of saddle sweat off their backs, drying them out. When he had finished, he watched them nose, then chomp their way through the grass for a few minutes, then folded his heavy cloth and dropped it. With a glance at the others he went to the boulder again and on hands and knees made his way out to its far point. There he sat, his long legs dangling in the empty air, the heels of his boots knocking together slowly, rhythmically.

Down a line off his left shoulder he saw black dots on a ridge, the town of Stewart, North Carolina, saw them intermittently through the passing mist that swept up to his feet, then past his face and over the bald, torn banners caught and spirited away by the wind. Stewart was a tiny, meaningless line of stores and houses from his high perch. He saw them laid out on each side of a threadlike trail that ran the top of the ridge like a chalk line. Starns thought the tiny buildings looked like a strung-out parade of wagons going over the ridge, stopped for an hour's rest.

Stewart. Now, is that the first town I ever seen? I do believe it was. I do believe it.

He looked straight ahead, out over mist-blown, clouded mountain country. He knocked his heels together and gently envied a large black bird floating almost level with his eyes. It was a raven, below whose idle circling, stretching away into the smoking distance, rolled the western Carolina mountains, ancient, aloof, indifferent. Under their thick, wet forest loam lay the great rocks, compounded, split open, riven each into the other a million times, then thrust high long before the Alps or the Himalayas stirred. Over the immense stillness the wind blew gently, until a faint, distant cawing broke the silence. Starns listened, cocking his head to one side. The cawing came again, and then a thin, faraway crack of a rifle. In places the sun was breaking through the murky tangle of heavy cloud banks; the wind-driven mist raced through its beams. The far horizon was cloudless but still blurred with smoky haze.

Bishop Ames, Starns remembered, had cleared his orator's throat and called it a blue sandstorm.

While Marcus Sales napped, while the Bishop talked with the earnest Billy Cobb about St. Paul and the true history of the Christian Church, a dark bank of clouds above Gelder's Knob whitened and parted. Shafts of sunlight slipped through its pale belly, fell down onto the slopes and fanned out as the clouds drifted apart. The wind rent the fabric of the mist, tore holes in it as it came by. Through the gaps Starns's sight leaped down into the chasms below him. With a careful hand behind him he held on to the rock.

Slowly the sun sharpened the vague outlines of the slopes. Starns saw a forest appear suddenly, its firs snapping into focus, ragged, tips sharp as dagger points. The air cleared, began to sparkle with moisture. On the slope just below his boots a bank of rhododendrons swayed under the wind, rose and milk-streaked purple, and he remembered, Why, it is summer. It is June.

Wasn't it June when I come down these slopes, down from my home after that circuit rider? It was, I believe it was.

He watched the sunlight pass over the land, bring it glistening into view.

Where was it? Now, where was it? I don't know, do I? No, I don't, I just don't.

He held on to the rock, gripping it hard.

Are they maybe still alive? It is a question. Most likely not. It has been a time since then.

Bright sunlight fell upon him. He looked up, squinting. It hurt, it sent tears into the crow's-feet cracks sprouting out of the corners of his eyes, it dazzled him. The light danced on the backs of his leathery hands and jumped away, spreading down the slope. His grip tightened on the rock, the knuckles were white and his forearm shook. For his senses were reeling, dizzy now from the quick onslaught of gusts of honeysuckle, of bright colors of the wild, livid azaleas, of shiny green laurel from whose tangle scarlet trumpet blossoms poked, as if to sound.

Well. Well, then. This is my place, all right, and I have come to be

back here after all this time. But where are they, my own? They, where
are they?

Leaning awkwardly from his saddle, Marcus Sales took a big breath and
shouted. He was calling to a gaunt woman hoeing a small, steeply
inclined patch of buckwheat shadowed by several large hemlocks.
"Madam!" he screamed. "Can you tell us are we on the way to the
home of Mr. Carford Dudley?" Marcus Sales was tired and worried. It
was late afternoon and they had been off the botanist's careful map for
an hour.

Pole thin, dressed in a baggy floursack dress and wearing a wagging
bonnet, the woman walked slowly to the split-rail fence between them,
set her hoe against it and stared. She looked at Marcus Sales, at his face
and shoulders, at his arms, hat, trousers, gloves, at his horse and saddle.
Then she inspected the rest of the party at that same pace, lingering
finally over the pack mule that brought up the rear. Then she looked at
Marcus Sales again.

"What was that?" she said.

Marcus Sales said: "I said, can you tell us are we on the way, the
right road, to Mr. Carford Dudley's house?"

"Who's he?"

"That's what I was asking you!"

"Then I reckon neither of us knows," she said, and she turned
instantly back to her field, dragging the hoe behind her.

"Madam, one moment, please," said Marcus Sales. He dismounted,
handing his reins to Billy Cobb. The woman turned again and stared
again. At the fence he said: "I want to thank you for your help, anyway."

She nodded.

"And while we are stopped, I would like to ask you something else,
if I may."

She nodded.

Fascinated by the botanist's tales of the heathen mountaineers, Sales
put a keen eye on the ragged, frail-looking woman and spoke in a full,

commanding voice. "Madam, I would like to know if you have ever heard of Jesus Christ."

In his saddle Starns squirmed. He was angry and embarrassed. He looked reproachfully at the Bishop, then back at Sales, thinking, Now, what's that for? What's he want to do that for?

The woman hefted her hoe and carried it back to the fence. She set it carefully against the top rail and opened her mouth, displaying a broken line of dark, rotted teeth. Her voice was thin and off pitch, almost whining.

"Yessir," she said soberly, "I have. I have heard of him." There was a pause. "He passed through here about a month ago."

Marcus Sales took a minute, then said: "No, I mean Jesus of Bethlehem, our Lord and Saviour."

Shadowed by the rim of her bonnet, the staring eyes neither wavered nor blinked. "That's right," she said confidentially, "Bethlehem, Pennsylvania. The feller was on his way home. Now, I'd a stopped to chat, but I got just too much to hoe here. Anything else ye want to know, Preacher?"

Marcus Sales stomped back to his horse, mounted stiffly and rode off, indignant. Behind him Bishop Ames and Billy Cobb tried not to smile. Behind them, bent over in his saddle, Starns was convulsed, thinking, Well, that's one of my own, yes, by God, that's one of them. He turned, stood in his stirrups and waved to her.

From her steep and shadowed field the gaunt woman waved back, her bonnet wagging.

Early the next morning they emerged from the house of Carford Dudley, got on their horses and left, gladly. In Stewart they had been told that Dudley lived in the only comfortable home in the mountains. It had been described to them as a towering brick palace on the banks of the Watauga, surrounded by rain-fresh orchards savory with the perfume of green apples. When they rode in, late in the afternoon, they saw no orchards and no palace. They saw only a squat, unfinished brick building hiding from them in the spreading dusk. It was true that it was brick, but they also saw patches of crude, discolored plaster, unfinished walls with gaping holes boarded up. It was a great hollow shell of a house, and they had decided it was deserted when they made out the still figure of a man sitting on the shambling porch that was held up by wobbly stacks of chipped bricks and uneven rocks. In silence they rode up to the porch. There, in the last light of day, sat a huge, hairy man, his eyelids half closed, doing nothing at all, paying them no attention. The Bishop spoke sharply. "Good evening. Would you please call Mr. Dudley for us?"

"Dudley?" said the hairy man, eyes half open. "Carford Dudley?"

"That's right," said the Bishop tartly. "Please call him."

"Well," said the hairy man, "if that's what ye want. I might find him, don't know, though. Sometimes he answers me, sometimes he don't. I'll give her a try, though." He got up slowly from his chair, making a pretense of brushing off his stained jeans. He looked around, called himself, answered, looked back at the Bishop and roared with laughter.

Again Starns's face brightened. He put a big leathery palm over his mouth. "Hee hee," he said.

Inside the house Dudley's wife served them a full dinner of fried salt pork, apple butter, cucumbers, potatoes and thick crusted pie with buttermilk, then coffee. She served it and removed it without speaking. The Bishop, over the pie, attempted a conversation with Dudley, managing to tell him where they were going before the hairy man got up and said he was ready for some sleep, for them to finish their coffee and he'd show them their beds. That night they slept on thin mattresses, piles of cornhusks covered with thin strips of flour-sack cotton, each one tossing and turning, even young Billy Cobb. Finally, one by one, they dropped off. The Bishop slept last, listening as he closed his eyes to the gurgling river flowing swiftly by the hollow mansion.

After their breakfast, which was much the same as dinner, the Bishop paid Dudley the seventy-five cents he charged for each man's board and room. Dudley walked out onto his porch with them and watched quietly while Starns brought the horses around from the barn.

When they were saddled and ready, Dudley suddenly lumbered down from his porch and held a beefy arm out to Bishop Ames. In his hand was a dirty piece of paper. "Something for ye," he said.

Bishop Ames took it with surprise. It was a map, drawn up in berry ink, without a scale of any sort or even boundaries of what it was supposed to chart. Useless, thought the Bishop, but he quickly realized that Dudley must have risen early or stayed up late to do it for them.

"We are greatly obliged, Mr. Dudley," he said. "We already have several maps, but yours is a welcome addition. Thank you, sir."

Dudley climbed his porch again, saying: "Shore. But none of them other maps will do ye, Bishop. I don't care where ye got them neither. Half a mile up from here there ain't no roads no more, and what sled trails and paths there be get washed out and slided over from time to time. That's right."

Holding the map with one hand and looking at it, Bishop Ames swung the bridle with the other, bringing Henry, the bay, about to face the porch. Henry was stamping nervously, restless in the early-morning dampness. "This is very thoughtful of you, sir," said the Bishop.

"Indeed," chimed Marcus Sales, "your efforts will be remembered, sir. They help the Lord's truth to shine in this wilderness." He shot up on his horse like a cavalryman.

Carford Dudley eased his hairy bulk down into his chair and sucked up a great blob of phlegm. He spat, sailing it out from the porch to the feet of Marcus Sales's horse.

"Now, listen," he said, wiping his mouth, "damn fool preachers. Why go up there in the first place? I made that there map so's ye wouldn't get lost and starve, but the best thing is just not to go at all. Ye ain't the kind of men for that country, I mean it. So why go?"

"Why not, Mr. Dudley?" said the Bishop quietly, stroking Henry's neck.

"Because it's dangerous, that's why. That's pagan land. All them people up there, they be heathen. Don't have no churches up there, don't have no marrying, funerals neither, much less no preachers. Ye'll come on things up there just benasty a man's mind, that's right."

His resentful, sleepy eyes began to droop shut as he squirmed his bulk deeper into the chair. From behind the house, carrying a large wooden bucket, the stooping figure of his wife passed into the forest. When Dudley spoke again, it was as if he were sleeping.

"No, don't go at all," he mumbled. "Why, Christmastime is the worst, yessir, it is. Christmas Day they do things a man just can't talk about. Don't go there." He waved a thick paw at them and disappeared into his huge, hairy body, oblivious.

Bishop Ames swung Henry around. "Starns, are we ready?" "Yessir," came the answer. "Very well, then," said Bishop Ames, trotting his bay handsomely away from the squat, empty shell of Dudley's house, the map fluttering in his hand.

They climbed up from the river cove in raw and wet early-morning weather. Soon they faced the ancient and unpeopled slopes that yawned above them, dwarfing their tiny horses, swallowing the scuffling sounds of their journey. Single file, they wound up a narrow sled trail, following Dudley's map, grateful for it now, for its crude precision. The Bishop rode in front, then Sales, Billy Cobb, Starns bringing up the rear, leading the pack mule that carried their equipment: food, medicines, camping gear, one shotgun, one bottle of whisky. They had been climbing for half an hour when the Bishop looked back and could no longer see the brick house or the river. He felt like a swimmer in the sea who turns shivering in the water to find that the waves are hiding the shore from his eyes.

The ancient, virgin forest, somber, drenched in summer rain, went passing as they climbed, met itself and closed arms on them. On each side of their trail the tangled, massive forest heaved up, then dropped into chasms where trees and brush and long vines seemed to grow on top of each other. They climbed through woods of dripping maple and ash, rode under towering oaks and walnuts, past the graceful sycamore and chincapin. The Bishop's imagination began to stir and trouble him. He tried to lull it by recalling his botany, and he spotted yellow buckeyes a hundred feet tall, birches with white trunks smooth as linen, wild cherry pines whose heads were lost in the great masses of soaked leaves moaning far above them. He watched the ground, saw passing under his stirrups parades of many-colored trilliums, trailing arbutus that Rachael loved, Dutchman's-breeches. Once he thought he saw the ginseng root, the mountain mandrake.

Then, with a sigh, he let loose his leashed imagination, let it flash images and impressions unhindered through his mind, each one lingered over a little longer than the one that preceded it, before being dismissed with a smile. The botanist had told him of the astounding number of plants and flowers native to these mountains that were believed to grow only in the Orient, in the wastes of China and on the islands of Japan. Of these the prize was the ginseng root, in the superstitions of China called *jen shen,* the root of life, prized and even worshiped for its powers of physical vigor and longevity. When was it that the Frenchman Michaux taught the mountaineers its value? Bishop Ames could not remember, but he did know that since then the poverty-stricken mountain people had swarmed over the slopes, grubbing for it, digging it out of the dark, wet mountain dirt to change it at some nameless store for flour and coffee. Smiling at him, the botanist had put a wooden box on the Bishop's desk. From it he took a ginseng root and held it up. It was split, had two legs, looked like a tiny man. "Interesting," said the Bishop, and the botanist said: "Isn't it? But it takes another form sometimes. Look." From the box he brought out some corn shucks kept moist in a surrounding cake of damp earth. He peeled them away, displaying a prize ginseng root, the dampness of the earth still on it. It was the size and shape of an erect, foot-long penis, with bulging, tubular testicles.

As the Bishop swayed in the saddle, thinking about the ginseng phallus, about passports to eternal youth, rich men's aphrodisiacs, his mouth went slack and he imagined himself suddenly a Mongol potentate riding up a giant, leaf-roofed corridor to give thanks at an unknown shrine. Through a stand of hemlocks he saw empty air, two ravens playing as they do on the updrafts, sailing up and down on the currents, like rafts on the sea. Then he thought himself a sailor, with sunburned neck and knots for knuckles, plotting their capture into cages, where he would teach them to speak his native tongue on foreign waters.

At this he guffawed, snorted at himself, then surrendered entirely. He was eight years old again, a child burrowing into a wondrous country, led by his wild and deeply satisfying imagination. His loose smile became that of an indulgent, dreamy, senseless man; he rode drunk and reinless. The smile spread on his face, for he was hearing the voice, the voice of his father, coming again through the clopping of hoofs, speaking to him through the cold New England morning air, saying, *Look, son, look! The sun's up and, god damn, it is fine out here! Get up, slugabed, come on out here!*

Above the tangled forest and the great mounds of the mountains, the clouds hung dark and low. A storm rumbled three miles east; around their heads the wind said it was coming, then dashed away to announce it elsewhere. They rode by a sudden gorge, somber and redolent with the stench of festering weeds and trapped air. The Bishop's smile faded away, his handsome face locked itself into a fixed stare.

He was hearing the ax blows again. The blade cracked into the wood and the echo rang in his brain. *No, Nahum, god dammit, look at the tree, boy, not the ax! The tree, boy,* said the voice, and the Bishop's right hand gripped his saddle horn, clenched at it with his right shoulder hunched forward. From the depths of his past he heard the tree creak again, heard something in it split with the last, desperate sound of falling timber. He lifted his head, childish again, and saw the great cluster of leaves begin to move, the trunk begin to lean. He pushed at the saddle horn and with the thin, frail arms of thirty years before he pushed the trunk, then turned before it fell, turned away from its slow, timeless fall, turned his beaming face to his father again, saw him sitting on a log, the jug jauntily upturned at his mouth, the gurgling sounding at his moist, beaded lips. *Good, by God! Right good, boy!* the lips said, and the Bishop's flushed face smiled again, his father's bright eyes glittered with pleasure and affection. Bishop Ames felt warm waves of comfort creeping down his backbone. Thank you, Father, he said.

Roaring through the air, the tree crashed to the ground.

"Hold up, there!" Starns yelled. "Bishop Ames!" He jumped his horse up the trail, slashing it with his reins, shouldering alongside the bay and smacking Henry's rump. They sprinted wildly up the trail, Henry almost unseating the Bishop. When they had stopped and looked back, Starns said: "What in the world? Didn't you hear him cutting?"

Bishop Ames mumbled something purposely incoherent, realizing how shamefully he had wandered. Across the trail below them, with the startled figures of Billy Cobb and Marcus Sales on the other side of it, lay the trunk of a fallen tree. The ax blows were real, thought the Bishop, momentary as well as timeless and false. They cut down that tree.

Hands over their faces, Billy Cobb and Marcus Sales walked their horses through brush and vine, circling the tip of the fallen tree, and joined Starns and the Bishop. Their horses milling awkwardly on the narrow trail, the four men peered into the woods. They heard a loud scuffling and stirring, heard the soft, mushy sounds of crushed wet brush and twig. Starns motioned, and they rode up the trail a few yards and waited.

The stirring came louder and the forest moved, the brush parted. From it stalked several head of scrawny, underfed cattle. They lumbered up to the fallen tree, which was a young linden, and began eagerly to munch the branches, eating the fresh shoots, which were tender and moist.

"I see him," said Starns. "Through there. Now, everybody just hold still."

Through the tangle of dripping leaves Bishop Ames saw him standing in the shadows of the forest, holding an ax in one hand. His eyes glittered. The Bishop shuddered and chased away the returning memories of his father, of wet lips and wild eyes, of mud-stained denims smelling of raw whisky. He forced himself to look into the brush. The man returned his stare without moving, holding the ax up stiffly.

None of them saw him that clearly, they said later when they talked it over. They agreed he looked young, and his hair was long and matted, some of it hanging down his forehead, and his clothes ragged and filthy.

That was all they agreed on, except for the wild fierceness of his eyes staring at them through the brush.

Bishop Ames raised a hand and called to him, his voice unsteady. The man did not answer, but in a moment he raised to his eye the long barrel of a rifle.

"All righty," said Starns gently, turning his horse casually up the trail. "Let's us go on now, he just don't want nobody to fool with him, that's certain. So we won't. Come on, now."

They followed Starns up the trail. The man in the forest stared after them, eyes blazing, watching them grow smaller and smaller as they worked their way up the slope.

Pale and shaken, the Bishop did not look back.

Billy Cobb's thighs were aching from the constant upward surge of the horse under him, from the uneven jerking of the saddle. He had been sweating hard for an hour, and when he wiped his face with a soft hand, it came away damp with cold, unsalty moisture. Heavily he gulped air through his mouth, keeping glassy eyes fastened onto the back of Bishop Ames riding in front of him. To himself Billy Cobb kept saying over and over, like a jingle to horse-clop rhythms: Billy follows, Billy follows. Only because the boy worshiped Bishop Ames, avidly treasured his opinion of him, could he keep from yelling: Stop, I'm not going on anymore, I don't care what. Christian or heathen or what.

The leaden sky drizzled steadily. Large outcroppings of rock became more and more frequent. The horses stepped warily, careful of such ground, so different from the casual hills of eastern Carolina. Behind them, led by Starns, the pack mule slopped his way up, mountain-born and unconcerned, his head nodding and bobbing, his hoofs clanking forlornly against the rocks.

Billy Cobb had decided that his spine would crack any minute when the Bishop looked back at him and pointed ahead. Except for a misty vapor on the wind, the rain had stopped. The boy nodded vigorously and grinned, his pains forgotten, seeing the trail run out of thinning forest into brush, cut through it and slip over into what they all hoped was the valley of Heathen. A few yards from the top the Bishop reined in. They gathered around him. "Well, gentlemen, let's hope we are here at last. I trust you are as thankful for that as I am. And I think we need a prayer." He looked at the boy. "Go ahead, Billy," he said, and bowed his head.

Blushing at this favor, Billy Cobb lowered his eyes, bent down his head with the shock of cowlicked reddish hair. "O Lord," he said in his trebled voice, and then paused. Then: "Let us just do what is good in thy sight amen."

"Amen," said Bishop Ames. "Thank you, Billy." He rode ahead, slapping a tired Henry to the best trot he could manage, then galloped over the top of the mound.

Heathen greeted the Bishop with thunder and a swirl of dark, ragged clouds. He saw an upland valley, two hundred acres of bottomland, boxed in on all sides. Parts of the valley had once been cleared, but most of the stumps had been left standing. They stuck up like black pockmarks, between them a few uneven, random clusters of sprouting corn. There were no other crops and no cabins visible. It seemed deserted, barren land, but in the damp evening air there was a harmony to it, there was a still beauty that awed them, hushed the aches and pains of their journey, made them forget to long for the sight of man-made homes, cabins to rest in.

Down the two high ridges that shut in the valley from the east and northwest flowed two rivers, small but fierce now from the rains, tumbling along mud-stained and angry in deeply cut beds. They met at the center of the valley bottom, mingled in a pile-up of brownish currents, and flowed out of the valley through a south gap. Above the swirling place of their meeting, as if gathered there in a ritual, hung the mist, long gray strips of it, banners of a hidden people, moving gently, floating in the evening sky.

To the Bishop's already leaping imagination they seemed incredible, foreign. Fantastic dancers, amorphous, otherworldly dignitaries, serenely parading themselves past each other, weightless and proud, scornful of the cares of the earth. Billy Cobb rode up next to him, the boy's horse bobbing its head and twitching its ears. Billy's pale face was still, rapt. Bishop Ames saw that his head was slightly tilted; like his horse, Billy was listening to something. It was the water, sounds of it coming from above, below, all sides. Bishop Ames heard the bass roar of a waterfall some-where across the valley up the slopes, heard the tinkling of rock-shallow streams and branches, and below them the angry, harsh rhythms of the two flooded rivers, smashing together like cymbals where they met.

Above it all, idle and careless, hung the mist.

"Heathen," whispered Billy Cobb.

They sat for some time on puzzled horses, resting and watching.

4

CIRCLE FOUR

Harlan

I watched them go toiling up the slopes. Soon they looked like ants.

Whilst my cow brutes ate on the tree, I stood pushing some dirt around with one foot. Ants, I thought. And worms. Creatures of the dirt, pass me by.

Orlean was only twelve and Joseph six, and I was down there in that field, hoeing. Over the head of Gore's Knob, as far off as Mary's Pass, it was rainy, and the clouds was heavy over the valley. I was studying the day, wondering when it would clear. That was when I heard the first shot. I figured it might be Tate Benson, shooting up the woods like he does, but I knowed Tate wouldn't be that near my place. The second shot come to me on the wind and it was at my cabin, all right. I dropped the hoe then and run.

When I come up on the yard, Margaret was standing there on the porch, one hand holding her arm where it was bloodied. When she seen it was me, she just pointed.

Now, I had built a swing for Orlean, hung it from our hickory. Little Joseph was hanging from it by one arm. It looked like he had got his hand caught in the rope where it went through a notch in the seat board. But whilst I looked on, he come loose and he slid down on top of Orlean. She was lying there right under him, face down in the mud. That swing I had fixed for my young'uns commenced to sway above

them, mocking their bodies. Under it they was all twisted and muddy,
like baby grouse a man sneaks up on and kills on the ground.

I carried them into the cabin and Margaret, she commenced to wash
their hands and faces and all. She wouldn't let me touch her. Her arm
was bleeding, but she wouldn't let me do a thing.

I didn't have to ask her was it Daniel Larman done it, I knowed that
right off. When I took that cornfield away from him, I knowed it was
part of it rightfully Daniel's, but then I never thought he would do what
he did. I went out and looked down into the valley and seen him down
there waiting.

"How did he do it?" I asked Margaret.

She had Joseph's shirt open, washing his chest.

"They was fooling about on the swing, Harlan," she said. "Daniel
come up and they was all laughing together, and then he shot them."

On my way down I lopped off the swing ropes at hand height. Then
I throwed that seat board as far off down the slope as I could. I left my
horse behind the cabin and struck out on foot.

Daniel was setting his big roan, expecting me to come right down at
him. Setting up there, the big roan twitching his ears, Daniel holding his
rifle gun, waiting for me to come on so's he could do me, too. Thinking
I'd run wild and come yelling down at him with my knife or something
and he'd get me then. Well, he figured wrong, Daniel did. I cut up over the
east ridge and bore down on him that way. I had to get down and crawl
the last part, but the stumps still standing in them fields was good cover.

When Daniel's time come, he was fooling with his shoe. Had one
leg flopped over the saddle horn, shoe off in one hand, shaking something out of it. Now, I knowed that field was rightfully his field as well
as mine, and I was still grabbing out for what was right and what was
wrong in the thing, yes, I was. But by that time I had crawled too far, I
was tired and weary of it and all of it was wrong, like my boy and little
girl twisted all crooked in the mud underneath that damn swing.

His shoe satisfied him and he was putting it back on and lacing
when I shot. Daniel come off that saddle like he was getting down quick
just to look at something. He held on to the horn with one hand, look-

ing around to see where I was, holding his hip. I got my rifle gun ram-rodded again and shot again. I hit him in the neck that time. He fell down like a tossed-off sack.

I got that big roan and rode him home. When I come riding into the yard, them rope ends hung down from the tree like legs.

Inside the cabin my Margaret had taken to bed. Orlean and Joseph was washed clean, lying there on the floor in front of the fire, the big coverlid over them up to their chins. A man does not ever expect to see his children that way. All I could study was that they was mad with their pa, disgusted with him, tired of the tales he told and the play purtys he made. It was like they was listening to some other storyteller then, who made all my tales not worth much.

I set the bed next to Margaret and seen right off she was fitified. She wouldn't do nothing for that arm. She fell to thrashing and moaning, so I made her let me pour some whisky on it. But she wouldn't tell me if the ball was in her or not, and I couldn't tell.

Night was coming down, the fire was most out, it was frosty in my cabin. I had to take the coverlid off Orlean and Joseph and put it on Margaret. She didn't like that, but I did it anyhow.

I looked in the crib once and seen that baby Jean, she wasn't well neither. Her little cheeks was all sandy and she coughed a time or two. Then I vowed it was bad in my cabin, and what would I do with Margaret gone? I always said this, Margaret never stinted on my Jean, even if I did get that child out of Cora Larman and it wasn't none of Margaret's at all. Margaret had been good about that. And my babies out of my Margaret, the ones lived on after birth, had only been two. Orlean and then Joseph, both lying cold at my knees whilst I built up the fire.

It got some warmer. I set the bed again and put one hand on Margaret's leg. Through the coverlid it was like a rock and she wasn't breathing hardly at all. Her chest was still as a plank. Her lips was all mashed together, little lines a-lacing up her mouth like thread stitches, just like she was some old, old woman.

So I asked her if there was anything she wanted me to do. Spells or charms or such. She shook her head.

"We always said we was above that, Harlan," she said.

I felt love come up in my heart for Margaret then. It was the first time I had felt that way about her for the longest time, but it happened. It happened when she said I wasn't to pass no spells. We had always said they was foolish and harmful, no good for the dying nohow. It made me ache and love her then, that she held up to what we had always said. Not even dying did she put no trust in spells.

But she thrashed about again and looked so bad I wanted to make sure, so I asked her again and she said, "Oh, Harlan. I don't want no fuss from ye now, Harlan."

And I recalled the day we had decided about that. Setting the bed, my hand on her cold leg, I recalled the day.

I recalled the day he died and how it had been with me and Margaret then, watching him on his last bed with Ma half wild all that time. We was near Orlean's age then, young'uns both, her some older than me. We held on to each other's arms whilst Ma called in that mess of moaning fools, coming in there trying to hex a deathbed to life again. And afterwards it was worse, because when they had gone, she made us turn and conjur over the body of our own pa.

I recalled the smelly roots and weeds she made Margaret cook. I recalled the charms she boiled and laid on his chest. I felt Ma's hand on my shoulder again, and her saying, "Hep me now, hep me now! Lift this quick, Harlan." And her sweating and straining at the foot of the bed, trying to lift it. Then, when we had got it moved, with him on it screaming, Ma saying, "Begone, Harlan! Git that ax, boy!" And me running out to the woodpile under the lean-shed, crying. Me pulling the ax out of a log and running back in with it. Her saying, "Now, Harlan, we will save him. Now you and me and Margaret here, hit will be us to do hit. He won't like that much, but ye be my witness, boy. Hit was me saved him, me he has to thank now. Be my witness, sonny, now do what I showed ye!" Her throwing back her head and wailing, me with the ax making the biggest swing I could, slicing smack into the cabin floor, right there in the dust and dirt where the bed had been. Then her, sweating and straining again, saying, "Quick, 'fore the power goes out of hit," and then Margaret and Ma and me lifting the bed again and setting it back, down on top of the ax biting the floor. And her saying, "Now git the razor, boy!"

I recalled handing it to her. Her throwing back one of his arms, whistling through her teeth whilst he spit blood, and then her shaving the hair from the dark hollow under his arm. Then handing it to me and me running with it, out to the white birch tree beyond the clearing. Her watching at the cabin door, all glittery-eyed and whistling. Me knifing a hole in the white bark and shoving the hair in it, then sealing it up in there with mud and bark and a little rock.

And that night, when he died, her beating us. Saying we had faulted the spell on purpose so's it would kill him. Margaret was in the corner, she wouldn't move from it, holding her hands over her face.

Watching Margaret on her last bed, I recalled all that. And I recalled what a long time it took Ma to see that he was gone truly, and how when she finally come to endure it, had him taken away in his winding sheet and wouldn't suffer us to come when she took him off in the wagon.

Margaret's arm was around my neck whilst I was crying after that wagon, and one of her hands at my cheek. She comforted me best she could, saying we had learned never to do spells like that, but to die quiet. Won't we, Harlan? she said then.

So that was one thing I loved about my Margaret, and I was glad she wouldn't suffer me to pass no spells, no charms for her. It brought up a great love in my heart, the kind of thing a man should feel for his closest in such times.

"Harlan," she said.

"What?"

"I hears it, Harlan."

"Hear what, Margaret?"

She stared up at the roof. "Somebody's tearing some cloth," she said.

I hung my head.

"Harlan."

"What?"

"Do ye curse me about that field, honey?"

It was Margaret told me to take the damn field away from Daniel Larman.

"No, now, Margaret, don't bother about that."

I said no and I meant it, too. There is no way of tracking down the blame of things. No trapper ever tracked that down, no. I promised her I would never try.

Then there was a noise, a funny noise. Something fell out by my springhouse. I had some feed and meat in there.

"Margaret."

"What?" she said, staring at the roof.

"Something's at the springhouse. I best see to it."

"Go on, then."

When I got out there, there wasn't nothing. No cats or razorbacks, which was the most likely. It was just a split-rail piece I had put up to run rain away from a bad place in the roof shingles. It had come loose somehow and then down. I had put it up there with staves, too.

That rail, it baffled me. How come it to fall? I looked at my staves and they was in the same places, nothing had moved them. I calculated the wind and it was blowing, but not much. I had already satisfied my senses that no beast had been there.

I squatted down by the log and felt awful strange and nervous about it. There wasn't no reason, not one, why it should have come down like that. But it had. I set it back on the roof, caught it in them staves good and tight.

Laying it up there, the moonlight all over one side of it, I recalled the night Margaret and me lay alone in the cabin, Ma having gone on. Margaret, some older than me, had scorned a passel of boys. To listen to her, she had, anyhow. She was a fury the day after we buried Ma. She was a fury in that cabin, changing and switching things thisaway and that, whipping about in the yard, cleaning and piling and throwing away and cussing me for being worthless. Then, that night, pulling away from me in the one bed she'd left standing, teasing me about my great youthfulness, calling me gazer eyes and baby brother and such. Laughing under the quilt, pulling my hair and kicking me in the back, not about to hear a thing from me, though I had some fine tales I wanted to tell her. She hit me then, right on the nose, hard, and then did it again, and I felt strong of a sudden and then it was that we first come together. When we was done, the moon was hanging outside the window, its light falling all on her face, showing me her eyes big and wide open, staring at the moonlight, her not so frisky or know-it-all then. She made me stay on her, holding me tight with both arms.

I knocked in one more stave for that log, to make sure it would hold.

When I got inside the cabin again, I was rubbing wet bark off my hands with a rag when I recalled Daniel Larman's big roan horse. I went over to tell Margaret I might give it to her when I seen she had gone on. Them tiny little thread lines had come undone from her lips, and her hands lay open on the coverlid.

I took some cloth from the back of Margaret's loom and made her a winding sheet. When I tore it, it made an awful noise.

Then I sat the night with my three. When morning come, I loaded them onto my sled and carried them down to a corner of that field Margaret liked so much, and put them down. When I had laid the last clod, I leaned on my shovel. It sank down through that soft, rained-out, upturned earth and I knowed I was wishing hard it might move, turn again. I couldn't help myself. I couldn't stop thinking things like that.

Well, that shovel hit one of them down there and that was my last touching of my own. I didn't know which one it was, whether Orlean or Margaret or Joseph, but I dreaded to pull that shovel up after that. So I left it there.

When I looked back, it comforted me. I hoped Margaret wouldn't have faulted me for leaving it there, that one charm to watch over them when I was gone.

When I got back to the cabin again, I fed Jean in her crib. I couldn't bear to hold her none. I fed her and thought I wished she had been out of my poor Margaret instead of Cora Larman. Then, rocking Jean, I was thinking of Cora, thinking of her and nothing else at all, though I had just done what I done. And I knowed that deep down I was glad it was Jean, Cora's child, had been left to me. It was a bad time. I was thankful Jean went off to sleep and didn't see me then.

After a while I recalled my cow brutes way down below Gore's Knob, where I'd put them out. I rode Daniel Larman's roan horse down there and with my ax cut a linden so's they could feed some off the shoots. It was hard work and I'd had no sleep and I seen terrible things chopping away with that ax. Then, right when the tree fell, I seen them men and I near throwed the ax at them. But I seen they was outlanders, so I hid and readied my rifle gun. But they passed on, crawling up the slope, looking like ants after a while and I thought, Ants. Ants and worms. Ants and worms and creatures of the dirt, pass me by. Never stop for me.

Juba

When my old boy Tate come back from hunting the hog and seen me setting them outlanders, two on the porch and two more in the cabin, like they was all best of kin, well, he was struck dumb on the spot. I did my best to make him come back to this life, but he wasn't ready. All he did was set in the corner and watch the two men was inside, like they was fixing to steal the fireplace if he looked away once.

Now, these men had been a-roaming the valley for three days, without a soul speaking a word to them, though they tried hard to talk to somebody. I had just took pity on them, that's all, they looked like decent men to me. But then I had to get Tate to talk to them, and it wasn't easy.

Finally I says, "Well, Tate, did ye get a whack at the fiend?" I was bound Tate should be decent and friendly, that's why.

The fiend is Tate's old razorback hog he hunts near ever day. That beast has been living well off this family for one whole winter and one spring and part of this summer. Tate swears there's a fiend inside the wild creature. Says that's why he can't get no killing bead on it. Ever day out Tate stomps and I listen, while I'm working, to him blasting away. And ever day when he comes back it makes good sassing for the both of us, me hooting at him and him telling me how the fiend got away this time.

So that brung him back to this life again.

"Well, I laid eyes on the monster, Juba," Tate says.

"Monster?" one outlander says. "What kind of monster?"

Tate didn't say nothing right off. Just stared that outlander down. Then, after we had endured the time a-waiting on him, he throwed up his hands, sudden like, like he was holding his rifle gun.

"I'm gonna have me a bead on his big old ear," Tate says, "one of these days. I figure if I mark him, knock off part of that ear, he won't be so uppity no more, he'll be branded and all. That's the way my pa took care of wild razorbacks, yessir. It plumb dispirits them. Ever hunt a wild razorback, Mister?"

This outlander, name of Ames, says no, he hadn't. I was feeling pretty good then, because Tate had gone and spoke to the feller.

"Thought ye hadn't," Tate says. "If ye had, ye'd know my trial with the beast. Lord God, he's ornery. There's witchery in him for certain."

Both outlanders perked up at that, and the scrawny little feller that was with this Mister Ames, the one had the milky face and strawberry hair, he says, "What makes you think it's witched?"

"Why, boy," says Tate, and I felt he was friendly now, "I seen it cross the line. Yessir, I seen that thing step right over the line twixt hog and fiend. Day before yestiddy I was down on him. Had him setting my sights like a bird on a limb. I was one little squeeze from putting a ball in his fat old neck, but, boy, just when I triggered, he turned around and stared at me. Eyes like hellfire. My rifle gun went off and tore off a maple branch a smart fifteen feet above him, that stare was so powerful. Then he stood up on his old hind hoofs like a man and growed these bloody wings and rose up in the air like a baldy eagle, and if that ain't witchery, boy, what is?"

The puny milk-faced boy giggled some at that, but this Mister Ames looked him down. He seemed like he'd swallowed Tate's old story about that hog like it made best sense ever. But he was meaning to get something else besides Tate's old whoppers about that hog, I could tell.

Then I opened my mouth. I had to open my mouth and say something, I still don't know why. Just felt like it, so I said, "We calls him old

Job," I says, chattering on like any bird, and I reckon it was that let Mister Ames in the door he'd come knocking on all the time.

"Job?" he says. Then he wanted to know how come we named him Job. Where we had heard that name.

Oh, I hung my head. Job was a boy who come twixt me and Tate years ago. I finally got him out of my blood, but old Tate, he was wild about me then and had to make a fuss. Come right near killing that lover I had. It was years ago, the both of us young then, me not having had neither of our boys. A long time ago, that's right, but even now Tate remembers it, calls that hog Job, did right off when the beast began pestering us, just like he calls anything that bothers him Job. Course I couldn't say that to them outlanders, so I mumbled what a nice name it was for a big razorback and felt like walking through the wall. It give Tate something to hoot about for days and days.

The milk-faced boy says that Job is a name out of a book he shows us. It was a Bible he had, and then they asked us if we had one. Got no answer there, so asked us if we'd ever read the thing.

Well, Tate give me such a low look then, just like I had set fire to the cabin. He was disgusted with me and I didn't blame him a bit, I was so mortified. I could have jumped in my own pot and boiled myself away, yessir.

"We don't read nothing," Tate says.

Mister Ames, he looked at us real gentle then, like we was young'uns. He had a kind of hurt look about him, too. "But are you Christians?" he says. "Don't you remember it at all?"

Tate set his rifle gun on his knees and allowed as how it was time to go hunt some squirrel. "I go ever day about this time," he says. "Been a downright pleasure to talk with you men."

Didn't do it. Mister Ames stayed right where he was. He was a fine figure of a man and I had thought he was pleasant to have to set until he commenced saying then that he was a man of the church.

"King's Church?" says Tate, quick as a bug.

He allowed as how it had been the King's Church but wasn't his no more. It was called something else now, I couldn't get the name. Then he went on, saying he was Bishop of this church, and that he had come here to see us about finding Jesus Christ, and that tore it, all right.

Tate shot up out of the corner and ramrodded his rifle gun, looking at me whilst he slammed the rod down the barrel, like he meant, See what you done? Flap that tongue some more, woman, and I'll poke it down in here for gun waddy.

Mister Ames had kept right on talking, but he stopped when old Tate leveled on him. That puny boy turned a shade or two whiter than he was, which got him awful white. The two other men on the porch come in then and Tate leveled on them too. He was through being friendly, and my little socializing was over, I seen it.

"Who the hell are ye, anyhow?" Tate says. "Don't give me no foolishness, neither."

So Mister Ames, he pulled this ring out of his vest pocket. It was a plain ring but a big one. Said it showed he was truly Bishop in that church.

"I might have knowed it from the first," Tate says. "Now just turn yeselves around and git out. Before I breathe twice, I mean, and don't come back. I done breathed once. Git."

The puny boy and the other two men, they got out quick, but that Bishop Ames he took his sweet time, I'll say that for him. He wasn't showing no fear. He stood up nice and easy and thanked me so purty for being nice to him, and then started out the door slow. Things would have been all right, I reckon, if he hadn't stopped on the steps there and done what he did. He turned about there on the steps and raised his hands and said something soft to the cabin. It scared Tate to death.

Tate turned four shades whiter than that boy, run to the door and stuck his barrel in the Bishop's ribs, screaming that he had hexed the cabin, that it takes demons and devils to put such charms on a man's cabin.

"Stay in there, Juba!" Tate yelled. "Don't come out! When the boys git back, keep them in there, too!"

"Hey, Tate!" I yelled. "Hold on, now!" But I knowed my old boy. When he takes an idea into his head, it is going to be there for a while. Tate, who tells whoppers all the time, will swallow other people's the same way they swallow his.

"You four men git on them beasts there," Tate says. "We'll all just go see Jacob Larman about this." So I knowed it was bothering Tate, that he would take them to Jacob Larman. But I felt easy then, because old Jacob Larman would fix it, and smooth Tate out a little, too, which he needed.

"Now, you creatures don't go racing," says Tate. "I'm old, but I can still hit a squirrel and you are all a damn sight bigger than that. Git on, now."

Well, the Bishop got more and more dignified all the time, but he seemed satisfied they were going to see Larman. Whilst Tate chattered on, he got up on his big reddy horse and set there, preening like a peacock. The puny boy and the other two men saddled, and Tate, puffing and wheezing, got up on the mare and they was off down the trail.

Now, right when they took to galloping, Bishop Ames's purty roan horse broke some powerful wind. Made the biggest, fattest bust ye ever heard. And the Bishop setting up there on him like a peacock.

I knowed my old boy was doing the right thing, he generally does somehow, but them fellers didn't seem like no devils to me.

Cora

I stood outside his cabin three nights and he never come out. Never made nary sign. Harlan stayed in there whilst I stood in the night and waited, wanting my baby, my own now his woman was finally dead and gone. The third night, after standing the longest time, I couldn't bear it no more and I yelled out, "Harlan! Harlan! I want my baby! Harlan, you hear!"

He heard, but he never made nary sign. Once Jean cried, just like she knowed it was me outside, but I still couldn't go in, not until he opened that door to me. Harlan was still scared of me, scared of snarly Cora that pulled him on her the night he come up Sand Mountain in midwinter. He was drunk and mindless that night, it was me done it to him, he hardly moved at all. Scared of Cora, yes, he was, and that is the way I have always wanted it with men. But when I had the baby and had already named her Jean after my mother and Harlan come to see

Grandpa Jacob about taking her back, I knowed that he would do it, that it was his more than mine because he had a place for it. And Grandpa Jacob said that the seed is the man's and only property is the woman's and I had none of that. And that a baby with no place for it don't make sense, and that what kind of a woman was I for a young'un to grow up with, and so I give Jean back. And I never faulted nobody for it except Harlan's woman that put him up to it, even then I never made no demands whilst she lived, that woman. But now she was dead and gone, it was done, Daniel had done what I meant him to all along, but Harlan was still setting in that cabin playing with my baby like I was dead and gone, too.

Then I had to contend with Cief.

I never thought the day would come I'd hate Cief, but it did. Ever since I was the smallest girl I'd play with my brother and try to make him learn to behave. It was just a thing I did and cared to do. But that third night, standing there shaking in the frost, I commenced calling Harlan and there come a yell from the bresh and out of a pokeberry bush busted Cief. He put his hands on me and tried to pull me back up the mountain with him. He knowed my feelings then, knowed they had nothing to do with him no more.

I hated my brother Cief then. Hated him and all the times I had played with him. I hit at his face and he backed off. But when I turned to call again, Cief cried out like them times he'd bash hisself or cut his foot on a stob or something, and that time when he grabbed me I knowed Cief my brother hated me, too.

Cief hit me on the shoulder and once up side the head. We both went down and I saw Harlan's cabin door come open and my baby's father standing there, wild-eyed and fearful. Then I was flat on the ground and I tried to roll away, but Cief, he scrambled after me and hit me in the side and I thought I would pass on, he did it so hard.

Maybe it was seeing Cief killing me made Harlan come between us. I like to think it anyhow. And he did, he got between me and my brother and pushed Cief off with his rifle gun long enough to get me inside the cabin. He did it, and that's all I wanted. He slammed the door and I seen my baby, sleeping in the nicest crib, under a little quilt all beautified with thready birds and tiny apple trees, and I got down on the floor and hung on to that crib whilst Harlan stood at the door with his rifle gun, listening to Cief scream for me.

Cief went away soon, but we could hear him for the longest time. After a while he sounded like a dog barking from a far distance, his yells and screams come up the slopes that way. I didn't mind it none. I wanted him just to keep right on going, my brother Cief I'd played with when nobody else would, when it was plain he was pitiful. My brother Cief who doted on me and who kept me good company all the times before I met Harlan and had his Jean.

Harlan built up the fire and then he give me a drink of applejack. I took some but not much. His cabin was all warm woody and the cleanest thing I'd ever seen. There was a rug on the floor and many chairs and two tables and over the fireplace hung shiny pans and stirring sticks and in the corner a big loom with bits of thread hanging off it and a set of cardings with a pile of wool stuck between them. The wood floor was so smooth and fine, it was like cloth all stretched out, and the firelight on it was just like a red moon on a stillwater pond. I was warm from the fire and the applejack whisky, and I stretched out my arm and wriggled the fingers of my hand. Little Jean, my baby, she come awake when her ma did that and I put my hand over her and wriggled it some more and she reached up and took hold one finger and wouldn't let it go, not for the longest time. I played with her and hummed to her and all this time feeling so sure I would never leave all this until the day I died.

Harlan set and drank some more and wanted me to drink, too, but I wouldn't. I shook my head, smily and humming, and wouldn't have none. Well, he got up and commenced taking steps all around like he was a-dancing. He'd come at me, then back off, stop, then just stand around, then do it all over again. I never took no notice of him, I just set there on the floor with Jean holding my finger, my cheek resting on the edge of the crib, counting apple trees on that quilt. There was no use him taking on that way.

So after some more fooling about, Harlan went outside. I heard him trampling around out there the same way. That left me all alone in that cabin with my baby, there where his woman had kept house for him, made him handsome things on her fine weaving loom, carded the wool from his sheep right there all them years I was playing with Cief, running with my brothers Cief and Shad and Cardell, living on Sand Mountain with Earl and Grandpa Jacob, wild as hogs, all of us saying we was having grand times. I stayed down on that floor that was warm and smooth and I knowed I had just come in, new to the world, that I was a younger woman than my Jean even. I heard Harlan stomping around outside, kicking the side of his springhouse, cussing me, and I could have laughed and cried both at once, I was so glad I had come down from Sand Mountain to stand there three nights in the cold until Harlan opened his door to me.

When he got tired out, Harlan come in to warm hisself at the fire. He made some coffee and drank it, the firelight running across his face, him staring at it, drinking his coffee. All this time I had not moved one bit, I had not stirred. My Jean, she got drowsy. She puffed herself up, meaning to commence bawling again, but all of a sudden sleep come down too hard on her and she opened her little mouth and sailed right off again. I watched her sleeping like that.

Harlan finally brought hisself to the point of looking down square at me. He seen I had not moved none and it bothered him. He said, "Move, Cora, ye make me nervous."

And I said I would if I could choose where. I said if I couldn't choose where and if he put me out of that cabin, then for me to move was for me to die, and I meant it, and Harlan, he seen that. And he said, "Cora, do what ye please." Then he looked back at the fire. It run all over his face, that face still like any boy's, like the face of his little Joseph I seen once at Jimmy Rode's store. That face, mightily played upon by that fire, it was a fine sight.

So I moved and stood up and said, "Harlan, look here at me." He did and I peered into his eyes and they was swimming in misery, but I seen it was all right for me to do what I did. I had to look to find it, but it was there.

I leaned over and pushed that fine quilt about Jean's neck and kissed my baby and went in and laid down on her bed, his woman who had died. I laid there and it was a good enough bed when I went to it, but best after I was on it awhile, making it come alive again. I laid there where she must have died, me just born. I felt that bed go warm and I looked out the window and seen the blackness and the cold I had stood in and I listened to the hickories groaning and the whippoorwills and such as that, warming up his bed.

Then Harlan stood over me, staring at me, asking if I would ever want to go back up Sand Mountain again. I said no, not never again, long as I lived.

Why not? Harlan asked me, frowning, and I told him best I could why not. Because I had come into his cabin and seen my baby in the crib and because it was all just as pleasant as the flowers are made. And Harlan, he screwed up his fine face and I seen his hands clenching and his arms go big with blood. His breath, with applejack on it, washed over my cheek like warm water.

So when he come on me that time, there was no strife, no fret to it, no crying neither. He was free from his and so was I free from mine. So there was no call for no fret, nor crying neither. We was all cut loose from everything, and his body weight on me that night was what was holding me on this earth, and my arms around his back was what held him down here, too.

In the morning, when I come awake, he was looking at me, laughing, and I laughed, and we was both glad I had come down to him three nights running from my home on Sand Mountain.

There was only the getting up before they come. Before they called out from the yard. It was Shad calling, and when Harlan opened the door a slit, I seen Cardell and Earl, too, and Cief crying, and even Grandpa Jacob hisself, sitting up in his sled, the wind blowing his beard. They had their rifle guns slung in their elbows all, pointing down, and they said there'd be no shooting. Harlan commenced to open the door and I said No, Harlan, but he did it anyhow.

"Snarly bitch!" yelled Grandpa Jacob, shaking his dried-up, bony hand at me. "There she is, that snarly bitch. Cora, come on out of there!"

Harlan put his arm around me and I let him, knowing he'd take it away soon enough. I wanted to go get my Jean, but there was no time. With Harlan holding me, they told him what I had been doing to Daniel. How I had been at him, chiding him about that field, saying he'd let a woman, Harlan's Margaret, take it away from him.

I said, "Harlan, Harlan, I didn't think he'd do what he did. I didn't, Harlan." But I did. And then, if Daniel had of killed Harlan, too, it would have been all right with me. That's what I had got to, missing my Jean, and wanting Harlan so bad.

I felt Harlan's arm go slack on my shoulder whilst they told him how I had dug up a little early bloodroot and planted it in the yard with a tiny fence about it, saying to Daniel he should see if he could farm that without getting run off it by some conniving woman like Margaret, and how three days ago Daniel got mad at everybody and went off with his rifle gun.

"So what's this bitch been up to, Harlan?" called Grandpa Jacob. "And where's my Daniel now?"

Harlan took his arm off my shoulders and he told them where Daniel was. The rifle guns come out of them elbows and up, but then Harlan told them what Daniel had done, how he killed little Orlean and Joseph, and caused Margaret to die from sorrow at it.

Grandpa Jacob put out his skinny arm, made them hold.

"Margaret?" he said. "She's dead? And them young'uns, too?"

Harlan nodded, and they all looked at me. I wanted to run to Jean then, my baby older than me, but they would have shot me down, I think.

"Well, Harlan," Grandpa Jacob muttered, "will ye take me to Daniel, then?" He looked like some old woman. "And with Cora ye can do what ye please."

I looked at Harlan then and seen the meanness and the hurt in him when he said yes, he'd take them to Daniel. I jumped then, went in and took up Jean, but Harlan's hand come heavy on my shoulder.

He said, "Snarly bitch. Leave her alone." I cried then.

So we rode on down to the field, Grandpa Jacob stewing in his sled, swearing and cussing, howling that all of us should be shot, that we was all worthless, ever last one.

Jacob Larman

The valley was wet, full of rot. I'd thought never to see it again. Thought it was all over twixt me and this land, but I was wrong. Clayton Gaines met us on the trail, said they'd found Daniel and had him at Jimmy Rode's store. Said that Tate Benson had caught some outlanders fooling about, maybe they had done it. I said no, knowing no outlanders killed Daniel, nor even Harlan, knowing that the land done it, that my hotheaded Daniel wanted a field so bad he killed for it. Cora was some to blame, but mostly the land, yes. I told Clayton Gaines we were coming and tried not to look at Cora or at Harlan, scared to death. I said, "Cardell," and he said, "Yessir," and slapped the gray pulling my sled, and we went down.

I seen the slopes a-stirring, and I knowed others would be coming to that store too. They'd all be bound to know by now, and we'd have another meeting, a grand commingling of us all, but me the only one to know what a far cry it'd be from the times we was all young here, and that land young, too.

It was Harlan's grandpa and my pa who come first. I am the only one left to recall it. Different men and different land then, and smart work to clear it. Harlan's grandpa and me, we was friends then, and sometimes when we was able we'd sneak off from the work and, like young'uns, fool around until they caught us out and yelled us back to work. That's the way we did, and I am the only one left to recall it.

"Grandpa, how's your comfort?" said Shad, and Earl reached over to fix my blanket, but I pushed his hand off. I was all right, not coming to pieces like they thought, my fool young'uns. "Git off, I'm living yet," I told them, and they said, "Yessir." There was a rainy wind blowing the valley, and I recalled Harlan's grandpa and me when we was little, and we rode on.

Going down to Jimmy Rode's store, I recalled how good it was here for a long time. Even with all my fool young'uns about me, I recalled that. How the new outlanders come in cheerful and neighborly, how fine the big valley meeting was, the raisings we had then, and the women's bees, and the times they'd be fiddles and dancing around a new cabin just put up, and a big bench lined with applejack jugs, jerky and ham smoked and ready, and the slippery possum meat, too. My easy-eyed Debra teased me once too often on one of them days and that night it was me and her until the day she died. Nobody faulted me then, or fretted about my comfort, I had plenty of comfort with Debra. Long time ago that was, she was.

"Grandpa Jacob," said Cardell, "yonder's the store."

"I see it. I ain't blind," I said.

The wind blowed the rot smell as we went on. It come into my beard and stayed there. They got me out of the sled and we went in the store.

Everbody stood up when I come in. I seen that there was some there I didn't know. That's what it has got to around here. And there was four outlanders, too, under Tate Benson's rifle gun, Tate foaming and yelling that they was demons and such. I have always enjoyed Tate and his Juba, but he is a fool, no way around it. One outlander was looking at me queerly. He was powerful set in his stare, brainy, too, I could tell. With him was a reddy-haired boy, a frog-eyed feller scared to death, and a big, mournful-looking man who kept looking at the floor. Tate Benson foamed on about them, and I had stopped to listen when I seen Daniel's face behind him, staring up in the air from his plank.

They had laid my grandson out on the plank counter. There was a hole in his neck big as a corn stob is round, and ants was in it. He had been in the rain three days, they said, and I seen it was so. Dusk on the back steps my boy's face was, and his eyes like two little stones with the skin pulled down over them. I put my hand on his leg and couldn't help but shake it some. I knowed I had come undone at Daniel's time and I stood there shaking his leg until Cief and then that snarly bitch, they commenced to whine about it. So I told them hush up, and they did. Everbody did. They all knowed I was undone, womanly I was over Daniel, but Jacob Larman I still was, still alive after eighty-four years of this life, and they knowed that, too. They hushed up and waited for me to say what was to be done now.

And I didn't know. I just didn't know. My hotheaded Daniel didn't leave it simple for me. Him and Harlan had both killed, and Margaret and Cora had put them up to it, and so where was the blame? Earl and Shad and Cardell, even Cief and Cora, they was waiting for me to say, Take Harlan out and hang him now, but it was not so simple. I did not know what was right, and they seen me falter and I knowed Earl wanted to take it over and say what to do, but I couldn't let that happen. So I said Hush again, and they did and I turned to them outlanders to see who they was whilst I gave myself some time to think.

"Who be ye and what be ye business?" I said.

The lead man, that brainy one, stepped up and spoke. I had figgered his talking would give me time, but I found myself listening to what that man had to say. Because he come right out and said we was all of us to blame, which is what I knowed was the only right of it all. Then he said it was because we scorned the gospel and the will of God. I had not heard anybody talking like that in a long time. I let him go on, and he did, talking a blue streak.

Whilst he talked I kept thinking of Harlan's grandpa and me when we was little. Something we did. Then I recalled it. We had run off to Moore's Fork that day, the both of us, to the place where it turkey-tails off into little streams. Earl says they still bite there in the mornings, and I reckon they do. We was on a crossing we had made, fishing and fight-ing with each other like boys will when they ought to be working, when we seen that thing in the water. It was a big black thing, and it washed up against our logs. We rocked at it and poked at it, and then pulled it out. We went running back to the clearing with it, yelling, "Look what we got! Look what we got!"

Harlan's grandpa and my pa, they turned sober when they seen it. They shook their heads over it, saying not a word. But there was one man who said something. Benjamin Cutbirth, standing there leaning on his broadax, he said something all right, he said, "Boys, do ye know what that thing is?" I didn't, but Harlan's pa, he nodded and said, "Yes, a Bible."

And Ben Cutbirth, who had big, long scars on his arms from the wars, the man we was wild about because he had led us into the valley away from the King's Men and the Indians, he said, "Looky, boys, how it's still black. Still black after being washed all down that stream, and no wonder. That's the very thing has caused all ye troubles, boys. That's what ran ye up here."

"Who throwed it away, Ben?" I asked him, and he told us, Some man with good sense. Called me little Jeb, and told me some man who knowed it for what it was, the King's book. The King's book that sounded just fine when the King's preacher read from it but which wasn't fine at all. It was rules for the tax, he told us, reasons to set the tormented Indian against the decent, said Ben Cutbirth, who'd killed both Indians and King's Men in the war. "The King's book, boys, no wonder the damn thing's still black."

Harlan's grandma come out of the half-built cabin and said, "Benjamin Cutbirth, you hush," but he wouldn't. He told us about the English Church, how the King made it speak fair to dissenters, saying they could believe what they pleased, but slayed them when they did. Not manly slaying neither, Ben Cutbirth said, no, with the damned tax took away their own, stealing their food for fat, worthless preachers, men meaner than wolves, saying, Shore, go on and dissent, but give this church everything ye have, and do it on ye knees.

He got so mad he scared us and we looked at our pas, who said, Yes, he is right. Then my pa held out his hands to me, that ever since I could remember them had been all black and twisted in the palms, where he'd burned hisself making a fire once, he always said. But that day he told me the truth about his hands, about them awful scars, worse than the ones on Cutbirth's arms even. "The King's Men come, sonny," he told me, "they come when your ma was still with us, and you a baby. They come because I wouldn't give what they wanted of my crop, a tax for a church I didn't even hold with. They made me grab on to two burning sticks they took out of the fire, hold them in my hands until I said God Save the King three times. Then I could let go, not until."

He looked at his hands and I got sick almost, and Ben Cutbirth slammed his ax into a log and stood spitting. And my pa said, "That's when I decided to leave all that, Jeb. Come someplace like this. That's why we don't have ye ma no more. She stayed behind, saying she loved Christ, not because she was sickly like we said. But, boy, we wouldn't want her here in this fine place, would we?"

I said, "Nossir," and Harlan's grandpa and me, we was quiet then, and we took that black thing back to Moore's Fork and throwed it back in again, like some fish we didn't want.

So I recalled all that whilst the preacher talked on, and I seen that black book tucked under his arm, too. And I tried to figger how I was going to keep from having Harlan killed, or Cora killed, or anybody killed. Another preacher wanted to talk some and I let him, but he was a mess. His name was Sales, and he was all peach-faced and full of his-self, and made no sense. The mournful-faced man, when I shut Sales up and asked if he had anything to say, said, No, sir, to me, I don't. Then there was the reddy-haired boy and I asked him if he had anything to say and he looked at the lead preacher and said Yes, he did. He then come forth among us and be dog if he didn't commence singing a song. I commenced to get mad about it, but I was listening all of a sudden to that song. Plainsong, they said. Song of the church.

Now, it had no right words to it, what the boy sang, but it was something, once going, I did not know how to stop it. Old it was, older than me, so I listened, and took the time it give me to think a little. When he finished, there was a spot of peace in the store, and I seen we had all listened. I seen Earl's gun hand loose on the stock, seen some puzzlement flickering in Cardell's mean little eyes.

And it give me time to think, but I still couldn't come up with nothing. Except one thing. Harlan's face. It hurt me looking at him. He has a fine head, Harlan, a good face. It is like his grandpa's face. When I look at Harlan, it is like looking up to his grandpa again, from the height of that little boy I was all them years ago. Daniel dead or alive, I knowed I did not want Harlan killed, too, what kind of an end would that be for what we started here? Who'd be left? Earl and Shad and Cardell and a few others, and they're not much.

I said, "All right, Preacher. Now what?"

"I'm not a preacher," he said. "I don't mind if you call me one, but I am a bishop. I want you to know what I am."

We took that in.

"And what I want to know is this. What are you going to do now?"

I thought, Yes, that's what I want to know, too, and didn't say nothing.

"Kill again?" he said, looking around angry like.

Earl's hand slid back up the stock and everybody stiffened up, but I waved them down and didn't say nothing.

"You don't know, do you?" he said. The man was mad. "Well, do you?"

That burned me a little. I was getting riled myself. "No, we don't," I said. "Who in hell does?"

He fair roared at us. "The Church!" he said. "What else is there, do you think, can make men out of dogs!"

I said, "Earl! Be still. Cardell, you too. Best set them guns on the counter. I said do it. I let this man begin, I will let him finish. Go on, I am waiting."

I give them that minute to see what they would do. They looked their hate at me and I suffered the burning of my heart and bile until they put the rifle guns down. My old legs was a-shaking like I was a jumped-on boy again, and I knowed I couldn't go through much more of this thing. I looked back at that man, thinking, You best know what you're doing, or it won't matter what they called you, preacher or Bishop or what.

I said, "Now, just listen here," said it calm as I could. "I don't know what ye think we are, but all of us here have good knowledge of the King's Church. That's what we run away from. You say it knows what to do. Well, sir, my pa had his good hands burned black by your damn Church knowing what to do. So I think there is some question as to who are men and who are dogs, I shorely do."

He nodded and took on some of my calm, and then looked at us like we was all children. "There's no King's Church anymore," he said, "not in this nation. It is your Church, if you want it, ruled by its bishops, who are voted for, elected. I am one of them. I don't like kings any more than you do."

Clayton Gaines, with his hands folded up under his armpits, in his rusty voice he said, "Then it is you we make up our minds about, is that it?"

The Bishop, he nodded like that should have been understood, and said, "That's right," and stood there looking us down.

We took that in.

I said, "Well. So what's to be done by this fine Church? And let's don't have no singing about it, neither. Just tell a feller."

He walked over to the counter and looked down on Daniel's gray face. He turned and looked at us, then back at Daniel again.

"That field," he said. "The Church will buy that field. Through me it will pay both families for it, equal price. And square in the middle of it, before this night comes down, I will hold decent Christian burial for those who died over it. That is first."

Earl said, "Look here, Grandpa," but I said, "What is second?" real quick, and the Bishop went on.

"Soon as it can be done, the Church will put you up a schoolhouse and a place to worship there. It will build you a mission."

Earl spun around and said, "And what will that do?" and spit on the floor.

The Bishop never blinked. "It will bless the children when they are born. It will teach them how to behave in this life. It will marry them and it will keep them married. And when the time comes, it will show them how to die. Then it will bury them in peace and bless their spirits."

"No!" somebody said. It was Harlan.

It took me a minute to realize it was Harlan. I said, "No, Harlan?" because if it was no, he was the one to suffer. I didn't comprehend it.

"My Margaret and me," said Harlan, "we never held with charms and such. Do what ye want with Daniel, and I'll even sell that field if you want it, but I have already buried mine in the ground, and I'll have no spells said."

The Bishop looked at Harlan, and his eyes was wide and soft. "Charms?" he said. "Spells?"

"That's right," said Harlan. "I'll not have it. None of it."

The Bishop talked to Harlan like a man talks to a boy who is hurt and won't say where. "When you buried them, your wife and children, do you mean to tell me you just put them in the ground and walked off?"

"Yes," said Harlan. "It was all Margaret wanted."

"You didn't leave anything to mark their graves? Nothing?"

Harlan swallowed and said yes, he had. Said he'd left the shovel there, didn't know why.

"Bishop," said a new voice. I turned, and it was the big, mournful-looking man who hadn't said nothing before. He was staring at the Bishop. He said, "Bishop, leave the man alone."

The Bishop said, "All right, Starns," to him, and then, to us, "When the mission is built, it will have a backyard. That is the place where people should be buried. We can mark that yard off right now, and bury this man, and I will say the service for him. We can bury all this hate with him, if you want. Now, is that a spell, a charm?"

I said it didn't seem so to me, and Harlan, he looked at me, and he said, "Well, if you will all leave me in peace."

The Bishop asked him where he buried his Margaret, and Harlan said it was at the far end of the field. The Bishop said we could bury Daniel beside them and mark it as the burying ground of the mission when it got built.

Then he looked at me and said, "That is what the Church can do. Wants to do. Wants very much to do." Then he set down on a box there and looked at his hands.

Then everybody looked at me.

Well, I wished my pa and Harlan's grandpa and old Benjamin Cutbirth had been there, but they was gone long ago. They might have told me what was best, but they was gone. Now I did not know whether to believe the man or not, but his was the only way out of our troubles that I could see.

I looked my wild young'uns over, looked at Earl with his tight mouth and twitching hands, at Cardell's black eyes, at Cora squirming about. I looked at pitiful Cief, scared and whining. My wild and helpless children, standing around Daniel laid on the plank.

Only Daniel knowed anything for sure, and he didn't care what I did. Only Daniel was peaceful now, all the hate and meanness gutted out of him. I stared at him and then knowed all this had to stop somehow. My Daniel's scowling face, it would never be nothing but gray, like dusk.

It tore me all up, what is left of me.

I spit, and said, "All right. Thank ye, Bishop. We will hear some more."

5

CONVERSION

STARNS STUMBLED ALONG after Cora Larman, like a drunk following the back of a man in front of him, wandering in a crowd.

He was dazed and lost, angry with the Bishop and with himself. He was ashamed of the proud heads of his people, bent down beneath the Bishop's outstretched, graceful arms. It was all wrong. It was shameful. The sinking ache in his stomach told him that.

He had loved them when they stood spitting through mouths of stone while the Bishop talked. And he had been thrilled by the old man, dry and frail, who looked down at the corpse laid out on the plank counter as if inspecting a hole in the porch instead of a dead grandson.

He knows what my father knew, Starns thought, watching Jacob Larman. What I left behind and haven't never come on again. The hell with it, how to say that when it's your own flesh and blood that's running off into the ground like paste and water. When your own, your son or wife or father or daughter or little girl you love dies, and though you yourself don't think about dying much except like tomorrow it is going to happen and like tomorrow happen to everything that breathes and lives, though you hold no more with it than that while the rest of them preach and howl, still it is hard to do what you know how to do, look down on them dead that you have loved, saying the hell with it and meaning it.

Running, stumbling down into a dark, rocky gorge after the woman, Starns was obsessed by the figure of Jacob Larman. When he turned and stared at the strangers who had witnessed his sorrow, he had towered over them. He looked into the Bishop's eyes like a man who catches another man stealing from him, and Starns thought then that the Bishop was out to steal, steal away the vast and arrogant pride that allowed an old man to relish the death of his grandson, the last wiping away of that seed, and to have only contempt and loathing for those who try, by lament, to forget.

And then the Bishop had done it. He had gone right on and stolen it, not only from the old man but from them all. Bishop Ames, with his witching voice, his vacant, depthless eyes and his graceful arms. He kept at it until they went to their knees to pray with him, to say yes to whatever he said, calling Jesus with him, saying, Help, oh, help me, Jesus.

And pale Billy Cobb, spindly-legged and girlish, singing again the chant with no words to it, looking up at the roof of the store, his eyelids fluttering. And they, wide-eyed and anxious when he finished and when the Bishop finished, having seen the Heavenly Kingdom, been told about its great peace and its merciful Saviour, bending their heads and clasping their hands, whining and bleating like sheep, looking up at Bishop Nahum Immanuel Ames like that many dogs who have not been fed yet, like babies or puking kittens in a basket, how it had disgusted him!

Sheep! Sheep!

And when old Larman made his speech, told them that the Bishop was right, only the Church knew what to do, not he himself anymore, when he put his old knees to the floor and said, Bishop, help us, pray for me and for my boy Daniel over there, Starns fled.

He ran through the door and stood trembling outside the store in the gathering dusk. He was in agony. Once again he had witnessed what had dogged him all his life since he followed the circuit rider away from his home. He had seen the truly hungry fed with worthless food. He had watched their pride and manliness stolen away, and to its place, shrieking with glee, flocked the nameless specters, vanishing into the spirits of the kneeling, the penitent, the remorseful, with that fool Marcus Sales grinning at them, nodding his empty head, yes, yes, yes.

He stood with his arms flung round himself, in a rage, swearing he would never see it again, the shame and cowardice of any such truce with cold mortality, whose stark beauty his father had shown him in barren fields years ago.

Then he saw her shadow at the door. She stopped there and looked until she saw him, then passed over the threshold.

She walked up to him quickly, a tall woman and big-boned. She pushed her bonnet off her head, letting it hang from her neck streaked with dirt, tangled in her dark, thick hair. She stopped a few feet away from him, bold eyes stared him down. "What's ailing you, Mister?" she said. A twist of a smile, saying, "Whatever it is, maybe I can help it some." Her tongue came to her lips and with a big hand she gently grazed the swell of her breasts, full under the floursack dress.

She stood waiting, one knee bent slightly and turned out from the other. Starns looked at her and saw that she, too, was troubled, desperate even, he wasn't alone.

All right, all right, just what I want, yessir.

He grabbed her. Strong as a man, she broke his hold, saying, "Not here. Come on with me."

She took his hand, her skin tough and hard, and jerked him off balance as she stepped off toward the woods. When they passed the clearing in front of the store, in the first thrusts of high brush, she turned and kissed him, her mouth wet and open. His long arms went around her, and with a big hand under each of her buttocks, he lifted her and slid her down him. She slid down kissing him and laughing, but when her feet touched the ground she tried to get loose. Starns held her tight until she grabbed at his crotch and squeezed him, hard. He yelled. She broke his hold again and ran into the woods and he followed.

She climbed the slopes effortlessly, running full tilt as if in daylight. In the shifting dusk he lost her over and over again, but blundered on and would almost bump into her, standing somewhere waiting for him. She spat on him once, she'd been that close and he hadn't seen her, and he swore and followed her. Once she was sitting on a rock, her legs spread apart. This time she spat at herself, jumped off the rock like a cat and ran on again, down into the gorge.

It was a descending stairway of broken, jutting rock steps, a dry creek bed that the hidden machinery of stones had long ago drained of its burden. He stepped awkwardly, sometimes crawling, moving down to the bed of the gorge, meeting her at last on a flat piece of damp ground. He reached for her, but she pushed his hands away. They stood breathing hard at each other in gulps and gasps, Cora Larman giggling and choking and wiping tears from her eyes.

"There," she said. "That's it." She pointed behind her to a looming shadow in the night. "I come here all the time. Mister, we can do what we want to in there. Come on."

She led him toward the shadow. It was a cabin, set back twenty yards from the dry creek, empty, its vital organs long ago torn out. A tongue of moss reached out of the doorway. As they went in, a salamander darted past them, slipping under a log soaked flaccid by years of rain and snow.

Starns did not look at the cabin. All his senses were on the woman leading him, gloating over her, glad that her eager devilment had come his way, to banish all the nameless specters until sex and sleep were gotten through, and by that time it would be morning.

Inside the cabin a wooden bed with a pile of sacks on it lay against one wall. The sacks were mildewed from the rain that leaked in through the shredded roof. He took off his coat and shirt and laid them on the bed. Without a word Cora Larman lay on them and spread her legs. In one swift, ruthless motion she pulled her long, tattered skirt up to her breasts, moaning, "Well, come on, Mister, come on."

Starns hesitated, then put one hand down on her chest. She cried out, "Oh, Mister, stop fooling and come on!" and he slid down on top of her.

Starns woke slowly from a short, deep sleep, his body's retreat after its stuttering and spurting. One of his huge hands lay on her throat, loose, his grasp weak as sleeping. Her skin was cool and moist. He moved his forehead against her cheek and came awake.

It was still dark. He cursed his waking and wished it was morning.

He moved to get away from her, but she slid her arm under his chest and held him without opening her eyes.

"Mister," she mumbled, "where you going?"

"Awake, are you?"

"Yes."

"Well, I best get back to that store." He started up again, but she held him.

"Hold on, it ain't morning yet. I need some rest. I don't feel good. Stay awhile."

"What for?" said Starns. "You don't need me. You finished with me before we went to sleep." But he lay back down beside her.

Cora turned her face to him and spoke softly. "I am sorry if I was hateful to you. I get mean sometimes then. I don't know why. I am sorry if I hurt you."

"Hush," Starns said, "hush." He slid his arm across her stomach. Cora rested one hand on it.

"You sure were good to me," she whispered. "You made me think of them, my baby and my man, and I guess it was that made me mean and do what I did, made me turn hateful on you. I didn't mean all them things I said and did. You were good to me, Mister."

"It's all right, honey," said Starns. "I have never been much with the ladies. It's all right."

"No, I mean it. You were good. But I got to thinking on them, you see, and that was the trouble. Now, did I make you feel bad? I am sorry."

Starns smiled. "Hush. What was that you said about your baby?"

She blinked, rubbed her eyes. "Well, after we got started last night, I got to thinking the same thing over and over. His, not mine. His, not mine. I kept thinking that."

She yawned, tightened and relaxed the muscles of her thighs. "His, not mine. That's what made me mean. Because Jean, that's my baby, I give her away."

"Well, why'd you do that?" Starns asked her, thinking, There are things you can say and ask strange women after it's over, and it seems just fine. It is funny when people can talk to each other and when they can't.

She lay quiet for a minute. "Oh, there's no telling. I reckon ye either have both or none, that's the way I feel, anyhow."

"Where's the man now?"

"Why, down at the store. Harlan, the one killed Daniel. I didn't think it would go that far. It was my doing, some of it."

"Well," said Starns, "it's a mess, then, ain't it."

"That's right, Mister," she said, and started to sit up. But Starns held her down and rubbed his forearm over her belly gently. She put her hand back on his arm and smiled. "All right," she said.

Outside the cabin, a moonless night shut them in. Cora stroked the arm that held her down, rubbing it absently. They lay still for a while, then she said, "Why'd you run out of that store? I was about to come say something to you when you flew right out. Was it me coming made you go, or what?"

"You? No, ma'am, I'm afraid it wasn't. It had nothing to do with you at all."

"Well, what, then, Mister?"

Starns sighed. "Well, it was because I got so mad at the Bishop, preaching at them like that."

Into his eyes came a glazed look of fear. She saw it and wondered.

"All them folks acting like that," said Starns. "Like sheep, like damn sheep a-bleating. Tell me, what the Bishop said, did you believe it? Tell me that."

She snorted. "Why should I? I'm too young for that. There's no pleasure in that, not for me. Too many fine men like you around. Too many around here thirsting for Cora's tits, Mister." She turned her head and licked at his mouth, then held one breast up with her hand and squeezed it. "See?" she said.

"Don't do that," said Starns. "Come on, stop that."

Her face darkened. "What for, Mister! You was after it yeself, little while ago! You damn men. You run after it, then get mad with it. Harlan was the same! Worthless men! No, I'm sorry, I didn't mean that. I don't mean you, Mister. I'm sorry."

"I am sorry, too," said Starns. "That just bothered me, I'm sorry. But

I'll tell you what, I am glad to hear you say you don't hold with what the Bishop said. And I'm sorry I can't tell you I run out of that store wanting you to follow me. But, then, I reckon it wasn't exactly me that made you come out, neither."

"Huh?"

"I mean it was more your man in there and all your troubles with him. You thought I could get you free of them for a spell. Wasn't that it?"

She smiled and looked at the sky through the shredded roof. "I will allow you that," she said.

"Well," said Starns, "we was both mistook, then. I figgered it was maybe my fine good looks done it, but no, it wasn't that, was it?"

"No, sir," whispered Cora, "it was not." She waited a long time before speaking again. "You are a good man. I wish you was Harlan."

She turned her face into his neck and closed her eyes. Starns lay holding her, uncomfortable. He stirred once and she raised up and looked at him.

"They have always called me the snarly bitch. What do you think about that?"

"Well," said Starns, "you have snarled at me, that's true, but I will stay until morning. Is that all right?"

She put her face to his neck again. "Yes," she said. She rubbed his arm with her hand. They slept again.

When he opened his eyes, it was morning. Through the cracks in the roof he saw the vague pink dawnlight creeping. He turned his head away from Cora and looked through the open door, saw faint spirals of mist outside, rising and floating away over the wet dew. Cold morning air slipped between their bodies and drew away the warmth of their night. Starns lay on his back, drinking the morning air like spring water. He felt refreshed, ready to go back to it, the valley, the Bishop, the store.

So the people had turned Christian, been bleating sheep, well, what was it to him? Time to get up, Starns, he thought. Time to go somewheres again. Who cares where?

He nudged Cora awake. She mumbled something, snorted delicately and tossed, then sat up suddenly, holding her head with both hands. She looked at him, blinked and said, "Well, it's morning, ain't it?"

"Yes, ma'am, it is," said Starns, and he sat up with her.

Outside the open door he saw the close forest pressing in on the cabin. Must have been a good clearing there once, he thought, a big one. Then he wondered why he should think so. The brush was high and thick, reaching to grow up against the cabin and engulf it.

Whoever lived here must have cleared him a big yard. Of course.

He gazed out at the brush, disturbed without knowing why. The interior of the cabin was still dark. Something is wrong here, thought Starns. What?

Cora climbed over him and stood on the flat dirt floor of the cabin, pulling at her long hair, dark with dirt, tangled and matted. She bent over and shook it out, stood straight and scratched herself. She walked to the door and looked out. The sunlight beyond was almost bright, she stood a morning shadow against it, leaning in the doorway, yawning.

Starns's hands moved out from his body, exploring the rag-padded bed. He had not looked at it the night before, or at anything in the cabin. He had just thrown down his coat and shirt, then himself on the woman. When they woke for a while and talked, it had been too dark to see.

The bed was wide, and he knew his long legs did not reach the end of it. His hands closed on each edge of the bed, measuring by that grip the thickness of the flat log slabs he suddenly knew were pegged together nailless from below. Above him the light of the morning began to find its way down from the edges of the holes in the roof, fall upon the dirt floor, the walls.

Cora walked out of the door, saying, "I'm going to the spring over here," and he said, "What spring?"

"There's one right here, I think," she called, and Starns gripped the slab edges of the bed in panic.

For the second time in twenty-four hours he was brought low, struck into agony. From watery eyes the tears came, for now it was not anger that tore him. His tense thighs shook and trembled, even though he had lain back on the full length of the bed, measuring it with a body that had measured it many times before, yet each time finding the bed much larger, for then the measuring body had been smaller, much smaller.

He lay there, saying, "No, no, no, it ain't, it just looks like it." But when Cora walked back in the doorway and stopped there, her hands wet and dripping from cold spring water, rubbing its aching freshness into her face, he knew it was so, knew where he was.

He cried out and sat up like a man suddenly aware of a ghost standing by his bed, a specter more real than the morning calling him awake. Cora stopped rubbing her face and gazed at him, saw the stare of panic and the open, gaping mouth as he looked wildly about, seeing again, gutted and forsaken but corporeal and still standing, the home of his childhood, the cabin built by his father. From the bed they all slept in through the long mountain nights, father, mother, son and brother, he looked about and began to cry. To sob. To bleat like a sheep.

"I've told ye fifty times," Cora called. "Nobody knows about this place. Not even Grandpa Jacob."

She was sitting on a stump in front of the cabin, knee hooked inside clasped hands, leaning back, taking the sun. She was waiting for Starns to quit scratching and digging about in the cabin.

"We come a lot further than you thought last night. Three miles over a big ridge from Jimmy Rode's. None of us ever come over here until I did one day. Whoever was here left when the creek went dry, most likely. So come on, Mister, there's nothing in there any good now."

He yelled something from the cabin she could not understand, and she thought, Well, if he growed up here, I will just have to wait and let the man look. He'll never find his way back if I don't.

With her knee she pulled against her hands, stretching her joints in the sun. When she fell asleep with him the second time, she had been drenched in sweat and ease, her joints melting. Like when I had Jean, she thought.

Waiting for him, Cora thought of her long walk to Harlan's cabin when his wife and children were still alive. She remembered the flaming sourwood and gum trees ablaze, the purple-red dogwood berries through which she walked to his cabin, carrying the baby not yet a month old then in her arms, the child his, not hers.

She walked with her big strides like a man up to the porch where he stood with his frowning wife and two half-grown, fine-looking children. She stood before him smartly, pretending no one was bewildered, and handed him her baby, and said, "Here. Her name's Jean. You take her, she's yours, I think."

On the stump Cora remembered the long walk back, her arms loose and awkward when she stopped for berries. Red leaves and gold were hurtful to her eyes. That winter, watching them fall, she took pleasure. She smiled when the trees emptied their arms of such life, stood imprisoned in dry and wrinkled coats of bark, waiting for cold winds, ice and snow.

I did not want my baby then, she thought, pulling against her knee. That's what I said. But I did, and I do now. Maybe I could steal her back and run off with this man here.

The sounds in the cabin stopped. Starns walked out into the sunlight, blinking, holding something in his hand that reflected the light like a mirror, something bright and shiny.

Cora stood up. "What's that?" she said and walked to meet him. He held out his hand. In it was a belt buckle, tarnished and green except for the shiny spot where he'd polished it with his shirt.

"Is that silver?" said Cora.

He nodded and rubbed it against his coat. The edges of it left a dull smear on his coat, but the center came away brighter than before.

"If it's silver, it's worth something," said Cora.

Starns said, "Well, they have been killed, then. This here was my pa's. He'd never have left it. They're gone, then."

"Well," she said, "you can't tell that for certain."

"Yes, I can," said Starns, looking about. "I wish I could recall more of this place when we was here, but I just can't. It has been a time since then. You sure nobody of yours knowed them here?"

She shook her head. "That's a big ridge we come over. Do you remember where you people traded?"

"In the Watauga bottom," said Starns. "I do remember that."

"We never go down there," said Cora. "I'm sorry, Mister."

Starns sat on the stump. "So am I," he said. "I don't mean to blame you, but it would have been better if I had stayed in that store."

He turned the buckle in his hand, looking at it like a man whose treasure, unearthed, rots away in his hands at the touch of air and light. He looked at the cabin again. "If I'd stayed in that store, you see, I would have kept on thinking they might still be around here somewheres and I'd come upon them one fine day."

For the first time Cora felt she understood the man. She put a hand on the back of his neck. "Maybe, maybe not," she said. She waited a minute, then said, "Anyhow, come on back now. I best show the way."

He didn't answer. She bent down and took his hand. He followed her like a child into the woods. She waited patiently each time he turned to stare back at the falling cabin until finally, from the top of the gorge, he saw only the sparkling leaves and the choked laurel, their dew drying rapidly in the sun.

"Well, that's it yonder," said Cora when they topped the rise over Jimmy Rode's store. "Looks like they took to it early today. Or maybe they never stopped."

Starns saw that a crowd was milling about in front of the store, some sitting or squatting in the dirt, others standing around idly, a few motionless on horseback. On the steps he saw Billy Cobb with his red hair, and Marcus Sales standing behind him, a fresh white collar shining. In the doorway, his arms moving gracefully, his quick, delicate hands pointing, opening, gesturing as he spoke, Bishop Ames preached the gospel of Christ Jesus.

Starns leaned against a birch tree and glanced sheepishly at Cora. "You must think I am a great baby," he said, turning the silver buckle in his hand.

With one finger she reached out and touched it. "No," she said. "It don't take a big seed to hurt a sore tooth. I reckon I know that."

Starns slipped it into his coat pocket. "That's right."

"See that clump of hickories yonder?" said Cora, pointing across the valley. "That's where Harlan lives, right there is his cabin. That's where he is bringing up my baby Jean, bringing her up to hate me, her ma. Mister, it is just all of it so messed up and benastied, I don't know what will happen, I just don't. My life is worse than yours, Mister."

"Well, I don't know about that," said Starns.

On the soft, hot wind, snatches of the Bishop's sermon drifted up to them, the words strung out like commands from a field. His figure filled the doorway. His arms moved in broad, exalted gestures.

"Good-by," said Cora.

"So long," said Starns.

They turned from each other at the same time, Cora to climb Sand Mountain, Starns to descend to Jimmy Rode's store, to the graceful arms of the Bishop waving over the heads of his idle, absorbed congregation. No one paid him much attention when he joined them. Billy Cobb blinked and said, "Starns, where you been?" and Marcus Sales frowned at him. But the Bishop went on as if he had never left them, and nobody else knew him enough to wonder.

He sat on the steps by the Bishop's feet, his eyes lowered, not looking at the silent listeners. He thought of Cora and the futility of his hands on her wrenching, twisting body. He thought of the cabin, gutted, and of the times he had stared with the serene eyes of a child at the dripping clay of its now scattered chimney.

Finally, he looked at the people gathered around the steps of the store, his people, sheepish. In their shy, hungry eyes he recognized his own stare as he had searched the cabin like a mole and found the buckle. He slipped it out of his pocket and rubbed it hard. Something began to work inside him, cutting like a scythe.

Bishop Ames preached for four days in Heathen. Then his party crawled down the slopes to Dudley's house by the river, then to Stewart, where they rested a day, and then back to Raleigh. Billy Cobb was sent home to prepare for the next session of the seminary school. Marcus Sales collapsed in his study over a bottle of May wine and set out to forget the trip from beginning to end, and a fretful, troubled William Starns went back to his basement room in the church.

In his study Bishop Ames took up his pen. He averaged ten letters a day for over two months, sounding the depths of his influence, checking on the condition of friendships, greeting debtors vaguely, saying to all: Pay attention to me, I'm going to do something, watch.

In December a pastoral letter circulated through the diocese, announcing the need for a mission and describing the forsaken mountaineers who had responded so definitely to his visit.

"My emotions," wrote Bishop Ames, "were aroused by the sight of their enormous destitution of spirit, by the pathetic superstitions they cling to, yet my frank and immediate admiration was also awakened by the simplicity of their character and the deep earnestness of their petition for instruction."

In January, at the General Convention in Philadelphia, he provoked remarks from the bishops of Virginia and South Carolina on the general backwardness of his diocese, his state. He stored away in his memory the soft, patrician slurs he provoked, and thought cheerfully of his congregations when they would hear them. Nobody supports you like the righteously indignant.

On his way home from the Convention he stopped in Washington to visit Statius Collins, a tart-tongued mountain lawyer who had sung his way to Congress from fly-blown, up-country courtrooms. They chatted about the mountains, about the Congressman's pioneer childhood and then about a mission for some of the people Statius Collins had left behind him.

Philanthropic activities, thought Statius Collins. Christian philanthropic activities. On top of a mountain. Who could miss that? Bishop Ames is right. I owe something to them, my people, salt of this earth. Here's a bishop talking some sense. I don't know what to make of it.

The Bishop took his slaps on the back and his support, smiling.

In March he went to New York with Rachael to visit her father, Bishop Mullen of New York. He came across a book in his father-in-law's library, a large, ornate volume of etchings and descriptions of old monasteries in Wales. As a young man he had visited England and Wales, and he remembered the wildness of the country of Wales and thought about its similarities to the mountains of North Carolina. In the book he found a rich, deep-toned etching of a ruined monastery, abandoned now in a desolate Welsh valley. Under the picture he read: "Cistercian Abbey de Valle Sanctus. Founded 1200 A.D." It had once been a great and powerful monastery, he read, where the hospitality of the abbots was compounded not only of holy benedictions but also of four-course meat dinners in silver dishes and sparkling claret in dazzling goblets.

Valle Sanctus, he thought. Valle Sanctus.

"Valle Sanctus," said the people when he began his sermons. He preached daily, on a wide and tireless circuit from New Bern to Fayetteville, Charlotte to Morganton, talking all day and sipping hot coffee at night with honey in it for his itching throat.

"Valle Sanctus," said the diocese, impressed. Soon it was talking of little else, talking cautiously, as he knew it would, but talking.

It's a Christian scheme to be reckoned with, they said. He's a good man and powerful, they said. God knows this state could use something like that, they said.

"He's impossible!" said Marcus Sales. "Impossible, impossible!"

He was talking to his wife, striding up and down in his parlor four days before Good Friday. Rolled up and gripped in one tight fist was a sheath of papers. It was the sermon, carefully wrought, that he would now be unable to deliver in his own church.

He slapped it against his thigh in frustration, like the rider with his crop who has been thrown and stands smarting, watching the victorious horse canter away. "Absolutely impossible!"

"Well," said his wife from her sofa, "what are you going to do?"

"Do?" said Marcus Sales. "Do? Do?" He swung the sermon viciously. "What can I do? He's the Bishop. He's my superior. Can't you understand that?"

From her soft mohair sofa his wife looked at him with the black eyes of a hen. Your superior, she thought, yes, I understand that, all right. She said, "Well, does it make so much difference, after all?"

He stopped his pacing and gazed at her. She stared back from the sofa and bunched up a pillow under one arm.

"Can it be that my own wife doesn't see what he is doing? Is it possible you are taken in by him, too?"

"He's preaching in your church on Good Friday," she said. "So?"

"So blasphemy! Nothing less. He is going to change the order of worship, change it all around to suit himself. And for what purpose? For the remembrance of our Lord on Calvary? Hardly, hardly. No, for the remembrance of this wild, wasteful scheme of a mountain mission. For such nonsense the order of worship is turned upside down on Good Friday. Blasphemy!"

Outside, in the tall oaks that grew around his parish home, sparrows in a rising wind fluttered their wings in nervous frenzies and puffed up tiny, ruffled breasts. Inside, Marcus Sales chatted and paced, his wife watching him in lazy comfort from her cushioned sofa, speculating on the facts of blasphemy, and envy, and the all-canceling finalities of marriage.

For three days before the Good Friday service Starns worked furiously, cleaning and polishing. Often, when he would stop to wipe his face with a dirty kerchief, he would gaze at the dignified old church, scoured now and dressed up like a boy for Sunday school, and think, I bet you never expected nothing like this. I bet you are aching like me, and a little put out, too. Don't blame you, so am I. Whew! Shoo!

On Friday the windows sparkled, the floor was spotless and silky with wax, the drapery soft and lustrous. Starns himself, by that time, looked like a coal miner.

It's as though he has cleaned the church by making all the dirt stick to him, thought the Bishop that afternoon when he handed Starns the shroud for the cross.

"Starns, I see you have been doing some work," he said, grinning. "I see it all over you." And he laughed.

Starns took the shroud and grinned back. "I am glad you are enjoying yourself," he said. "Now, what do I do with this here?"

"It's for the cross. Put it over it and tie it with the little ribbon there."

"Yessir." He stood on a chair and slipped the purple velure shroud over the cross carefully and tied it on. From a front pew the Bishop watched him. When Starns tied the ribbon, he felt waves of black fatigue coming upon him. He thought, Hold on, not yet, and he said to Starns, "Not so tight, Starns, you're not tying a sack. That's better."

When he had dressed the cross, Starns came down from his chair, picked it up and carried it past the Bishop. Going by, he said, "Well, I do hope all this turns out the way you want it to. I can't take much more and that's a fact."

Bishop Ames smiled and listened to Starns's heavy footsteps pad up the thick carpet of the aisle. He thought, Neither can I, Starns. Then he straightened his back, shook his head slightly and plunged into prayer.

On the altar the cross stood enshrouded in its purple robe of mourning. Before it sat a huge congregation, packed into the church to hear Bishop Ames.

In his pulpit, waxed by Starns until it glittered like a golden chariot, with the sorcery of candlelight streaming down across his snow-white bishop's robe, with his handsome, intense face and the bearing of a prophet, Nahum Immanuel Ames was persuasion enough for most.

As he spoke, they saw the savage wilderness parting, saw in its depths a Christian mission. Even those in the congregation who liked neither the Bishop nor the idea felt the call of it working in him, never doubted the wan, desperate faces he described, turned to him, saying, Christ, who is he? Tell us.

"Now you tell me," said Bishop Ames, his arms outstretched, his voice leaping over their heads. "You tell me what a church without a mission is, and I will listen. But when all the talk is done, I will think that it isn't much more than a place where the proud amuse themselves and the jealous bicker. A place where ruffled peacock feathers get smoothed out again. That's what a church without a mission becomes, you and I both know it. God forbid that in this diocese, but it could happen here, as it is now happening, has already come about, in certain other places familiar to us all." Virginia, thought the congregation. And South Carolina. Pride, sinful pride. They listened, silent, on their haunches, spirits ready to leap.

"The true Church is nothing if it is not hope," said Bishop Ames, and he held on to the railing of the pulpit, felt the black waves of fatigue drawing away his strength. A feather slipped up into his throat. He cleared it away and said, "Hope for the destitute," and something in the back of the church caught his eye.

The vestrymen were milling about quietly, preparing for the offertory, and he thought he saw a familiar, frightening figure pass through them with unkempt hair.

He cleared his throat again and said, "Hope. Hope for the bloody who are dear to Christ, who wander and die lost and alone." Feathers and dry quills choked his throat and he coughed and his voice failed him.

He motioned then for Billy Cobb to step up before the congregation and sing. They had planned it for the end of the sermon, during the offering, but he thought it would give him time to get his voice back, and Billy Cobb saw that and stepped up from the front pew and sang. His shock of red hair carefully slicked down, he sang the plainsong chant the mountain people had liked, the eerie glissandos that had touched the unplayed string in them as ancient as itself. Billy Cobb's voice that night was clear and sweet. His pale eyelids fluttered as he sang, and when he finished and the last note sank into them, the congregation was silent.

Bishop Ames nodded, and when Billy sat down again, he resumed his sermon, refreshed. He preached to them as he had to the mountain people, not so much a sermon as a quiet recitation of the parables, and the people thought, How grand!

Grand, they thought, not what you usually get. A lot different, they thought, than circuit-rider rantings, wastrel preachers or wild Baptists. This is something else again.

They considered his plans, the land he told them was already bought from his own funds, the buildings he wanted put up, the school for a native ministry and for the children of the poor. Seated on their cushions, the well-fed congregation listened as the mountain people had listened, squatting in the dirt or perched on their mules or horses or oxen. Like the heathen, they listened, those who were proud and envious and ruffled and angry, they listened and they were proud of him.

The dust in his throat told him he could not finish. He thought, Well, it's enough. It's going to be all right. They are willing.

He pointed to the cross in the shroud and told them Easter was near, that on Sunday, when the purple shroud was withdrawn, he hoped the great arms of the cross could be seen from remote Valle Sanctus, the valley of Heathen now. And he told them that for human miracles, humans must sacrifice.

He exhorted them to give him money to build the mission, hating the old, tired words that always performed so well. Finishing, he said, "Without a mission the Church is neither true nor false, it is only a sapless tree, a rootless branch drifting in a stream."

Enough, that's good enough, he thought, and gave a short prayer. When he said "Amen," his bleak eyes found the vestrymen and he nodded and stepped down from the pulpit.

He stood by Marcus Sales while the offering was collected. He listened to the rustling of the people, sensed their sympathy and support. He felt empty and full of peace.

There was some confusion among the vestrymen, but finally they came down the aisle. Bishop Ames grabbed Marcus Sales's arm. From his dry throat came a wet sound, like the mushy cry of a gigged frog, and Marcus Sales, astonished, had to keep him from falling.

One of the bearers of the offering, out of step, was shambling along behind the rest, wobbling about in the center of the aisle. He tottered along behind the others like a frantic child trying to walk. Bishop Ames shuddered. The white cloth of his robe began to shake. Into his dry nostrils crept the familiar, sweet, stinging breath, whisky-laden.

Trailing along crazily after the orderly procession of the offering, stomping clumsily toward him over the red carpet of the aisle came the haunting figure with blood in its hair, the ghastly apparition of his dead father in stained denims, holding out in both hands, full to the brim, the polished offering bowl.

There was a raft crossing a river. Water green and swirling but deathly still in places. In one glassy spot a face beneath green water, looking up at him, trying to surface. It was his brother, a face Starns had not seen in twenty-five years, disfigured by time and water, imploring him. Starns felt great sorrow, knowing he could not pull him out of the green water where his arms waved like shallow-river grass. From the raft Starns saw the riverbank, dark and somber, scorched. Forests burned for clearings that no one farmed. By black stumps stood this person and that, he recognized some of them. Farmers who hired him, a man he killed with a plow, a girl standing by a dead dog with a pitchfork sticking out of its ribs, carrying a window frame and yelling soundlessly through it, next to her Cora Larman with one hand rubbing her face and the other lifting up her skirt, and the sorrow came again. Wind blew. The figures turned black as the stumps, and the wind blew off their heads and arms, blew them away like soot.

When Billy Cobb began to sing the plainsong in the church above his room, Starns dreamed of wind whistling through warped cabin logs. When Billy stopped, the wind stopped, and he was suddenly awake and very cold, sitting upright in his narrow bed with all his clothes on.

He rolled over on his side, reached under the bed for the jug. He drank from it steadily, in sucking, smacking drafts, until the cold dampness in his stomach was gone.

What would I do without some whisky? Some men live without it, I don't see how.

Upstairs in the great church the Bishop's husky voice droned on, rising and falling like the endless buzz of a restless hornet.

When he had come down to his room, as was his unyielding habit just before every service, Starns had thrown himself on his bed, exhausted. Now he was wide awake, fumbling in the pockets of his work coat hanging on a peg until he found the silver buckle and drew it out. He had clipped it to a scrap of leather, an ancient noseband for a long-dead mule. He clutched it like a charm, gripped it like a last talisman that might banish the cold, dank, desolate wretchedness he had brought with him out of his dream.

He looked at the close walls of his room.

I got to get out of here.

He wandered about the churchyard, came to rest leaning weakly against the wall of the rear of the church. Above his head, through one of the great windows opened to the warmish night, came the sounds of many people breathing and the glow of candlelight. Framed in the window was the pulpit, the golden chariot in which Bishop Ames was preaching the last of his sermon. Starns listened to his voice, buzz, buzz, and smelled the warm breath of all the people inside listening to him, and then he twisted his head and pressed it against the hard wall of the church.

A nailhead stuck up out of one of the frame boards. It cut his scalp, a trickle of blood ran down over one eye. He turned and leaned against the wall, staring into the darkness of the warm night.

Oh, where are they, my own? What am I supposed to be doing in this life?

Against that cry the sanity and order of his senses could not stand. Behind the church was an empty field, and when he looked at it, he saw a tree that had not been there before. Around it, waving full tassels in sunlight, was a field of high Indian corn. Above towered the tree, with giant arms sticking out, a massive cross with beams like two arms. With a shapeless hand he wiped the blood from his eye and saw his mother standing with her hand at her bonnet, looking for him, and against the trunk, leaning idly and swishing a stick, his speechless, ragged, proud father. Starns's arm jumped, he waved a weak paw at them and they saw him, waved back and pointed up above their heads, his mother with her hands, his father with the stick. There was something there, but he didn't know what it was. Above his head, through the window of the church, the Bishop's voice spoke the name and then he saw the name sitting in the great tree, sitting not at all the way he would sit in the Bishop's sermon but perched casually like a man sits on a split-rail fence in the afternoon. It was the white figure with the long hair he had seen so often in the big Bibles when you turn the black cover. Above his mother and his father sat Jesus Christ on a beam of his cross, smiling easily and waving to him.

When the offering was taken and the vestrymen stood in line at the rear of the church to march to the altar, they were amazed to see him. He came through the oak doors and stood there blinking, just as they were ready to begin their procession.

"It's Starns," one of them said. "You suppose all the creeks are running backwards, too? Hey, Starns, what you doing here?"

Starns did not answer. He put a great hand on the man's shoulder and gently but swiftly took the offering bowl from him.

"Excuse me," he said. "I will do this now. I thank you."

The procession began. Down the aisle marched the procession of offering, Starns at the end, reeling. The people stared at him, wrinkled their noses at the whisky on his breath. Bishop Ames, hallucinated, held on to Marcus Sales and saw his father bear down on him. Starns himself stomped on, like a tired horse to the barn, his bleary eyes fastened on the high pulpit and, behind it, unseen, the shrouded cross.

Interlude

TUNE THE FIDDLE

YOU STAND under my wet hickories with gray rain in your eyes, under halos of mist, my friends and ghosts, specters all, and I am wondering if you remember any of it now. Do specters remember things when they stand by a man's bed in the night, lean against his trees in the rain and walk across his yard while he sits drinking on his porch? You don't smile at me none, but there's something around them bloodless mouths, some kind of a pucker or something, tells me most likely you do.

Then, do you remember the day Marcus Sales preached his first sermon and, thinking it should be clear, he brought along a little Negro boy with a tin horn, had that boy climb a tree and when he preached how the doom and the judgment could come just any day, that Negro blew that horn and scared everbody senseless, so that men fell off mules and women wailed and all the dogs ran away? And what you did to him later in the creek? And do you remember how one of you—Cardell, was it you?—taught him later what a stump-broke mare was, stood him on a stump and had some old mare back her sweaty bottom up against him and him not knowing why until one of you—Shad, was it you?—called out: "Now all ye have to do is open ye britches," and how that preacher swore then?

Rachael, you are wearing your soft woolly shawl and your cold fingers are there on its fringe, do you remember those fingers rippling, playing the foot organ, me pumping it for you, with Starns standing around mocking the thing because he was puzzled and happy at its sound? Jimmy Rode, do you recall cheating the hell out of us at your store, figuring that practicing Christians wouldn't be thinking about such things, until the day Starns busted your plank counter and said, "Do you think God give me this big arm and this fist to be cheated every day by a damn little storekeep?" and how you said later, "That's the man for me," and joined the church?

Harlan, do you remember Cora now, Cora, do you remember Jean?

Bishop, you are the only one will not look at me. No, you stand turned away from me, like a preoccupied father, looking after Starns where he disappeared into the brush. Standing looking after him, with the mist crawling up and down your arms, curling around the black sleeves of your frock coat like smoke. Look at me, remember me.

I recall myself so clearly then, you must, too, a little. Spindly-legged, redheaded Billy Cobb, with the high tenor voice like an Irish boy, and the disposition toward you of a spaniel toward his master. Have you forgot all the coffee and all the books and bags I carried for you? I reckon you have, but, oh, God, I did always mean to please you.

All you had to do was whisper and I jumped. So did a lot of other people, but me quickest of all. Like the day after that first Good Friday service, when you said, "Billy, I need your help," and I jumped like I was stuck with a needle, saying, "Yessir!" And you, "Did you see the ruckus Starns caused in the church last night?" And me, "Yessir, I did, and it scared me," and you, "Yes, it scared me a little too, Billy. But nobody is going to push Starns around because of it." And me, "Who could push Starns around?" and you, "There are some who'd like to. They call him ignorant dirt, Billy, but it's not true, not anymore. Starns has had a change of heart." And me, "What?" and you, "Yes, it surprised me, too, but he has. Billy, he came to me after the service and told me he wants to learn to read and write better, and to study the government, and do whatever it is he has to do to be a good man."

And me, I was sad then, thinking of poor old Starns saying that, and I said so. "Poor old Starns."

"He's not so old," you said. "He just looks older." And you smiled that far-off, superior smile, like you was looking down from some great height. "There are still things he can do."

"What?" I said, and you, "Well, he knows a good deal about handi-work and farming. He picked up a lot just drifting around. Now, about thirty-five acres of the old Johnson farm has been given to the Church. You know that land, Billy?"

I said, "Yessir, it's not much, though, I used to play out there some. Awful rocky." And you, "Yes, but it's a start. I gave it to him to look after and work any way he pleases. That's one thing. But there's something else I want him to have, and, Billy, you're about the only one can give it to him. Yes, you're the only one can help me."

"Well, yes, how?" I said, not breathing, and you, "I want you to teach him, Billy, tutor him."

Did I fail you, Bishop? No, I didn't, it was me and Starns an hour a day, three hours on Saturdays, for one year. Pretending I was doing it for fun, but Sundays after church taking from you the one whole dollar a week salary you gave me. Yes, we worked. Over Rachael's oilcloth kitchen table, in his basement room at Marcus Sales's church, out at the little Johnson farm. Or, rather, he worked while I watched him. I never saw anything so painful. Two books and a ruler, a coal-oil lantern and a quill pen and some paper and sweat.

I thought it was crazy, and for what? I said to myself, but you wanted it, and that was enough for Billy Cobb then. At least, I thought it was crazy until I saw his first harvest.

I met Starns one day out at that farm supposed to be worthless, and saw it waving wheat and corn and great big cabbages with leaves like elephant's ears, and the few peach trees there giving again. Those crops waved at me like a crowd of people at the fair, and I looked flabber-gasted at the man I thought was crazy, heard him say, "Thanks be to God and Bishop Ames, Billy, it's a good first crop."

Often you'd ask me about him. The things he said and did. When I would tell you some of them, and how well he was getting along, you'd sit back in your chair like a man whose horse just won the race. One time you said, "You see, he never was insane. They were stupid, all of them."

I said, "Yessir," thinking you meant Starns, but knowing it didn't sound quite right, the way you said it, and the smile you gave it.

Bishop, when you smiled like that, who knew what you meant? Your tactical smile, you said, and laughed it off. I was only a boy then, I am glad I did not know what it hid, that smile, about the mission, about God, about Rachael, about Starns, about yourself. I wonder if Starns ever knew. I don't think Rachael did, your own wife, and maybe not even those strange beings you went to at the end. Maybe not even them, though I reckon you thought they did.

The mist curls around your ghost like smoke, and you will not look at me. You stand looking off after Starns, and I think it is strange you are now the figure you were in the early days of the mission, tall and commanding, your black coat hanging down you straight as a general's uniform. In your office you were like a general, impatient and fed up with maps, who wants to take to the field, or maybe a ship's captain pacing a tiny cabin, wanting the wheel himself.

You knew you'd made a mistake, sending Marcus Sales up there to start the mission. Why did you do that? Did you feel guilty about the way you'd treated him over Starns, or what? Anyway, you knew you'd made a mistake the day you saw him and his proud wife, Vida, off in that buggy of theirs bought for the trip. You bought it, as I recall.

When Marcus Sales's reports stopped coming, in the winter of '51, you were like a wild man, wanting to go back up there. His other reports, the few you got, they all but said the mission was an impossible failure, and it drove you wild. But you couldn't go. The general had to stay with his maps, and the captain get in his own reports, and there was already too much talk about the diocese being neglected, anyway, because of one tiny, impractical mission.

So you sent Starns. He didn't want to go, as I remember, said he'd seen what there was for him to see in those mountains, but you said go and that was enough for any of us. You gave him one of your best horses, and Starns went off, after that snow-blasted, late-thaw winter of 1851, to see what had happened to Marcus Sales and the Valle Sanctus mission.

So many stories were told later, about Marcus Sales and what happened to him, and about Starns when he first got there. But neither

Starns, or you, there, Marcus Sales, would make it plain, and I still wonder about it myself.

Marcus Sales, with your black hands and martyr's eyes, you still won't talk. None of you will talk to me about anything. You lean against my trees in the rain and say not a word, specters all.

But there is so much to recall. Speak to me, friends and ghosts, speak to me out of your mist and gray rain.

Part Two

SAVIOUR STARNS

1

CIRCLE FOUR

Harlan

At the bluff, down under the poplars, I had Jean on my side, standing in the thin sun watching them men a-building. Her little legs was astraddle my hip, and I held her to me in the crook of one arm. She was fooling with a hole in my shirt, pushing a finger through it and poking me. "Jean, quit," I said, and she stuck up her face and made a little o with her lips and tore it open some more. Then she laughed and flopped down her head, all bushy now, on my shoulder. Not two year old, Jean, but like a woman already.

I hefted her and put my other arm under her legs. She got content and, with her eyes closed, turned her mouth up to the sun and was drowsy. I watched her for a while, sharing the sun, thin as it was. We was content there for a time, and I forgot them men down in the valley bottom.

But soon she commenced to shiver and press her ear into my neck for some more warmth. I felt the damp coming in on the wind, which was low, moving the bottom branches as the top, reaching into the valley like a man scrapes the bottom of his seed barrel. It was after them men, and I wanted to see it get them.

Not long for you, I thought. A few more days, it'll chase you out of here, swarming and a-building on that field with their grave markers right there. Yelling and pounding and running around them where they lie, it will soon stop.

I had watched them with Jean many times. Watched them come last summer after the big meeting when I killed Daniel, and they cleared the bottom then. In the winter I most forgot about them, living alone with my Jean, but then they come again when the wind stopped blowing and it was spring weather. Now all this summer I have watched them, when the Bishop in his long black coat riding his bay horse was here and there, talking and arguing and laughing with them strange hired men he brung up here, waving his hands over them and all that. Once they all got mad and bunched together in a crowd and stood all around him, pressing in on him and his big bay horse. But he just talked and waved his hands and charmed them and they went on back to work. That is what he can do, when he wants to.

He left after some time, and the other preacher come, and he is not the man the Bishop is. No, he don't have the powers. All that hired help, they run around more now and do less. And now Jacob Larman has brung down some boys from the slopes to go to that school when it is finished, and so now they are all down there, running and hollering and pushing stone and timber, trying to get something finished before the winter comes down.

They won't do it. This wind, when it is ready, it will dig them out of there a-yelping. It will scour that field. It will reach into them half-built houses and get them. Then all their running and yelling over the graves of my family, it will be for nothing. Slave and strain, you damn little bugs, chop and carry and jump around, go ahead. All your sweat will turn to ice when this wind tells it to.

Whilst I was watching, and holding my Jean, one of that hired help put his coat over Margaret's gravestone and leaned against it, spitting. I thought hard on her then, Margaret come back to me strong, and with her, all bones and dust in their winding sheets, stood Orlean and little Joseph.

I shook Jean awake then and carried her home, saying, "Talk some to me, honey, say something. Talk to your daddy, talk to him."

Cora

Both them two summers and winters Harlan's door stayed closed to me. He would not wave when I come by, or speak, or let me see Jean. There was nothing for me home on Sand Mountain, them that come wanting me, they had nothing for me. So when Grandpa Jacob decided that of the boys it was Cardell needed most to go to that mission school, and when he asked me, by hinting at it, to take Cief along and see if they would take him, too, I went.

Preacher Sales and Mrs. Sales, they made it plain they didn't want Cief, that he scared them. I told them they'd better take him, whether he learned anything or not, or they'd have trouble from us, and so they did. I didn't mean Cardell to have something Cief didn't, and I wanted a reason to go there now and again myself.

I took to going down there more and more, to see about Cief, I said, until that Mrs. Sales kept me on to help her in the log kitchen. I'd sleep there by the stove, or sometimes sneak out with one of the boys, or maybe stay up through the night with Cief, watching the iron stove they had there burn itself out. Sometimes there was two boys, once three. Preacher Sales, he knowed what was likely in that kitchen at night, but he was too scared of them boys to do nothing.

In the daytime, in the big room, I took to standing in the back and watching them say their words after Preacher Sales. All but Cief, I mean. His big head stuck up above them a foot or two, and he just set there and stared. But he did like the sounds of it all, it was company for him, he never give no trouble. Preacher Sales and Mrs. Sales, they just acted like he wasn't there, except sometimes they'd be going some-wheres and see him, and then turn like they'd forgot something and head somewheres else quick.

I got so I could say some of them things, too. Almost as fast as them boys. Like when Preacher Sales would say, "Who are the Three Persons in one God?" well, I could say back, "The Three Persons in one God are God the Father God the Son and God the Holy Ghost," and get through it about the same time as the others. And when he said, "What does the word God mean?" I knowed to snap right out, "He who is Good!" mak-

ing the last word loud and long like he wanted, but there wasn't nothing in it for me. It was just something to do while Mrs. Sales rested,
which she did a lot of the time.

But Cief and me both, we liked them pictures the man showed. I
could tell when Cief puzzled at them, pictures of folks dressed in long
white things, sitting around talking or going somewhere together. And
most of the time it was all right, because the boys was all tired out from
a morning's work on the buildings. They was plumb happy to be in
there where it was a little warmer than outside, and they most of them
slept a lot then, while he talked and showed pictures. It only got bad
when they was all awake at the same time.

Now, I knowed it was just the cold wintertime held them boys
down. I figured I would just stay until spring anyhow and see it all bust
loose, the way men and boys will do when the wind turns warm.

It come sooner than that. I hadn't been there three weeks before
Preacher Sales got mad at Thurmon Gaines's backtalk, Thurmon being
a puny, feisty little thing, ready to yell at anybody because about anybody is bigger than he is. Preacher Sales got mad because he wouldn't
say what he was supposed to, and made Thurmon get down on the
floor to pray with his hands folded and all. Thurmon did, but he got
right up again and told Preacher he was sick to death of working and
sitting in the cold, jabbering things he didn't know the first thing about
nohow and didn't care. He got red-faced like a little raw baby, and he
looked back to where I was standing and said something about Mrs.
Sales and looked at me again and told the Preacher he should get him
some of that and maybe he wouldn't be such a damn old woman, and
then he started out.

White and fitified, Preacher Sales run after Thurmon and dragged
him back by his shirt collar. It tore, and the shirt, it ripped open down
the back, and when Preacher Sales grabbed again he sunk his thumb in
Thurmon's eye, and Thurmon howled like the dead and dying then,
and them boys went wild.

I run to Cief and grabbed him and held his hand, him scared and
whining. Them boys would have done I don't know what, but I hollered

at them and they hushed and I said they'd get flayed alive by their folks if they did anything, and they thought about it. I took Cief and left, knowing there'd be trouble soon and that there was nothing in it for me.

Me and Cief went on up Sand Mountain. Stopped by Harlan's cabin to see if he would let us in, but he wouldn't. He did let me see Jean, though, for a minute, and I wished he hadn't. He brung her out on the porch holding his hand, with that coverlid all around her, her hair like a little yellow bird's nest and her little mouth breathing steam. She has growed a lot and her hair, it's bushy now like mine, only a lot more yellow. I was glad to see her, but she was thin under that coverlid and her cheeks was dark and her eyes, too. I could tell from where I was that she was puny. She coughed and he took her back in before I could see much more about her.

So I went on up the mountain with Cief, not caring if we got home or not, knowing there wasn't much reason for it even if we did. At the falls I said, "Cief, you know where you are now," and left him there and commenced to run, but not to get home. Cief slopped along and I run.

The snow bit my feet, but I didn't care.

Jacob Larman

When the Bishop sent that preacher named Sales up here to learn the young, it turned out he couldn't even make them sit still.

But I said, Well, it is cold down there, them cabins wasn't put up right nohow, and it is hard on them boys. I said, Patience, all.

Then, right after the first blizzard, I think it was, he come up here the first time. Wanted to know why nobody was coming to his church meetings.

"That wasn't the bargain," I told him, but he didn't comprehend it.

"Preacher," I said, "the bargain was this. For that field, sold to him, the Bishop was to put up this school. We was to send young'uns down to it, which we have done."

"Yes, a school," he said, "but a church, too, Mister Larman."

I smelled it coming and I said, "Yes, but not like the King's Church, I hope. Where a body must go, want to or not. Not no church like that, I hope, Mister Sales."

And he said, "Well, no," and then, "But you see," and so we skitted along like that for a while.

Finally, to shut him up, I said I would see somebody of mine went on down there the next time. Earl was standing the porch watching us and I told him he'd go. He said the hell he would, and I got mad, and while we was talking it over, the preacher, he left.

Earl never did go, but it wasn't the bargain he should, so I didn't blame him. And I couldn't do it, sick as I am now with this bad bile and all. So we let it ride.

Then he come up the second time, not two weeks later, telling me that little Thurmon Gaines just tried to kill him with a barlow knife. Well, Cora had told me how he'd treated Thurmon once before, so I didn't say nothing, but my patience was going fast. I felt it going right out of me like water in the morning, with him talking how they was all ready to kill him first chance they got. He went on and on, until I was sick to death of it.

When we got ahold of them fourteen boys and sent them down to him and to that school, which ones did he think we was sending? Them that mind and do right? What for? No, we sent down them that needed to learn, them in trouble all the time, them that reach for a stick when any soul says nay to them. Hoped it would do them some good, like the Bishop said. But no, now they swing barlow knives instead of sticks.

Preacher Sales just kept right at it, he would keep talking, and I seen then I had been wrong about trusting in people like that, even when I had to. He jabbered on and on about the laws of his very good friend Jesus Christ, about God's awful power and holy this and that.

Well, I knowed I didn't know what he was talking about, and I commenced to wonder if *he* did.

He was proving this to me and proving that, saying if this here was so, then that there had to be true, and such. I couldn't stand it no more and I yelled at him and he stood blinking and Earl and Shad come out on the porch with us and I yelled at them too.

I told that preacher that all his jabbering didn't have nothing to do with the truth at all, that it was just calculation, which is something else. And if he thought we don't know what calculation is, well, he might just stop and figure, calculate, how much Jimmy Rode has been a-cheating him at his store. Calculation we know, truth is something else, I told him.

So then he pulled up a chair next to my rocker, lit on it and then he asks me, What is truth, then?

I thought, Aw, hang this man.

Shad and Earl gathered right around, interested, and Earl spit and said truth is knowing when to run, and both him and Shad looked the man over like a cut of beef until I yelled at them to get on the hell off the porch and let us talk.

I knowed I shouldn't have gone on like that, a voice said, Hold on, old man, but even tasting my own bile couldn't stop me from being so mad at that man, preaching to me.

Truth, I told him, is a fight, and which man stays alive and which man don't. It's a childbirth that looked likely but wasn't, it's a crop acting different from the weather. It is why some young'uns turn out the way they do, why Harlan, whose father I loved, killed my grandson Daniel and lives alone now with my granddaughter's child and talks to not one soul. It is what has come of all of us here, of my pa and Ben Cutbirth who brought him here, it is what has happened to the brood my Debra give me out of her fair sweet body in clenching and in yelling, and why they have now come to live like dogs around me. Why Callman, Cief and Cora's pa, was such a fine figure of a man, yet Cief's tongue is like a mashed stick in his mouth and Cora's legs fork open to any man.

I raved on, couldn't stop. I said, Well, yes, we are interested, well, yes, we care about the truth, but not God's, because what do we know about that? No more than you. No, we care about the truth that comes from our cabins and homes, where we know the placing of things, or anyhow the way they was meant to be placed. We know what we meant to come about, and we measure it against the way it did come out finally, over the years, and yes, we want the truth about that difference, ignorant though we may be. But that we don't get.

"Least of all from you," I said, tasting bile and near foaming at the mouth.

I tried not to fall no deeper into that fit, but then he commenced being real nice to me. Thought I was just this old fool with sons mean enough to make people pay attention. I near puked right down to that bile watching him try to pet me like a damn dog. He hadn't heard a word I said. He just would not have another man talking, couldn't stand another man speaking out his heart, that wasn't to be done, especially an old man like me, dried out and sick. He said something sweet about a man at my time of life, and I hit at him with my stick and tried to bash in his high and mighty Jesus Christing face. I was on my feet swinging and puking, and I seen my stick go tumbling down off the porch and the preacher was holding me up and yelling for Shad and Earl.

They come running and took hold of me, and then that man, he run. Just run off, as soon as they were there to take me off his hands.

Shad and Earl carried me in the cabin, with me trying to yell for that preacher to send Cardell back up here from that school. I couldn't make no noise, but I kept thinking I could, trying to yell as they laid me to bed, yell at that man with God's beautiful truth just handed to him at birth and kept from us, the ignorant. That man who didn't have no cabin hisself and didn't want one. No, him, damn people like him, they live vagrant, under a mess of roofs they never look at, on floors they don't know who cut and laid, in beds where strangers have and will sleep when they are gone, strangers they'll never know nothing about.

I wanted up. I wanted to go beat that man with a stick, because when people like him talk about the truth, it means let's you and the other man fight, and I have hated that kind of little meanness all my life.

Then, in the bed, I seen the way Shad was a-looking at me, and I got scared and tried to call myself up out of my fit. I thought on my Debra. How she could calm me down. I felt better for a while until something sharp turned behind my eyes and something sharper yet come crawling up my side like a serpent.

Juba

Tate and me come awake together when we heard them outside call-ing, but both the boys was up and out the door before we was out of bed. When Tate went out, they come a-running back in, snow in their hair and snivelly at the nose. They got the rifle guns down from the deerhorns.

"Hold on," I said, "what's transpiring here?"

But they paid me no mind, my boys. Kept jumping about, eyes beady, on the run, so I worried a little. My boys know better than to get so flustered unless there is some reason.

Outside, I seen Tate standing by John Barco's horse, holding the bri-dle and talking to him. Behind them was a whole bunch of men, sitting their horses in the falling snow, all riders, all with rifle guns. Jimmy Rode was there, and Clayton Gaines, and such. The snow was heavy-flaked and wet, coming down like big white leaves, and I could hear the hickories freezing in the wind.

When I got out on the porch, I heard Tate say, "Well, she'll do what she can," and I wondered just what it was he said I would do in such weather, and whether I would do it for a bunch of fool men out in the freezing night up to no good.

But then the back horses moved and come up dragging a sled and in it was the mission people, hurt.

Tate was saying, "Well, something must have happened to old Jacob. He would never have tolerated this. Think he's dead, finally?"

John Barco said, "It is hard to believe, but if he is dead, then we will have to find Earl and Shad and Cardell and all their wild friends and calm them down. We can't have them on the loose without Jacob around to hold them down."

All the men said that was right.

"How'd you find these people?" Tate said, nodding down at the mis-sion man and his woman on the sled.

"Heard her yelling," said Jimmy Rode. "All the way from Sand Mountain ridge. One of the boys told Clayton that they'd been taken up to Jacob's during the day. We was all standing around at the store wondering what to do about it, when we heard her yelling where they say Earl and Shad left them. Got the sled and brung them here. Juba, if ye can keep them while we go up and see about Jacob, we'll appreciate it."

Now, all this time them poor people was just lying on the sled, catching snow. Them men, they would have talked right on while they froze.

"Lafe and little Tate," I said, "get inside and hot up the fire." They did, but they took a minute before doing it, and I wondered about that.

When the men got them mission people inside, I seen that the woman, she was all right, just scared senseless. But the man was a-moaning like a wild thing and I couldn't see why until John Barco took hold of his hands and turned the man's palms up so's I could see them.

Well, sir, both his palms was scorched, just burnt black.

"What in the world has this man been doing?" I said. "Holding fire?"

John Barco said, "Yes, ma'am, I think that is just exactly what he's been doing," and him and me and Tate all looked at each other and remembered that Jacob Larman's pa, so the story goes, had his hands burned like that, by men of the Church.

"Now you see," said Jimmy Rode, "we have got to go up there and find out what has happened to Jacob. I don't mean to have any Larman do this to me."

The rest of the men muttered and I seen there was going to be trouble. We have always tried to tolerate the Larmans and their wild doings on Sand Mountain in midwinter. Yes, and some of us have even gone up there a time or two and joined in with them in their sprees because old Jacob, he would never let it get out of hand. But this here was something else, this man being treated like this, something set on fire for the fun of it maybe. I knowed the men was mad, the way people get when neighbors go too far with wild times. Especially when the neighbors, they have wanted to join them wild times but have been ashamed to, or scared to, like Jimmy Rode. They are the quickest to get mad, want to stamp out something they can't have.

My boys got the fire hotted. Soon as it blazed up, they looked away from me, paid me no more mind, made it plain that if there was something else I had for them to do, they wasn't a-going to do it. Stood there waiting on the men, guns in their hands, ready to go out and do whatever it is won't wait until morning. They figured they was men now, ready to move quick, and what did a woman know about that?

Good boys, the both of them. I knowed better than to regret it. Let them go when it's time.

Tate said, "All right, let's go see, then," and all the men started out the door.

On the steps Tate slipped on the snow, and Lafe caught his arm and kept him from falling flat. Slip-sliding about, old Tate, he is at the place in life where because he is still lean and light on his feet he thinks he ain't old. Acts like he don't need to look where he is going, but then he has always been like that, Tate has.

The boys got on the mule and Tate on his sorrel, sitting up there jerking it about a little and calling it Job. Calling it Job, like he calls the razorback hog that plagues us, like he calls any other low-down beast, just to remind me of my lovemaking years ago when I run out on him for a while. He talks to me that way, Tate does.

"Here, Job, ho, Job!" Tate said, his way of saying, So long, woman. I hooted at him, told him not to fall down kill hisself, and then he was gone into them big falling snowflakes and I couldn't tell him from the others.

My boys rode off last, two straight backs and four legs on the mule, and not a look back when I waved to them.

I went in the cabin quick.

Something had to be done for the man, so I did it. I got down and scraped off some soot from the fireplace and then cut some lard. I recalled the day I burned my foot so bad and fixed it this way and then fell to hoeing corn on it and it got all right.

So I packed the man's hands in soot and lard, and wrapped them just a little. He howled, but not so bad.

When it was over, he sat on the floor with his head resting on the edge of my bed, and I didn't try to move him. His woman, she was in the bed and didn't want to look at nothing.

I put great store in boneset tea, so I made some and give some to her. She come around then and said thanks and helped me get some down the man. Once she reached over and dried off his mouth, but the way she did it, it was funny. It was like a woman dries the mouth of somebody else's child, one suffered, not cared for.

He was hurt so bad, and she was having no pity for him, and it troubled me. So I asked her why, right out, and then she looked at me like I was the world's fool indeed.

"Do you know what season this is?" she said.

I said, "Well, winter," and looked out the window at the snow coming down and felt foolish.

She looked at her man on the floor there and said, "It is the Christmas season."

I allowed it was that, too, for them that wanted to fool with it. And she, looking at that man all the time, she started telling me all the fine doings that were going on in far-off places, talking about all the great gatherings and mighty churches, and all the wonderful things happen this time of year down off these mountains. Talked about food and fine clothes, she did, and men who preach so that other men cry, and things like that. People singing in great bunches together, around big bowls of hot, sweet things to drink they all laugh over, and when she finished telling about that, she set my cup of boneset tea down on the floor.

She got out of the bed and come to stand by the fire, and she told me then how Earl and Shad come down to the mission to get them, saying they wanted Preacher Sales to come celebrate Christmas with them because old Jacob, he couldn't move and he needed the Holy Ghost. Preacher Sales, he was pleased by it, and he went and took her with him and when they got there, there was the big cabin with cedar chips laid all on the floor, and a big fire blazing in the tall chimney, tables with jerky and likker on them, and for a minute, she said, she didn't feel so sad about not being in the city for Christmas.

"Well," I said. "That's good, then."

She looked at the fire like it was somebody she hated and went on, with her hair still wet and scraggly from the snow, went on to tell me how they had fallen among thieves, truly. She went on to tell about just another Larman midwinter spree, but to her it was more than that. In all them wild and worthless slope folks that come to the Larmans' then to get drunk and roll around with each other and rut about in them cedar chips, she seen something even worse. To her they was like Tate's demons and devils when the spell is on him, except this was the first time she'd ever seen them that close.

She said how awful it was to watch them raising such hell, crawling around and throwing food and likker at each other, and rutting, and running out into the snow and grabbing and beating on each other.

I said, "Well, it's only once a year."

Then I thought about old Jacob, and I said, "But where was old Jacob? He has always kept them down some up there. Is he dead, finally?"

Truth is, Tate and me snuck up there one winter, like a lot of folks at one time or another. It was wild, all right, but we felt like it then, and had a good time, too. Old Jacob was there and he'd kick the fierceness out of anybody got too mean.

"No, he's not dead," she said. "But he might as well be. He's in his bed and can't move. They all talked to him, but he couldn't answer. His sons would ask him if they could do something, then go ahead and do it just as if he'd said yes."

"Grandsons," I said. "All his sons are dead, except Earl. Now, what was it they did?"

Then she told me what we'd all suspected. They made the Preacher hold on to some burning sticks and say god damn the King three times before he could let go. Then they'd laid ahold of her, and she would talk no more about it. I knowed it must have been bad for them up there if Earl was free to do what he wanted, but still that woman wasn't hurt all that bad, it was the man, he was the one. And her paying him no mind at all. So I said, "Well, anyhow, ye ain't hurt none."

I had only meant to commiserate with the creature, but it was like I had said something awful. She was that mortified. Wouldn't talk at all then. I hotted some more tea.

Preacher Sales commenced to sweat when I give it to him, and that was good. The poor man would moan and jerk his arms about, and at last I had to get right down and hold on to him. Otherwise he'd have hit them hands on the bed pegs or the floor and been yelling the rest of his life. I held on to him, and soon I was in as big a sweat as he was.

I was glad to do it, mind. But it did seem to me his own woman should have been at that instead of me. But no, she was on her knees the other side of the bed, hands clasped together, praying hard.

A time come when the Preacher cleared his head a trifle and looked at me, smily. Smiled at old Juba, the man did. His look was so clear and sweet. I reckoned he figured something like me a-holding him couldn't be earthly and he was already a long ways past dying.

"Well, now," I said to him. "Well, now." Just like he was any child.

He studied me then and mistook my gray old face for somebody else's, maybe his ma's, I don't know. He whispered real low to me a big secret, that he was hurt.

So I played like I was the one he took me for, and I will allow it, it give Juba comfort to do that right then.

"Oh, I am so scared," he told me, and his eyes got big and round.

"Well, now," I said, humming like it was just the usual sort of day. "Well, now, that ain't no way to be. Ain't nothing to be scared of. Ain't no boogers in here."

Then I stretched my neck like an old turkey and looked around the cabin like I was looking for some boogers. Then I was going to say, I don't see no boogers, do you? But the only thing wrong with that was his woman on her knees, fussing and praying hard. A booger for certain. So I let that pass by.

I recalled a story then. One that was told to me once when I was hurt, had been scared like him. All about a boy who went off somewhere and how his girly waited for him to come back. It was the only pleasant thing I could think of, so I told it to him.

Well, sir, there was Juba, plumb carried away with storytelling, thinking about her boys gone off with guns in the snow, holding the mission man like he was her own, telling that tale with him out of his head and the both of us a-sweating like horses.

I was about halfway through my story when the woman commenced to pray that much louder, and the man heard her and then he just give out, her calling for Christ and him hugging me hard. I stopped my fine story then, and thought then of the seven young ones that have come out of my body, of the two that lived, and how they were gone from me that night to fight and maybe kill on Sand Mountain. I laid my quilt over the man. Then I grabbed that woman and slapped her hard.

"Hush up!" I said. "Get on up and help me make this man something to eat on when he wakes. You ain't hurt none."

She did what I said then, I was that mean about it. But I was plumb fitified at her coming in here to torment herself and her man at my fire. When you don't have big worries, you can worry like that, but when you do have them, it will kill you.

She stepped then, me chasing her like after the wily hen before supper.

Later on she did feed her man like a woman should, and I was watching them and wondering about them when we heard gunfire commence on Sand Mountain. John Barco and Jimmy Rode, they was right about it. There was a ruction up there, and there was old Tate and my boys, all three being men and, like men must, killing when they had to.

That calmed me down some and I fell to cooking for them if they ever got back, but still wondering at them mission people, whose demons and devils are worse than ours, wondering what in the nation they reckon everything is all about, anyhow.

2

THE SOWER

THE RIDER dropped the reins onto the mane of his horse. In two strides the animal stopped and settled his weight, bent a long neck down to his forelegs and then shook himself violently, spinning sweat off his flanks. Up in his stirrups, the rider held the saddle horn, letting him shake, thinking, Yes, I'm hot too. Wish I could do that. When the shiver passed, he eased back into the saddle on one thigh, unhooked a foot from a stirrup and let it hang. From the spot where the Bishop's party first saw the valley two years before, Starns, alone, gazed down on it again.

On the slopes the late afternoon sun was gliding down the still barren limbs of the trees, spreading out on the uneven ground, tinting the forest loam light amber and soft green. The steep ground that plunged into the valley was spotted and mottled by spurts of bloodroot and white hepatica, blossoms that cheat their way up before the leaves sprout, thus gaining the sunlight that falls straight to the ground.

Well, Starns, he thought, it will behoove you to look close at that before the leaves come, hide everything. Early spring, it's the time to kick over some dirt, see what's there. That ground looks rich.

He held his hat up to block the sun and looked at the three dusty brown buildings. That's the schoolhouse, that must be the chapel, and there's the log kitchen. And all in adobe, just like the Bishop said. What got into him to do that, build in adobe? Lord.

He started to snug his hat back on his head, but took it off again quickly and held it up. Two small figures were running around, darting out of the chapel and back in again. He heard thin, high-pitched laughter and then the crack of wood splitting. He wiped his forehead with his sleeve, eased his head into his hat until it suited him. He took up the reins and nudged the horse on, thinking, What are you getting into, Starns? The horse looked back at him regretfully as he lurched off, and Starns thought, That's right, I don't want to go no more than you do. Giddup.

At the juncture of the two rivers, over the sounds of their meeting and over the whistle of the sharp early April wind, he heard a rhythmic knocking, like shutters flapping on an empty house. When he rode around the log kitchen and faced the chapel, he saw a clumsy cross hanging by corroded wire from the adobe wall above the door. It had been fashioned by the nailing of shares to the sides of a split-handled plow. Now it rocked loose in the wind, knocking one arm, then the other against the wall, digging out bits of adobe and sending them running down the wall to the ground.

Adobe, thought Starns. Lord save us.

As he ambled his horse around, a small explosion burst out of the chapel door. Two boys, fighting. They had begun it playfully, absently, but when Starns reached the chapel they had slapped each other into anger. Starns pulled up, watched them kick and swing with abandon. They hit and spat, stood and wiped their noses, and fell on each other again, oblivious of the man standing his dusty horse to watch them.

One boy swung a stiff-armed haymaker, missed, got knocked flat. Starns smiled, but when the boy came up with a large, sharp-sided rock, he kicked the horse again. The boy was running after his opponent, screaming.

"I'll bust ye damned head open," he howled, swinging the fist that held the rock.

Starns trotted his horse in between them and they scattered. He reined in, looking down from the saddle. The mellow glare of the afternoon sun, skipping off leaves and stones, hit his new spectacles and they went opaque. To the boys he looked like a man with tarnished disks for eyes. They gaped at him.

"A fist is one thing, a rock's another," said Starns soberly. "What's the trouble?"

The boys stepped backward. Like canyoned animals, they eyed him.

"Who be ye!" demanded one.

"What's ye business!" the other spat at him.

"Give me that rock first, before somebody gets a head knocked open."

He held out his palm, the skin hard and smooth, like pebbles washed and tumbled in a creek. He waited patiently.

From the high slopes came a faraway cackle of crows.

"Get out, Mister!"

Now they both held rocks and they stood together, hefting their weapons, tossing their threats up and down in their tough and dirty hands.

"All right," said Starns, "kill each other, then."

He flicked the reins and passed on. At the schoolhouse he dismounted in puffs of dust and a painful screeching of leather. Looking over the top of the saddle while he loosened the cinch knot, he saw that the boys were side by side now. They hooted at him in unison, then threw their rocks, which looped up in the air and landed a few feet away from him, frightening the horse.

For a moment he stared at them, seeing in simplicity and in miniature that which in size and complexity had so terrified and defeated Marcus Sales. The boy who had swung the vicious rock now had one arm slung across his enemy's neck.

Starns calmed the horse, untied a saddlebag and swung it up over one bony shoulder. He walked to the empty schoolhouse, thinking, Yes, ain't that always the way, though.

At his bedside in Stewart a week before, Starns had tried to understand Marcus Sales's failure. The minister lay in a bed at the Stewart parish house, rigid in a pose of tortured, death-mask martyrdom. His arms terminated in two swollen bandages. He looked both impotent and formidable, like a figure with white cannon balls for hands.

Starns had trouble getting Sales's wife to let him in, but she finally relented, grumbling. He took a chair by the bed and she stood at its foot, her arms folded.

Well, she looks all right, thought Starns. But what in the world happened to him? Lying here like he wants somebody to come throw dirt on him, get it over with.

"Hello, Reverend," he said. "I'm sorry I took so long to get here. How you feeling?"

"Oh, my God, I didn't think anybody would ever come," whispered Marcus Sales. "I hope you didn't expect us to stay up there and wait for you. We couldn't do that. Hardly."

"Nossir," said Starns. "Well, how you feeling?"

Marcus Sales did not answer. He pursed his lips and said, "All right, you can tell us what His Holiness has decreed now."

"Huh?" said Starns.

"The Bishop, what does he want me to do now? Go back up there, I suppose. What's he been saying about me?"

Sales's wife barked out a short laugh. "Mister Starns won't tell you anything," she said. "Because the Bishop has made him a missionary, for one thing, and because your question is a little beyond him, for another. You might ask why they sent him at all and not a doctor."

"Now, Vida," said Marcus Sales.

"Reverend," said Starns, "all I know is that Bishop Ames sent me up to help out. He reckoned you had come down sick and needed a man. Now, as far as I know, you are just to get yourself well and then go home, see him about it then. He didn't give me no letters for you, nothing like that."

"I've gotten plenty of letters from him in my life, thank you. I certainly don't need any more."

"Yessir," said Starns.

"Vida said a missionary. Is that right, Starns?"

Starns grinned uncomfortably. "Uh, yessir, it is."

"Well, congratulations," snorted Marcus Sales. "That's quite a step up from your last position, as I recall it. Just how did His Holiness manage that?"

Starns kept on grinning, bound to be pleasant. "Well, now, some of it I did myself, Reverend. Improved my reading and writing and all, worked on that some. But it is sort of with the understanding I will be up in them mountains, not nowheres else right away."

Sales smirked and snorted. "I see," he said.

"Well, no, maybe you don't. It is official, all right. I even had to preach two sermons. They sure weren't much, but people said they would do. For the mountains, anyhow. So I am a missionary now, legal, with a salary the Bishop set up for me. A missionary, never thought I'd see the day when that would happen. And I bet you didn't neither."

"Well, with His Holiness all things are possible, Starns. You bring your gun?"

"Huh? Well, yessir."

"Fine. That's the first thing a missionary needs. As long as you keep it handy, you might be just the man for that place. I wish you lots of success."

"Why, thank you," said Starns. "I appreciate that."

During the frozen silence that descended upon them Starns looked from one to the other, from the death mask in the bed to the smoldering wraith standing at its foot. He could not understand them.

Maybe they're just mad, he thought. Mad because the likes of me has been sent up to do what they couldn't. Dealing with people like this is just not easy. No wonder a lot of folks won't try. Just burn down the church and shoot the preacher, it's easier.

Finally, he decided that they were not going to tell him what he had to know. He stared at Marcus Sales's bandages and thought, Well, I will just have to ask.

"What happened to your hands?" he said.

"Oh, please!" said Vida Sales, glaring at him. "It's been horrible enough without talking about it. We don't have to do that now, not for you."

"Fine bandages," said Starns, without looking at her. "Does it pain you much now?"

Marcus Sales's death mask came open. Under it his face was that of a child about to cry.

"Yes, they do!" said Vida Sales. "They pain him a great deal. He can't move his fingers. You'd think they'd send a doctor."

Starns turned in the chair to stare at her. "Mrs. Sales," he said, "you folks have been up there and are back, now it is me has to go. I don't much want to, and I sure don't mean to put you out any, but can't you just tell me what happened? That's all. The rest is none of my business, but I do need to know that much. Now, is it a whole lot to ask?"

"Yes!" hissed Vida Sales. "For you to ask us, yes, it is a whole lot too much! Even if you are the Bishop's janitor, or whatever it is you are."

"Hush, Vida," said Marcus Sales. "I'll tell him, you just be quiet. I've got nothing to hide, Starns. Now, I didn't want to go to that godforsaken place, Starns. But when the Bishop asked me to, I went. My qualifications for other positions notwithstanding, I went. I did not complain. I did not argue or bicker about it. I went."

"I know you did," said Starns, "yessir."

"Well, we rode into that valley to face three half-finished, already crumbling adobe buildings and a crew of drunken workmen. They left before anything was properly completed, and then I had fifteen howling boys to handle, one of them a hopeless and disgusting moron. My wife and I were in constant terror of what they might do at any moment. It snowed the second week in October and we froze. Everything wooden was always wet. We began coughing the day we got there."

"Don't excite yourself," said Vida Sales. "We don't have to talk to him."

"All right, Vida," said Marcus Sales, now anxious to release his grievance and his bitterness. "Starns, after the first few services no one came to church. When I tried to talk to them, they insulted me and made me stand and listen to long, utterly senseless arguments. One of their women came down to spy on us, pretending to help my wife. She completely corrupted the boys, if that was possible."

"Cora Larman," said Vida Sales. "A harlot."

"Yes," Starns said softly, "I remember her."

Marcus Sales rushed on. "Later the Larmans called me to come to their home to celebrate Christmas with them. Now, I did not ask one question or entertain one suspicion."

Yessir, thought Starns, you just went. But what happened when you got there?

"We were taken into captivity amid an unspeakable drunken riot. I was made to stand witness to the—well, to the abuse of my wife. Then I was forced to hold in my bare hands two burning sticks from the fire, curse God and the King of England three times before I could let go. When they had finished with us, they threw us out into the snow. Then, in an ignorant old woman's filthy cabin, I had these hands smeared with grease and soot. And when we left the mission itself, Starns, all the boys I tried to teach the gospel of Jesus ran after the wagon, throwing rocks at me, trying to hit my hands."

"Marcus, be quiet," said Vida Sales. "You're a fool to talk to him. I'm not going to listen to any more of it, do you hear me?"

"Now, Vida," said Sales, a faint smile suddenly on his childish, self-pitying mouth, "what makes you think you'll have to?"

"I said be quiet, Marcus. Now, Starns, is this enough for you? Can't you leave us alone now?"

"Well," said Starns, "yes, ma'am, except for just this one thing. I hate to bring it up again, but, well, Mrs. Sales, just what did they do to you? Now, I am sorry to ask, but I will need to know. It might come up again, and I just can't be wrong about a thing like that."

Vida Sales glared at him, and at her husband, and swept out of the room.

Starns threw up his hands, thinking, Now, what kind of hateful stuff is this? What a pair of nanny goats they are! I didn't give her no cause to act like that.

Marcus Sales raised one of the swollen bandages. Now that his wife was out of the room, the childish quality of his self-pity went out of him. He was suddenly, cynically amused. He spoke to Starns in a low, bitter whisper.

"You see, Starns, they got some of her clothes off and stood her out in the snow. Then they brought her back in and the big man named Earl got her to drink their whisky that way, because she was so cold, you see."

Oh, thought Starns. Oh, oh.

"You have no idea what it was like in that house. Pretty soon my wife lost all control. She took off most of the rest of her clothes by herself."

"Yes, well, you don't have to say no more," said Starns, looking at the floor, but Sales, smiling, kept on, his voice tinged with hysterical glee.

"You see, Vida came to expect that she'd be violated. Then—well, she wasn't. That man named Earl, he just laughed at her. Then he told her about some dream he had, about witches that rode him in the night, and asked her was she one. My wife said Yes, she was."

"Reverend Sales," said Starns, "I shore didn't mean—"

"So he sat on her back and rode her around the room. Incredible, Starns. Drunk as she was, she carried him like he weighed nothing at all. They all stamped and laughed, and she even neighed like a horse and laughed, too, like a witch. Cackled, you know. Then they got tired of it and turned to me. Vida begged him then, that man Earl Larman, tried to make him take her out of the room. He laughed and made fun of her and tied her up. A woman you have to tie up with a rope, they all said."

Starns, miserable, hung his head while Sales finished his confession.

"After that they turned to me. I only wish I had enjoyed my ordeal as much as my wife did, Starns."

"Yes, yes, I sure am sorry," said Starns quickly. "But, Reverend, why did they treat you like that? They was all right two years ago. And when the Bishop come back after getting the building started, why, he said everything was fine."

Marcus Sales laid his head back on the pillow and said nothing for a moment. Then he turned and looked sharply at Starns. He was still smiling.

"You poor soul," he said. "You are like them, and like my wife. You believe in that man. A fool botanist tells him about romantic mountain pagans waiting for nothing more than his magic presence to turn them all into devout Christians. So he goes up and preaches for a few days, waves money at them, buys land. They played the part he wanted them to. They are savages, but not fools, as he is a fool and you are a fool and my wife is a fool. You all believe in him. Tell me you believe in him."

Starns considered Sales. "Yes," he said quietly. "I believe in him, all right. Because not long ago, Reverend Sales, I didn't believe in nothing, or nobody. Now I have come to believe in him, and because of him, maybe in a few others, too."

Sales's lips trembled. "He will betray you, Starns, as he has betrayed me. He will do worse than that. He will lead you into betraying yourself. Consider my wife. Consider me, now, in this state. It will happen to you, too."

"Well, maybe, Reverend, maybe," thinking, Now, what is this man talking about? Lord.

"When the great speeches are over, Starns, when the great orator, the great magician Bishop Nahum Ames, has grown tired of it and left, then what? You are a plain man, no magician. And so am I. All I had to offer was the teaching and salvation of my Lord and Saviour, you see. That's all. They do not want it. They are animals. Shrewd and cunning and utterly immoral. They are like the vermin that cling to them. He will deliver you up to them, as he did me, and my wife. I shudder to think of God's awful judgment when it falls on them, and on him. I shudder."

"Well," said Starns, tired out, "I am sorry I had to make you talk about it."

Vida Sales appeared in the doorway, behind her the minister of the Stewart parish. She pointed at Starns, and the minister cleared his throat gently.

"The Reverend's wife thinks he should have some sleep now, Mr. Starns. Can I offer you some coffee, perhaps?"

"He won't need that where he's going," snapped Vida Sales. "He'll need hard whisky, and I'll warrant he's got plenty of that with him."

She should talk about whisky, thought Starns, getting up. "I am sorry to have put you to such trouble," he said. Then he took a long look at Vida Sales and left the house.

His horse had lost a shoe and while it was at the livery stable, Starns went to the Stewart general store, carrying a bag of seed corn whose side had split open on him. In the cluttered store smelling of leather and coal oil a man with a wrinkled face waited on him. Starns was angry and out of sorts with himself after the meeting with Marcus Sales and his wife. He told the storekeeper to give him a new bag and turned curtly away from him.

Man looks like an old seed hisself, thought Starns, that dried up.

Scowling, he walked about the store, looking at things and touching them, sometimes slapping at them. Holding a harness and looking it over, his eyes wandered and a brief smile lifted his mouth.

I try and I try, but I can't for the life of me see Vida Sales with some man riding piggyback. He slung the harness back on its nail. Sure wish I'd a been there.

But then he thought of Marcus Sales, with child's tears in his eyes, and he frowned and spat on the dry man's floor and scuffed it with his boot.

He was walking back to the counter when he heard something. He turned, listened and then looked out the back door.

He had heard a thin voice singing to the thrusts of a broom, singing the old song about Joseph and Mary and the cherry tree. When he looked out, Starns saw a young girl, about fifteen or sixteen years old, sweeping the stones that made a back porch for the store. Her back was toward him. Her figure was stooped and bent, and she clutched the broom hard, but her voice was sweet and free. Long black hair hung down loose over a faded dress. The porch was clean, but she kept on sweeping it, singing Joseph, Mary and the cherry tree.

"Want to hire her out, Mister?" said the storekeeper, his wrinkled face appearing at Starns's shoulder. "She's a little daft, but a good worker. Hey, Ellen!"

The cramped figure stopped singing, turned and stared at them, hugging the broom handle. Her face was pinched and narrow; only her eyes, frightened, showed any life.

"Ellen, show this man how ye can work. Go on. Sweep!"

She looked toward Starns in a dim panic and began to jerk the broom about the stone porch.

"That's all right, honey," said Starns. "You don't have to show me nothing. Best you just sing."

Then, to the storekeeper, curtly, "No, I can't use her. But she's for hire, is she? How's that?"

"That's right," said the dry man, "for hire. I've took care of her three years now. If I didn't, she'd starve. Only right she does some work. If not for me, she'd live like a dog, Mister."

"All right, all right," said Starns. "How much do I owe you?"

"Twenty-five cents. Here's your seed."

On his way out of Stewart he stopped his horse by the store and listened to her thin voice singing again, lulling herself as she worked, crooning the same song over and over. Joseph, Mary, the cherry tree. Starns looked at the gray mountains looming ahead of him and listened.

Pagans and heathen, he thought. Or filth and scum. They ain't neither one. Bishop and Reverend, you are both wrong. They are just poor, and poor folks has poor ways. Why can't nobody understand that?

Shaking his head, he rode on toward the mountains, the frail, repeated song echoing in his mind.

Rid of their rocks, the two boys turned away from the mission and started back up the slope. Starns watched them go.

A heavy padlock, smashed to pieces, lay scattered on the schoolhouse porch. With his boot Starns swept the rusted fragments off the porch and kicked open the door. A little lizard performed a split-second about-face toward him, started one way, stopped, glared at him with bright, outraged eyes and then vanished.

He stood inside the door for a moment, looking at the tangled underbrush of smashed tables and broken chairs. A large, split bookcase lay on its back, littered with torn bindings. Pages from ripped-apart books lay scattered about the room like leaves. Starns swore softly, bringing a hand to his nose, and coughed. Just ahead of him were several deposits of human excretion.

He set his saddlebag on the one table that was still standing, bent down and picked up the dusty cover of a hymnal. He blew the dust off it and then tossed it back on the floor again.

He began to kick his way through the rubbish, stepping carefully, wondering what could be saved and used again. There wasn't much. Every table and chair leg had been broken in two. There wasn't a stick of furniture over a foot in length.

Under a pulled-out drawer on the floor he found a pack of white papers tied by a string. He slipped them loose and unfolded the papers. They were covered by an elaborate script and signed, each one, by Bishop Ames. They were his letters to Marcus Sales, dated during August, September and part of October, sent up by rider from Stewart.

Well, he did leave in a hurry, then, thought Starns, to leave these lying here.

He took them outside and sat on the porch steps. Slowly he read them through, straining his eyes in the swiftly descending dusk. When he finished, he crumpled them up, knocked a hole in the dirt with his heel, took a metal box of lucifers from his coat pocket and burned them there, all but one. That last letter he held up to the quick flare of the fire and looked at it again. Starns smiled at the orders written there, in the sweeping, commanding ink.

1. By oral catechism, teach the fundamentals of our Christian faith.
2. Conduct three services daily. Upon arising, before the noon meal, before the evening meal. Prayers before sleep.
3. Teach the fundamentals of grammar and simple calculation.
4. To those who are able to receive them, teach the classical subjects.
5. Search out the human material from which a native mountain ministry may be formed.
6. Devote two full hours each day to the physical improvement of the mission, that is, to hard manual labor.
7. One evening each week if they desire it, though I do not think they will, the boys may visit their homes.

Yessir, Bishop.

In the last flickering of the fire he read the note at the bottom of the list.

Marcus, if you can do it, try to get at least one barn up and whatever
sheds are needed and one springhouse. In the spring I will be with you.
We will plant then and see to the orchards, livestock, and so on. I am
sending a man up to help you in April, but I won't tell you who he is
except that it will be a surprise. But I have no doubts he will work hard,
as we all must work hard, to make this mission an independent colony,
worthy of the task it has taken up for the glory of God.

Starns ticked at his beard with the edge of the letter and looked at
the valley, at random underbrush, unpulled black stumps, at the heavy
mountain bottomland, soggy and idle underneath the scurrying of
insects and the flourishing of weeds. Around the land, in the shifting
light of mountain dusk, stood the black, stark silhouettes of the slopes,
rising imperious and tyrannical out of the last light of the sun.

Bishop, you have done me in this time, you sure have. You think one
way and this land thinks another. And I am in the middle. I wonder
what Sales did, read this damn list at them? Whooee!

He put the letter in his pocket and saw to his horse and bedding,
cooked himself some supper. Because of the stench in the schoolroom,
he bedded down on the porch, stacking saddlebags and supplies around
him against the night wind. Before he slept, he combed the short,
bristly beard he had grown to hide his weathered cheeks and chin,
grown at Rachael Ames's suggestion. By his head lay a pair of steel-
rimmed spectacles. The Bishop had gotten them for him when he realized Starns was farsighted and was trying to read print that swam
before his eyes. He had objected to them at first, but soon was using
them every day, washing the lenses each night and polishing the steel
rims with a rag soaked carefully in coal oil. In one of the saddlebags
was a pack of books bound together by a piece of rawhide, books on
the Bible and the Church.

Starns was thirty-two years old that night, but he looked fifty. He
was like a much older man who comes late in life to what learning he
possesses, and therefore has no fear of what he knows he will never
understand. The ideas of men on paper he had learned painfully to

decipher, and the holy word of God he read daily and dutifully, but none of it bothered him, caused him any anxiety. The words he read, words so quick to convince by their logic and sound and grace, were for him frail and incomplete, utterly apart from the world as he knew it.

He pillowed his head on bags of seed, and he stared out into the black mountain night and was afraid. He hoped the mountain people would stay up their slopes and leave him alone. He did not want to face them. He knew their life and knew there was nothing he could tell them. He thought then that he was a man of things, not of people. All his people were gone. He had lived alone and apart from them too long.

When I lay something down, I want it to be there when I go to pick it up again. Things stay put, people won't. What is it them old men in the towns would say? Oh, yes. Seed grows where you plant it, but a woman's belly opens on the wind. That's true.

He fell asleep, smelling the dry mystery in the bags that pillowed his head. On the slopes a cat screamed. In a moment a hoarse-throated hound answered. Later the soft slithering of a screech owl's wings passed over the porch.

Everything then was silent, like the seed that has just been put into the earth.

3

THE SEEDS

STARNS BUILT his fire at the steps, where he had burned the Bishop's letters. Frying bacon and boiling coffee, he watched the mountain sunrise fool him, watched it shift its early promises of brilliance from one peak to another, creating a glow of warmth and then dissolving it into pale dawnlight again and again.

In the night he had heard the thudding of hoofs several times. Cooking his bacon, hung in strips over a stick, Starns wondered who it was crazy enough to ride a horse that fast in the night over such land. Once the pounding hoofs had sounded so close he'd thought he heard the horse breathing, or even the man, but when he got out of his blankets and looked, he saw nothing. Now, as he cooked, with the teasing sunlight glowing and fading around him, he wondered at those hoofs, coming and going in the night, out of the dark and back into it again, at a madman's speed, and it bothered him.

On the fire the bacon fat began to curl and brown. He waved the stick over the fire three times, draped the bacon over his knee and threw the stick away. He had his coffee at his lips when he saw that the sun, like a masterful hunter, had come up on him unexpected. It commanded the peaks brazenly, its entrance accomplished with slow, sly skill. Starns, cold, blew on his coffee and welcomed it.

You take your time, but when you are here, you are here. It's good you know what you are doing. That wild bastard last night, he sure didn't.

He chewed his bacon and looked at the empty, dew-soaked buildings about him, admitting to himself: And neither do I.

After his breakfast, hedging in his fire with some rocks from under
the porch, he saw two figures standing in misty brush about a hundred
yards away. One of them moved idly to a tree. He saw the skirt move
and watched her tear off a strip of bark and take it to the tall, slack-
armed man, who rubbed it against his mouth.

Starns squinted at them nervously, then went into the mission
schoolroom with his ax and began to break up the remains of the furniture. When he came to the door with pieces of tabletops and chair-
backs, he looked at the brush. Each time he looked they had moved, but
only slightly, and each time they stood facing him, like good children
awaiting instructions.

At noon, with a split drawer bottom and some table legs, he built up
his fire again and heated coffee and cornbread. Then the woman
approached him, walking firmly away from the tall man, who stood
alone and made no move. When she got to the fire, she stood there
calmly and watched Starns until he looked up at her. He did not know
what to say to Cora. She had to speak first.

"You've growed a beard," she said. "If you are the man was here two
year ago, you have. Are you the man?"

"Yes, I am," said Starns. He pulled a spotted kerchief from his
pocket and blew his nose. He motioned at the fire, said, "You want
some? I got plenty."

"I would. Thank ye." She squatted slowly, folding her hands over
her knees. Starns handed her coffee in the one tin cup. She nodded to
him and drank it quickly, though it was scalding hot, and gave him back
the cup.

"Don't seem like two years, now, does it?" she said, rubbing her eyes.

"Does to me," said Starns. He glanced at the saddlebags on the
porch, at the one containing the books bound by the rawhide thong.
"Yes, it does. I been through a lot since I seen you."

She considered him, looked him over. "Got religion, did ye?"

"How did you know that?"

"You look like it. And you're back here. Can't think why, if not that. Are you a preacher now, or what?"

"Half a one." He turned the kerchief in his hand and mopped his face and beard. The sun was hot, he was close to the fire and perspiring.

"How can you be half a preacher?"

"Well, I'm a missionary. Half preacher, half hired help. It's hard to explain."

She nodded, said, "Uh-huh." Starns held out the pan with the bread and fatback in it. Her hands stayed folded. Starns cut the bread and bacon in half with his knife and held out the pan again. She took her half from it and stood up.

"I'll take some of this to my brother," she said, looking toward the brush. "He thanks you for it."

Starns nodded and began to eat. "That's all right," he said.

"If you got religion now, I guess you'll have no use for me. I guess you're a different man now, that right?"

Starns did not know what to answer, so he chewed his bacon and looked at the fire. Cora waited a moment, then shrugged her shoulders and started off. A few steps away she turned back and said, "You know, you don't have to cook like that. There was a big stove in the log kitchen. Earl and Cardell tried to haul it off, but they got mad with it. It's lying down by the river now. You seen it?"

"No, but I'll go get it. I thank you for telling me."

"I'll come show you how it works, if you want. I cooked a lot for Mrs. Sales when she was here."

"All right," said Starns. "Suit yourself."

Through his glasses he watched Cora walk back into the brush, thought of her long legs under the swaying homespun skirt.

Watch out, missionary, he thought, and then took his ax and began to split up the rest of the mission furniture.

Night came fast, the sun's gradual descent blocked by a clouded afternoon sky. The schoolroom of the mission house, swept clean, with its one table standing forlornly in a corner, was as cold as the yard, but Starns had scattered some needles and cedar chips about and it smelled clean. After his supper he stuffed the stone fireplace with wood, and later he bedded down before it. He lay on his side, facing the slow and scattered fire, his eyes unfocused and full of tired peace, watching the wood sputter and snap and burn.

When he heard the heavy footsteps on the porch, he turned only slightly in his blankets, sliding the barrel of the rifle he slept with across the floor until it pointed at the door. When the door came slowly open and he saw it was Cora, he started to slide it back under the blankets, but another figure in the doorway behind her made him slip it out again and rise up on one elbow.

"Now hold it. Who is in here?"

Cora came to him and squatted easily by the blankets. She put a warm hand on his neck, and her long, matted hair touched his beard.

"Well, didn't you know I'd come see you tonight?"

"Maybe, but who's your friend?" He looked around her at the figure standing in the doorway.

"That's just Cief," she whispered. "He won't hurt nothing. He just needs company. You don't mind if he stays. He'll be quiet."

She turned and spoke to him. "Cief, you sit down somewhere, now."

The shadow lurched into the room and slumped soundless against the far wall, out of the firelight except for his feet. Starns saw they were bare and hard, but overlapped one upon the other, like a child's. Starns sniffed at a strange odor that had come into the room. It was faintly like the smell of the hide of a goat.

Cora's hand was still on his neck. He could feel her forearm trembling. He lay back and looked at her face, dark and somber, brooding over him in the flickering light of the fire.

"There ain't much in this world my brother can have," she said. "A little company is all. You won't begrudge him that. Here, I'll fix the fire."

"You don't need to do that," said Starns. He put the rifle aside, undone by the warmth of her hand and by the sadness of her face. "Are you cold?"

"Yessir, I am," said Cora.

He pulled on her arm. She said, "Wait a minute," then sat back on her knees. Slowly this time, almost delicately, she raised above her breasts the long, tattered shirt. When Starns took her in his arms and spread the blanket over them, he heard a low whining from the shadow against the far wall. He started to say something, but Cora put one hand on his mouth, the other warm and busy on his body, and silenced him.

Let him yell, thought Starns.

In vicious waves the wind buffeted the adobe walls. Swift drafts cut across the floor of the mission house. Starns was reaching for his kerchief, half asleep, when he realized she had slipped away from him, was no longer sleeping by his side. He heard the whining sounds and saw, against the wall, a larger shadow than had been there before. The whining rose in intensity and in ugliness, then subsided, became sounds that were soft and gratified. The shadow split. When Cora crept back to the fire, she was wiping her hands on her shirt.

Starns jumped up out of the blankets.

"Now, look here!" he said, shaking. "Now, look here! This won't do! Now, you just take him and go on and get him out of here, and you, too. You hear me?"

She did not move or answer him. She sat still amid the tangled blankets, wiping her hand on her skirt. Starns felt sick. He went to the door and jerked it open, took in the raw night air. Around the valley he saw the high, dim slopes sentineled in the darkness, and he shivered. When he turned back, she was building up the fire.

"Never mind that," he said. "Just move over there somewhere. In the morning I want you out of here, the both of you. You hear me?"

She poked the fire and spoke softly, as if to the flames. "Go walk some. It'll be all right in a minute. You've got some religion, and you feel benastied because of me, but it'll be all right. You're just a man, that's all."

"What does all that mean?" said Starns, fighting the dark revulsion in his stomach.

She threw the last piece of wood on the fire and swung about on her knees.

"It means you don't care for them worse off than you! Means you will take me and grind on me, but, when you're done, think it benastying for anybody else to do the same. Means you're a man. With religion. Go walk some of it off."

"Religion ain't got nothing to do with it," said Starns. "In the first place, your brother is feeble-minded. In the second, he's your brother. I'm not mean, it's you. Why treat the poor man like that?"

"Why not?" Cora said. "What else, just leave him be? Let him hurt hisself like he does sometimes? What do you know about my brother? Are you going to be like that Preacher Sales and tell me, so solemn and sober, tell me, who's the only one ever to suffer poor Cief, tell me he's feeble-minded? I know that."

She threw his blanket away from her and spat into the fire.

"But he's a man, too. Just like you are. And on cold nights like this, when he is cold, what's the great difference? None, there ain't none. No, it's you, you're just killed dead to see a man like my brother get the same pleasures you get. With all your religion, you can't stand being that much like him. Now, that's it, ain't it?"

"I don't know what in hell you're talking about, even," said Starns. Then he stopped and listened. Cief's feet were sliding on the floor.

He whirled about, but the shadow was still slumped against the wall. Only now his feet were moving, the bare heels sliding slowly back and forth. In the light of the built-up fire Starns saw that Cief was asleep, his big, narrow face bland and his mouth and lips slack. He mumbled softly, saliva bubbling at his lips, and slid his heels up and down, pushing them against the floor.

Starns turned to the open door again and looked out, assaulted by memory. In his mind the large adobe mission-house schoolroom shrank to the close, cramped quarters of a moldering shack outside the city of Raleigh. He recalled himself, slumped against one of its crumbling, rotted walls, beside him the dark figure of Bishop Nahum Immanuel Ames squatting on a cracker box, talking to him and watching his boots dig and thrash at the dank ground.

Well, Starns, what's wrong with you? Didn't you scare and disgust the Bishop and Mrs. Ames, too? Just as much as these here do you? Yes, you did. Now, once you wanted your own.

He turned and looked at Cief sprawled against the wall, at Cora sitting alone in a tangle of blankets, staring vacantly at the fire.

Well, here they are. On the ground, just like you were.

He closed the door. "Well, Cora, is there anything he can do? Can he work at all?"

"Why, yes," she said eagerly. "He has lots of sense sometimes. He can carry and do what you tell him with it, most of the time. Only nobody but me will ever tell him nothing or fool with him at all. But he understands a lot sometimes."

"Well, tell me some more about him. No, you can stay there. Just fix them blankets a little."

Starns stood watching the shadow move its heels. When Cora said, "All right, I'm ready," he got back into the blankets and settled his head against her shoulder and listened while she looked at Cief and talked.

The next day Starns took Cora and Cief with him when he went out to girdle a stand of thick tulip trees. They watched him ax the notches into the trunks a few feet up from the ground, listened to him carefully when he told them it would kill the trees and make the wood straight and dry later.

Cora asked Starns how he came to know about such things, and he told her of his life before he met the Bishop, about all the things he had learned that meant nothing then but did mean something now. Once, while he talked, she took up a sliver of bark and gave it to Cief, who put it to his lips and rubbed it against them.

Starns leaned on his ax and spoke to Cief. "You get that, Cief, about the tree?"

Cief rubbed the bark against his cheek and mouth, his large eyes vacant. Starns stared at him a minute, and Cief stared back. Starns shook his head and dug into another trunk.

"Here," said Cora. "I'll spell ye." She held out her hands.

"What, with the ax?"

She took it from him, planted her feet apart and swung it in vicious sidearm slashes. The muscles stood up tough and stringy on her forearms. Chips, like flushed grouse, flew violently out of the notches.

Starns sat on the ground. Cora, whaling away, showed no sign of tiring quickly, so he sat there, sifting chips and dirt through one hand and watching the morning sun flirt with him through the treetops. He slipped his hand under his hat and rubbed his forehead, then walked his fingers along the edge of his retreating hairline. He fell dreaming, sifting the idle dirt.

Vaguely he heard Cora say, "Here, Cief, you try." He thought it was some woman could handle an ax like that, and smiled and spilled dirt off the heel of his hand.

Two great feet appeared before his downcast eyes. Above him, blocking the sun, loomed Cief, the ax held tight in confused hands, the blade Starns had sharpened that morning glinting dully.

Starns kept on sifting the dirt, held his breath a moment. "Go on, Cief," he said quietly, "hit right there where your sister did." With one hand he sifted the dirt carelessly, with the other gripped the ground behind him in panic.

"Cief?" said Cora. She started toward him, but Cief whined like a terrified dog, and she stopped.

Cief stood over Starns, his narrow face twisted into a bewildered grimace. Starns didn't move.

"Cief!" said Cora.

The muscles in his arms tightened. Suddenly he raised the ax and turned away.

O Lord, thought Starns, shooee!

In a rush of wind Cief swung at the tree, missing the notch, hitting on the slant of the blade. With a hollow ring the ax flew out of his hands onto the ground, the handle spinning around in the dirt. Starns got up on unsteady legs, picked it up and spoke as casually as he could, one frightened man to another.

"You have to watch the place you mean to hit," he said. "You have to look at it. Don't worry about the ax, it will be all right. Now let me show you, slow."

He swung three times, very slowly, stopping the blade just short of the wood. Then he put the ax into Cief's shaking hands and slowly swung it with him. Cora sat down and watched them.

The two men worked on, absorbed. Soon Starns felt a pleasant, relaxing patience soothe him. From intense concentration on hands and notch and blade he would awake suddenly to the pleasant calm within him. It seemed to him that all things, time itself even, had stopped for Cief to learn to hit his notch. Starns's fear of Cief was gone now that he was used to his appearance and his smell, and he soon began to talk to him without wondering what he understood and what he didn't.

Only when he felt the sun warming the crown of his hat did Starns realize they had been at it all morning. By that time Cief was swinging alone, weakly, missing and dropping the ax sometimes, but hitting the notch more often. Starns looked around for Cora, but she was gone. He saw smoke rising from the mission, then saw Cora bending over his fire by the porch steps. Spirals of thin gray smoke rose up into the clear noon air. Starns felt the muscles moving in his stomach and knew he was very hungry.

"Hey, Cief, time to eat!"

The bland, narrow face stared at him.

"Eat, Cief," said Starns, opening and closing his mouth. "Come on."

Walking toward the column of smoke, he thought, Wonder what she's put on my fire. Maybe I ought to go get her that stove she was talking about. Maybe so.

Behind him, shambling along, swinging the ax at weeds and dandelions, Cief followed.

When he went to Jimmy Rode's store to buy flour and coffee, Starns brought Cief with him and Cora, too, sometimes. Small, sallow Jimmy Rode greeted them affably, but he did not try to hide the contempt he felt for Marcus Sales and, by logical transference, for William Starns. But when they came by the third week, when Starns told Cief to pick up the flour and he did without being shown which it was, Jimmy Rode said, "Cora, I see your brother is improving."

"No, Mr. Rode," said Cora, "it is just that you are." Then she laughed at him and swished out the door after Starns, like a sassy child.

Jimmy Rode stood at the door of his tiny store and watched them walking down to the mission. Some parade, he thought. A whore, a half-wit and a preacher. Yessir, that's some congregation.

For his plow he dismantled the shares from the makeshift cross that had fallen down from the chapel wall, and for a harrow he used thorny branches, flailed by hand or sometimes tied to the tail of his horse. When the cold ground was open to the spring air and the clods were broken up and then furrowed again, Starns dropped his seeds with Cief watching, dropped them carelessly, as his father had.

He sowed maize, a little wheat to see what it would do, buckwheat and barley, beans, potatoes. Around them Starns sowed grasses and clover. From Stewart, ordered by Bishop Ames, came three wagonloads of young orchard trees. With Cief holding one end of a long cord, he planted them in lines and groups and hoped for apples, peaches and cherries in time to come.

In mid-May the first blisteringly hot day fell upon them, and the humblebees began their attack on the adobe walls. Bishop Ames, enchanted by tales of Spanish missions, had insisted on building in adobe. He had had the bricks made with mountain clay, and now Starns and Cief watched the tiny holes appear, Starns shaking his head at the little puffs of dust that came out in tiny, ominous challenges. He knew then he would have to rebuild the whole wall structure of the mission.

In June the tulip trees came down. Cief, with his own ax, worked independently and well. Starns was proud of it and admitted as much to himself once, watching Cief swing, sipping some spring water Cora had brought him, garnished with specks of rust.

When the logs were down, Starns measured seven ax handles on each and cut a band. "Score the bark off up to here, Cief," he said.

As they worked, two boys came out of the woods to watch them. Since they had thrown their rocks at him and run away, they had spied on him when they could get away from home. This was the first time they had decided to talk to him again. They stood by while Starns and Cief bent over the logs, slashing away the bark, stood there quietly in their woolen hats and stitched-down shoes with the seams turned out instead of in.

Starns and Cief ran a long cord through a pot of charcoal and powdered locust bark, laid it the length of a log and pulled at it until it was centered. With painful care, like a doctor over a critical patient, Cief took the cord between thumb and forefinger and snapped it. Then he smiled at the neat, straight chalk line that ran the center of the log.

"What are you trying to do?" said one of the boys.

"Talk, do you?" said Starns. "We are splitting rails. You never seen that?"

"We seen it. But you don't have to do all that. Just split them."

"Any fool knows that," echoed his brother.

"Can any fool make a rail that won't warp? That will always lie flush?" said Starns.

They shrugged their shoulders. One of them spat. The other said, "No."

"All right, then," said Starns.

He sliced into the chalk line with deadly certainty. Once on each end and once in the middle. Then he and Cief mashed a wooden glut into the center slice, put their ax blades in the other two. Starns picked up two wooden mauls and a stray stick that was heavy, and handed one of the mauls to the biggest of the boys.

"Take this thing and do something besides stand around," he said. "We will all hit at the same time, make it look good. When I say three.

You know, Cief, one-two-three-hit. Cief, you got that? AH right. One-two-three!"

They hit. The dead log fell open, splitting into two perfect rails. The boys got on their knees and squinted down the flat side, and one whispered, "He's right, it's straight."

The other stood up quickly. "It'll warp," he said. "First rain."

"That's right," said the other. "First rain it'll warp."

Then both boys and Starns turned and stared. Cief was shaking his head, his body trembling. Like the sound of wind through an empty house came his voice, mournful and blurred and indistinct, but Starns understood him.

"No, no, no, won't warp!" said Cief. "Won't!"

With Cief and sometimes the two Benson boys to help him, Starns rebuilt the mission house, adding two rooms onto the back. In one, after suppers, he made a large bed for Cora and for himself, made it of choice walnut. When he pegged it together, Cora came in with a big feather-and-husk mattress she'd stitched together without his knowing about it. He took it from her and put it on the bed, and they were happy about it.

But that night after their love-making, they heard the pounding hoofs again. Starns lay with his head on her stomach, listening. He knew who it was now, because Cora had told him.

"Oh, that's Earl, my uncle," she said the first time they heard the hoofs together. "He has done that most every night since his Hester died. Rides like a fool all night, sleeps in the day. Nobody knows how he doesn't kill hisself doing that. Says it's witches riding him, get him at night and make him go. He'll show ye tangled-up places in his horse's mane that he says proves it, because they are the witches' stirrups. Sometimes he comes home with scrapes all over his knees and elbows where they got him down and rode him like a horse, too. Seven years he's done that most every night. He's mean, Earl is."

In their new bed Starns lay listening, his balding head pillowed on the flesh of Cora's stomach. The thudding hoofs came louder and pounded up to the mission house. Outside in the night, Starns could tell that the horse was being jerked about irresolutely, hoofclops thudding, then stepping, then thudding again. Finally, after a long silence, in a chaotic burst the hoofclops pounded away.

Poor wild bastard, thought Starns. Witches riding him like a horse. I reckon I know what that is.

It was July, and he thought of the jug of whisky that sat in the log kitchen. It had lasted him over two months and was not yet half empty. Two months, one or two drinks a day, after dinner, just before bed and Cora. He remembered when it had been different, even after his conversion. He thought of the man in the night, ridden like his horse.

Both Starns and Cora had been uneasy in their big, new bed. She held his head on her stomach, feeling suddenly that she held a stranger. She rubbed his forehead and talked to him, disappointed, like a mother.

"What's wrong, what's wrong?"

He heard the hoofs again, far off. "I don't know. We had such pleasure making this bed, too. It's funny."

"You are just tired, Starns. I never seen a man work like you do."

The hoofbeats died away, like the patter of rain. "I wish that was it," he said, and sat up away from her.

She knew he was a strange man, and she knew when to leave him alone. She leaned back against the rolled blanket that was their pillow and folded her hands, chilled. He had made such a fuss over the bed, put it together in sound, tapered walnut. Now he sat in it like a timid stranger, thin hair tousled, his short, scraggly beard moving over soundless lips.

He sat listening for the hoofbeats, wanting to hear them come back.

"Starns?" said Cora.

"Well," he said at last, "you and Cief. It has been like you are my own, Cora, my family. But you are not."

She spoke quickly. "We could be, if you want. I am willing."

"Yes, I have thought about it. It's not the thing to do."

"All right, then."

"No, Cora, listen," he said, in a mumbling rush of words. "All my life it has been like I ought to be some other place from where I was. But not no new place, or strange. No, it was always some place I had some idea of, like towns I passed through once and don't remember except for pieces of them, like boards over a hole in a bridge, or somebody looking out of a store window, or the way a tree was scattering leaves on some man's porch. And then, always, the feeling you ought to have stopped there and seen the rest. But you didn't, you went right on."

Cora watched his short beard bobbing and thought, Men have so many ways to tell a woman they don't want her. She rubbed his shoulder with one hand, said, "Yes?"

"Well, now, here. I am stopped here for a time. And I have you and Cief, and things are going all right with this place."

"Yes, I know it," she said.

Hoofbeats, he heard them again, ghostly stamping. He got out of bed. He put on his boots.

"Cora, something else is going to happen. I feel it coming all around us, like a river a-rising. I have to wait and see about it, Cora. You see, Cora?"

"Uh-huh," she said, pretending to be asleep, because she had nothing to say to the man then. Soon she was asleep, a wry smile on her face. Starns watched her for a moment, but when the hoofbeats sounded closer, he went out on the porch.

He stayed there all through the cool mountain summer night, sitting on the porch steps, in boots, long Johns and coat, looking at his fields and waiting. Just before dawn the rider came close and stood his horse in front of the porch. Starns got up and they faced each other for a moment in the bleak darkness just before dawn. "Wait a minute," Starns called. "I want to talk to you. Want some coffee?" But the man swore at him and Starns saw in the darkness a savage jerk of the arm. The horse whinnied and turned, bounded away in pain.

"All right," Starns whispered, "all right. Take your time. You'll come back, like I did."

He walked around the mission to the log kitchen and fired the iron stove for his coffee. When he came out, with a steaming tin cup in one hand, dawn was up. He went into the mission house and looked in at Cora. She was a pile of blankets in the center of the big bed, her face turned away from the door. In the big room, when he passed, Cief, wrapped like a tight cocoon, slept by the fire, snoring gently and evenly. He went back onto the porch and stood there, his boots gleaming with dew, and watched the mist rise. Behind the steel-rimmed spectacles, squinting, his eyes searched the slopes, looking for smoke. He saw a few thin spirals here and there, rising above the treetops, breakfast smoke.

I want them all, thought Starns.

Light poured over the eastern ridges. The valley dew sparkled on the bottomland. Starns drank his coffee, his homely, lined face contorted by a rapturous smile.

The earth seemed to him dainty and soft, like the little girl he had loved when he was young.

4

CIRCLE FOUR

Juba

After that midwinter ruction on Sand Mountain everybody in these parts turned sour. Nobody was killed then, but my little Tate got his left hand nigh shot off. All for nothing, too. After they shot at each other some, Earl Larman said they wasn't mad at nobody but that preacher and let them all in to see Jacob, felled by a stroke and fast in his bed. So after that it broke up.

But my big Tate, he took to moping about mightily. He burned off twice as much likker as we needed and just poured it down hisself. Sour, like everbody else.

In bed one night, when the boys was sleeping, he told me it was because people here have turned so mean since them mission folks churned us up so, but I knowed that wasn't it. For Tate it was seeing old Jacob laid out like that, having to be fed and carried outside and all. I tried to tell Tate he was a long ways from that yet, but he wouldn't hear it.

He commenced getting serious about his demons again. It has always been his pleasure to delight in the old tales and to make out he seen this or that by the light of the cloudy moon, and to plant his crops by the laws of conjur, but this time it was different, it followed no laws or reason at all. He'd whoop and holler for no earthly reason, and run about the cabin looking for nothing at all, until even the boys got scared.

Then one day we caught him firing hair bullets into the springhouse door, a desperate charm to ward off the witches, and I knowed then he was in real trouble, my fool Tate. I did my best to calm the man, but what's a wife in times like that? Not much.

The razorback hog got to be the worst. It was on his mind all the time. He'd go out and shoot bark off half the trees on the slopes, trying to fell the thing, convinced right down through his boots that it was a deadly fiend. It put me right out, him doing that so fierce. I couldn't say the right things to him no more, all our hooting and joking was forgot. I knowed something had to be done the day he upped and killed our best cow brute, shot her down and butchered her, screaming he sure got him a demon that time, that there was one less to worry about now.

He was walking all about the place likkered up, with the blood of that valuable cow brute all on his hands, and little Tate, him and Lafe both said I should go down and get that new mission man and bring him up here to do something. They have been spending a lot of time down there with that man, and I have been just unable to make them do any other.

I said I will not, because I knowed that whatever was going on down there was as bad or worse than here. That fork-legged Cora Larman and her half-wit brother living down there with that man. And him, so they say, the new mission man, going all the way down the mountain to get yet another half-wit, that pinch-eyed, long-nosed, feeble-minded girl named Ellen, bringing her up to live with Cief Larman, having them together. Why, it give me and everbody else the shivers, such carryings-on.

Now, I allowed the boys his crops looked good, that he was a farmer, which Preacher Sales shore wasn't, and that he had been putting up likely-looking buildings down there. I allowed the boys that they had learned good things from him about that, and that the lean-shed they built here, after working with him some, it was sturdy. But still.

And when they told me how he got ahold of Earl Larman one night and the two of them got drunk together and the next day Earl was helping him build the mission up again, I said, Well, maybe he is a man, then, but something is still wrong about it, and wouldn't hear no more.

But with Tate raving, they went anyhow and got him. I couldn't stop them.

It was the day after Tate shot the cow brute that they brung him up to the yard. He called out, but I wouldn't move. The boys brung him in anyhow and said, This here is Starns.

I recalled him somewhat from two years before. He had been with that Bishop, one of them men. But he was different now, a scraggle-beard now, mournful-looking as an old hound, but sly, too. In a minute he had poor Tate talking about his fiends, him just nodding and considering like he believed it.

But soon Tate got mad. He'd been raving about the demon hog, and he finally seen that the new mission man was just letting him talk.

"If you are sniggering at me," Tate said to this Starns, "you got no call to. You damn mission folks are just as bad. Didn't my woman here have to abide them other mission folks when she took them in, them carrying on about torments and demons?"

I spoke up and said, "Yes, I did."

"Damn right," said Tate, surprised I'd spoke up so. "So you got no call to snigger, then."

This Starns creature smiled a slow, snaky smile. He said, "Well, Church people get scared like everybody else. Now, it is you says I am laughing, not me."

Tate didn't like that. "You're awful smart. If you're so smart, you go call that fiend and face him once. Catch that monster for us. Otherwise, get on back down the slope and pray and handle them big crops, and leave the tormented alone!"

That Starns, he didn't answer, he just set thinking, but looking serious about it, not smiling at all. He rubbed his scraggly beard and mashed his palm against his bald spot, thinking hard.

"I will try that," he said after some time. "If you will do your part to help me."

Tate, he howled. "Shore! Shore! I'll do 'er! Anything ye want. I just want to see ye confront that fiend, that's all!"

"Well, then," this Starns man said, "where is your still?"

"My still?" said Tate, blinking. "Why, out back a ways. Why?"

"Then have your two fine boys here go bring us a bucket of mash. I guess you got plenty out there."

Tate liked that least of all, but he'd said he would help. The boys was up like a shot to do what that man wanted, so Tate nodded, and they flew.

Made me feel powerful black, them minding that man that way. They wouldn't have run that way for me.

While they was gone for the mash, this Starns, he talked about how he was getting to where he liked these mountains. Told us he growed up not far from here and was satisfied to be back, but I didn't believe a word of it. Didn't even look at him, he was that hateful to my sight.

Well, I was about to go out to the shed and disdain the whole event when that man reached in his coat and pulled something out of his inside pocket and held it out to me.

He said, "Mrs. Benson, Cief Larman made one of these the other day for his girl, Ellen. But when we heard you lost a cow, we thought maybe you'd be interested in it. Here, it's for you."

I looked at his hand, and in it was a big comb. It was long and creamy-colored, with ever so many teeth.

He held it up to the light at the door and said, "Look what the sun does to it," and I did look, and through it the light was the softest, creamiest thing.

Now, I had me a big comb like that once, but it got lost somewheres. I touched it and then was holding it.

He said, "Now, you can make more if you want to. You just take the horns off the carcass of your cow and boil them about four hours or so. Then you cut them open and spread them flat under a clamp of some kind."

He was acting it all out, like a boy, waving his hands around like it was a great thing to make a comb, and I reckoned that it might be.

"You file in the teeth and set it in a cold spring and you will have another one like that. No, that one is yours, Cief means for you to have it. But if you do make another one, you might send it down for his Ellen."

"Cief Larman made this?" I said, and he said yes. I thought, Well, if Cief Larman can make a comb like this, who can't? But it was a fine thing, I had to allow it.

I swear I was mightily pleased by it. I said, "Well, thank ye," to the man, but I didn't know what else to say or whichaways to look or nothing. Truth was, I wanted to put that comb to my head and just scratch, like I did years ago, for hours sometimes.

"I will tell Cief and Ellen that it pleased you," he said, and then the boys come up onto the porch with the bucket of mash.

Tate went out the door and peered into the bucket.

"That's all good mash," he muttered, fearful it'd get wasted.

I went out there with Mister Starns and stood with him. He put to his eyes a pair of fine spectacles and looked out at the woods where they come up the slope out front.

"Where does this hog run?" he said.

"Hellfire," said Tate. "He runs right up to the door sometimes. We can hear him snorting nights. That monster's out there somewhere now, a-waiting for me."

Good Mister Starns give me a look then and I said, "Oh, yes, that's so."

And it was. I had seen the thing myself. Course I knowed it was just a hog, not no demon, but it had gotten powerful bold with us.

Mister Starns grunted and took the bucket and walked off with it to the edge of the front slope. Then he stopped, looked around him a few times, and poured the mash right on the ground.

"Hey!" hollered Tate. "That's all good mash! Well, damn that feller!"

I said, "Well, Tate, I think he is trying to help."

"Shet up," my man said. I did.

Mister Starns come on back and we all set the porch and waited, Mister Starns, Tate, the boys and me. Mister Starns took to chatting on like any kin, and it was pleasant.

It'd been a long time since I seen a big man enjoy hisself talking like that. You could see he was excited about what he was doing down at the mission, and when he talked about the mountains, about the big trees and the laurel, why, I went girlish and wanted to run look at things I have seen all my life.

I kept looking at Mister Starns this way and that, smiling and saying nothing but "Oh, yes?" and "Well, is that right?" and so on, making Tate mad ready to bust.

Tate was scowling meanness at me and hanging his head this way and that, when suddenly he tucked up his head and held still. He turned grimy white and said, "It's a-coming."

He stood up. "Now! Now, the fiend! Now, mission man, do what ye can!"

Mister Starns just set there. "I hope I won't have to do nothing," he said, but low. Uneasy hisself he was, looking hard where Tate was pointing.

Now the day had come right cloudy and the ravens was out. There fell this rumble of thunder and Tate's knees got the shivers and he went right down on them when the hog come up in sight.

It was a mean-looking thing, let me say it. Big as a horse's body it was, and its back curved up powerful spiny. From where we was we could see him through the bresh, saw them glittery black little eyes poked back in that puffed-up, hairy head. And I allowed Tate that them eyes looked a different kind of meanness than any man's, any human's.

Tate was gibbering and wailing, and I thought, Well, it's no wonder he never shot the thing. How could he, shaking like that? and Mister Starns kept saying, "Be still! Hush!"

Somewheres a raven squawked, and the monster stepped out of the bresh. Tate made a gurgly sound and bolted in the cabin and come flopping back out again with his rifle gun. Mister Starns was on his feet like a bobcat, and he wrapped both long arms around Tate and held him still, saying, "Hush now! You'll run him off. Be quiet and maybe we'll see some fun."

Tate wailed, but he had to stand and watch the monster, who was poking about with that long snout. Then the monster looked toward us and got still, and then he started at us, and then I was afeared myself. I wished I hadn't taken so to Mister Starns and let him get us into this. I thought my old Tate was not such a fool after all, when all of a whup that monster stopped dead.

He rooted around and then commenced eating on that mash.

"Huh?" said Tate. "What's it doing?"

Mister Starns was hugging Tate bug-eyed and talking to the hog, but in a low voice, saying, "Go on! Go on, eat that stuff, go on, now, eat it!" But then, in a minute, he seen the hog meant to finish ever bit of that mash, Tate didn't need Mister Starns to tell him about it, so Mister Starns let Tate go and set down again, grinning wide.

That monster ate it all and started at us again. And then it was a sight, let me tell it, yes, sir.

That monster took about ten steps when one hoof give out on him. One minute he was a-coming along fine, the next leaning over slant-wise, stopped. He looked at the hoof like he was puzzled about it, dug it into the ground and straightened up and started for us again, and another one give out. He lay there lopsided for a time, trying to under-stand his trouble. He strained and pulled with his big thick neck and got his great self off the ground again and come barreling at us this time, and this time all four hoofs give out at once and he come down belly whumpus with a powerful thump and lay looking around with red eyes, wondering why he was on the ground.

Mister Starns was going hee-hee-hee, and when the monster decided he'd just give it all up and stuck his little legs in the air and looked at them, and then rolling over on his back, then flopping from side to side, Mister Starns just busted out stomping and laughing and hooting like any boy.

Well, I couldn't help but giggle, and the boys was fitified a course, and finally old Tate, he went haw-haw. Then we was all of us roaring on the porch.

The hog looked like he was laughing, too, because he would stick his snout down in his belly and throw it back again and do that over and over, just as corned as any man. But it wasn't so funny for him, because Tate went down there and stood over him, shaking his head, and then laid his rifle barrel to that silly thing's big head and pulled the trigger.

We all went down, and that monster was a lot of meat. Mister Starns stood over the thing and said, "Well, anyhow, he had him a good time before he went, didn't he?"

Tate allowed that he had, and said Mister Starns could choose his side from that hog and we would smoke it for him.

Mister Starns said that would be fine, that he'd always wanted a demon for supper.

Jacob Larman

Nobody says yessir now. I talk and holler sometimes, but the faces that look down pay me no heed, don't hear what I hear myself saying. No, they just look down on me in wonderment.

Bedfast. Laid inside an old hollow log, and them coming to peer in at me. Lonely and beholden, holed up. Not always sure just what part of my life I go to sleep from or wake up to. Expecting to see Debra's face sometimes and sometimes even Callman's, surprised at Earl's and Shad's and Cardell's all the time.

Then one morning, or night, or whatever it was, there was a face I had not seen in such a time I didn't know whose it was. I watched it watch me, wondering at it as it wondered at me, and then, oh, I wanted to get up and run and jump because it was Ben! It was Benjamin Cutbirth, with his long face like bark and his big hands and steady eyes.

I said, "Oh, Ben, you have come back to see how we are getting along here where you left us." I turned my head and yelled, "Pa! Here's Benjamin Cutbirth come through Mary's Pass to see us!"

Nobody answered, heard, not even Ben hisself.

That face, so strong and fine, it moved up away from me and took on a pair of eyeglasses and a rat-tailed beard, and I seen Ben was old now, like me. Then I thought, No, you old fool, it ain't him, Ben was seventy years ago. Sixty now in the ground by the simmon tree in the Watauga bottom. You are daft again, I thought, and shut my eyes and took a swim in the darkness like I did as a boy in the deep hole below Carson's Fall, with Ben there one time, laughing at me from the bank,

tossing rocks, trying to hit my little white bottom when I turned it up
to dive.

Earl said, "We'll get the sled," and then that man I thought was Ben,
he said, "No, that sled will kill him. We must carry him down."

If it is you, Benjamin Cutbirth, I thought, then I will go. You will get
me there, wherever it is they must take me.

I felt big hands under my back, Ben's. They was lifting me up, and
the next thing I was going down the slopes in the daytime, slung
betwixt two poles like a carcass but lying easy all the same, watching
the sun shoot light at me through the leaves and branches. On the pole
handles by my head was them big hands like Ben's, holding me up with
that grip I remember on the ax and the puncheon, that I remember
reversing a bullwhip and with the handle striking a fractious horse in
the forehead, square and hard, until it went to its forelegs like a man to
his knees. That grip carried me on, then put me down in a big bed with
walnut pins in a room smelled of cedar and balsam.

I looked and seen the faces passing and buzzing like blowflies above
me. I seen Earl, looking mean as always, then Cora, and when Cora
moved, I seen Cief. Beside Cief's face was a girl's face, I didn't know her.
She was like Cief, I seen that right off, Cief's girl, I could tell. Narrow-
faced like he is, but fleshy, too, with them high cheekbones and slitted
eyes and long-nosed look you think ain't seeing nothing.

Ben's big face come betwixt them, and Ben pushed Cief and Cief
said, "Grandpa Jacob." It was the first time he ever said my name. It
wasn't that clear, but he said it, and I heard, all right. Ben pushed Cief
again and Cief swallowed and worked his throat and said, "Her name's
Ellen." Cief said all that.

Cora said, "She will see to you, Grandpa," and then Ben said, "We
mean to do our best for you while you're here with us."

I closed my eyes and thought, That's Ben. He has come back to
teach Cief to talk and he's brought Cief a woman with him, from Virginia maybe, where he has been, fighting the King's Men and Indians.

Cora said something and I looked. She was holding Ben's arm and
saying did I remember him when he come up with the Bishop. I said of

course I remember Ben, but not with no Bishop, Ben was long before that, and then I heard Debra calling, "Jacob, Jacob," and I said Yes ma'am and went swimming into the dark, deep hole to find her.

Then I thought the sun had come up sudden and I looked, but it was only Cief's scrawny, long-nosed girl, standing all alone, holding a saucer candle and looking at me scared. The rest of them was all gone, but she run out and back in, bringing them all with her, Earl and Shad and ornery little Cardell, and finally Ben again, then Cora with a smoky bowl she give to Ellen to give to me.

I heard a stool being hitched up to the bed and Ellen sat on it and put a spoon in my mouth, hot. The steam from the mush bowl made my eyebrows sweat. That scrawny face next to me, she was like Cief, but she smelled fresh. She had her mouth open a ways, humming as she poked at me with the spoon, and I looked in and seen her tongue, it was pink and flat, not like Cief's. Her hand was strong on that spoon, putting it in my mouth and pushing it down on my tongue and turning it.

Scrawny Ellen, you couldn't know this bedfast old man was wanting you to climb in with him, let him warm his cold hands on you, like he did on his Debra years ago, hands flopped down still after eighty-six years of touching, all of it now so hard to recall.

But scrawny Ellen, she seen I was watching her and thinking on her, and she commenced to hum louder and then sing. Ben, he made a lot of that and told her I liked it, and Cief smiled his lopsided smile and she sang, to me, and it was like Debra. I listened, and it was her back again.

> O Joseph was an old man an old man was he
> He married Virgin Mary the Queen of Galilee

She sang that, Ellen did, and Debra did, in the warm nights and cold I don't remember now, me saying stop that, her singing to spite me, holding me off in them nights I can't count now.

> O Joseph and Mary walked through an orchard green
> There were apples and cherries plenty to be seen

My hands, they thawed, they commenced to move again over

Debra, over her scrawny one night big the next, over Debra thin and Debra big as she give them to me, over Callman, Cief's pa, over sweet Jessie and Earl, and over them that couldn't live on. Frozen in the big bed, but Cief's girl sang Debra into it again, to give me my comfort.

> *Then Mary spoke to Joseph so meek and so mild*
> *Joseph gather me some cherries for I am with child*

Then the nights got counted. Jessie and Callman gone, and Debra failing in the bed, saying nothing but failing, me pretending to sleep but touching her legs with mine to see if they was still warm until they went cold out to the hairs and only mine warm. Jessie and Callman gone, and Debra cold.

> *Then Joseph flew in anger in anger flew he*
> *Let the father of the baby gather cherries for thee*

Well, Callman and my sweet Jessie, lost Daniel and Earl, Cora and Cief, Shad, Cardell, now scrawny Ellen and Cief, now Cora standing with this man I think is Benjamin Cutbirth come out of the dark wilderness to see me, well, who then is dead and who's alive?

> *O the baby spoke a few words a few words spoke he*
> *Let my mother have some cherries bow down low cherry tree*

Well, I see Earl there, he's alive. And sorrowful. I thought he would be glad when I die. But they are all here, tending to me, yes, and all our dead have come down to watch, because Ben come back to show them what a family is, something I somewhere forgot how to do.

Scrawny Ellen, she's singing, wiping sweat off my skull with a fresh-smelling hand, Cief's girl. Ben, I am obliged to you for bringing her. Ben, do you remember when we left for the mountains, you and my pa and Harlan's grandpa and grandma? When we left that little warm building I was born in and went out over the frosty ground and come to the great mountains, where nobody had been before, and cut our way into it, everbody scared but you? Well, if I must do it again, with you, Ben, I am ready. You take me, and I'll go. Because I can now, you have calmed my young'uns down, see, they are fine. You brung Cief his scrawny Ellen, and they will breed me a Callman and a Jessie again, yes, it's the truth.

That serpent in my side, he's waking up. He's ready to crawl. And the sharpness behind my eyes. My old flesh just fails me, that's right. Take me on with you, Ben. Sing, Ellen.

> *O I will be dead mother as the stones in the wall*
> *But I will come again mother come again for all*

Cora

So it wasn't never Harlan that opened the door to me, but me and Starns opened it for him. And Harlan come in it and took me, and I left Starns. But I left knowing that if not for him, all doors for me, for Harlan, and for Jean, too, would still be shut tight.

In the night he died, Grandpa Jacob finally broke his fit. We was standing there and his arm jerked out from his side, like he was cured. I took his hand and knowed he didn't mean it for me. Earl took it, and it was the same. Finally I seen what he wanted, and said, "Starns." Starns took his dried-up old root of a hand and held it in his big, smooth-skinned paw. We all thought Grandpa was well again, because when Starns took hold, it was like two men striking a bargain. But then Grandpa just withered up and failed, a body could see it happen right there. He turned into a dry, dead root in the bed, and it was over. Little Ellen kept on a-singing and nobody said nothing until Cief, he put his hands on her shoulders, and she stopped.

The rest of us slept some before morning, but Starns wouldn't. He took the stool by the bed Grandpa lay in, that walnut-pinned bed he'd made for the two of us, and sat there all night. I stayed for a while, but it got to be like Grandpa was still there, talking with Starns. It was like two men in the room, striking bargains. I got the shivers after a while and slept some, too.

In the morning we buried him next to Daniel, who was buried next to Harlan's Margaret and Orlean and Joseph. The sky was clear and blue. It was windy, but nicely so. A day more pleasant couldn't be. Shad and Earl made the box and we put Grandpa in it and buried him with the sun shining all around us. Then Starns, he read something from the holy books he has, and then stepped back while Earl and Shad shoveled the dirt, like he felt he should move out and let us have the last of Grandpa Jacob, because he was ours, after all, and not his.

Then we stood around, looking at each other, wondering what to do. Starns didn't say nothing, just stood, too, but those few steps away from us. Then Cief, and it was him alone knowed what to do, turned and walked to the mission house and took up his boards for the crib he is building for the harvest. When he did that, we all looked at Starns and waited.

He didn't say nothing, and I knowed he would have to be asked. That is the way he is. I said, "Tell us what to do, Starns," and Earl and Shad both said "Yes" at the same time.

So the afternoon of the morning we buried Grandpa Jacob we was all busy. I was in the log kitchen, and could see the sky still so blue and clear, and could hear them all at work. Cief, with Ellen to help, building harvest cribs, and Earl and Shad laying in a new floor for the church. Tate and Juba Benson had come down with their two boys, and Jimmy Rode, too, and Clayton Gaines and John Barco and some others, all to say good-by to Grandpa. They stayed on through the day to help, the Benson boys scoring timber with Starns by the rivers where he wants his sawmill, with Jimmy Rode bossy beside them, talking but not lifting a hand.

Juba Benson was in with me, helping me cook corn and bean bread she brung down to us. I left her there to go ask Clayton Gaines if we could have some milk from his cows for the big supper. Him and John Barco was in the church there with Earl and Shad and Cardell. Little Thurmon was jumping about a-squawking and making a show of his size, and the men kidding him about it. Clayton Gaines sent him on for my milk, and I stayed there and talked with them some and kidded Earl about building a church for Starns and him, Earl, the meanest man in the valley until now. His reputation, I told him, was plumb lost and gone.

Earl's grizzly face, with that white-bearded stubble, just looked at me and paid me no more mind than a pesky fly. He said, "Well, I am just *building* for Starns. I don't put him to bed at night. Don't you talk to me." And all them men grinned when he put his thumbs and fingers together in a circle and held them up to his eyes like Starns's eyeglasses and wiggled his hips. "Don't you talk to me," he said, kidding me back.

When the old adobe church was half down, Starns told Earl he would build the new one cornerless. That in a cornerless church there was no place for the devil to hide. That Earl could sleep there nights when the witches was after him. Him and Starns laid it out, the new one, with not one corner, and Earl has worked on it half of ever day since, and slept there at night like a bear. When I left them, John Barco was handing him another squared beam to drive down in the ground lengthwise. It was Earl's idea, so Starns says, to make the floor of log ends drove down deep, so's it will never rot and fall through. I left him and Shad banging away with them big mauls, Clayton Gaines and John Barco holding the log steady.

It ain't true no more, what Earl said about me and Starns. I don't lie with Starns no more at night, though they all think I do, and think it is all right for once. Since Starns went out in the night and pulled Earl off his horse, since he went down the mountain and brung back little Ellen for Cief, Starns has been different at night. He feels bad at night when I twitch in my sleep, and once he woke me up and said, "It'll be all right, Cora. Just you wait. It will. I told you once I was never much with the ladies. That's true, but you just wait."

I was thinking about that, going back to my kitchen, ambling on through the sounds and smells of that fine day back to work. Juba was getting on well in the kitchen, I was taking out some peels and went by the cribs to talk to Cief and Ellen when I seen they wasn't working. They was standing by the cribs, holding on to each other, pointing. They seen me and pointed and I looked.

I seen Harlan then, with the sweet blue sky all above him, holding Jean in his arms, her all wrapped in white. From one crook of his elbow, down hung her long yellow hair, and from the crook of his other, hung her little feet, bare and dirty. I started toward him, but stopped when I comprehended where he was a-standing.

He was there at them sunny graves of Daniel, of Grandpa Jacob, and of his Margaret, his Orlean and his Joseph. And he had my Jean in a winding sheet. "Starns!" I yelled. "Starns!"

Harlan

"Starns!" hollered Cora. "Starns!"

I know his name now, but then I did not know it. That morning, from my watching place, the clump of poplars, I seen them bury Jacob and shovel that dirt onto him. I seen Starns take his book of spells and conjur over the grave with it, and I knowed how wrong I had been two years ago to let that happen here. I thought on Margaret, when we was little together, saying we would never have that, and how she had held up to it, and how I had not.

From that place, with Jean, I had watched them graves so many times. There I had seen strange men build the first mission, and I watched Starns tear it down and build again. And there I stood that bright morning they laid old Jacob Larman in beside my own, not one cloud in the sky. Clayton Gaines rode by my cabin early, told me Jacob died in the night, so I come out to watch and seen them open up that ground next to my own. I felt awful bad, commenced to shake, when that hole appeared, when that ground come open. It was so close to them, where they lie. In my arms Jean got scared at me and jumped down like a kitten cat, and I let her.

When Starns conjured, from the grave just behind them all up come Daniel with my bullet hole in his neck, a-waving his arms like he did getting down from that roan the first time I shot him. They did not see him jumping around them, but I did. And he seen me, and he pointed at me up on the slope, and then from the ground Margaret rose into that bright and sunny daylight, with Orlean and little Joseph behind her, the three of them all bones and dust in their winding sheets, the sweet-

smelling wind blowing them sheets about them, flapping them. They
left Daniel jumping around, and they moved. Margaret held out what
was her hand under the sheet and Orlean took it and held out hers to
little Joseph and he took it, and they come moving up to me on the
slope, coming home to me.

I grabbed up Jean and I run with her through the woods, down the
east slope and up again to Gore's Knob. I knowed a place there, a place
Margaret never knowed about, a place I used to go alone, a cave hole
under a big rock. I hid in there with Jean and waited until Margaret
would get to the cabin and find me and Jean gone and then go back to
the ground again. Jean was hungry and kept after me for something to
eat until I slapped her and she crawled over against the rock and played
there alone.

I stayed there for some time, until it was into the afternoon, then I got
Jean and left. She had been playing with some old fox bones lying around
and didn't want to leave, and I slapped her again until she was quiet.

At the cabin I watched for a while and seen nobody. They had come
and gone, then. I left Jean in the yard by the white birch at the clearing
and went in the cabin, slow. It was the way I had left it. I knowed Margaret must have been pained to see it that way. I have not kept it up. I
looked at it, thinking of her, looking at the way things are, and I went
and touched her loom that is all fallen apart now. There was some cloth
still by it, in the box she had, and I opened it and took out some cloth
and looked at it. I still had it in my hand when I heard Jean crying, and
when I run out to see what was wrong with her, I pulled it with me
without knowing it.

I got to the clearing and I seen that Margaret, she had fooled me. In
the ground two years, she was still smarter than me. She had waited
somewhere for me, and now there was Jean at the white birch, kicking
and screaming and rolling on the ground. And Margaret in her wormy
white winding sheet, bony hands at Jean's throat, shrieking and squeez-
ing her, with Jean's tiny fists trying to get Margaret's awful hands from
her throat. Then Jean just flopped over in the dirt and lay still, the way
Orlean and Joseph had when Daniel killed them.

Margaret held out her hands under the sheet, and Orlean and Joseph come up and took them, the three staring at me. Margaret grinned, and then the three of them just went into that white birch tree, leaving Jean on the ground.

In my hands I held the cloth from Margaret's box. It was white. Margaret had willed me in there to get it while she struck Jean down, for it was to be my Jean's winding sheet.

So I wrapped Jean up in it. I couldn't bear to see her face then, I just wrapped her up in it and knowed I had to take her and put her there with my others who had wanted her and who had come and took her.

Down the slope I walked with her, on that fine, clear day, and, carrying her, I thought I felt her move in my arms. But I knowed that was what happens when your own die, that you think they are still alive for a long time.

I got to the graves and looked at the ground and thought, Turn again, dirt, so's I can put little Jean down in there with the rest of them and have done.

Then somebody was walking toward me and stopped. I seen it was Cora, snarly bitch Cora Larman, mother of my Jean. She looked and I wanted to talk to her, but couldn't.

"Starns!" she yelled. "Starns!"

We looked at each other there, while all them people come running out of the mission. Starns come out ahead of the rest of them, puffing and breathing hard. "Cora, what in the world?" he said to her, then he saw me.

He took hold of Cora's arm and walked her up to me, saying, "Hush, Cora, come on, now." When he got to me he looked at Jean in my arms and at me shaking like I was, and he said, "You best give her to me," and held out his hands.

I told him no, that she had to be put in with Margaret who had struck her down. I told him this time there would be no charms and no spells neither. I told him I would not falter this time, no, I would not.

"Well, just let me see, then," he said. I held Jean so he could see her little face clenched and blue like a dead baby's fist, and her mouth all smeared with dirt. He come right up and bent over her and put his hand on her chest and then looked up quick at me. He touched her throat, and then I hollered, because when he did that, Jean jumped in my arms, turned her mouth to Starns and spit hot blood on his face.

"God Almighty!" he roared at me. "She's still alive, give her here!"

He grabbed Jean from me and went running through that crowd and they followed him. I didn't know what to do. I went to Cora and told her what had happened, how Margaret come, and she held my arm and said, "Yes, Harlan, yes."

"Cora! Cora, god damn it, get in here!"

It was Starns, yelling at her from their log kitchen. She took my hand and we run to it and through them standing at the door. I looked in, and then I run in.

He had Jean laid out on a cutting table, had one of his big hands in her mouth, blood running out betwixt his fingers.

I jumped at him, yelling, but Earl Larman was there and flung his strong arms around me. He shoved me back against the wall and held me there, and I had to watch.

Starns said, "Cora, empty them pots!"

Cora, at the door, she said, "What?"

"Water, Cora," said Earl between his teeth, holding me down. "Get some water on that fire."

"Yes, yes!" and run to it while Earl held me fast and Starns worked his big hand in Jean's mouth. Her feet was kicking, and some girl I never seen before, that Cora called Ellen, she come and held Jean's legs down. I could hear Cief Larman whining the way he does outside, and Shad Larman trying to hush him up. The door next to me was full of faces, all watching Starns work on my Jean.

We looked and in a minute Starns's right shoulder jerked up hard, like he was pulling out her tongue, and in his fist was something bloody. Jean's feet went still. Her chest commenced to heave and then she was breathing deep and crying.

"Shad!" said Starns.

His face popped in there at the door.

"Get Jimmy Rode and tell him I want some of that arnica grease he has, and some hemlock. If he argues credit with you, knock him down and take it."

Starns didn't know Jimmy Rode was right there at the door. "No need to talk like that," Jimmy Rode grumbled. "Come on, Shad." Shad went out with him.

"Cora, let me see that bucket," Starns said.

She got the one he meant. It was half full of water, cold. He sunk his arm down in it and swished his fist around. When he pulled it out and opened it, there was something in it looked like a knuckle.

He laid it on the table by Jean's feet. I seen it was a knuckle and part of a splintered bone. Then I thought about that cave hole, and her playing with them bones there, and me slapping her.

Starns said, "Earl, let the man loose." I moved away from the wall, but could not look at my Jean. I did not feel like much right then.

"That thing is a damn shinbone or something," Starns said. "What kind of man are you, anyhow? What do you feed this child, rocks and dirt, that she'd eat on something like that?"

I said, "No, I am not much, you are right."

"We ought to take that child and keep her here," said Starns, "if you don't know how to take care of her."

I hung my head, said, "Yes, you are right, but don't do that."

"You shut your mouth, Starns," Cora said, sharp, and everbody looked surprised at that. "Harlan's grateful for what you just done, but you don't know what he has suffered through. And you ain't Jean's pa, neither! You got no right. Hush."

Then Starns looked at me and Jean and then took Cora by the shoulders and gazed at her funny like and said, "This here is your child, Cora, am I right?"

Cora looked at me, said, "Well, Harlan, is she?"

I couldn't say a word, and just then Jean coughed a little blood, but not much. I went to the table and Starns took Cora by the hand and brung her over, too. Jean was breathing like she does when she's tired after running. I leaned over her, and knowed how wild I looked, how witless, and I knowed Jean would be right to be scared of me if she seen me then, after all I had done in my miseries over Margaret. Then I recalled the way Margaret really did treat Jean, and I said, "I done Margaret wrong, seeing her like that, Cora. Why, Margaret never stinted on Jean, even if she was ours and not hers. She loved Jean, she'd never have done what I saw." And Cora said, "Yes, Harlan, I believe that." And I said, "Starns is right. I don't have sense enough anymore to take care of her." And I looked down on Jean, and thought what a sorry father I have always been to all my children, and how Jean would be right to be scared of me and want no more of me.

Then Jean, she opened her eyes, and blinked them, and seen me leaning over her, and all of a sudden her soft little arms come up around my neck and she cried for me. It was the most pleasant thing in all my sorry life, but I took her arms away after a minute and pulled Cora over, and the two of them looked at each other, Cora holding her breath. "Go to yore momma, Jean," I said. Jean looked and then busted into a wail and grabbed out and Cora took her and Jean put her face into Cora's neck and cried.

Cora lifted her and carried her out. I followed, and as I was going after them, Starns, he laid a big hand on my shoulder, hard. "Good," he said.

They put Jean in the big bed, the one Jacob Larman died in the night before, they told me. Starns said I should stay there and sleep the night with Jean, and I thanked the man. Then Shad Larman come in with the arnica and hemlock and Starns said, "I'll leave it to you and Cora now, I have some work." So me and Cora tended Jean, and that night when I was in the bed, Cora come in and we talked. I told her how scared I have been since Margaret died, how haunted scared like a baby. I broke down then and all my shakes come back to me, and my remembering of Margaret pulled at my innards so. I told Cora I did not know what to do, I just didn't. And she got in the bed with me then, got in with me and Jean her baby, and that night I slept in the soft crib of Cora's big legs.

So that was the first time I knowed who Starns was, that day.

Now the trees on the slopes, they have turned. Dancing in the wind and sun, some leaves are like sparks off flint. This afternoon I stood watching at my watching place again, at my clump of poplars, watching Starns on his mission-house porch. His big harvest, it's over now, and they say he means all of us to have some of it. Nobody ever growed nothing like all that around here. The whole valley had to come help him bring it in, there was so much.

When I watched this afternoon, he was just sitting there, harvest done, filing the big reaper he prizes so, the sunshine shining on his sweaty head most bald and glinting on his eyeglasses while he went scrape, scrape, scrape, him looking up to nod at them that passed while he worked.

I had gone down to the poplars to fell some timber, and had worked some, but mostly stood watching the mission and Starns, thinking about Jean, that I might just quit cutting soon and go home and maybe sing something to Jean. I knowed Cora would fault me for not working the day out, she needed the wood, but I wanted to see Jean.

Little Lafe Benson was down there, and I seen him bring around Starns's horse, saddled. Starns give the boy the big reaper to put away and said something to him. Then he got up in his saddle and headed toward the rivers, the east slope and Gore's Knob. They tell me John Barco's woman got milk sick up there and Starns goes to see her ever day, along with his others. That is the way he is.

I asked Cora about that, about Starns, the first night we come together again at the mission. "Why should he care about them not his own?" I said. "Why should he care?"

"I don't know, Harlan," she said, like it was sad. "He just does."

When we left the mission the next morning to go home, I seen Cora was right, there was no calculation in the man, he meant the things he said and did.

Before we left, Starns said he would marry Cora and me legal when the church got built. After that he said something else to me. He said I was wrong to go on so about my dead.

"You are a man that sees too much, Harlan," he said. "It's like you have two pair of eyes, and that second pair is the one you have to be careful of, because it can see awful things."

He knowed. That man knowed what my miseries were. The only one who ever has.

"Now, when you get to seeing things like that, talk to Cora. When she gets to seeing them, too, the both of you come down here and talk to me. And when I get to seeing them, and that can damn well happen, then we'll all go to church and let the Almighty bear the awful things we see."

Then I told him about Margaret and our ma, and how we hexed over the dying body of our own pa and then lived together after Ma died. And how I still could not hold with charms and spells, or angels and almighties and heaven and hell and such.

We was standing on the mission-house porch then, Cora holding Jean and waiting on me. Starns looked out on his fields, all swollen and waving then with them crops. He looked at Cora, then me, and rubbed his bald spot.

"I'll tell you something," he said. "I don't hold with them much neither. But this much I do know. Your Margaret and them young'uns, they are at rest now."

I shook my head. "How do I know that?" I said.

"Because I tell you they are," he said, and he put a big hand on my shoulder and looked deeper into me than any man ever has or will. "I have seen mine," Starns said, "and they were at peace. I have seen it."

I believed him. I just knowed he must be right. I looked out over his full fields, waving tassels of high corn, looked over them to the graves, and I seen Margaret again then, seen her the way she was when we was little, how she could sleep so sound in the bed with me. I seen her then, sleeping sound and quiet where I had buried her two years ago.

I thought about Starns telling me that, and what it meant to me, watching him ride off to the rivers, cross and head up toward the east slope and Gore's Knob.

When he got to the foot of the slope, somebody in the gristmill yelled at him. He stopped, reined in, his horse stomping, and yelled back. And everybody down there at the mission just stopped, too, and looked to him where he was standing up in his stirrups, turned half around in the saddle and yelling. They all stopped dead, all the men and women and boys that pass through there now, going in and out of them six fine buildings he set square and straight into the dirt of that field. And when he set back in the saddle again and rode on, they moved about again, chattering like they do, and the sounds of them drifted up to me like the pleasant wash of a full creek.

I took my ax and started home, thinking, To hell with this, I've worked enough today. I want to have a drink with Cora and maybe sing something to Jean. I felt good, going home again.

Walking, I heard them in the woods, all the little, fearful things you never see but who are there anyhow, who when it's howling storm and rain have no need to step careful, their little feet making no sound when they run wild over rotten sticks and cakes of moldy leaves, but now, having to learn to step careful and not make so much noise, snapping and cracking the things that have dried out again.

A pack of blackbirds busted up out of a clump of trees on the far slope, flying dead east, and I knowed something was running west. I put up my hands like a boy and went bang! and thought of Jean and vowed I would sing her something wonderful in a minute, and laughed a little, and felt just fine.

Where I turn off to home, I seen another flock of blackbirds come squawking up from the trees, going west this time, meaning that the fool deer or cat or bear or whatever it was was headed back east now.

I waited there and watched, and then I seen the horse and Starns hunched over the saddle, one arm fending off briers and vines. He'd missed the trail up to Gore's Knob and had to come back some for it. He was slapping at his horse and I could tell he was a-cussing the way his head was bobbing. I laughed at him then, until he was gone up the trail, and another pack of birds squawked at him and busted up out of the trees.

He couldn't hear me, but I yelled something at Starns anyhow, yelled for him not to bust his britches or something like that.

At that turnoff I watched the valley so dry and bright in the sun, watched it go all blue as it slipped on through Mary's Pass, flowing along like a smoky blue river.

Then I turned from it and walked to the cabin, already singing though Jean was yet to come.

Interlude

TUNE THE FIDDLE

CORA, do you remember Harlan now? Harlan, do you remember Jean?

Ghosts. Specters all. Memories standing mute and bareheaded in the gray rain and mist of my yard, how I wish we could talk. How I wish you could break those ghostly ranks and stomp up here on my porch, and have this last drink of my whisky with me, and belch and fart and laugh and hoot, and cry, too, why not, going over the old times. But no, you don't share my teary sentiments now, and there is no human telling of all the things you did. You won't speak at all, not even to me. No, the part of you that spoke is long buried in the rich black dirt of Valle Sanctus, your living flesh is sifted through it now, and harrowed, and before me only your specters, nightmares mute and dearly loved and past and gone.

But Billy Cobb, yes, he's still alive these twenty years after the last of you died, still alive, full of aches and memory. I will, tonight, be your earthly memories. I'll do some of it for you, like I sang for you when my throat was young, when I sang your prayers and dances.

So then, my gentlemen and ladies all, I tell you it was something, the Bishop's face, when he first laid eyes on that lopsided church. Yes, in late October of the fall of 1852, when we come up, it was just finished, built with not one corner, to keep out Earl Larman's devils. Well, Bishop, when you first looked at it, you stared and considered and then tilted your head a little.

"Starns," you said.

"Yessir."

"Where are the corners?"

"In hell, Bishop, I reckon," Starns said, and the giggles swept all the mountain people there, and me, too, as I recall.

Then Starns showed us around the place. Ghosts, it is a tasty thing, remembering the first time you seen a place that was to mean so much. I was up with you, Bishop, then, and you, Rachael, you come, too, for the first time, and with us was Statius Collins, the Congressman. I see he is not here with us tonight, my specters, and good riddance. Well, anyhow, in Raleigh we had heard Starns was doing well, Marcus Sales not able to believe it. So we got there, and after looking over that lopsided church we went out to his cribs and seen the size of his store there. I can still see you, Bishop, looking over the little ledgers, in painful, cramped scrawls, showing how much corn and barley and wheat was given out to who, and how much more they would need to see them through the winter. And we learned who had built what part of the buildings, the mission house, the log kitchen, the church, the sawmill, the gristmill, the barn. And who came down when, to help out and keep things going. Statius Collins, the Congressman, he was impressed, and he looked Starns over, said, "You are quite an organizer, sir," and Starns nodded, said, "Yessir," unaware the man meant a compliment.

No, he was a farmer, not no organizer, and his harvest was all of us. Because of him we grew, and gave up our yield, and grew again.

But none of us knew that right then. We thought Starns was just a man who'd found his place in life. And for that alone we were proud enough of him, a drunken drifter three years before.

Proud, why, Bishop, you were so proud of him you just shined like a new boot and didn't have a word to say. Not even when we finished seeing the place and Starns handed you the list of things to be done, the one you sent Marcus Sales and he left behind. You just shined when Starns handed it to you and said, "Here. This is yours."

Yes, he handed you your mission then, and you knew it, but didn't say anything, you just shined. And you chatted with the mountain peo-

ple and laughed with them the way you could with people, and finally
turned to Starns and called him "Nestor" for the first time.

"What's that?" Starns said, thinking it was something you wanted
him to get. And you said, "Nothing," and said no more until that
evening, when you preached for two solid hours straight, with all the
valley gathered in that church to hear you, preached like St. Paul himself on a good day. It was something, that sermon. I don't think you
ever did better anywhere. Except once, maybe, later. But that I will not
remember, not now, not right now.

At the end of your sermon you turned to Starns and told him you
would ordain him deacon for this church and that you would be proud
to do it. And you told him then, and it stuck, that he was Nestor, all
right, because Nestor was the world's greatest peacemaker, the best and
wisest man in the greatest war of the ancient world.

Earl Larman, you said, "Was he as ugly as Starns, too?" and the giggles went around again, and, Bishop, you said, "No, he wasn't as ugly,
but he wasn't any wiser either."

"Hello there, Nestor," said the people after the service, and Nestor it
was, Deacon Nestor Starns, the peacemaker. Rachael, you gave it a
woman's light laugh then and clapped your dainty hands, and we all
clapped, Starns, too, shrugging his shoulders and grinning, happy as
a boy.

Later, Bishop, Starns got sober with you, asked you if you would
grant them all a big favor. You said "What?" and Starns asked if you
wouldn't have nothing against it, he would like to have a big dance for
everybody the next night.

"There'll be no trouble," he said. "And they could all do with one,
Bishop. It would pick everybody up a lot."

"Go ahead, Starns," you said, and the next night was the first dance
feast, the first of two a month for six years. And Starns was ready. He
had brewed mountain beer for it, great barrels of it. Mountain lager
beer, just water poured over the combs of bumblebees and let ferment,
not long. Mild and sweet, it give a man just the right drunk to dance
right, without bringing out his meanness at all. Starns had got a big

dulcimore for Cief Larman's wife, Ellen, to sing to, and I played that, and John Barco sawed a gourd fiddle, and I called the turns.

It was a little hard at first, my ghosts, because your bodies then, they were stiff and awkward, hard as your lives. You were shy about it, snickered and scoffed a little. But Starns had brewed his beer with cunning, and soon, still a little stiff with your hunched shoulders and cramped, horny hands, you began to sway to my calls. And then you found your own grace, your own stamp and turn, and the breath began to whoosh in and out of you, and away we went, that night.

Without knowing it, you danced the old songs of weddings and feasts and days of joy, the old Infare songs, I sang them and called them. "Prince Charlie" you danced, and "The Chimney Sweep," "The Downfall of Paris," and the reels and quadrilles and boxes, me singing sometimes and Cief's Ellen sometimes while I called or played. I called them for you, I called "Swing around and a swap you've made, your pretty girl for my old maid," and Ellen sang, "There goes a man and I'll go with him, way off down the mountain," and I sang, "I'll be true to my love, if my love will be true to me," and John Barco sawed "The Downfall of Paris" like he'd been there when it happened.

Cora, you were beautiful dancing with Harlan, and, Harlan, I can see you waving to Jean from the floor, then breaking out and sweeping her up on your shoulders, and dancing again, with Jean squealing with glee, her long whiteblond hair tossed out behind you. Earl, you had some god-awful-looking woman with you with great squaw breasts and dirt an inch thick, but you danced her like she was Egypt's queen. And, Cardell, swinging the little Barco girl, your black eyes flashed, but not with meanness. And then, Juba, Lord! you and your old Tate stepping out on the floor, him looking about, sheepish and suspicious and grumbling but stepping with you finally, the both of you worn and thin but coltish, too, and ancient and stately in the dance.

And Starns. With his honeycomb beer and wide grin and bald spot and eyeglasses. At home and happy, though he wouldn't dance himself, until, Cora, you whispered to Harlan and took Starns out and made him step with the rest, until his bald head was wet with sweat and he puffed and spewed like a sea beast sounding. And stomped and swung you, until finally he swung around once too hard and he tripped and fell and lay down and then got up, laughing with all the rest of us.

When my throat and lungs gave out, I remember I put on my coat and went out to take the night air. Bishop, you came, too, I know you must remember. We walked a ways and found ourselves by that little graveyard with those five fresh graves. And we looked around us, shivering a bit, because for a minute we were part of the dark night, with the mission house far away from us, though only a hundred yards off.

It was like we stood atop Sand Mountain, or any of the peaks bordering Mary's Pass, watching the tiny glow of light that was the mission-house door. Faint was John Barco's gourd fiddle, and hardly heard the stepping of the dancing feet, because the night wind of the mountains blew cold in the blackness over the great slopes and risings, over the dark, deserted steeps and ridges and caverns, but heard it was and we saw the light from the doorway, and that mission-house dance beat in the dark valley like a heart in a strong body.

Then the door opened wide and Starns came out, putting on his coat and sniffing the air, and with him was Statius Collins, his cheeks red above his whiskered jowls. They turned when we called, and came up, and we talked quietly for a while. And then Statius Collins, a little nervous about the people still whooping it up in the mission house, said, "Hadn't you better go back, Mr. Starns, before they get out of hand in there?"

I will never forget him then, saying, "No, they won't get out of hand. They are all good people."

It came burning out of his words, the passion he had that night for his good people.

Those were the years, yes. Six long, full years of it. And Starns our fool and our king, because we laughed at his awkwardness, but to his perfect honesty we bowed.

For those six years, counting them from that night on, under Deacon Nestor Starns that mission was something. It was a school that taught, it was a hospital that healed, it was a store that didn't cheat, and it was a church that didn't presume. Six years it was all that, and I wonder now who else has done all them things all at once for that length of time. What great men, tell me, in the ancient world, or in the pages of leather-bound books, claim that? I don't believe there can be very damn many.

Oh, how can you not remember it? Cief singing in church like a lonely cow, with Ellen's sweet voice mixing in with his, and Earl sleeping there every night. And Rachael bringing up that ornamented foot organ for me to play on Sundays when I stayed up as schoolteacher for the boys, and how Starns made such fun of the thing, but fixed it every time it broke down.

And the sermons. Ha, I remember one time a circuit rider came by and asked Starns if he could preach a part of his service, and Starns said, Well, yes, well, all right. And the circuit rider, with a flaring beard and the eyes of Moses watching God burn his word into the mountain-side, he got up and spoke first to the ladies.

"Ladies," he said, "before I commence here, when I say go, will all of ye please cross ye legs. Go."

And the ladies, puzzled, crossed their legs.

"Now that the gates to hell are closed tight, I'll commence," said the Moses-eyed circuit rider, but he didn't, because Starns had him by the neck and beard on his way out, and threw him out down the steps and went back to preach about cherry preserves, apologizing to the ladies, and then about the use of hemlock for great pains of the body.

Six years of it. How can you not remember? How I wish you could stomp on up here, my ghosts, and hoot and fart and drink and cry with me. But you can't.

You can't even talk. You just stand there, bareheaded, and the gray rain falls through you, mist streams down from your eyes. Mute, and dearly loved and past and gone.

Starns, where are your own now?

Bishop, where is your ring?

Part Three

BLACK CASSOCKS

1

THE SMILE OF SAUL
AND DAVID

ONCE A YEAR, on the day Bishop Ames rode to the mission from Stewart on his spring visit after Easter, Starns declared utter holiday. No one worked, no one prayed, no one studied anything at all. Preparations for the Bishop's coming done the day before, on the day itself they all loafed, Starns lazy as any, an event so remarkable that curious and incredulous souls were known to journey two or three hard miles just to see him on his back in the sun, sleeping in the daytime.

In the six functioning years, then, of the mountain mission, he loafed six days.

This spring morning, 1858, was bright. Starns came rested and joking to a prayerless breakfast, saying it was loafer's glory for God, too, if He needed it and Starns reckoned He might, took coffee in a tin cup and walked, grateful, idle, into the sunshine. He fooled about, wandering, finished his coffee standing by Two Rivers, tossed the grounds at a trouty ripple and hooked the tin cup into his belt, then headed up toward Harlan's cabin, his boots half laced and flapping, sock tops soaking in dew.

He had the rest of his breakfast with them. Bean bread, bacon and more coffee, bark bitter, as Cora made it. When Harlan left for his field, saying, "Preachers have holidays, farmers don't, come on, Jean," Starns sat with Cora and the new baby under the hickory trees.

"She still goes to the field with him, does she?"

"Oh, yes. Where Harlan is, there's Jean," said Cora, smiling.

Cora's first lawful child from Harlan came a year after Starns married them, a girl who did not live. The baby she held on this bright morning was the second, and after five long barren years he came early, a boy, ferocious and squawling. There was no doubt about him, and they immediately named him Jacob. He slept now, cradled on Cora's thighs, his head resting between her knees, his tiny feet in her hands. Cora sat on an overturned crate, toe-gazing, while Starns lay back against the hickory, his head propped on his coat.

"That Jean," said Cora. "She must be with him and trot along, no matter. Harlan swears she keeps up, but, you know, they just sit around half the time."

She smiled and jiggled her knees, looking at Jacob, who gave a tiny cough and wondered in his sleep what was happening.

"Harlan and Jean, it's a caution," said Cora. "You know, he cut a slice out of his leg a few days ago on that old piece of plow wire lying over yonder, and I swear Jean tried to do the same. That child."

Starns rolled half over and looked down the slope. Through the trees, from where he lay, he saw a part of the field and then the two of them walking into it from the valley bottom. They marched even for a minute, then Jean fell behind, then she was running ahead, stopping while he passed and pulling at his hoe, then running ahead again, white-blond hair bouncing against the back of her neck, thin, strong legs pumping her along and kicking out the back of her ragged skirt.

"Well, Cora, there are reasons, I reckon."

"Yes." She laid one finger along the little row of Jacob's toes, measuring their slant. "She knows him better than I do, my Jean, and I allow it, so things go along fine. I give her that, and she knows I do, and it's enough for her. She's smart, Jean. And he has been good to both of us because of it. Jean knows that, too."

Jacob's toes stirred just a little in her hands. He jerked his head sideways against one of her kneecaps and came awake. A sudden mass of wrinkles instantly distorted his face. Throat, lungs and little belly went into flawless action.

Starns laughed. "I'd shoot a child bawled like that." His eyes sparkled. He put mocking fingers to his ears. "Why, Cora, it's awful."

"Yes, we throw him up on the roof come nighttime," said Cora, holding the baby's feet.

O Lord, just look at this, Starns thought. So soft and still with that child. Them big hands, holding him so nicely.

He remembered those hands, clenched behind his back, her face plunged sobbing into his neck during their night in the moldering shack, his birthplace. He remembered the bed he made for her at the mission on those first nights, where they lay while Cief slept the hearth like a hound, and Cora's hands again, digging into his flesh, as if she had to reach through to the bone and shake him. Her great body pressed against him he remembered, twisting and pumping through the night, in dry convulsion, like a snaky coil that even in sleep could not give up the struggle decreed for it.

Lord, how she scared me! Oh, Starns, never much with ladies, who could have foretold this? Not you, anyhow.

Sitting on the overturned crate, Cora brooded quietly over her baby, big hands holding his feet, beautiful, mother and child still one thing. Though the rope had been cut and flung away, the nourishing blood still seemed to flow, uniting them. Jacob pushed his fist across his face and bawled, wondering who he was. It was there, on Cora's hard face, brooding just above him.

"Yell, Jacob," she said. "I'll hear ye." She grinned. "So will Starns."

"Yes, he shore as hell will," said Starns, making a gruesome face, thinking, This here is the best day ever. Ever.

After a while he left them, saddled his horse in the mission barn and rode slowly down to the Watauga. There he unsaddled and left his horse to graze and sat again by a tree, but upright this time, his eyes fixed in confidence and contentment on the turning of the road from Stewart, where it rounded the mountain. He knew he would see the wagon appear there soon, as it always did about this time, on the same day for six years, knew he would see on its seat the frock coat with one tail flapping and the bright bonnet. He always came early, to sit and indulge himself in this great pleasure of his new life, to sit and wait and know that the good thing he expected would happen.

When the wagon appeared, he sighed happily, got up and stretched. He followed his ritual, saddling the horse again and climbing up while the wagon came closer though hidden by brush and a turn down through a ravine. He was in the saddle, riding gracefully and waving when the wagon appeared in full sight, coming toward him along the riverbank.

He met them at the same turn of the road, for his ritual was cherished and precise, and there he shook hands with them, from the saddle, and turned his horse to ride with them to the mission, quietly relishing these first moments of their meeting.

Yes, the herd's fine, bred well. The land will be all right, not enough rain quite, but I got it turned. The boys are working hard as ye can hope for. Cora's had her baby, yes, a boy, come two weeks early. Jacob. Billy Cobb's just fine. He's making a fine preacher, Bishop, everbody knows him, of course, so there's been no standing off from him at all. You was right to send him on up here. The gristmill, yes, the roof will be done by harvest, oh, yes. Bishop, you look a little puny. Have to get you behind a plow tomorrow. Why, that's pretty. Yes, ma'am, Ellen will love that. Oh, yes, she still sings the same. No, they've had no children this year, neither, but they are getting along. Yes, it is all just fine, yes, it is.

When the wagon with its familiar outrider topped the rise, the people were all gathered on the mission porch, waiting. They swarmed about the wagon before it stopped, and greeted Bishop Ames and his Rachael with a warmth unknown elsewhere in the hard highland country. They did not hold themselves back, and Starns, as he surrendered his Bishop to them and drove the wagon to the back of the mission to unpack it, relished this, too.

He was working on the wagon, replacing a board in its bed, when Rachael came out to see him, waving to some of the women inside that she'd be right back. She had taken off her bright, spotted bonnet and was hatless now. She held a woolen shawl over her shoulders.

"Well, now, you seen everybody already?" said Starns.

"I have. Now I want to see you, and the organ. Can we go now, Starns? I want to see it. I've been thinking about it all the way from Stewart. Is it fixed yet?"

He hopped down from the wagon and walked with her toward the chapel, rubbing his hands on his trousers.

"It's just like new. Had a little trouble at Christmas, that's what I wrote you about. But it's fine now."

They went in the narrow door of the chapel and walked down the single aisle to the polished wooden box set high up on long, slender legs, standing across from the pulpit. It was a strange-looking thing in the mountain chapel, spidery on its thin legs, a contrast to the rest of the furnishings, thick-wooded and sturdy. A silver key stuck out of the bronze-rimmed keyhole on one of the two front panels, where a desk-top would have been, had it been a desk. Rachael turned the key knowingly and the two panels swung open, revealing a four-octave ivory keyboard under a set of tiny pipes.

The organ was Rachael's gift to her husband and to his mission, shipped down from New York in the fourth year. It was an heirloom of her father's family, willed to her at his death, a perfect specimen of Post-Restoration miniature organs, built by a nameless English organmaker in the 1660's.

Above the slightly yellowed keyboard stood the row of tiny pipes, set so that the larger were at the outside, set so that the size of the pipes diminished from each end until the two smallest pipes reached center. The whole framework was artfully painted to make a perspective of these pipes, with curving gilded beams painted above them and the parquet squares of a royal flooring below. The pipes, when looked at from center, seemed like inlaid screens standing down two walls of a miniature baroque hallway. At the center of the perspective they met beside an altar of ivory, still dazzling white, on which, four inches square, was a tiny and delicate oil portrait of Virgin and Child.

Rachael took the shawl from her shoulders and handed it to Starns, who had pulled up the bench for her. He stepped to the side of the organ and gripped the pump, working it tentatively a few times, then pumping twice with a full stroke, but she did not reach for the keys. She was looking carefully at the paintings on the two panels.

When these panels swung open, as they did when the instrument was to be played, their inner surfaces presented, within two dark arches, two battle scenes done in rich, durable oils. The left panel showed the giant Saul standing in front of his mammoth tent of still bloody skins and furs, looking over his shoulder with a scornful, derisive smile at the pale, thin, serious young man in a goatskin approaching him with a slingshot.

David was in the other panel, too. He was older, his beard the painter had flecked with white. He stood among spear-gripping, glitteringly armored soldiers, one forearm reaching up to the high saddle of a proud-maned black horse, ready to mount. At David's feet, head almost to the ground, knelt a slave holding the harp, whose strings by the painter's art gleamed sharply, as if vibrating in the wind that ruffled the mane of the black horse and pulled at David's beard. King David himself, caught in the instant before swinging up into saddle and battle, was staring down at the harp, a scornful smile on his lips.

Rachael looked back and forth, back and forth. Yes, she was right, it was the same. By some whim the painter had put that same smile to the mouths of Saul and David. As many times as she had watched these panels, she had never before noticed it. Only in the wagon, riding up from Stewart, had it occurred to her. She sat back and thought about it, and then laid one hand on the keyboard.

Starns pumped, but she hesitated.

"How does it sound?" she asked. "All right?" She seemed afraid to touch it.

"Just like new. Better, because Billy Cobb says it gets richer with the years. Well, well, go on. See for yeself."

She pressed one high key. Starns pumped. The wavering note sounded.

"Such a delicate thing. What was wrong with it, Starns?"

"Some little hickey in there broke, I don't know what, exactly. I give it to Cardell and he whittled a new one. It fit all right and seems to do. Sounds good, don't it?"

She pressed another key and made a harsh dissonance. Starns jumped.

"What happened there?" he said.

"Nothing, nothing, that was me. The organ is fine. I'll play us something now, if you'll pump for me."

Well, what do you think I have been doing? he thought happily, and he pumped, watching her hands ripple slowly and gracefully over the yellowed keys, listening to the hymn she played. When she finished, she put both hands in her lap and looked at them there for a moment, and then gazed up at him.

The buoyant gaiety and devotion that were her stamp had left her face. For the first time Starns saw Rachael Ames look her age. She was gray and tired.

She held out her hand to him. "William."

He took it and sat down beside her on the bench, clumsily, abashed by her sudden intimacy with him.

"Why, yes, ma'am?"

She rubbed her fingers against his and thought for a moment, and then spoke with slow deliberation.

"William, a lot will depend on you. He needs this rest. He needs it very badly."

"The Bishop. Yes. Yes, I seen that when you drove up to the river."

"I'm going home at the end of the week. I'm sorry, I must. But I want him to stay here for a while. He loves it here, and I hope it will do him some good. It has to do him some good."

"Well, now, what in the world?" Starns had never seen her so dispirited.

Rachael smiled quickly. "Oh, nothing so serious. I'm just fussing. But he had, well, disappointments this last year. Nothing all that important, you understand, William, but he took them hard. The future means a lot to him, and his ideas about it and programs. You know."

"Yes, he always has something for somebody to do, that man," said Starns gently.

"But people don't always want to do it, William, and he can't always see it's not because of him. Anyway, he is tired and needs this rest. I'm depending on you to see that he gets it. Can you promise me that, William?"

"Yes. Surest I ever made. But there's no call for you to go back down the mountain. Both of you stay and do nothing at all, all summer. Now, why not?"

She lifted her hand from his and stood up. Absently she touched her shoulder, and Starns laid the shawl there and she pulled it close in to her throat.

"No. I will go home end of the week. He'll rest better alone." She stared at Saul and at the bitter smile on David's bearded face, then quickly shut the panels and turned the silver key.

After supper, under gleaming, softly glowing saucer lamps hung cunningly from chain pulleys on the sloping roof, Starns and Bishop Ames sat on the widened veranda of the mission. This was their time alone together, to go over their business, and everyone left them alone. It was the hour for rancher and foreman, officer and sergeant, architect and builder, bishop and deacon.

It was clear. Bits of sharp starlight pierced the thin, frayed sheets of mist passing overhead, and the dark slopes were quietly stirred by cautious creatures testing out the spring night and what it held for them. Noises of dogs and children and pots and kitchen axes traveled from one end of the valley to the other. The Bishop sniffed the dry, comforting scents of evening smoke with pleasure, sitting in one of the rockers while Starns sat on the veranda flooring, his back against one of the post beams at the steps, a large leather-covered ledger in his hands.

In six years the porch, now veranda, had been rebuilt and added to four times, just as the whole mission four times had been gone over from post top to foundation stone, joint by joint by matching joint, every log, board and peg shored up, repaired or ripped out and replaced, on Starns's barest suspicion of its fiber. And, every time, something was added, something got changed about. The veranda now, from the Bishop's chair, spread wide and spacious to its outer corners, where shady vines clutched a lattice framework. Six sturdy chairs, with rockers curved like scimitars and with great flat armpieces, their backs ornamented by carved leaves with graceful stems, sat regally down the veranda in a leonine row. Starns had fashioned the first one, and when he'd finished and sat trying to carve a little leaf on the back of it, he became aware of Cardell Larman's black eyes on his knife. Since then, one a year, Cardell made the chairs and discovered in his idle, relaxed hands an agility with blade and wood that made Starns whistle. Bishop Ames sat rocking in the newest and mort ornate of these chairs, sniffing the evening smoke.

There were fourteen regular students living at the Valle Sanctus mission now, candidates for the ministry. A few were mountain born, from the richer lowland settlements, but most came from other parts of the state and two or three from the north, drawn to the mission and its work. With Billy Cobb, now ordained, wearing a hectic red beard about his pale cheeks which strangely enough only made him look younger, they ran the mission under Starns's supervision.

They taught a day school of forty-seven mountain children, boarding thirty-five of them during the winter. They rode out with Starns and Billy Cobb on a sixty-five-mile preaching circuit. They studied the rudiments of medicine Starns had laboriously culled from experience and a strange assortment of texts, and kept up a rough, ten-cot hospital with a thick pine table familiar with blood and bone. They kept the profitless mission store in full supply, though it was run by Jimmy Rode, hired and paid and forbade any cheating, which was hard on him. They learned their sacred theology and their Latin from Billy Cobb, and from the long, detailed sheets of instruction sent up each month by the Bishop.

And then, four hours out of each day, they saw to the mission buildings and worked the land, sweating in the big barn and in its outlying pens of pigs and chickens and goats, herding the growing stock of sleek cattle, pruning the fruitful orchards of apple and peach and cherry, following the stooping, balding figure of William Starns out over the entire reach of his mission kingdom, three hundred and fifty-five acres now of wheat and buckwheat, of sturdy maize and coarse barley, of potatoes and beans and clover and hay and the long, soldierly rows of choice, sound-headed cabbages he so loved and prized.

Bishop Ames, wherever he preached now, managed with considerable skill and sometimes strained invention to mix into his sermons the image of the mountain mission. He pulled it miraculously from unlikely texts, and it lurked behind the polished arguments of his science, theology, like a philosopher's birthplace. The donations from congregations left stricken and starry-eyed by his oratory paid all expenses, and with enough left over during the year he went to New York to buy their first stock of cattle and have them shipped down from Pennsylvania.

The Bishop sniffed and rocked. "All right, Starns," he said, and Starns opened the big, leather-covered ledger.

"Well. Ah. From September first until January first."

He cleared his throat self-consciously and read.

"Baptisms, sixteen. Confirmations, ten. Marriages, six. Burials, eight. Offerings, four dollars and fifty-eight cents. Divine services have been held at the following places, that is, not counting the ones here at the mission. On September the tenth at Henry Thorne's store above Carson's Fall, and there one person was received. On September twenty-second, in front of a cabin owned by a Mr. Hartfoot, I don't know just where but it's marked on the big map inside. There no one was received, but many stood and listened and received our talk in a kindly way. On October the eighth..."

A child ran across the mission yard, a jangling bucket jumping in his hand. Bishop Ames watched the sure-footed little shadow go by in the clear night and then closed his eyes and rocked the big chair.

On his third visit he had mentioned to Starns that it was not necessary that he verbally account to his Bishop for every activity of the mission during his absence, but he got such a look from Starns then that he never said it again. He could have told Starns that he trusted him as he would trust an archangel, but not even that would have taken the place of this verbal, minute, yearly accounting. It was an excruciating performance, for it tallied each sacrament, each service, each lesson, each penny, each nail, and though Starns sweated while reading it out, it was a necessary agony, crucial to his well-being. So Bishop Ames sat and tried to listen carefully to it all, sometimes succeeding, but not on this night.

Pluck from the mind, he thought, the rooted sorrow. But therein the patient must minister to himself. But canst thou not, but therein the patient must minister, but canst thou not?

"...on November the twentieth, at a farm owned by Mr. Norwood Ackly, which is twenty miles up east ridge from the Watauga. Billy Cobb preached for me, as I was sick in the throat. He sang the chants, and we were pleasantly welcome. Mr. Ackly has visited the mission twice since then, and his farm is now on the circuit. He has been supplied with number-three line of medicines, and with ten copies each of gospel, hymnal and prayerbook, which he can't read but wanted anyhow. On November the twenty-fifth..."

Pluck from the mind, thought the Bishop, drawing in the smell of evening smoke, listening to the night of the darkened valley, and wondering how long it would take the surrounding mountains to calm him down, to give him that belief that nothing lay beyond them, to give him again his love and affection for fellow humans learned only here, in this savage country of animals and mountains. How long this time? Longer, surely? When? Pluck from the mind the rooted sorrow.

His eyes followed the spill of lantern light out to the yard and then went on past it, into the darkness and up to the peaks, lying shrouded but there, his memory of their shape giving him sight that pierced the night. The wind moved past the veranda and he thought with delight of the land it stirred, thought how envious a Frenchman he knew once would be of this utter, unforced nonchalance, of this giant refined indifference, forever out of the reach of men, no matter how hard they tried to feign it, this superb and brutal elegance of the great mountains.

He sighed and pressed his head against the carved headpiece of the rocker. Tiny, spiteful figures danced on his brains. They stamped their feet with vexation and puffed up their chests like men in a fight or in a useless argument. Marcus Sales, now priest to the largest congregation in the state, stood on his brains and looked at him balefully. With him stood a long line of little men and women, and, as when he spoke to them, their mouths came open and then clamped shut as if they were biting something. He thought of the tedious parades of women, well fed and nothing else and on the borders of derangement because of it, talking to him endlessly, reciting the confused, senseless litany of their boredom and despair. He thought of his fellow bishops and clergymen, and his increasing lack of contact with them, his slow realization of the depth of their jealousy and rancor for his ideas, his office, and, above all, his hopes.

He listened for his heart, heard it too loud and too quick in the cavern of his chest. When he raised one hand from the flat armrest, it shook. He watched it. He shifted his weight in the chair, testing the taut wires strung through his stomach.

On his brains the tiny people fretted and vexed themselves and him and each other, their faces dark with envy and spite. He was weary of them, weary to the bone of their suspicions and petty hatreds, utterly tired of those people, the fearful, vicious creatures who can only gain their repose by the judgment of others.

Heal me, mountains. Animals, teach me to love man again.

Bishop Ames was a lover of poetry, and when he visited the mission and sat on the porch after supper, he tried often to compose it himself. He always ended by embarrassing himself and opening his mind to bits and pieces of other men's work. On this night he remembered devotions by George Herbert, whose life and works he admired, saying some of the words silently with his lips, letting them sift and mingle and come fresh, not as written but as remembered.

He listened to his heartbeat, to George Herbert, to the grinding cadences of Starns's report and to the valley wind.

He rocked and remembered, Yet now in age, I bud again, after so many deaths I live and write, once more smell the dew and rain, and relish versing.

George Herbert, he remembered, died when he was young, but foresaw that experience for an aging, tired bishop. Nahum Ames relaxed in the big chair, into a sudden moment of grace. A warm swelling rose moist in his chest, hushing the beating heart, and his handsome, strained eyes blinked tears.

Oh, my only light, it cannot be, that I am he, on whom thy tempests fell all night.

He sat very still in the rocking chair and raised his hand. It did not shake. In the darkness beyond the mission the great peaks seemed to bend to his gaze. The wind urged him forward.

Will You come into my heart and arm again? Can it be?

"Marriages, three. Burials, four. Offering, two dollars and thirty-nine cents. That's all, Bishop. Tomorrow we'll do the store finances and some of the farming, if there's time."

2

CIRCLE FOUR

Jimmy Rode

It worked out slick as a lizard. And James Rode, that's me, has his place now, sits where he should in this valley.

Now, I had commenced to ponder it when he didn't leave, when he stayed up here. It got on into summer, and there the man still was, in the house there, living in that big back bedroom made into a place for him to handle his books and do his writing and all. His woman went home, too, long before, but he stayed on, and I pondered it.

So whenever he'd come in the store, I'd prick ears and listen. I seen how the man was living in close to hisself more and more. Ye could see him come to silence with us and not wish to squander his opinions. One day he got powerful vexed at something somebody said just to be pleasant, and talked long and loud about it, but made no sense at all. He was talking something clean another way from that little joke or whatever it was, and when he come to hisself and seen the fact, he got beety red and mumbled something and left quick. Now, James Rode is nobody's blind man. I knowed something was out of the barn, all right.

Then, there was the preaching. He didn't do much at first, because we all figure if preaching must be, let Starns, he's the one. Now, I have had my troubles with William Starns, and he has pestered me to screaming more than once, but a man can partake of his words. Afterwards ye know what he has said, and it makes sense most of the time. So it was Starns preached most of the way, and the Bishop only some.

Well back when we was about knee deep in August, there was this big call for everbody. Starns rang the chapel bell on that big post like he was making thunder, and I swear it sounded that way before he was through. Everbody came on down the slopes and we gathered. Then the Bishop, he got up and talked some more like the day in the store, and nobody knowed what it was. It took us some time to see it, but we did finally and commenced to listen close, because he was vexed, powerfully so we come to see, about the fact that we had only begun what was to be done up here in this valley. We had this whole lot more to do, he said.

It was that whole lot more that made everbody sit up, because he didn't mean work. He meant that we was all getting along too good and fine. He meant that we was to think about giving up a few things for the Lord, and changing our ways of looking at life.

Now, we all got that much, but ye couldn't tell just what it was he had in mind. He didn't say. He just kept on talking sacrifice and the changing of ways, and we all looked around flat-faced at each other and wondered what the man meant. I seen a chance for gain then, and took it.

I stood up and said right out that it didn't sound outlandish to me, that it was a fine way to talk, and how I wanted to give up something for the Lord but didn't know what, and could he help me? Well, he just looked right through me like I was a glass window, and I seen I didn't fool him, so I set down. But then he said maybe I would be doing something like that soon, and smiled at me. I got the jitters and my feet was hopping with curious taps on the floor, I was so about ready to bust to know what he was a-doing.

Well, after some more of that talk nobody knowed what it was, he got down to cases. Told us we was to live this new life, a way that would please the Lord. Said we was to march on out of these here swamps we was in, swamps of riches, and that to begin with there would be some changes in the mission and we'd be told about them later, but that for now it would start with me.

I smelled a loss of some kind to that somehow, and I said, "Well, why me?" and he said, "You will see tomorrow, at credit time."

So the next day, when everbody was to the store there, to get credit against the harvests, he was there, too, and Starns, looking pretty sad about it but working for the Bishop like always, seeing things went right.

What I was to do was give away the damn stock. Most near all of it. When they told me that, I near had a heart failure, and it was a black day until later, when I come back into my own.

The people come to the store like usual, but when the first family's goods was laid out and John Barco saw all that he was a-getting, he said, "Hold on, here. Starns, I don't know as I want to sign up for all that. My crop just might not be this big this year."

Then Starns rubbed his head and started in real soft and easy to explain things, but couldn't seem to get it said. The Bishop waited and then cut in and, with no fol-der-ree about it, spelled it out like to little boys in the school. And Starns screwed up his ugly face and waited for trouble.

It come. The Bishop made it clear to John Barco that this was to be the end of the mission store. That most all of these goods was to be given away free to the poor and needy.

The poor and needy, Bishop Ames said, and Starns closed his eyes.

John Barco had a pair of new boots in his hand. "I will be damned if that's so," he said. "Poor and needy yeself!" and he flung them boots to the back of the store, where they hit the shelves and knocked things flying. Then he stomped out and stood outside with the others for a time, all of them muttering, Poor and needy. Then they all took to their teams and wagons and left.

"What did you want to say that for?" Starns asked the Bishop, and he didn't answer for a minute or two, but then he said, "Please pick up the boots, Starns. Mr. Rode can sell them at cost."

James Rode seen his move then, and I want to tell the world I didn't wait for nobody.

I said, "Well, I will *buy* them boots, Bishop, just to oblige ye."

Starns didn't like that, he knowed what I was after, and he said he didn't like it, and I said I was only trying to help, I didn't care who got them old boots. But that by the time they took things down to Stewart to sell at cost, the trip would be a loss, and especially if a lot of stock had to go. So I said that just to help out I would be willing to buy everthing right now, at cost.

"With what buy it?" said Starns, looking awful surprised, and I said, "Never you mind. I got it." Over the years I have managed to get a little here and save a little there. You can't keep a good man down.

Starns was about to cuss me some when the Bishop said, "All right. Mr. Rode, if by the day after tomorrow no one has taken what we offer, if by then we have anything to sell, you may have it all at cost, sir."

Starns stood there like a bull losing a heated heifer and tried to talk the Bishop out of it, but he held firm.

I said, "Don't get mad with me, Starns. You heard the Bishop."

So that begun it, and now it is finished fine. Six years ago Starns closed me out by setting up that mission store and that heavy credit and I had to go work for him. Well, now I have me some stock again, and nobody else to sell but me. I have moved it all back into my own place now, and will deal as I damn well see fit. James Rode is nobody's milksop, and he will do business as men ought to do business, hard and sharp right down there on the counter and not in no ledger book somewheres.

And the people here, they will come back to my store at night, to sit and ask me about things, because I will be the man to tell them, from my perch in the world of business and high finance, yes, and there will be no hundred-fifty-year-old Jacob Larman to lord it over me neither. I'll do that myself, in his place which is mine now, and tell them what is what, and they will listen.

Juba

My boys come home some time ago.

I was carrying from the spring when I seen them standing the yard, and them supposed to be helping Mister Starns that day. I commenced to lay into them, but they said yes, they had been there and had come back. Tate come out of the cabin and listened and then said, "Well, Juba, looks like they don't need no more help down there at the mission."

"Well, why not?" I said to the boys.

"Don't rightly know," said Lafe.

"Pa's right," said little Tate. "Bishop said so."

I thought it sounded funny. "What did Mister Starns say?"

"Nothing."

"Well," I says, and then they went in the cabin with Tate.

That was some time ago. Now Tate and the boys are thick as fleas again, and they don't farm hardly at all, just drink the corn and go hunting. It bothers me, it does.

Not because of Tate. He is an old fool but not so bad. He is good to our boys and all, but it was Starns, you see, could be counted on. I could count on him teaching them boys things they'll never get from Tate, good man though he is, just foolish.

No, they'll never get it. I recall a few years ago, one fine, sharp morning in the turning of the bright leaves, Mister Starns was here and went hunting with the boys just for a short turn down the slopes. They come back without a shot, but just when they stepped in the yard, a big old grouse thundered up and Lafe shot him at tree height and the bird fell and Lafe whooped.

He run off to get it, yelling away the hound we had then, who'd a-gobbled it like a lost chicken. Starns went with him and they was in the brush there where it fell for some time. When they come walking back, Lafe had a powerful stare in his eyes, down at the bird he had in his hand. When they got up to the porch, Starns took the bird and hefted it, said, "Your boy has a good eye, Juba, he can shoot. Here's a fine grouse for the table tonight." Then he give Lafe back the grouse because it was his, and Lafe give it to me to pluck and cook.

Now, that little thing there of the handing about of that bird, it wasn't much, I know, but it was the way it was done. It was done in a soft way that pleased me. He done it, Mister Starns, and he smiled at me when I took the bird, when I seen that my boy Lafe understood it wasn't him killed that grouse, but that the grouse was delivered to his hand by what laws there be of this life, just as he, my boy Lafe, would one fine day be delivered into the hand of that other hunter hisself. And that it was proper, and right, when he handled his kill, to do it with some thinking on the matter and some gentleness, too, against his own day, when it would not be so fine for him, and brave.

Mister Starns, passing my boy a dead bird, put that in his hand, too, without a word. And Lafe, he understood it and give me the bird for the fire with such grace I was a happy woman that whole week.

Now, Tate, who is good a man as there is but foolish, he takes the boys out and they shoot up anything they see and come back like the king and his men, dragging in whatever they've been lucky enough to hit, and sit around then, big men together, talking about what they'll get tomorrow, what mighty doings await their pleasure and deadly aim.

And me, I watch them, and I wonder, I do, what has happened to Mister Starns, why he don't come to see us no more.

Cora

When the leaves turned and the red and gold run all up and down the slopes, I went up to the old home one day to visit with Ellen and Hester, who is Shad's young wife now. I was with them when Cief fell from the loft of the old barn. We heard him holler, and I give Jacob to Hester to hold and run out there and come on Cief lying in the barn.

He was piled up in the hay and seemed to be getting hisself untangled all right, but when he seen me he laid back like some old scarecrow, half in and half out, and I couldn't help but giggle. But then he let out his old bellow, and I knowed he was hurt.

It was his shoulder. I couldn't tell what was wrong, or where it was busted, and he just laid down there whimpering like when he was so little and none but me to suffer him.

Ellen come and Hester with Jacob, and I told them I would go down to the mission for Starns. They said but no, that Earl and Shad and Cardell was down to the Watauga, had took both horses and the mule and both sleds.

I said, Well, I have walked it before this many a time, and told them not to move Cief, and took on down the slope to the mission.

I run at first, but then walked. It got far into the afternoon, and I knowed we'd never get back afore dark, not the way I was going. I was so slow, and the rocks and stobs hurt my feet. I wondered then at the times, just yesterday they all seemed, when I run that slope top to bottom a mile a minute, day or night.

Once I just had to stop. I lay flat down in some balsam shade and had to rest.

And I missed them times when I run the slopes, the way Jean does now and Jacob will. I lay there missing them times of chasing and scrambling wild up and down, over creek beds and balds. When Harlan first come up to the old home the midwinter night he held me and give me Jean, just before it I run out into the woods and tore up the snow, and he stood watching me at the door until I went back to him, my feet and hands and face red and my hair wet.

I got up then and walked on, mad. That was no way to be. Because there was other things to miss, too. The way we lived then, not so fine to think about now, and how benastied my own life was until Starns come and took me and Cief to hisself for a time, and then I got awful mad at myself. How terrible it would be, Cora, I thought and knew, if ye still had to scramble and run, like in them days of young wildness. What if ye still had to do that, changed as ye are, now? I was mad at myself, then, for missing it.

I recalled then the day I married Harlan and come to the life I live now. The day before, the Bishop had talked to us a lot, and his wife was there on the porch with us, me and Harlan and Jean, too, though we wasn't married yet. I watched her look at her husband the way she did, listening to ever little word and smiling when he said something she thought was good. She had on a long wavy dress with little dots peppered on it, turned about here and there with ribbons and fastened to her in a fine way. Her bonnet was so clean and new. She stood there without no airs at all, but so straight and easy, watching her husband talk. I felt my own dress then, and seen how the three of us looked like three tough chickens out of the pen and lost. So that night I scrubbed Jean till she yelled murder and death, and made Harlan help and then go to it hisself. That night we went down to service, and come into the chapel there and sat with the Barcos, and everybody looked and didn't know me, and I felt better about things a good deal more than usual.

When service was over, Mrs. Ames, she stopped me and talked to me right out and said I was a lovely woman and mother. Said that to me, snarly bitch Cora Larman, standing there holding Harlan's bastard child.

Then the next day we was married. And everybody who come was washed and scrubbed to their eyeballs. A body couldn't smell the flowers for the soap. It was the cleanest group of humans ever gathered, so Starns said, who was jittery because it was his first wedding as well as mine.

I thought about that, and did not regret it, and moved on slow and steady, and soon I come to the mission. I hadn't been down since the end of summer, when the day school was broke up, and hadn't seen Starns since then, neither.

There wasn't nobody in the mission house when I called. The big porch was bare and I wondered about Cardell's pretty chairs. I stood there and called again and then somebody said, Yes, yes, and I seen a man's head sticking out of the chapel door.

I went over and told him. He didn't seem like he knowed what to do, so I told him what to do, get Starns. He said, "Well, I'll see," and went back in.

I thought I had seen him down here before, but, dressed the way he was, I couldn't tell. He had on a long black dress thing, and a big white rope was tied about his waist, with knots from it hanging down. He'd cut his hair real short, too. I reckoned him to be one of them young fellers the Bishop brung down in the summer, but I didn't worry about it much, I wanted Starns to get on up to Cief.

So I stepped up and on in the door. All the men, they was in there, kneeled for prayer. The Bishop was standing up before them, dressed that same way. His hands was clasped hard and his eyes shut tight. There was big hollows, dark as holes, in his cheeks.

The man I'd talked to was just standing, not doing nothing. I poked him in the back, said, "Go on! Tell them to get Starns."

The Bishop heard it and opened his eyes. He looked like a man who has just bit open a hard, sour nut. The man stammered and stuttered out that I had come to see Starns about some man who'd fallen and hurt his shoulder.

"Not some man," I said. "Cief."

Then I seen him turn around from them that was kneeling. It was Starns, and he was dressed the same. He stood up.

The Bishop pointed to the man I'd poked. "Brother Horace, you may go with her," he said. "You are able."

"Bishop," said Starns, and everbody looked at him then, Starns, like he'd said something wrong.

The Bishop sighed and looked pained about it and said, "Brother Horace can go." He looked at Starns the way ye do when ye talk to a child ye love but must punish. "Brother Nestor, you have been too many times away from us. We need you here. Brother Horace?"

"Yes, Father," said the man I'd poked.

"Hold on, here," I said, and then Billy Cobb got up and came to me, and said soft, Now, Cora. Little Billy Cobb, a scared, milky-faced boy when I seen him first, now telling me, Now, Cora. I pushed him out of the way.

I said, "Bishop, I want Starns."

He said, real soft and pained about it, said, "Brother William, take Cora out now."

Brother William was Billy Cobb, and he said, Now, Cora, and this time I pushed him hard and he sat down on the floor.

"Don't nobody now Cora me no more!" I said, mad. "Starns, Cief's busted his shoulder and is lying in the barn yelling for you, not nobody's brother. And this here is Cora, not nobody's sister neither, and you come on!"

I wished then I hadn't yelled that out so mean, like the snarly bitch again, because Starns looked more miserable then than I ever seen human man. Standing there in that black dress that didn't fit him nohow, his bony shoulders all humped up with it and his baldy head sticking out like an onion, he was just swimming in misery.

He looked to the Bishop, whose eyes was closed again.

"Bishop," he said. "I will have to go. Tell me I can."

The Bishop commenced to pray again, and the rest jerked their heads down and kneeled praying with him in words saying I don't know what, because I had never heard them before.

Starns watched the Bishop for some time and then moved out of the pew there, not one of them men pulling back theirselves to make it easy for him to pass.

He come up to me and said, "All right, Cora. You got a sled?"

I said, "No, Starns. And I'm sorry if..."

He said, "We'll take mine. Come on."

He went and got out of that dress, and we went on. He didn't say nothing all the way.

We got there just after dark.

In the barn, Cief looked at him, hopeful, and Starns said, "Well, Cief, what have you gone and done to yourself this time?" and it come out harsh.

I said, "Starns, I have not meant to make nobody mad."

Cief whined then, and Ellen looked awry at Starns, and he shook his head. "I'm sorry to be this way, Cora," he said. "Don't pay me no mind. Go get them books from my bags now, and, Ellen, get us some more light."

It took him about an hour. He felt Cief's shoulder and felt it some more, and then took a long time in the books. Then he was ready, and he smiled then for the first time.

"Cief, I swear," he said, "you ain't broke nothing. Hold on, now."

He commenced to move Cief's shoulder a little. He looked into that book he says a man wrote about Indian medicine and then got Cief over on his stomach and pressed all along his backbone and then pounded him and kneaded him. He got Cief up, and Cief moved his shoulder and looked at it sheepish, wondering why it didn't fall off.

So Ellen cooked a big meal for him, and Starns ate it smacking and slobbering. Ellen cooks a good and tasty meal, but I'd never seen Starns eat like that. When I said it must have been some time since his last meal, he laughed and said no, it was just that he hadn't lately been able to eat the way he wanted, with noise and some appreciation.

He took his coffee out on the porch and I went out with him, carrying Jacob. Ellen and Hester and Cief stayed inside, and it was me and Starns and little Jacob then, out watching the night all clear and starry, with no mist at all. Them stars was sharp and glittery, and Starns sat and looked up at them, his worries passing across his face, one after another.

I said, "Starns, I could have swore Cief was hurt bad."

He said, "He was scared, Cora. You come in on him there, and it was like him when he was young again and kept hurting hisself. You know how it was. He's all right now, and don't worry about getting me up here, I'm glad you did."

He leaned against the post there where Cief used to sit and watch me play. I sat in Grandpa Jacob's old chair and held little Jacob up to suck. There wasn't enough, I didn't think, but he went on to sleep anyhow, and me and Starns sat there at the old home under them stars.

He was so glum, it bothered me bad. I was trying to think up something to say when we heard hounds down in the valley.

I wondered about it to him, and Starns smiled then, a trifle, and said, "Possum." I said, "Shoot, how can ye tell?" and he said, smiling and musing, "Well, it is Clayton Gaines's pack. You hear that one hoarse barking there, like a cow?"

I listened, and he cocked his head, smiling, and I heard it.

"That's old Bob," said Starns. "That's Clayton's old yellow-eyed hound Bob he swears is twenty-three years old. That dog is cautious, I'll tell ye. So if he is out with the pack, then ye know there is nothing more dangerous than possum. So it's possum." He smiled on for a while, thinking about that hound, I reckon, then it faded off his face and he was glum again.

I felt so for him. "Oh, Starns," I said, "what's wrong with the Bishop?"

He looked at me then and just nodded and asked if Harlan wouldn't be fretted about me off from home this late. I said, yes, I had told him I'd be back tonight, and he'd most likely come up soon to take me home, and Starns said, Oh, good.

Then I felt worse, because the man had as good as told me not to step where I didn't belong. He was right. A woman asking "What's wrong, what's wrong?" is a trial, so I stopped that.

I held up little Jacob and said, "Lord, he's a-growing, Starns. This boy is on his way, he is. Reckon he'll live as long as Grandpa Jacob? The way he has commenced here, ye'd think he was knowing he would live that long and was anxious to get it over with. Yes, Jacob. How about that, Starns? You think he'll live as long as Grandpa Jacob?"

Starns just stared at them glittery stars. "Cora," he said, "hush."

Harlan

I was out with Jean. On the slopes we seen Starns. He waved and come riding over to us.

I could tell even afore he was close that he was feeling low. There has been trouble down at the mission house since the leaves commenced to turn, so Cora says, and things ain't going to suit Starns at all. I allowed Cora must be right, because I could see Starns was not riding easy, he was stiff in the saddle and handling his horse a lot rougher than he usually does.

I told Jean to speak nicely to him when he got to us, and she said why. I said Never mind why, just do it, and she said was it because he's been feeling sick lately and it would make him feel better, and I said Yes, that's why we will speak nice. Then she told me she reckoned that was always the best reason to speak nicely, no matter who it was. She is a smart trick now.

Just afore he got to us he called out, "Harlan, have you and Jean seen Bishop Ames this morning?"

I yelled, "No, we ain't, Starns!" and Jean, she sung out, "No, we ain't, Starns! How are you, Starns!"

He shied his horse around sideways to us and leaned down from the saddle to take the little hand my Jean was a-holding up to him.

"I'm just fine, Jean," he said. "How are you?"

"Fine as I need to be, I reckon, Starns," she said, smiling up at him with her face squinty and her nose wrinkled up, and on her his eyes went pleasant.

Yes, my Jean is a smart trick now. Ten year old and as pretty as a yellow flower in a red pot. Her hair just will get longer and longer, and so blond now it goes shiny white in the sunlight. Her eyes are blue like a high-meadow gentian, and her little arms and legs have growed out round and strong but soft and slender, too, like willows. She is a joy to her pore miserable daddy, she is that.

Starns took pleasure in her greeting, as everbody does, and then commenced to tease her some, which she just loves, and reached down and pulled her hair a trifle.

Jean squealed and picked up a make-believe rock and held it ready, and Starns put up his hand and said, "Look out, now!" and she make-believe throwed it at him and he grabbed his bald spot and yelped, "Oowee! I quit! I quit!" Jean laughed at him and come up to me and took my hand.

Starns set back in the saddle and looked around at the slopes. His face emptied its pleasure looking at them, and he stopped smiling.

"Well, Harlan," he said, "the fact is, Bishop Ames went riding this morning without telling nobody. Ah, there's some things we need him for."

"We'll shore tell him if we see him, Starns," I said, and Jean, real sober, said, "We will do it, Starns, for certain."

"I'm obliged to you both," he said, and swung his horse to face up country and rode on.

Jean watched him go, and then said, "He didn't tease with me as long as he used to. Why is he feeling sick?"

"I don't know, honey," I said. "Come on, now."

Jean thought about it some as we went on, but soon it left its place in her thinking and she was free of it and took off running. She is like that. Will walk a ways with me, then go like the wind, then come dead stop and stand there like a dog wondering if the next piece of wind will have scent, then tear out again and stop again, her head cocked to one side, listening and looking at goodness knows what. I take such pleasure in her doing that, and I watch her and wonder what it is my child does and I can't know. But it affects me powerful all the same, and when she takes off a-running again I go with her and the wind plays my face the same as hers.

When we got to my squirrel tree, I said, "Fool about where ye please, but not too far. And when I call, you answer. And when you come back, call out all the way so I'll know it is you and not something else coming up on me. You hear, now?"

She endured all that with this great patience, and said, Oh yes, like I was the fussiest old woman.

"Oh, yes, nothing," I said. "You come creeping and I'm like as not to shoot me a Jean instead of a squirrel. Then it's Jean soup we'd have to have tonight, and who wants that?"

She squealed and laughed and run off.

I let Jean go when I'm out with her. She knows what is on these slopes and what she is doing here, and she has no fear of it. That is what counts, and I see she has it. Now, me, I'd perish with fear and the pounding heart if I didn't have my rifle gun, but Jean loves it up here, and that is better than any gun any man ever bought or made.

I settled down and got my back eased against my tree the way it is supposed to be, and felt my ease coming to me, and looked around for a squirrel or two. Soon one come skittling along a branch, tail sassy like Jean's hair. I yawned and thought of her, and called.

She called back and the squirrel shot off the branch and was gone. I smiled and took my ease.

After some time I reckoned that I had better shoot something to take home or Cora would get mad. But I didn't care to disturb myself. The sun was slipping down in and through the fine colors of the turning leaves and was good and warm. There was some chill in the wind but not too much, and it swept low, pushing at the leaves, making them hop and dance. Their shadows just washed the ground, that's the way it looked. I was content to lie right in the middle of it, with Jean close by, but I knowed Cora would say, Well? and I knowed I couldn't tell her I spent the day lying down getting washed by no shadows. So I sat up and put my eyes to it.

Mr. Squirrel come soon and fidgeted about on a root not far off, but I couldn't see him clear because of some brush. I waited until he scatted up the trunk, and when he popped up in a crotch between trunk and limb, I had him, just right, on my sights.

Then I seen Jean standing right there. I wasn't aimed that close to her, but oh, Lord, it scared me.

I got up quick. "Now, Jean, hellfire!" I yelled. "You come here! Didn't I say call when you come up on me, didn't I say that? You come here and answer me!"

But when she come, I seen something was wrong. She was all puzzled, and her little lips was white as white ashes.

"Honey, what?" I said when she held out her hands to me.

"I found Bishop Ames," she said. "But I was scared to tell him. I was scared to tell him. Even if I did tell Starns I would, I was scared."

She held my hands tight.

"You come tell him," she said. "I know I told Starns I would, but you do it."

I said all right, where was he, and she said Come on and led me a ways, saying we'd best be quiet, quiet.

We went through some brush and down past the creek there and back yonder behind it till we got to a stand of chinkpins. She pointed through them, and said, There.

"Stay here," I said.

I couldn't tell just what he was doing at first, because of the brush, but it was something funny. I moved in a ways.

He was on his knees there in this little clearing, like a little meadow sort of place. He had a big black coat spread out and he was on top of it. He didn't have no shirt on, but was wearing boots and trousers. The sun was full on him, and ye could see the sweat shining. He was making noises like he was hurt.

I got closer. His head jerked back a bit and he hollered, but real low.

I got closer yet, then I seen it mixed with his sweat and I knowed what it was.

The man had in his right hand a piece of rawhide. The ends of it was all shredded up, and tiny little beads was fixed to them ends. He was kneeling on his coat there and whipping hisself with that thing.

Now, I know about this. There is something to it sometimes, I know that. I feel like beating myself a lot of times, and sometimes my Cora and me will slap a little, when it makes things better.

But this wasn't like that. This was all thought out and calculated, and he was too old a man and too fine a man to be doing that to hisself, I thought. It did something to my innards when I seen what ran with the sweat on his back.

Jean come up quick beside me and grabbed my hand, and just then he raised that thong. It whistled like birdsong and slapped along the other cuts on his back and we seen them black buckshot bead things bite into him.

I whispered, "All right, that's enough of this. Come on."

"But Starns said to tell him," she said. "I'm not scared to, now you're here." And afore I could stop her, she sung right out, "Bishop! Starns wants to see you!"

"Jean, hush!" I said, but he had heard it. He sat back on his haunches and looked at the brush where we was, glared at it. It scared me so, that look.

"What?" he said, hoarse as a cow. "Who's there!"

He looked at the brush, his face all twisted. I had seen that look before. Long ago I knowed it. From the time Pa took sick I seen that twisted look on Ma's face, when she made Margaret and me conjur over him. She looked just like that, trying to hex his dying body to life again.

I picked Jean right up and off the ground and moved back in the brush and out of that place. When we was hid from him completely, I set her down and said, "Home."

We went down, and for a time we heard him calling in that hoarse voice, "Who's there! Who's there!"

Halfway to the cabin we seen Starns, with Billy Cobb this time, riding a ways off down to the valley. I shot off my rifle gun and they seen me waving and slapped reins up to us.

When I told him what we had seen, Billy Cobb went pale and

bowed his head. Then he had to raise it and move, because Starns had already whacked his horse and jumped it into the brush like it could fly.

From the yard of my cabin, standing there later on talking to Cora, we seen them taking him back down to the mission. Starns was walking the Bishop's horse with the Bishop up on it, and Billy Cobb led Starns's horse. Sometimes the Bishop would set up all right in the saddle and sometimes not. But I don't reckon he wanted nobody to help him, so it seemed, because once he went over to one side and slipped right off. He would have fell flat if the horse hadn't stopped and he grabbed the stirrup. Starns run to help, but I reckon they had words or something, because Starns stepped back then and waited. The Bishop hauled and pulled hisself back up on that horse, though even from where we was we seen it was a-killing him to do it. When they finally got to the mission, he got down by hisself, it seemed to us, and went on in the door.

"Harlan, Harlan," said Cora. "What is wrong down there?"

I said I didn't know and didn't want to know.

I walked down to my fence and stood looking over the valley. The clouds was rolling about and I followed the sunlight they let fall here and there. Some of it went along and then spread out back of the mission, and I seen the graves then, brought to light and my eyes by the roaming sunshine.

And it brought Margaret to my mind again, and what she had always said about charms and spells.

3

FATHER NAHUM

SITTING on the edge of the veranda, Bishop Ames watched the sun go down over the western slope of Mary's Pass. Above the mission, stretching almost to the horizon but cut off just above it, clouds swirled in a confusion of changing winds. The sun hung just above the slope, beginning its blatant descent behind the darkening peaks. For an hour low winds had swept the valley, scouring away the mist, and Bishop Ames had watched the sun slip flaring from behind the cut edge of the cloudbanks, skipping dull red reflections off the seas of leaves, warming the chill, blue mountain dusk. He watched without moving, his eyes fixed on the sun, red now as the skin of an October apple, sat and watched it and did not move.

Billy Cobb and Starns walked into the yard and Billy Cobb began to unwind the rope from its hitch on the post. While he rang the bell for evening prayers, Starns sagged one shoulder against the post and looked through the dusk toward the veranda.

Bishop Ames sat with empty, upcurled hands in his lap, like an old, bent woman inscrutable on her evening porch. His handsome head was bent forward slightly, as if he were napping and dozing, but he was very much awake. His black eyes stared at the horizon, as if boring through to the core of its apple-red sun.

"Well, my dear sir," said Marcus Sales. "Why beat around the bush? We all know why we are here, at least generally. It is now time for some specifics."

Facing him across his parlor in Raleigh, a priest with white hair blushed and set his teacup down on a mahogany table. His name was Thackery Curry, and he had a small parish in Tarboro.

"You're right, sorry, sorry," said Curry. "Old men, Sales, old men do beat the bush. That's because they've seen some fearful things come out of it. But sorry, sorry, Sales."

In the room Curry was presented with a polite array of tight smiles. Marcus Sales smiled, too, thinking of Curry's age. He had been alarmed when Curry walked in, but now he was comforted by the old man's obvious immersion in his own age. Not far from downright senility, thought Sales, smiling at the old man. Curry's hair sprouted outrageously, like a white weedpatch, but his clean-shaven cheeks were gray and sunken, his mouth wrecked by whistling, ill-fitting dentures. And most grotesque of all was the pendant flesh of his throat. From a point just under his chin, a long, bloodless flap of skin hung down like the sweep of a valance curtain and was caught to his Adam's apple by his tight collar. The old man constantly rubbed and pulled at it, the gesture in the course of fifty years of meditation and perplexity having shaped it so, but the seventy-year-old hands that pulled at it were still strong, the bones firmly encased in hard flesh.

Sales thought he looked like an old turtle, which was not absurd because a lot of people thought so, too. A turtle, thought Sales, except not bald like he should be. Has that rampaging white bush up there instead. I never thought he'd have the strength left to drag himself here, but it won't matter.

The old priest's admiration of his young Bishop was well known. Bishop Ames had often visited Curry's small parish and stayed with him lengths of time irritating to some of the other, larger congregations. Now Curry sat at his ease and smiling, though around him, aloof from his aged nonchalance, the others had thought to make him feel out of place. They sat around the parlor watching Marcus Sales, propped up by stiff white shirts and dark suits, by pins and stays, gay ribbons and bright curiosity.

"Reverend Curry has mentioned that it is a very unusual thing to have such a meeting as this without the presence of the Bishop," said Marcus Sales. "Now, nobody in this diocese would want it that way more than I. But it is only because—"

"How can you talk to a man that's never here?" snapped Vida Sales, gripping her delicate teacup. "That's it, Reverend Curry. If he was just here, we wouldn't have to do this at all, perhaps."

"Yes, indeed," said Marcus Sales. "We must admit that here is the very center and crux of our problem, although we should not—"

"It certainly is," said Vida. "All he does now is send down pastoral letters from that mission house. Like Moses on the mountain."

"Vida," said Sales. "Ladies and gentlemen, my wife is a trifle vehement about the matter. Yes, you are, my dear. But yes, you are. Far be it from any of us to judge our Bishop."

"That's what I was beating the bush for," said Thackery Curry, sitting back and smiling.

"Nevertheless," Sales said quickly, "we cannot in good faith submit without an examination to what many, many good and reasonable souls consider and pronounce a, ah, severe theological indiscretion."

Curry put his strong old hands up in the air and waggled his fingers. "Yes, exactly, precisely, of course," he said.

The room stirred with the purposefully incoherent noises of righteous people reacting so that, if you wore God's ears, you could not tell which side of anything they were taking.

Sales spoke sharply. "Reverend Curry, if you wish it, we can postpone this meeting while you try to get Bishop Ames to come down from his mountain and attend it. Attend to anything else, for that matter. Do you realize, sir, that it is now the end of October, and still our Bishop has chosen to remain absent from his flock, and to communicate only by pastoral letters, which are in themselves very puzzling indeed, if not downright suspect, in the doctrines they propound."

Curry waggled his fingers. "Yes, that's it, all right," he said.

"Well, sir, what is it you want?" demanded Sales, exasperated.

"Well," said the old priest, peering into his cup, "some more tea, please, Mrs. Sales."

Marcus Sales smiled in pain and forced a laugh. He knew he had already stirred the indignation of the others, by calling the meeting itself, and that it was essential that they go away with the one unutterable thought he had for them. The proof he had for them had to be presented delicately and with great dignity. This great dignity, he feared, was being quietly tapped away by the old priest and his antics, and all that was carefully built up by the atmosphere of European teacups and Vida's new furniture and drapes was going fast.

"Well, I got something to say, if nobody else will!" said Mrs. Oscar Johnson. She was wife to prominence in Raleigh and firm holder of a central pew in Sales's church. Her dress was as plain as her speech.

"We all know," she said, "that we are in strange times. Funny things are going on. *The Christian Intelligencer,* to which I subscribe, said right out that the way they are carrying on in England now, we just as well better get ready to kiss the Pope's foot tomorrow."

Oh, dear, thought Marcus Sales, and he rubbed his eyes. His wife, however, sat up eagerly in her chair.

"That's right," she said quickly. "It says the same thing in the *Banner of the Cross,* to which I am a faithful subscriber. I have seen it in the last issue, which is right here in the house now."

"Well, but, ladies," said a sober, hawk-nosed young minister from Charlotte. "I don't believe the magazines go quite that far. One periodical, the *Churchman*—which, by the way, as far as I can tell, is certainly the most impartial of the group—seems quite favorably disposed. Indeed, the Oxford reforms now being debated by members of the mother church have attracted many impressive adherents from the highest stations of English life."

"Well, that may be," said Mrs. Johnson, glaring. "But I don't want to kiss no Pope's foot, even if some do!"

For goodness sakes, thought Marcus Sales, everything is going all to pieces.

"I think we must admit that there is disturbance, Reverend," said a stocky, methodical-eyed man, a minister from New Bern, addressing the young minister from Charlotte. "Unless I am mistaken, which I often am, just this past month a young man was refused ordination in New York by four examining bishops. The issue, I am certain of this, was doctrine propounded by the Oxford Tracts. Am I correct, Reverend Sales, on this matter?"

"You certainly are," said Vida Sales. "That's in the *Banner of the Cross*, too." She joined Mrs. Johnson and they both glared at the hawk-nosed young minister, who lifted his eyebrows and stared above their heads.

"Four bishops agreed?" said Thackery Curry. "Four? Great day!"

They ignored him, the ladies plunging into sacred debate and question.

"Reverend, what should we think about this?"

"Reverend, where does this diocese stand?"

"Reverend, what would Christ say?"

Same thing I would, thought the old priest. Help!

"Now, you see!" said Marcus Sales, grabbing his chance. "It is just such discord as this, just such bewilderment, that is the fruit of our Bishop's prolonged absence. We need him to make the decisions only he can make. We need him, and he is not here. I am not able to speak for him, but concerning the Oxford Tracts I can say that they are stressing a return to higher ritual and objecting to undue domination by the state. It would seem that this could not concern us in this country, but I lack the wisdom and authority of our Bishop, to whom alone such authority belongs, to make any definite statement."

His right hand, the palm still scarred and blackened in spots, reached to a side table and took up a set of papers. He thought it was time to begin.

"Seeing that Mrs. Johnson has kindly mentioned this matter, the Oxford disturbance, perhaps we can arrive at our own problems from a view of our friends' problems across the sea. I have here a sketch, a draft, of a paper to be finished by Bishop Ames, on this subject. It is a proposed history of the origins of the movement, and, though unfinished, our Bishop's familiarity with English ways make it very definite."

Thackery Curry said, "What are *you* doing with it?"

Sales blushed and looked in forced amazement at Curry. "Why, I have had to be his secretary since he left. Who else has a better right, after these confusing months, to bring to your attention something that I know, were he here, he would . . ."

Curry raised both hands, and waggled his fingers. "All right, all right, that's enough," he said. "I'm an old man."

"Very amusing," said Marcus Sales. "But I know my right and my duty, sir. I can only hope that you will know yours when you leave this house today. Ladies and gentlemen, shall I proceed?"

"Yes," said the righteous, united, on fire.

The paper began with the 1829 apology of the Bishop of London to the House of Lords for daring to oppose the Prime Minister who had been responsible for his appointment. It ended with quotations from Newman's *Tracts for the Times*.

It was, throughout, stamped with the flaming idealism of Bishop Ames. It brought him into the room and disturbed them by a vehemence of passion and accusation more severe and more savage than they had ever heard from him before, even at the height of any of his many crusades. He denounced the slovenly and disheveled state of sacred liturgy, scornfully attacked ecclesiastical cowardice before secular authority, and made specific mention of certain organizations and men in England who made, as he said, "a deceitful and disgusting living, highly comfortable to be sure, off the body of the church, who make no efforts for spiritual progress and allow no one else to do so."

It was a fiery defense of the Oxford Movement, and Thackery Curry, listening, pulling at his chin, was very sorry to hear it.

Sitting with them, Curry remembered himself sitting in St. Mark's church, bored, summoned and dutifully arrived to listen to the opening-gambit sermon of the new and very young Bishop of North Carolina. Curry had been against his election, and when he first glanced at Nahum Ames that day, he sniffed and thought, The whelp can't be a day over thirty, though he had heard the young man was then thirty-five.

He pulled at his chin and thought of the things waiting to be done at home. Only when Bishop Ames poured forth his first torrent of words from the pulpit of St. Mark's did Curry really look at him, look and then approve and then grin with that delight that fifty-year-old men can have when they realize someone can still make their last active years exciting.

Bishop Ames, in the pulpit then with eyes flashing and white sleeves billowing, his quick, silvery tongue not obscuring the fundamental grasp and power of his reasoning, gave not a careful tribute to his new diocese and his predecessor, but instead a ringing challenge to the state itself, demanding that it abolish a law then up before the courts, a law that punished thieves by the cutting off of one or both of their ears.

Thackery Curry, enchanted, thought he would have to find out about this young man, his new Bishop.

This he did by patient work in slow, casual conversation and post-scripts to letters to friends. Even before the Bishop came to realize the older man's regard for him and spent time with him in Tarboro, Curry knew as much about him as anyone in the state.

He knew that Nahum Ames came from one of the oldest families in America. Its founder, one Mordecai Ames, was born around 1609 and sailed into New Bedford harbor on the ship *Truelove* in 1635. In four years he was recorded as one of the freemen and landholders of the colony of New Haven. He died in 1648, leaving one son named, pro-saically, John, who was the father of another John Ames (1669–1738), who handed down the same name through three more generations until 1785, when the spell was broken and a firstborn son, father of the Bishop, was named, again, Mordecai.

He married and lived and farmed in his native state of Connecticut until the end of the century, when he became embroiled in much court litigation and, disgusted, sold his land and moved with his wife and chil-dren to New York State, near the mountains, where he built a large house and took up his farming again. Curry found out very little about this second Mordecai, father of Nahum, because the man's personal reputation and ways of life were dwarfed by the act of violence that brought his days to an end. His farm projects raised some comment, but only because of their imaginative, consistent failure. He would never admit the failure of his new farm methods, whatever they were, and ruined crop after crop by their use until, in 1815, he committed suicide by drowning himself in a creek that ran through his farm. He left ten children, the eldest being Nahum Ames, then eight years old.

In 1841, at the age of thirty-five, the Right Reverend Nahum Immanuel Ames came to his Bishopric after a vigorous and romantic youth. He had worked his way through common day schools and then gained admission to an academy at Lowville, in Lewis County. There his mind began to shape itself. His record was brilliant until his final year, when something went wrong and he was very nearly expelled in disgrace. Curry could never determine what it was, but guessed it was the old song of teachers who cannot bear their students' demands about the extracurricular realities that have frightened them into pedantry.

He left the academy and joined the U.S. Army, lying about his age. He received promotion to the rank of corporal and was offered later a decoration, which he refused. He was involved in a camp incident when a drunken fellow soldier attacked him with a steel pipe. He was forced to defend himself and did so with a hand spade, with which he penetrated the man's neck and killed him. He was acquitted by court-martial and honorably discharged soon afterward. In conversations with Curry, Bishop Ames never talked about the army or military life, and he was not happy when anyone else did.

He resumed his studies and prepared himself for college, determined to enter the ministry in the faith of his family, which was Presbyterian. He was enrolled in Hamilton College, Clinton, New York, but left within a year because of a nervous disorder, the nature of which Curry never determined. When he regained his health, he began a course of study that led to his priesthood in the Episcopal Church.

In 1832 he was ordered deacon by Bishop Mullen in New York City and, in the following year, priest, by Bishop Moore of Pennsylvania. His first charge was a coal-mining missionary station in Pennsylvania. He became briefly famous for a daring descent into a shattered mine shaft, and later made trips and speeches denouncing the conditions of the miners. Someone with an eye for his future intervened, and he was appointed Rector of Trinity Church, Philadelphia. He served a parish in Lancaster, Pennsylvania, and then went to New York as Assistant Rector of Christ Church, then Rector, St. Luke's, and finally, from that church, justly called the "Mother of Bishops," went to North Carolina, a bishop at last, carrying authority into a new country, where something might be done.

During this time in New York he plunged into a pleasing scandal that ended well, his furious courtship of Rachael Mullen, daughter of the Bishop of New York. Directly after their marriage they went abroad briefly, and returned and settled in New York. They had two babies within a year of each other. Both died at birth.

Then, in 1841, to the pulpit of St. Mark's in Raleigh, denouncing laws that cut off men's ears while Thackery Curry listened in delight, came the Right Reverend Nahum Immanuel Ames, S.T.D., LL.D., Bishop of North Carolina and twenty-fifth in the succession of the American Episcopate.

When Marcus Sales finished reading the Bishop's passionate defense of the Oxford reforms, he knew he would have no further problems about his meeting. Every eye in the room was fixed upon him, and they were the eyes of birds in awe of the snake. He saw no reproach in any of them for his reading of the Bishop's unfinished paper, and even Thackery Curry seemed hypnotized.

He knew he could go on. He put the manuscript down on the small table and picked up another.

"I will not comment on what has just been read to you," he said. "I believe this pamphlet says it very well."

He waved it before them, handling it with great care and respect.

"It has not yet been distributed to the public, due to the author's respect for this diocese. This, ladies and gentlemen, is the reason for this meeting. We must decide whether or not to allow the author justice in his conclusions."

In his scarred hands the pamphlet took on the value of a new gospel, or a treatise snatched from the fires of Alexandria.

"As you see, it is entitled, *An Examination of Superstition, being An Objection to the* Powers *Claimed by the Right Reverend Nahum I. Ames, Written by One who signs himself, A Layman of the Protestant Episcopal Church in America.*"

He looked at them from a very high place, and his pause ushered into the room the absent, powerful author.

"Ladies and gentlemen, who do you think this Layman of our Church really is?" he asked.

"Moses?" asked Thackery Curry mildly.

Marcus Sales looked dangerously at the old man. "I am shocked," he said. "Your irreverence is unheard of in a priest, and unbecoming a man of your years. And I am sure we are all growing very tired of it. This pamphlet, ladies and gentlemen, was written by United States Congressman Statius Collins. I suggest to you that the printed word of a man who has devoted his entire life to the service of our people and our nation is not to be lightly regarded."

"Statius Collins," said Curry, "stole a horse from a man in Tarboro once. Stole from behind the man's store, June twentieth, 1824. I saw him do it. But it is God who will punish him, as he will punish all men who speak well and do evil."

He looked at Marcus Sales, his ancient eyes burning.

While visiting Curry, the Bishop had once fallen ill. The doctor had pronounced it a nervous disorder brought on by overwork and to be cured by simple rest, but Bishop Ames was convinced that he was going to die.

He had spoken to Curry then of his childhood, told him wandering remembrances, half confession and half memoir, of his father's death and last days. His mother had been a very devout woman, and his father quiet and submissive to her piety in the home but not outside the farmyard.

On the day of his death the Bishop's father took the eight-year-old eldest child hunting with him, into the frost of a New England morning. It was not the first of their trips, and the boy both dreaded and welcomed it. He loved the traveling with his father, and the camps they made, and the talk they shared, but dreaded the kill and the brutality with which his father insisted on showing him the facts of life and death in the forest. On their last trip he had been forced to gut and strip the body of a deer, and the smell of its blood and raw hornroots he had endured while his father talked of his frustrations, of farm methods and treacherous weather and envious friends. He poured into the boy's ears all his bitterness, while he, the boy, gutted and stripped the body smelling of deer and death.

It was the next week, the Bishop told Curry from what he believed to be his deathbed, that he went out with his father for the last time. They had no luck and, before going back, stopped to cut some timber. The boy swung with all his might, to please his father. He tried so hard he did very badly, and his father railed at him and then spent a long time trying to teach him the use of the ax, smelling of the strong whisky he drank and, when tipsy, spilled down the front of his shirt. His father finally sat down on a log and watched him work, and then, smiling a warm and affectionate smile, told his son he was all right, that he would do fine. The boy almost fainted with happiness.

Then he sat and was quiet for a long time while the boy worked. When the boy looked up after slicing through one fallen log, his father was gone. He was very frightened and did not know what to do. He called, but got no answer. Then he ran toward fancied sounds and became lost.

When he came upon his father, brought by the sounds of cursing, he saw him standing by the edge of a newly dug ditch, muttering and swearing blasphemously. He hid in a thicket, and watched his father get into the ditch waist high and look about him at the little sticks and pegs with ribbons and streamers that he had posted in the dirt, very neatly and according to some scheme, around the ditch. The boy was puzzled and so interested in the sticks and pegs and colored cloths that he did not realize what was happening when his father set his feet wide apart and drew the razor-sharp hatchet he always carried at his belt in a shining, much polished leather holster. He saw only after staring and blinking that his father was hitting himself in the temple with the hatchet.

His father fell and got up again, still cursing. He rose up, again waist high, blood streaming down his chest, and, still cursing, chopped himself in the face until he collapsed again and disappeared into the ditch.

There was a creek twenty yards away. The boy pulled his father's body from the ditch, his feet stepping on the ropes and sticks and madman's colored cloth. His small weak hands grasped the heavy boots and he pulled his father's body to the water. He rubbed wet, cool mud on the agonized face and then pushed him into the water and watched the cold creek seal the wounds of his head.

Then he went back and got his ax and drove the wagon home and told his mother Father was lost.

A day later he heard as if from a great distance the proof of his father's death by drowning. Nobody thought much about the cuts on his face, but they knew for certain he died from water in his lungs. Then the boy felt rising in his childish heart a terrible rejoicing: Father, you are dead, I am rid of you!

After the Bishop told Thackery Curry this, the old priest stayed by his bed for four days, until he was well again.

"'. . . Therefore it seems beyond denial that he, the Right Reverend Nahum I. Ames, has, in the mountains of this state, instituted and enforced obedience to a monastic order, a blasphemous society within the sacred bounds of this our holy church, composed of deluded young men bound to his personal authority by the medieval vows of poverty, celibacy and obedience. He is known there as Father Nahum, his priest as Brother William, and his deacon as Brother Nestor, for some reason, and to each member of this society, called the Order of the Essenes from a pre-Christian Jewish society of "Healers," he has given for their raiment a black cassock, girding them from throat to ankle, in exact replica of that worn by the Romish Order of Jesus.'"

Marcus Sales, almost finished with the pamphlet, read quietly and calmly. His passion, cold and deadly, had not yet thawed from six years of resentment and icy shame.

"'Upon the altar of his mountain chapel, he allows a pyx, in which repose the remaining consecrated elements after communion, a practice of the Roman Church but disavowed and forbidden by our own. Committed to memory by every member of this Essenean Order is a manual of devotions, whose existence the Bishop, when I spoke to him in Valle Sanctus a month ago, emphatically denied. It has been recited to me by two different ex-members of this sect since then, young men who have rightfully forgone all practices of this misguided man. The manual contains, in language beautifully ornate and deceitful, prayers to the Saints, the Virgin Mary, and to the souls of the dead.'"

Marcus Sales looked at Thackery Curry. The old priest was sitting back in his chair, eyes closed, breathing calmly. But the hand that stroked the flesh of his throat trembled.

He read on, and into his cold voice now came the ugly, flat cadence of spite, of his fury against the idealistic Bishop and his wandering, picked-off-the-roads drifter who won the love and faith of people who had tortured and despised the Reverend Marcus Sales.

"'Father Nahum, then, has rejected voluntary confession of the penitent as sufficient for salvation, and insists, on pain of anathema, that each member of this Order of the Essenes submit to his ear enforced and regular confession of their sins, and, further, that until they receive his personal absolution and blessing, their certain destiny is damnation in the eternal fires of hell.'"

"Oh!" said the young hawk-nosed minister aloud, no color in his face at all.

Marcus Sales looked again at Curry, thinking, Well, how do you like that? and was comforted by the old man's visible shaking. The thin lids of his eyes now were closed, sad as those of a dove just shot from the air.

Through Curry's mind ran all the failures of Bishop Ames, the ambitious crusades attempted and almost won but aborted and frustrated at last. Slaves' churches, criminal law, education for the poor, homes for the insane . . . He heard the silvery tongue cry out for them.

Criminal punishment free from vengeance. Let the man stand up who has not lashed his horse and beaten his dog and cursed his wife and children out of his own torment.

Churches for the slaves. Let the man stand up who is himself free from bondage, who holds the right to forbid a mortal creature the search for his Maker.

Education for all children. Let the man stand up who in his heart truly wishes his son to live the same life he has lived.

Comfort for the insane. Let the man stand up who is certain of his own mind, who does not avoid the depth of the swamp, who does not hide from the black wind of confusion.

Curry saw him again, striding to the pulpit of some church somewhere only a year ago, eyes flashing, sleeves of the white robe billowing, breath short and jerky, mind and heart and being plunged into a fight for one state home for the insane, a fight he was to lose.

By the Providence of God, I am today the voice of the maniac deserted, oppressed and desolate, and today at least his piercing cry will get through the door of this Temple. I will not spare you, or myself, from the pitiful hopes of those poor crazed beings who face the corners of cells and stalls and cages, who lie in the foul waste of poorhouses and jailhouses. I will speak, and shriek their cries if need be, for some comfort to give human dignity to their misfortune and some hope of cure. Not, however, because I want only to tax you with their burden, but because, my people, I am afraid for you and for myself. Who among us is so strong that he may not become weak? Let the man stand up whose reason is so firm that it may not, in one hour, be overwhelmed by swirling madness.

Biting his lip, Curry remembered the flashing eyes and the billowing robe.

"'... Therefore, it is the duty of this Layman of the Church, as well as the call of this public servant, to object and utterly protest against such abuse of youth for whose religious instruction Bishop Ames is responsible. It is my hope that this earnest protest may bring to an immediate conclusion a chapter dark with strange perversities that may well have reached terrible depths in the immature minds and bodies of these unfortunate young men.'"

"Oh, my," whispered the hawk-nosed young minister in a blushing realization of what he heard.

Thackery Curry croaked, "Rubbish, Sales. That's rubbish and you know it."

Marcus Sales waited for anyone else who wanted to speak. No one did, they were too shocked to remember their own righteousness. Marcus Sales waited, sober pain on his face while in his heart a gleeful, destructive child hopped and whistled and swung a white rope that fired everything it touched. He waited, and then read on.

"'If, then, this man is not, as he claims, spiritual lord and master over us, subjecting us to the shiftings of his unlawful doctrines, if he is not, as he seems to believe, in a state of Papal authority over us, then I ask that we conclude this matter, and demand his immediate and final resignation. Not to do this is certainly to subject ourselves in passive submission before Roman superstition, and perhaps place our diocese and its faith at the mercy of a man, I greatly fear, who suffers from a dangerously unbalanced mind.'"

Sales finished and looked at Curry again, but the old priest's back was to him, at the door. He left and did not look back.

Bishop Ames raised his head. Gathered in front of the chapel, dark figures in the mountain dusk, stood the candidates for holy orders, waiting for him. He stood up, the hem of his long black cassock falling straight down to the ground, covering his sandaled feet.

Beyond the western slope of Mary's Pass the peaks still glowed, lit from behind by the last thrusts of the sunlight. A few clouds gleamed faintly there, and he remembered the sunset and wished he were a poet. His eyes were wet, and the night wind caught the sleeves of his cassock.

> *Beyond a horizon of ashes burns an unbearable sun,*
> *Like a golden entrance into the mind of God.*

He stood for a moment, still as stone. Then his poem embarrassed him, as always, and he went into the chapel.

4

CIRCLE FOUR

Cora

We come to the mission that day because Harlan wanted to make peace with me. Lately he has been bothered recalling her, his sister Margaret. It has just been on his mind, and that spell of his means misery for me. He rebuilt her loom and fooled with it a lot, wanting me to make him something on it, and got the silences when I couldn't manage the thing and stopped trying.

But then, one night in bed, Harlan woke me up and laid hold of me, and I knowed something had come around right again. And when we heard that Billy Cobb was bedfast with chills and fevers, Harlan took up Margaret's pretty coverlid and gave it to me, saying, Let's us take this down for Billy Cobb, Cora, if it would please ye. He was making peace, and I felt fine about it. So we all went.

We was sitting by Billy's bed, Billy sweating under the coverlid and joking with us, feeling lots better, he said. He was poking his finger at my Jacob, saying, Cora, what a horse you got there, and such. Starns was sitting with us, telling me about something or other, when Harlan looked around, said, Jean?

We looked and she had slipped on out. Starns said, Oh, she'll be all right, and we talked some more, then Harlan went to the door and stuck his head out of it and called.

I told him to let the child be and stop acting grandma, and Harlan laughed with us and said, yes, it was true, and we all talked some more.

We was ready to go home, and still no Jean. Starns went to the chapel and she wasn't there. Some of them men in black was in the barn and they said they hadn't seen her. Harlan commenced to call out from the yard and still she didn't answer. The Bishop come out of his studying room and said, What's this noise? and we told him, and he said, Oh, and commenced to look and call with us.

We was all there in the yard when Jean come running to us from the riverbank, out of the gristmill there that they don't use no more. She was running and skipping, happy as she could be. Harlan stepped ahead and grabbed her arm and was set to scold, but she just smiled and laughed the way she can, and he couldn't help but feel silly the way he had carried on. He was looking at us sheepish when there was a noise of something falling over in the mill.

"Who's that?" said Harlan, and Jean said, "My brother."

"Who?" said Harlan, and she said it again, her brother. She had been playing with him in there. Starns and the Bishop walked to the mill, and we come after and looked in too.

In the mill, sitting on a barrel, was this man they call Brother Horace. He was pretty drunk. Had him a big pot of likker and was sitting up there singing and coughing. Jean run right in and up to him, and when he seen her he gave her a big, shiny smile and held out his arms for her, but then he seen us standing there and put them down. He turned pale and all that beaming smile and high spirit went right out of him. He got off the barrel and put the likker pot on it and just stood there, hanging his head.

Harlan grabbed Jean and cussed the man. Starns hopped in there and started talking, smoothing things over, and got Harlan and Jean out, and we left the Bishop and Brother Horace in the mill alone.

Jean cut up a little about it. She liked her Brother Horace and said so. She was a little fired up at Harlan for acting that way, and she told him what fine stories Brother Horace knew, and Harlan swung her around by the arm, mad. Starns cut in on them, saying he hoped the

Bishop wouldn't be too hard on the man, that he was a good worker and all, but that he feared the Bishop expected just a mite too much from him.

"A man just needs to sit and drink and sing now and then," said Starns, looking back to the mill there and sighing some. We could all hear the Bishop's voice, not mad exactly, but sad, and without no let-up in it telling the man he was letting everybody down and all of that.

Now, I thought it was funny, myself. Brother Horace, he was a gentle soul, anybody could tell. Sitting up there like a king singing, and all of that. If just that little bit of drinking hisself silly was bad, I wondered what the Bishop would have thought of Sand Mountain on a midwinter night the way it was before Starns came.

But Harlan, he didn't think it was funny at all. Halfway home he commenced. Kept asking Jean what the man done. Jean smiled and giggled and started to tell part of the stories he told her, but Harlan didn't mean that. She tried to show him how he drawed people for her in the dirt, but he didn't mean that neither. When he got mad and said, "Tell me where he touched you," I sent Jean on home ahead of us and had it out with Harlan, saying such things, and he took to his silence again.

Now, I talked to Jean myself. She is all right. That man was a good feller, he never touched her. And what if he had? He would not have hurt her. She is still a child, but it won't be long now afore she's ready for some man, and what will Harlan think then? Lord, I recall once, almost as young as Jean, with legs that never seen my own blood yet, in the old back shed to the barn at the old home with some man I forget his face even, yes, I listened to stories and touched him and him me and it did not kill Cora. Jean is all right, and will be all right later on, but how can I talk to Harlan about that?

Since then it is Margaret, all the time. Not even Jean can please him no more. And in his bed, neither can I. He mumbles on about Margaret and her grave like I should be in it, and wakes up sweating all through the night.

And me, in his bed awake with him, though I cannot show it, I do not know how to tell him. I would tell him if I could that my own body was benastied, yes, many times, but it don't matter now, that it will be for Jean like it was for me, just some stains that one rain washed away, once Harlan was mine, and no more than that for Jean, too, someday.

But you can't say that to Harlan.

Jimmy Rode

Yessir, that tears it. Oh, yes. I will smoke a cigar and open store brandy, I will for a fact.

It give me my place, and a powerful boost, when Starns come in today asking for credit. Oh, yes. He come in here and said, straight off and stony-faced, "I have come to do business with you, Jimmy."

I said, "My name is Mr. James Rode, if ye please," and he swallowed and tucked in his chin, said, "I have come to do business with you, Mr. Rode." I said, "Starns, that's better. I'll be proud to. Sit down."

He stood, though, and took his credit that way. And I clamped it on him, and he said nothing, and couldn't say nothing, he knowed it was my bargain this time, not his, oh, yes.

Now, I felt for the man, some, I'll allow it, because this wasn't his fault, not his doing, God knows. All summer he was jittery about them crops, with the Bishop cutting down on his field hours and Starns having to run after them men to get them working right. And when one of them sudden seen the holy ghost or whatever, just before the haying or such, well, he had to go pray and seek the spirit, and Starns had to let him. That happened a good deal, right about harvest. Starns cussed, but not to the Bishop, and it just went on that way.

The crop came and it was all right, even so. A trifle puny set up against his others, but not so bad. But then all that money the Bishop was used to getting from his home city, it didn't come, and he knowed it wasn't a-going to come, so Starns had to come and do business with James Rode, oh, yes.

Smoke, cigar. Brandy, fire my fine body, it's a cold night in the dead middle of winter.

Harlan

It was the time of dry storms. I was out all day, hunting meat. Everything darkly cloudy, and so the night caught up with me still chasing that deer, and I come to the thing that way.

I was ready to go home with no meat when I seen them just step out of the brush like dainty story-tale people walking home. There was five of them, one a great big buck. I seen his horns through the brush and leaves and could not count the points, but I figured ten, anyway. One doe come walking close to me and I whistled low and she jittered and moved off, giving me a shot at him. I took it and missed, and they crashed out of there. I ramrodded quick and shot again, to scare them so's maybe they would head up and I might get one of them when they had to come down. Because the creek at Carson's Fall now, it is flooded fierce with the rains all last week. It is dry storm now, but that creek is still raging, and I calculated they couldn't jump across now and would have to come back, to me.

I went on fast, and the sky was fired over and over with the dry lightning, but no thunder, and I went quiet. That is the thing, to be quiet, and not just in the forest neither. I hunted quiet, watching my steps but moving on, too. It was quiet, and the forest still, with that hushed lightning going all around the mountains as the dusk come down.

I parted brush and opened up a spruce thicket. For about the flick of one eyelash we stood together, me and that big one. I hadn't no more but blinked when he blew hisself out of that thicket and flashed away up the slope. I never got the gun to my shoulder.

Then I was after him, and it was the way it is in the forest when ye hunt mad. Something else is there, and ye don't have to worry about doing the right things, because it does them for ye and moves ye on. I never yet had that feeling but what I didn't bring home some kill. I let it take me and moved on fast and quiet up the slope to Carson's Fall, like I was part of it all now.

The slope narrowed and headed up, on each side the plunge got deeper, its sides stuck with them undercut rocks that stick out like big iron spikes. Three of them got by me, and I didn't even shoot. I was far from wasting on them, I was after him now. Dusk was not far, and I knowed I was fool enough to stay out and get caught by the dark, but I didn't care, I wanted him.

I almost hit him all right, but with me and not my rifle gun. I heard this fidgety slicing thing in the brush ahead, and raised my gun, and then he come sailing down, right at me, them antlers held high and scared, his white eyes bulging, leaping down from the raging Fall. I shot and missed way off, but blowed some bark off a tree. He came to a stop right on one bound and swung his big head, and slow and brazen he made up his mind. I was ramrodding when he turned and jumped and sailed off like wind back up toward Carson's Fall again.

I run and come on him once more, trying to get by me. He near did, but I fired and most hit him that time. He wheeled and took off back up, and this time I knowed he wouldn't stop for that creek.

But when I got there, breathing hard, he was still this side of it, standing there the way a man will wait to buy something, fidgety at the counter, and move backwards and forwards. I dropped and steadied on my knee and fired and missed him again, and swore. He heard that bullet, though, he heard it and then he went.

His legs blurred moving him back and then digging ground, and he jumped the creek and did not make the other side. He went into the raging waters and they drug him down and off the Fall, and when I got to where I could see down, I seen where he hit, and then I seen the Bishop down there, too, with both arms raised up in the air.

I figured to see the deer a-floating in the pool down there where the Fall crashes, sometimes in early spring one will have tried to jump and missed, like mine, and you will see them there. But no, he wasn't floating. I laid down and hung my head over the rock to see clear.

He had been slung out from the waters and had hit the rocks to one side of the pool. There was this great splinter of stone sticking near straight up, and he had hit that. He was hanging on it when I looked, and it had run him through, stuck him and held him up clear of the water, like meat on a knife.

Now the Bishop. He was staring at the thing, and then he whipped off his long rope belt he had on, that tied the black dress he wore under his coat. He crept out on the rock and tied the rope to the deerhorns hanging down and tried to get the thing loose.

I yelled down, loud because of the roaring water off the Fall, I yelled, "Hey! God damn you, leave my meat alone!"

He stopped and looked up. The dry lightning flared, and all around the creatures of the woods was stirring and cackling and running. The lightning flared, and he dropped the rope then and run into the woods, leaving his horse.

I went down and pulled it off the rock and shouldered my kill and went home. I stood in the door and Cora almost yelled, the way I was, standing there covered with deer and blood.

Juba

Tate and the boys found him roaming the slopes at night, horseless and lost, and brung him in here. Lafe took a saucer lantern and went down to the mission and got Starns, and he come up with some of the others and they took him back down.

When Starns was here, I said it was good to see him again after such a time, and he grinned, but not smiling, and said, yes, it had been a long time.

Now, I had been setting my cabin with the Bishop whilst they was gone for Starns, and I knowed the man was not right, no, not right. He tried to tell me all about praying at the water and then this animal from the sky and his pa after it, and such as that, and couldn't make sense of it hisself, much less have me abide his reasoning.

So I just said to Starns, I said, "Starns, look here, this man is not right." I told him what all the people are saying now. That the Bishop is agin them, because lately he has stopped the store, and there are no more circuit rides, and nobody will go to see Starns when they are sickly, and all that. I said right out that best he get the Bishop on back down the mountain.

Mister Starns, he listened, and pushed dirt with his boot. Then he said, "Juba, there was a time when I was lying down in a hole, ready to die. That man come to me and sat there and talked me up out of it again. This here mission, it is his. He can do what he wants, and I will go with him, I don't care what. If he wants to burn it down, then it'll burn, and I will tote the kerosene for him and throw down the first match. Juba, ain't no use talking this way to me."

I said, "All right, Starns. All right, all right." Then he seen he had spoke too bold and testy to me, and commenced to say he was sorry. It got so messy then I couldn't abide it, and broke off, and they left.

All I got to say is this. In one year this neighborhood has just gone down a whole lot.

5

THE APOSTATE

STARNS HAD THE wagon loaded before dawn. Packed with trunks containing the Bishop's clothes and all his books and papers, it stood ready as the morning light stole down into the valley. When Bishop Ames came out onto the veranda, dressed in a plain traveling suit with his frock coat over his arm, Starns was already up on the wagon seat, testing the brake with the toe of his boot.

The trip to Stewart was not an easy one in March. Starns had been against it, as Bishop Ames had been confined to his bed for the past month. But they had little choice, and he saw that, too. The last communication from the standing committee of the diocese informed them that there would be a General Convention in the middle of March. The committee stated that it had reached an impasse in its investigations, and demanded the presence of the Bishop. The Convention would be held in Stewart, for his easier arrival, but if he was not present they would have no other choice but to consider it his final word. Then, they said, they would be forced to ask another bishop to take his place until such time as he found himself able to give them his resignation.

"All right, I'm ready," said the Bishop. "Are you?"

"Yessir," said Starns. "May as well start."

Bishop Ames shook hands with Billy Cobb and the three young men who stood with him on the porch, put on his frock coat and climbed up onto that wagon seat. Billy Cobb held the Bishop's hat, which he gave to him, and Bishop Ames jammed it down on his head, pushing up the brim against the wind that would surely find them before they got down the mountain.

"Very well, then," he said.

Starns murmured softly and flicked the reins several times. Both horses responded calmly, and the wagon went away from the mission without a jerk or a lurch.

The Bishop turned in his seat and waved at the men standing in front of the porch, and they waved back violently. Three students and Billy Cobb were the only ones left by March. The rest, alarmed by the growing reputation of the mission as reported to them in letters from friends and parents, and finding themselves unable to follow their Bishop in his search, left when the snows cleared. Upon each application for separation from the mission, Bishop Ames, whom they all expected to be fiercely outraged, only nodded, told them to think about it another day, then gently gave his consent.

"Will there be ice, Starns?"

"It is likely. But maybe not. You warm?"

"Oh, yes."

When the wagon topped the rise, Bishop Ames asked Starns to stop, and he turned and stared a long moment back. Over the valley moved a dark pack of clouds, dense and sluggish, slovenly in its drift and bulk, trailing jagged gray streamers that joined in the idle, careless sail of the mist. It was, he thought, like the hangings from a hairy, bestial underbelly of something that loomed above, and he remembered his hope and joy when he first saw it, on the day when he spurred his horse, in the vigor of health, over the rise to look down upon the botanist's valley, Heathen.

He touched Starns's arm and they rode on.

He kept his hat brim down into the wind and fastened his eyes on his boots. Around him, passing back away from the lumbering wagon, the sullen forest retreated, dead as slate. That the seals of frost and ice would soon be broken, that the frozen ground would live and breathe again, that warm spring rains would stir it and turn it over and over within itself and send up rhododendron and gay azalea, and mushy, sharp-edged crabgrass, that the naked trees would then be stricken from within like astounded young lovers and wave their arms, amazed magicians, palming apple blossoms and fruit, peaches and bright cherries, these confused images Bishop Ames, in his descent, found excruciating.

Over the valley, soon after they left it, the wind picked up. It attacked the slovenly pack of dark clouds and broke it open. From the descending slopes, his eyes on his boots in the wagon, Bishop Ames listened to the thunder, fierce and far away.

They reached Stewart late in the afternoon. Going down the single street, they became aware of men standing in long coats before houses and stores, watching them, staring in silence, then bending heads in quick conversation, breaking and rejoining groups, a few quickly crossing the street.

Starns halted the wagon in front of the Stewart parish house, across the road from the small church. In the side yard of the parish a group of men, boots and canes and red handkerchiefs, were playing horseshoes. A flying shoe, short, hit the edge of the dirt box, but then flipped up and clanged around the pole.

Man made a ringer, thought Starns. He waved and called cheerfully, "Do them kind count hereabouts?"

The men did not answer, did not wave back. They nodded carefully and soberly to the Bishop, ignored Starns completely, then, with great dignity, went back to their game.

Starns kicked the wagon brake down. He turned to the Bishop to say, "Well, we made it, after all," but did not speak. The Bishop was hanging his head and biting at his lip.

Nothing was happening. No one was saying anything at all.

The Bishop sat in the wagon, trapped there by silent indifference, surrounded by a tense hush broken only by the murmurs and thuds and clangs of the men escaped into horseshoes. The door to the parish house stayed shut, but Starns saw the faces at the windows.

He started to jump down and curse them and welcome his Bishop by himself, but he knew he could not move until Bishop Ames did. God damn these people, won't one of them come and shake his hand? he thought, and his stomach began to hurt. This is awful.

They sat there for several minutes.

Then, down the street toward them in a merciful rush hobbled a grotesque old man with a head of bushy white hair and a flap of dangling skin at his throat. Behind him, walking as fast as she could, came Rachael Ames, and with her two or three men Starns did not know.

With a determined grunt Thackery Curry grabbed the wagon, stuck his foot on a spoke and pulled all seventy years of himself up on a level with the Bishop. He grabbed at the Bishop's hand, caught it and shook it as hard as he could.

Then Rachael was standing by the wagon, hands at her shawl and bonnet, smiling. "Nahum," she said, "you must be tired. Come take me to supper and then we'll rest. We are staying at the inn, my dear, it's very nice,"

The Bishop's head came up then, and slowly he climbed down from the wagon. The three other men greeted him warmly and respectfully, even effusively. The door of the parish house came slowly open then, and the minister walked out. Stiffly but politely, he welcomed his Bishop to his parish.

The horseshoe game, Starns noticed, went right on.

Misery, thought Starns, misery.

When he had the wagon unpacked and the horses barned, he went to the small room they gave him, off the livery stable, and lay down on the bed. Rachael Ames had told him to come to the inn, where some supper would be waiting for him, but he had excused himself. He was not hungry, he said.

He lay on the bed and closed his eyes, but could not rest.

What now? he thought. Starns, what now?

But for occasional trips down the mountain for supplies and two quick journeys to Raleigh, he had not been away from the mission for seven years. On his bed, in the damp, close room where he could hear the weight-shifting and snorting of the horses only a wall away from him, he felt the seven years suddenly annulled, vanished and traceless in the workings of his memory. To his mind, in their place, came the years of his wandering.

That's just because I got nothing to do now. Nobody to cuss at, fret about.

His hands, by his side on the rough, patched quilt of the bed, lay large and empty.

I don't know what the Bishop means to do now. I shore don't know what these people mean to do now. But me, well, I am bound to it, what they do, I reckon.

He opened his eyes and stared at the uneven, badly wrought beams of the bunkhouse roof.

When will they let me go back? Lord, I don't know that, neither. It is them will decide all, hired man.

His heart sank under the sudden, unfamiliar burden of his past life, under the hopeless weight of those old ways that he had so easily and gladly forgotten. He felt young again but very weak, born of helplessness. The expression on his face, as he lay chilled by the icy desolation of his life before the mission, became stony and implacable with the attitude of fatality, god of his youth, his salvation when he lived his days for no good reason whatsoever.

Oh, my Lord, thought Starns, lying weakly on his bed.

In a moment he sat up, surprised by rapping. Someone was at his door, calling him and knocking loudly. He knew the voice, but couldn't place it for a moment. Then he knew.

It was Marcus Sales, demanding entrance.

Starns turned up the lamp by his bed and said, "Come in."

The door creaked open and the pale face, familiar but heavier now, with no martyrdom to it, looked at him again. Starns stood up and said nothing.

Marcus Sales came into the room carefully but firmly, looked at

Starns quickly as if to see it was him and not somebody else, then grabbed his hand and pumped it fiercely.

Starns was apprehensive. What's this? What's this? he thought, and he shivered, feeling the threadlike scars on Sales's hand rubbing against his palm.

"Deacon Starns! Will you please accept my sincere apologies, sir, for these accommodations. The town is overcrowded, but I had no idea you would be put in here!"

"What?" Starns almost said, but caught himself. He looked around. "Suits me," he said. "Bed's good. Suits me."

"Well, we should have been able to do better, Deacon."

"No, it's fine," said Starns. "But I thank you for thinking of me."

"You're sure it will do, Deacon?"

For the first time Starns liked the sound of his title.

"It will do fine, thanks. But I tell you, I am a little hungry. You reckon they got anything left in the dining room?"

"I'm positive of it," said Sales. "Come on, I'll go with you."

On the way over, Sales stopped two passing men and introduced Starns to them in such a way that they quickly took his hand. By the simple act of saying Starns's name Sales connected to it all the worth and value of all missionary work, of all self-sacrifice, of the Church itself. When he quickly and deftly told them of Starns's work, Starns wondered, Who's the man a-talking about now? But he was very pleased.

"The whole diocese is proud of you," Sales said, scarred hand on Starns's back, as they went into the inn.

In the dining room of the Stewart Inn sat tables of raw, once varnished pine on a floor whose boards in places had warped an inch apart. The food, when it came, was limp as a swimmer drowned in grease, and it challenged inspection. Nevertheless, in the room, sitting comfortably in dirty chairs and talking briskly and affably, sat a large number of men and quite a few women, seemingly quite content with their lot.

They had come for judgment, a tribunal seriously to ponder and weigh, and were, therefore, appropriately humble. There were no complaints about the wretched food or slovenly rooms or suspicious beds, no, it was fine. The ugly room was alive with smiles and gentle looks and tranquil forbearance.

Starns, when he entered the room, spotted it immediately. This, too, he remembered, and he sniffed like an animal and almost turned around and left. But Marcus Sales quickly took him by the arm and led him from table to table, introducing him the same way as before, arousing the same warm and instant respect. The ladies, especially, beamed when Sales told them of the spiritual wilderness Starns had conquered.

When the introductions were over, Sales smiled and said quietly, "Deacon Starns taught me a great lesson, my friends. It is contained in the nickname he has now, among many people—Nestor, the peacemaker. A man must be a brother before he can be a priest."

He turned to Starns, who was flushed with embarrassment and deep pleasure.

"I have behaved badly to you many times, Deacon Starns, Nestor. I ask your forgiveness for it." He held out one scarred hand. "Let us be brothers in Christ," he said.

Starns blushed violently, a confused, warm feeling spread like the warmth of whisky in his stomach. Confused, he took Sales's hand, and then he was pumping it hard, overwhelmed with contrition for his hardness of heart toward the man, ashamed of his bitterness and self-pity in the livery-stable room.

Oh, they mean well, these people here. Oh, I have been wrong about him, and them, too, yes, I ain't been fair, no, I been wrong.

He held on to Marcus Sales's hand until he could stammer, "Yes, yes. I would like that, yessir."

Smiling discreetly, the others took up their table talk, and Marcus Sales, with a gentle pressure on his arm, led Starns to a table, sat him down and recommended possum. It was the one thing, he told Starns, they couldn't make any greasier, didn't try, and it was pretty good. Starns laughed and nodded, and Sales called the sleepy-eyed, loafing man from behind the high plank counter where he was hiding, and ordered.

While Starns ate his dinner, Marcus Sales drank three cups of coffee, talking casually. Looking occasionally at other parts of the room, smiling and talking effortlessly, he was as smooth and delicate as a matchmaker, keeping Starns amused and attentive. Farming, teaching, yes, even the weather, it flowed interesting and pleasant and carefully considerate. He told Starns about the newest things in farm machinery down from the north, describing them with such accuracy that Starns would stop chewing now and then, seeing the thing work in a field. Then he would smile, amused at Marcus Sales's new interest in farming, and chew on, nodding his approval, while Marcus Sales moved deftly on to another description, taking quick sips of tepid coffee.

Starns finished his possum, pretty good, just as Sales had advertised, and was having his coffee. The conversation had gone from farming to mission farming, and Starns began to talk, warm and full and easy, about its problems. He talked about the land and the mountain weather, and about working with part-time preacher-farmers who, to speak the flat truth, didn't know half the time what they was about, why, once...

He suddenly became aware that he was the only one in the room who was speaking. Marcus Sales was staring at him, rapt, his eyes wide open. Still talking, Starns tried to undo his sudden confusion. What was he saying so fast and free?

"For them last prayers, of course, some stay up all night. So you have to figure who can work the next day and who can't. Of course they'll all be there, but..."

Then he almost choked. He had just described the daily schedule of the Order of the Essenes.

Around him now the quiet people were still as death, leaning forward in their chairs. Marcus Sales, smiling. Yes? Yes? Then what?

Starns blushed again, but now in anger and mortification. Throughout his being swept scalding, stomach-burning shame. It burned him, and it made noise that rang in his ears.

His chair scraped and fell over behind him when he stood up. His voice sounded across the room like the ugly crack of a thick whip.

"You! Damn loafer behind that counter. Come get my money and come quick!"

He stood waiting, his homely, lined face livid with humiliation and wrath. When the man came up, frightened, and told him how much, Starns counted it out to the penny and threw it on the table.

For a moment, then, he looked at them, cold and suddenly poised, staring them down. It was the face of his mountain childhood that they saw, as stern and implacable as the certainty of man's mortality, as aloof and scornful as only a man can be when he has accepted the word of another mortal man and found it worthless.

He walked out, leaving them in silence. At the table Marcus Sales gaped like a toad.

At the livery stable Starns turned. Someone was hobbling after him, calling his name hoarsely. He could not see who it was and did not want to, so he went into his room and shut the door. In a moment he heard faltering footsteps, knocking, and quick, reedy breath.

He lit the lamp, taking his time about it. He opened the door and stood blocking the entrance. "Well?"

Before him was a head sprouting a thatch of white hair, with a face old and lined. A flap of skin dangled down from under the chin. The old man at his door looked so much like an ancient mud turtle, Starns could not help but loose some hold on his anger.

"Uh, Deacon Starns, uh," the old man puffed. "I must speak to you, uh. I am mortified at the treatment you just suffered. Uh."

"Mind your own business," said Starns. "I ain't a-going to fool with you people no more."

Thackery Curry nodded and regained his breath. "Don't blame you, Deacon. Don't blame you one bit. If it had been me, I'd have hit some-body just as hard as I could."

The idea of the mud turtle swinging on them, maybe hitting Sales, was again disconcerting, then funny, but Starns kept his anger bright.

"I don't care what you'd have done."

"Course you don't, why should you? But I must hold my ground with you, Deacon. I mean to tell you something about this Convention, like it or not. It is for our Bishop's good, just as much as yours."

Starns considered this. "All right. Say it and good night."

Curry set his frail shoulder against the door jamb. "You and the Bishop both, Deacon, have got to understand that this Convention is not, completely, a stacked deck. Yes, I know it sure looks like one, but it isn't. A lot of us worked hard to make it that way, and we did pretty well."

Starns held up the light. Furious as he was, there was no gainsaying the old priest's sincerity. But Marcus Sales had been sincere, too.

"Deacon, we are concerned about Bishop Ames. And, it seems to me, rightfully so. Now, how about that?"

Yes, I am, too, Starns thought, and nodded.

"The peace of this diocese is broken, and it has got to be mended up again. That comes first, like it or not, and there are plenty here who don't like doing it this way any more than you or I like seeing it done this way."

The old priest gathered himself and spoke firmly to Starns, who was listening.

"Then there are some others, the lint pickers. You know them, there must be some where you come from. They are the servants who bury the talent, you know them. They are terrified of a man like Bishop Ames, because he is original and they are not, because he loves his work and his duties and they do not, because his passions are young and theirs are old. They are afraid, and I am too a little, that he has been trying to do something terribly right up there in your mountains, and they don't want to face it. It might shame them too much. So they have reveled in these tales of perverse monasticism and Papal invasion and the Lord Himself only knows what else. It has gotten badly out of hand. And now we must get to the bottom of it, Deacon. We must, both those that hate him and those—like you and me, I think—who love him. He has got to come clean. I'm sorry, but he does."

The old priest's passion, spurting from him so fresh and lively, drew

Starns's anger after it. Both men stood looking at each other, somewhat exhausted.

"You must help him see this, Deacon," said Curry. "You mean a lot to him, I know this for a fact. He was a sick man when he met you and hired you, did you know that? He put a lot of store in you, and what you did up in those mountains, it tacked years onto his life, he told me. But now it seems he is not well, sick again. Am I wrong?"

Starns put the lamp down on the bed table and said softly, "No, you are not."

"Is there anything you can tell me about it?"

"I wonder myself. All the time. I don't know." He sat down on the bed.

"Well," said Curry. "We'll find out tomorrow, I hope. We have got to."

"What will happen?"

"He'll hear the committee report first, and get straight what everybody's excited about. It is mostly doctrine. Then, tomorrow night, he'll say his piece. It will be fierce, if I know Nahum Ames."

Starnes nodded.

"Deacon," said Curry, "listen. If you possibly can, make him understand that there are plenty of us here who respect him. We will wait for him to tell us, and we will listen. I don't mean that we're not alarmed and upset, but we don't mean to let Marcus Sales run away with the thing either, even if he is chairman of the committee."

Curry pulled at his chin. "You know, once at these Conventions, before you came, Deacon Starns, it was fine. Most people couldn't wait for the Bishop to come and tell us what he'd been doing and thinking. I've seen them act like kids at a fair when he came, and sit listening to him for hours. It was good, then, when we all came together. Now somebody says benediction and you get knocked down by the rush to the door. God bless you, get out of my way, I'm going home."

On the bed Starns stared bleakly at the old priest. "Yes, I know what you mean," he said.

Curry nodded. He grasped the doorknob. "Well, anyhow, Deacon," he said, "don't feel too bad about us. Our wisdom is often ugly, but we have got to know about this. And don't you take them personally, Deacon. Sales or his friends."

The old man sighed. "I don't know that our Lord did so well with his people, either. One of them sold Him right down the river, too. Good night, Deacon."

He closed the door softly.

Starns undressed and got into bed. He laid the coarse quilt across his chest carefully and neatly, as if by that order to undo some of his confusion. His head was full of things he did not understand and did not want to understand, and behind it all stood his Bishop, at the mercy, it seemed, of fools and worthless men. But Thackery Curry was not that. So something was wrong, then, but what it was Starns could not fathom, any more than he could ever fathom the Bishop, the man he loved and served.

His head ached, and he wondered, Now, what was I so mad about? Oh, yes, Marcus Sales, them people. Oowee, I could have shot the whole bunch.

He thought of the old priest's mud-turtle face, and he turned over, rumpling the covers, grinning.

That old man, he's something. Starns, what you was so mad at, it was just you being such a fool. Big dinner-table mouth. All you have to do, I reckon, is forgive Starns for being such a damn dumb mule, not them poor people like Sales in their misery. The mud turtle, he's right, then, I reckon.

Utterly spent, he slept soundly for a long time, but, just before dawn, began to toss and turn, dreaming of a man he had seen hung when he was a wandering drifter, only instead of boots dangling in the air, around the dead man's feet flapped a cassock, black as the night.

When he went to breakfast, the Bishop was already up, finishing his coffee with Rachael. Starns joined them and told Nahum Ames about his talk with Thackery Curry. The Bishop smiled briefly, said, "He's a good man, Starns," and went on reading a pile of notes laid by his plate. When he finished breakfast, he got up quickly and left the table.

Starns did not see him again until the Bishop went into the church to meet there with the committee. Thackery Curry was with him and they both marched in with an almost jaunty step. Starns sat on the small porch of the inn and waited until they came out again at eleven o'clock. The Bishop passed by him without seeing him, on his way in to his room.

That afternoon, while the committee meeting went on, Starns wandered about like a boy who has skipped school and doesn't know what to do with himself. He walked back and forth on the porch, strolled to the stables a dozen times, his eyes on the church all the time. Finally, late in the afternoon, waiting for the meeting to end, he stood by the dirt box of the horseshoe game, kicking it gently with his foot.

He threw two shoes, missing the pipe both times, and then saw them coming out. The ministers moved out quickly and went directly to the inn. Marcus Sales and Thackery Curry came out arguing with each other, and then Bishop Ames, a large portfolio of notes in his hand. His step was light, his face impassive, and a sense of accomplishment surrounded him as he passed Starns by without seeing him.

Starns threw a few more shoes, waiting for the night to come and, with it, his Bishop's address to the members of his diocese. One of the younger ministers saw Starns and played a game with him, beating him badly.

"You have to live on the farm to know this game," he told Starns, and Starns said yes, that was probably right, he didn't know. They played together until supper, and the young minister went in, but not Starns. He stayed and threw the shoes at the pipe in the dirt box until the evening meeting was called, and then he went into the church.

Bishop Ames sat relaxed and outwardly calm in a large chair placed for him by the pulpit. A table had been set in front of the pews, and Marcus Sales sat there with the rest of the committee, except Thackery Curry, who, waiting at the door, met Starns when he came in and sat with him at the back of the church.

It was a business meeting, not a service, and Starns did not like the atmosphere. The church was crowded, filled with those eager to hear what the Bishop would say for himself. They were all familiar with the long and self-contradicting pastoral letters he had sent down from the mission, and they felt that, whatever he said, it would be the final word on the Valle Sanctus affair, and they panted to hear it. Starns didn't like it.

When the church was filled, Marcus Sales looked at the Bishop, who nodded tranquilly and rose. He gave a short prayer and then turned the meeting over to Marcus Sales and sat down again, the same gentle and nonchalant smile on his lips.

"Bishop Ames has drawn up this following report to the standing committee, and he has asked me to read it for him, which I am most happy to do at this time," said Marcus Sales.

He don't need no Marcus Sales to speak for him, Starns thought. I don't like this.

"Well," Thackery Curry whispered, "this should do it, Starns."

They watched Marcus Sales as he studied the paper he held in his hands for a moment and then began to read. It was written in third person, as a report by the committee, and Curry stiffened.

"Sales got to him during dinner," he whispered. "That's his, not the Bishop's."

But the Bishop allows it, thought Starns. Look at him sitting there like a boy on the riverbank, dreaming. I don't like this here thing at all.

"'The Right Reverend Nahum I. Ames, Bishop of this Diocese, makes the following statement concerning the alleged practices and doctrines of the Valle Sanctus mission founded by him in the western mountains of this state. It is made in spite of the fact, to be here noted, that such a statement might be considered humiliating. Bishop Ames, however, has declared himself compelled to do so, after hearing the charges brought against him, by his sense of duty both to himself and to his Church.'"

Gracefully the Bishop turned his handsome, haggard face toward Marcus Sales. His smile was limpid, his gaze detached.

"'Bishop Ames tells us that since his childhood it has been a favorite and cherished idea with him to bring about a union of all churches, Roman, Greek, Anglican and American. He now admits the idea to have become an obsession in mature years when it should have been more carefully controlled, and that in his zeal for such action he has overlooked the difficulties in the way, which he is now satisfied are insurmountable.'"

"Yes," whispered Bishop Ames softly, "yes, that's right."

"'That this tendency of mind toward a union of the churches, cherished but unadmitted to his practical mind, has been greatly heightened, and his ability to perceive the difficulties in the way greatly diminished, by a high state of nervous excitement, arising either from bodily disease undetected by physicians, or from a constitutional infirmity. That, in pursuit of this idea, which he decided could be begun in the Valle Sanctus mission life, he was led into opinions on doctrine, and to a public teaching of them, of the impropriety of which he is now fully satisfied, and, upon a review of these opinions, wonders that he should ever have entertained them.'"

Thackery Curry bowed his white head. Union, he thought. So that was it, then, Nahum. I guess you couldn't shame us any more than that. God help you.

"'That this final change in his views has been brought about, in part, by a return to a more healthy condition of mind and body, but mainly from having at long last perceived the tendency of these doctrines toward the Church of Rome, as demonstrated by the sad events in England known as the Oxford Movement. Bishop Ames now admits and heartily retracts the following notions, which he tolerated only because of his long-cherished, but totally idealistic and impossible, desire to bring about said union of all churches and worshiping bodies. They are as follows. One that on the subject of auricular confession and absolution, he now recants and utterly abjures...'"

Terrible, thought Curry. It's a recantation, a medieval witch list. Terrible.

Listening to the long list of the Bishop's doctrinal recantations, Starns, his mind hopelessly bewildered, felt like a man who has walked into a covey of quail and is frightened by their sudden, erratic flight and by the loud rush of their wings. He tried to remember something about the theological books he had attempted to read years before, and what they were about, but could not. The sharp, impressive words coming from Marcus Sales were to him utterly meaningless. He shook his head like a man will who has been watching something terribly small and finds that his eyes have failed him. He listened doggedly.

"'. . . Eight, that he had, at one time, under the influences before mentioned, entertained doubts whether our Church was in a state of schism. That he had never gone so far as to believe that it was, but merely entertained doubts. He is now satisfied, without a doubt, that she is not in schism. Nine, that he had never held the abhorred doctrine that has entrapped the minds of. . .'"

Schism? wondered Starns. Now, what does that mean? Seems I used to know. Something bad. Just can't recall it now. It's good these people don't know what kind of a sorry deacon I am.

"'. . . Bishop Ames concludes this statement with the assurance that the so-called Order of the Essenes is no longer in existence and that Valle Sanctus is now only a mission station. He requests that it be allowed to continue its services in that capacity only, and asks that Reverend William Cobb and Deacon William Starns be allowed to remain there, performing their former duties only.'"

Maybe this will turn out, then, thought Starns.

"'. . . and, finally, Bishop Ames has requested a leave of absence, for the duration of six months, to recover his health in restful travel, during which time he authorizes this committee to appoint to his place any Bishop of the Episcopal Church or any other qualified member of it, to discharge his duties during this absence. This request, made known to us, the committee, this morning, has already been voted upon and granted.'"

In spite of himself, Marcus Sales was pleasant. He had done his best, and now, he thought, time will do more than that. I won't have to wait long. He spoke in his richest voice.

"To our Bishop," he said, "we tender our joy at his return to his flock, and we clasp his hand. He has our heartfelt wishes for a quick recovery and a regained ability to take up his duties once again among his people, who have been so deeply concerned, this past year, for his well-being."

Travel where? Thackery Curry was thinking.

Six months, Starns was thinking, that's not long. I will have everything fixed up again for him, when he gets back. It will be just like it was, yessir.

Then they saw Bishop Ames get up from his chair and very slowly mount the pulpit.

He saw again the jagged rocks and thunderous plunge of Carson's Fall. Again he stood there, by the waterfall's deep, thrashing pool, his coat over the cassock whose rough embrace was dear to him. Around him the great forest was sullen, hushed and tenantless, very quiet but for that one roar, the thick plunge of icy water from the jagged rocks above. No birds. No animals. The trees and plants seemed made of stone. Brush and branch pointed upward in utter stillness. Silent gray clouds, dragging strips of mist, shut out the sun and bore down heavily. The late afternoon was dry as bone, only the water spoke and moved, and quick, faraway flashes of lightning flared. He stood there mindless, rapt, enthralled by the gigantic spurt and power of the water, his devotions themselves stilled in the deadly silence of this vast and unknowable cathedral. Slowly, throughout his being, memories of his childhood fears began to stir. From the roar of the water he heard strange sounds. They sounded to him like the bass rumblings of his father's deep voice, and he listened. Something was being said to him. He tried to listen. Then he saw it. His eyes opened wide and he pointed upward, quickly, without volition, like a surprised child. Above him, poised on a pinnacle of broken stones just above the mouth of the Fall, as if alighted there an instant before from heaven, stood a stag, a handsome, incredibly handsome beast with a crown of curving antlers and a majestic tufted, panting white breast. "Wonderful!" he said aloud. and in the roaring waterfall the voice grew louder. It thundered at him and then crashed, erupted into a hideous explosion, which he recognized immediately as the furious blast of a shotgun discharging both barrels.

The mountain forest, the Fall, the stag, all vanished and he stood, a child again, behind his father in a New England thicket, sweating in August, watching his father reload, and wringing his hands. "Shut up, Nahum," said his father's deep bass voice. "Stop that." "But it's not in there, Father," he said. "I told you, I saw it go in over there." "It's in here somewhere," said his father, peering into the thicket. "But it wasn't alive, Father. It crawled in there and died, it must have. Leave it alone." Then the brush stirred, and the rabbit, brown and tiny with one foreleg red, moved out in panic. His father almost upended the shotgun. "No, don't," said the boy, and in the mountain forest the Bishop heard his father fire hideously again and saw a bloody hole blasted into the dirt. The sound sank into the waterfall and rumbled there, and Bishop Ames saw the stag again, and the lightning flared. On the high, jagged rocks he saw the stag twitch in panic, then gather himself, step back and, with a ripple of slim and fragile legs, soar into the air, high over the raging water, and land heavily on the other side of the stream. "Wonderful!" cried Bishop Ames. "Free!" he cried. "Run, run quick!" Then he saw that the beast was slipping. In horror he watched the stag thrash his hind legs, slosh them against slippery rocks and cold water, and roll his eyes like a horse. He pawed stone with delicate forelegs and then fell back into the torrent. The water, cold and full of shock, swept him backward, caught his great horns on the rocks and tore them loose in the sockets of his head, bore him relentlessly to the mouth of the gorge and flung him out over the Fall. He hit one last rock and was thrown free of the water. He came down, turning in the air like a stick, ripped into a sharp-edged shaft of stone and hung there, impaled. To the roar of the water Bishop Ames spoke quietly, seeing again the senseless, bloody hole at his father's feet, stained by the torn and mangled carcass of a brown rabbit. "You didn't have to do that, Father. Why did you?" His father snorted and laughed at him, and his laughter passed into the bass roar of the Fall, and around Bishop Ames in the mountain forest the world came horribly alive. Birds and animals and creatures of wood and dust and rock, even the waving branches of graceful trees, burst into sudden, boisterous, hideous, rejoicing life. Turning crows screamed in the air and flapped their black wings, squirrels furiously chattered and ran their limbs, wild dogs and wolves began to howl, a thundering covey of mountain quail burst from the brush, a masked raccoon slipped thieflike behind a tree, and the wind, in sudden gusts, raked the laurel, sang in the branches of balsam and pine, and scoured the cold rock with savage shrieks. In the depths of his spirit Bishop Ames sickened with dark revulsion, and heard his father speak to him. "They're glad, son! Nobody's scared but you. You see how things are now. Don't let nobody fool you about it, this is the way the world is made." "No, Father!" cried the boy, and "No, no, no, no!" the Bishop years later in the exaltation of the forest, amid the screaming of animals. Around the impaled stag, life rejoiced in triumph and utter forgetfulness. Bishop Ames tore off his coat, and from his waist the knotted rope. He crept out on the rock and tied the rope to one dangling antler and tried to pull the beast loose from the stone stake that ripped its body through. "God damn you, leave my meat alone!" said the voice, and he squinted and looked high up to the jagged rocks of the Fall. Then, twisted as a crab's leg, a sudden streaking bolt of lightning exploded behind a dark giant of a cloud. Father you are insane Father.

The Bishop's smile was limpid, his gaze detached. He stood in the pulpit in his plain frock coat and did not place his delicate hands on the rail. His face was tilted down on them, his head meekly bent. His voice was a rasp of a whisper.

Thackery Curry stiffened. Bishop Ames was reciting bits and pieces of the Order for the Burial of the Dead.

Starns looked about. Puzzled at first, the congregation slowly understood and then began to smile and nod at the pale, haggard man droning now like a dying wasp in his pulpit, smiling their forgiveness of his great pride and impossible intents, understanding his need to exorcise his demons by awful recitation, nodding, Go on, go on, now you finally see what it is to be on your knees and so we will forgive, we first and then God surely, come on down a little lower and be forgiven, go on, go on, go on.

Starns stood up, jaws rigid with anger. Over the pulpit the dangling lamps cast deep shadows on the temples and haggard cheeks of the Bishop.

"It's the Order for the Burial of the Dead," whispered Thackery Curry.

"I don't give a damn what it is," said Starns. He moved quickly out into the aisle and walked to the pulpit, his angry back to the rapt congregation. He looked up at his Bishop.

For the first time Bishop Ames lifted his hands. He held them palms up, in a saintly way.

"Hear my prayer, O Lord, and with thine ears consider my calling."

"Bishop."

"For I am a stranger with thee, and a sojourner, as all my fathers were. Oh, spare me a little, that I may recover my strength, before I go hither, and be no more seen."

"Bishop, come on down from there now. These people don't care. You come on."

"Glory be to the Father," said Bishop Ames, and then he was racked by violent coughing. Starns reached up and took his arm, and the Bishop came down meekly. He stumbled, and Starns caught him about the shoulders with one great arm and walked him out, glaring at the congregation.

"World without end," whispered the Bishop hoarsely.

"Yessir, yessir," said Starns. "Now, you come on with me. Everything is going to be all right now."

In the dawn of the next morning a silent, swift exodus of buggies and wagons left Stewart. By early morning the town was empty again, its single street depopulated of strangers, quiet and calm in the shadows of the peaks. The sun rose over the mountains close and warm, bathing Stewart in gentle light.

Starns brought Curry's wagon to the inn at midmorning, the time Rachael and Curry told him they would be ready, and waited in the wagon seat until the priest came out of the inn and walked up to him.

"How is he?" Starns asked. "Can he go?"

"Yes, he's coming," said Thackery Curry.

Starns had loaded the Bishop's belongings into Curry's wagon and got it to the inn on time, but sat fretful and worried. Curry had been at the Bishop's bedside throughout the night.

"You sure he's all right?"

"Yes, he slept just the same until an hour ago. Aside from that, well, who knows, Deacon? Here they come now."

Starns jumped down from the wagon and trotted up to the porch of the inn. He nodded to Rachael Ames, gaily and cheerfully dressed in a fur-trimmed traveling coat and an embroidered shawl, and took up the small handbag from the gaunt, frock-coated man who held her arm.

They walked slowly to the wagon. Starns helped them all up. Then he stood back, looking at them, trying to smile.

"Well," he said, one hand on the wagon wheel. "You have a good trip."

"Good-by, Starns," said Rachael.

"Have a good trip yourself, Deacon," said Thackery Curry.

The Bishop did not speak. The wagon began to move.

"See you in six months, Bishop!" said Starns. "So long, everbody will be waiting. See you then! So long! So long!" he called.

Bishop Ames did not answer him.

Late that evening, from the veranda of the mission, Billy Cobb heard the wagon come rattling into the yard, saw Starns riding down from the valley slope like a bandit. At the veranda he hauled in the reins. The horses stopped and stepped the ground like they should still be running, white lather and foam dripping from their mouths. Starns got down and slapped Billy on the back, a great grin splitting his homely face.

He told Billy Cobb everything had worked out all right, that the Bishop would soon be back the way he was before, that they would have it all back again, that they would dance again and plant fine crops and build and go out to the mountain people just as before. But it's a lot of work in only six months, Billy, come on!

His furious and joyful energy carried Starns through the spring and summer and into the autumn. He planted what he could in the time he had left of the almost passed spring and brought up a decent crop. When the winter came, so to him came again the hungry people of the mountains, to the man who knew their pride and did not damage it. They came to his good crop, to his skillful healing hands, and to the chanting, easy services of his mountain chapel. Their resentment faded, and after a while they even smiled in church when Starns, marking a homemade calendar with a feather pen, said, "This is all the time we got now before he comes back. It won't be long now."

But Bishop Ames did not return to his mountain mission.

He spent the summer at his home in Raleigh, seeing very few people and reading a great deal. Books came by the boxload every week, and he read them all, sending some back and keeping others. His health did not improve.

He is dying, someone said, of theology.

In the fall he made the trip to New York City, and from that place wrote the committee that he wished to prolong his leave of absence and travel abroad.

The anger and the bickering began again. The committee met and was broken up and reassembled, giving full powers to Marcus Sales. They received from Congressman Statius Collins another demand for the Bishop's resignation, replacing the one he withdrew after the Stewart Convention. They wrote several letters to the Bishop's address in New York, but received no answer.

The letters followed him to England and the mainland of Europe, and then, on the twenty-second of December, were all answered at once by his own last communication with his diocese, sent from Rome, a communication that resolved, finally, all dissension and settled all questions.

On Christmas Day of that year, in the sober glory of the great Roman cathedral, a tiny figure, the terrors of his childhood whispering only faintly in his brain, knelt before a surprised Holy Father of the Catholic world and surrendered to that Pontiff his faith and, as tokens of it, his surplice and his bishop's ring.

Immediately afterward, in New York, in another cathedral just as glorious, just as sober, he was formally deposed.

Interlude

TUNE THE FIDDLE

WELL, my ghostly Bishop, spirit of Nahum Ames in your black frock coat, standing here in my yard with the mist curling around your arms and up and down your back like smoke, I do not see, on any of the fingers of your delicate hands, that ring you gave away. I reckon it is still in Rome, in St. Peter's, where someone told me they saw it a long time ago, in a glass case or something like that.

Bishop, how is it that standing here now before me you look as fine a ghost as you did a man? You are straight now and tall, not the bent man there at the end, and your frock coat fits you like a uniform. You stand erect and strong in my yard, just like in the early times when I was a boy, and worshiped you, and dated my life as a man from the day you handed me a thick Bible with my name written in it by you, and slapped me on the back, saying, "You will make a fine Christian minister, Billy Cobb."

And all around the yard, staring with ghostly empty eyes at the place where Starns went off into the brush just now, the people you left are easy. In the leaning mist and under this dark night sky still dripping a bit of rain now and then, they don't seem bothered much. They shoulder a tree or foot a rock, standing idly by. They don't seem to hold it against you now.

But then, well, it was something else again. I was there and some others. Oh, ghosts and specters, I have forgotten which of you was with me then, just who was there and who wasn't when Starns got that letter and read it, and then had me read it, then again out loud to him, and then took it and read it yet again, while we stood there watching him make himself understand it.

It was in that fine, sweeping script he wrote, dated Rome, Italy, the twenty-second day of December, 1859. It was to all of us, but addressed to Starns, Deacon William Starns, and it began, "Dear Nestor, dear friends." It was a long thing, full of very precise histories why this was better than that and so on. Only right at the end did your flavor, Bishop, and your substance come out of it to us, when you wrote that you had woke "from a pleasant dream to a frightening reality," and when you wrote, dramatic as always, "my heart is bleeding as I trace the sentence that severs all pastoral relations between us, and conveys to you the knowledge that I am no longer . . ." and so on to the end, where you prayed we would still allow you to subscribe yourself our faithful friend.

Most of us reckoned your heart might have been bleeding, all right, but we didn't see you subscribed as our faithful friend, and we said so, and got mad. But not Starns.

It took him such a long time. He looked at the paper, and at the envelope it came in, and just looked and looked. He rubbed his head and rubbed it. He took them glasses and cleaned them four or five times and put them on his ugly face and took them off and put them on and looked again.

Ghosts, whichever of you stood there with me then, it was like watching something pulled out of the ground, root and branch, was it not?

"Well," Starns said after the longest time. "I reckon he won't be here for Easter, then."

He stared at the letter and took a deep, quick breath and said, "It will be a little longer, I reckon. Italy must be a long ways. It'll just take more time. But he'll get back soon enough. And we got lots to do until then."

And somebody, I forget who, said, "Starns, I don't think that can be right."

And Starns commenced to get mad, until I opened my mouth, me, who God knows should have known better, and said, "Oh, Starns, he has just quit us. Can't you see that?"

And he stood there mute and unbelieving, and then carefully, very, very neatly, folded the letter up and put it back in the big envelope, and said, "I don't have time to stand around here reading letters all day. There is a whole lot to be done, and we will commence doing it now." And then, quietly to me, as he walked out of the room, "Don't never say such a thing to me again, Billy," and he walked out and left us standing, and in a minute we heard him, out in the freezing January wet and cold and storm, riding off with his saddlebags of medicine books and old Bible and bottles of herbs and lotions, going out to see who was sick now and how could he ease them.

And it went on that way for a short time, Starns not about to believe the Bishop wouldn't be back soon, and me wondering about Bishop Ames and what he had done, afraid of him as a Popish devil one minute and jealous of him in the glory of Rome the next, until I finally came to my senses and felt for him, and hoped I would see him again someday and talk it over.

Then another letter came, to me this time, from Marcus Sales. I had been called to other duties. The land had all been sold to a man in Stewart, and one James Rode was to be his tenant. The mission station was, as of the day I got the letter, closed down. There was nothing in it about Starns at all.

I could not tell him that night, because he was happy about something, I forget what, and I just could not tell him. So I waited two days, and thanked the good stars I did, because then another letter came, again to me, from Thackery Curry this time. He had a knockdown fight, he said, with Sales and he won. True, I had to leave, and, true, all the land was sold, but Starns could stay on as missionary and deacon to the mountain people just as long as he wanted, at his new salary, which Thackery Curry had boosted up from 100 to 150 dollars a year. How the old man did it I know not, but he did, and Starns, when I told him, said, "Well."

So then I left you, my idle ghosts come back to my yard this night, left you and went down the mountain. And not so long after that I saw that this fine nation was about to have a war between the states. I planned to go on in as chaplain, but my heart wasn't in it, not at all. And then, one day when a man told me about the deposing of the Bishop, how he had been there in New York at that awesome thing, and how all the bishops joined in it and how it showed the terrible might and power of the Church, I lost my faith, too, and went into the army as soldier and fought like the rest.

Ghosts, at night during those years, in my tent with cigars and whisky, among jackboots and polished buttons and caps, with torn uniforms and torn flesh and the smell of sulphur and smoke, I thought of you in Valle Sanctus, thought of Starns and the mission with its one bell on the post in front of the chapel, me ringing it in the afternoons and early mornings and easy nights of summer and spring and fall, and I tell you now, it was hard on me.

I could not know then that it was hard on you, too, them days. Only later, when I came home, did I learn that.

Harlan, where are you? Oh, yes, I see you now, leaning on my hickory tree, with Jean holding your hand, looking up at you like the last time I saw you both together, with her bright yellow hair and smooth brown skin and eyes blue as sky. And, Cora, where are you? Somewhere near, surely. Oh, yes, there behind them, looking, strong legs set apart like a man, looking.

Cora, do you still so love this ghost of your Harlan? Sweet little Jean, with your whiteblond hair flowing into the pale mist, do you?

Part Four

NESTOR'S DEATH

1

SANG

THE DEEP-SET ROOT of the ginseng, by a decree centuries old, belongs to the Emperor of China. Wherever it grows, it is his, and one legend of the wild plant, even older, says only a pure man can find it.

It comes up out of the ground once in six years and does not stay long. On a slender tan stalk its leaves and blossoms grow quickly, but not toward the sun. It rises carefully up in the deep shade of the forest, in rich, cool woods, where it will not be challenged by weeds and grasses, or ruthless heat of the sun, where the earth is moist with woods dirt and the yeast of rotted leaves, on the banks of steep ravines, under the heavy branches of ancient trees.

Quickly, carefully, the slender tan stem rises, and at the center of its height it spurts out a solitary whorl of jagged-edged green leaves. They hang, indolent and graceful; above them the stem reaches up to support at its top tiny white flowers in pale green cups. The fruit, when it comes, is small and bright red. Below this exquisite delicacy, deep in the moist earth, is the root, sometimes forked, sometimes not, two to four to six inches long, often thicker than your thumb.

This is ginseng, *jen shen,* the root of life. That it and its elixir belonged to the Emperor of China, even though he paid well for it, was truth; that only a pure man could find it, legend.

With Jacob in her arms Cora walked through the silent grounds of the
deserted mission. Past the barn, infrequently used now by Jimmy Rode,
past the mission house with its windows broken and boarded up, past
the quiet chapel. She headed toward the old gristmill sitting on the edge
of the river. She moved quickly, looking behind her for someone who
should be there but wasn't.

Behind the slopes of Gore's Knob, steaming, the sun was coming
up, and the light spread itself down into the rising mist. At the sawmill
she lifted the flap of rotting canvas tacked where the door had been, in
late winter ripped away by someone cold, marauding for dry wood.

"Hoo-oou," she called, not loudly. "You in there?"

There was no answer. She stood uncertain whether she should call
again.

The logs of the mill were straight and still sturdy, laid flush against
each other, unwarped. But the chinking and daubing had fallen away
and the roof sat aslant, cock-eyed, tattered and ragged. At her feet, just
outside the door, rusted pieces of iron, a few rods and cogwheels, lay
half buried in the dirt, sticking out like collapsed, forgotten signposts.
The mill stood, a gaunt wartime soldier at attention, its vital organs
long ago ripped out but still there, unreasonably erect. A lizard slithered
out of the gaping mouth the canvas only half covered, and Cora kicked
dirt at it with one foot.

"Get on, hateful thing," she said. Then, softly again, "Hoo-oou. Are
you in there?"

She heard an equally soft reply. "Yes."

She lifted the canvas, ducked and went in.

Against the back wall a small plank platform had been set a foot or
so above the damp ground on rocks of various shapes. On it were a bed
and a homemade dresser, a rack for work clothes, a large box for a few
books, and shelves for rows of medicine bottles.

Since the mission land had been taken over and tenanted by Jimmy
Rode, Starns had lived here. He would not live in the mission house
itself, even though Jimmy Rode said he would rent a room there to him
same price. Starns told him he had built that mission, he never would

rent out in it, and lived in the gristmill. He only used the chapel for his services, to which some of the mountain people still came.

He was sitting on his bed, one boot on and one off, when Cora came in.

She moved quietly to the platform, wondering why he didn't look at her. He was sitting there dressed except for shirt and coat and one boot, hands on his knees, bending himself slightly forward. He looked like he was studying something in the board at his feet, staring at it with intense and rapt scrutiny.

"Well, morning, Starns," she said.

For a moment he did not answer or look at her. He drew in a slow breath and let it out again, then breathed half of a quick one and looked up as if listening to something. Then he smiled and looked at her and belched slightly.

"Morning. A little misery in the stomach, Cora."

He drew another breath, a deep one, and relaxed. He reached down for the other boot. "It's moved on now. How are you, Cora?"

She nodded that she was all right. "But, Starns, I need to stay with you today. It is Harlan again."

She put little Jacob down, and he stood on wobbly legs, holding her hand and watching Starns's huge fingers lace up the boot.

"Well, I got to go to the slopes today, Cora," he said, nodding his head at the bottles of medicine on the shelves. "I'm most out of a lot of needy things here."

"Can we come, too? I'll keep up, Starns."

Starns finished lacing the boot. Little Jacob, fascinated, staggered over to him and stuck a finger in between the thongs and pulled. Starns picked him up, sat him on his lap and grinned into his face. Jacob grinned briefly back, then looked down again, still thinking about the laces.

"Well, do you reckon it's all right with Harlan?"

He pushed a huge hand through the boy's thin hair and pulled at his ear. Jacob squirmed and pushed Starns's chin with his hand.

"I know Harlan has bad feelings about things now, the way they are and all. I'd hate for him to think I was talking against him, to you and his Jacob here."

"Oh, Starns, it is long past that," said Cora. "Don't worry. I just don't know what he thinks about no more, but it is long past that. I need to be with ye today, Starns."

He looked at her over the boy's head. If Cora said something was needed, it was.

He slapped huge hands under the boy's arms and swung him down to the floor. He got his coat, a big thick belt with several knives sheathed in it, a canteen and bread bag, and a large gunny sack.

"All right," he said. "Fine. You ready now?"

She nodded.

"Hey there, Jacob, go to your momma and we'll all take a stroll. It has been some time since we've done this, Cora, ain't it?"

"Yes, Starns, it has," Cora agreed. She picked Jacob up and sat him legs astraddle her hip. The three of them walked out into the valley morning, into the arbitrary and teasing light of the dawn.

They stopped on Gore's Knob while Starns filled his canteen at a spring. He knelt and swept away some branches and sank the empty canteen into the water. It was cold and clear, aching with purity. He drank a little, gave Jacob some and Cora some, and drank some more himself. It hurt his stomach. He belched again slightly, smiled at Cora, and they went on.

The spring season of 1863 had come very late and very sudden. The winter, tenacious, had passed, it seemed, in a day, and now the slopes fomented their gorgeous rebellion unhindered. A striped warbler flew over their heads and sailed to rest in a dark spire of rust-colored spruce. They listened and heard him sing, a jumbled and confused singing, a mixed hissing and trilling and buzz. They walked on, watching the white dogwood wave, the redbuds, the snowy trillium. Starns pointed once and Cora looked and saw, high in the crotch of an elm's branch, another warbler choking out his strange songs beside the bright orange fire of an oriole, which stood it for just a second and then, like a stone from a slingshot, spun away down the slope.

But most of the time his eyes were on the ground. Now and then he stopped, pulled something up, hefted it until most of the dirt fell away, then either threw it down again or cut it up with one of the knives from his big belt and put it in the gunny sack.

These were the plants from which he compounded his medicines. Pinkish-white bowman's-root, Indian physic. Purple foxglove, it gives a lift to the spirits. Deadly nightshade, makes a fine ointment for inflammations and corns. Leopard's bane, good on bruises and cuts, jimson root for the palsy, bloodroot for corns, hemlock for the great, deep pains.

He stomped on through the brush, head down, eyes sweeping the ground, slogging along like a dreary workhorse until suddenly he would bend, plunge a hand to the ground and come up with a dangling, valuable plant, tell Cora what it was, cut away the useless part and dump it into the sack. As it went in, he attached it immediately to someone he knew who needed it and sooner or later would get it, whether they might want it from him or not.

The clouds flowed to the smoking horizon and hung there. The midmorning sun was hot and fierce over the spring-wet, steaming brush of the slopes. Starns sweated and mopped his face, walking on with Cora and the boy behind him, and after a while the uneasiness in his stomach went away. Both he and Cora, who said nothing while she followed him, began to whistle and hum. Little Jacob flexed and unflexed the tiny, knotlike muscles of his legs, hugging his mother's hip with them, and gazed about with the slow, absentminded delight of childhood at the world to which he was born.

They followed a creek into a small bottom. In the meadow there, close to the ground, rippled a burnt-orange blanket of black-eyed Susans, receiving the full impact of the hot sunlight, reflecting it in a hot explosion.

The sudden colors, the orange flowers with their jet-black centers, were so fierce in their assault that they undid Starns, and they brought momentarily to his mind all the days such as this when he had ridden a fine horse through this bottom, going home to the mission rejoicing in his strength.

The outrageous blossoms tossed their burning color to his eyes, and his stomach gripped him again, the wrenching ache seized the folds of his belly.

"Lord a mercy, Cora," he said. "Them Susans are pleasant."

"Yes, they are, Starns."

And awful, too, he thought. "Cora, let's us find some shade and sit down. I'm ready to take some ease on this hot day."

She followed him out of the meadow, walking calmly, with her boy on her hip, after the bent, bald man who stumbled now from the orange fire of a field of black-eyed Susans.

They went to a stand of spruce, their bodies tingling with relief when they walked into its shade, out of the sun. They sat gratefully on the cool, soft needles. Jacob wobbled off to play ball with the fallen pine cones, and Cora settled beside Starns, who was lying on his side, head resting in the crook of his elbow.

He napped, and Cora watched him. All his hair now was gone, except for a little above the ears and the scraggly beard. He was forty-two years old and looked sixty-five.

He lies there, she thought, just as easy, just like he used to when he first come here, with me in that big walnut bed he made for us before Harlan was mine. I will never understand this man. Sometimes he is the oldest and the knowingest, and then sometimes the shallowest boy, nothing on his mind but sleep and the pleasance of flowers. How can he be such different things? And how can the man be what he is here now? How can he be something low when he has been high? How can he scrape and scrape around here, him who was once everthing to everbody?

Jacob tossed a pine cone. It landed a few feet away from him, hitting the soft needle bed with a whisper. Cora turned and looked from Starns to her son, and then back, and thought of her grandfather, and Starns in the room with his corpse, and how it had seemed to her then.

Like they was talking, him and Grandpa, striking bargains. Well, whatever bargain it was, God knows he has held to it.

She thought of the dances, the services, the one bell ringing the people down from the slopes. She thought of clean bonnets and smiling faces, of people humming and winking and playing jokes on each other and on him, and of his laughter.

Starns coughed and brushed his face with a leathery hand, one fingernail black where he'd mashed it working on the back of the chapel a week ago. He worked the muscles of his stomach, coughed again and turned away from her.

What makes a man keep on? Cora wondered.

When Starns returned from Stewart and rode to his people, he knew he would have to be quick, and knew he could not be quick enough. He was right. The Bishop had passed into myth, into legend, into instantly accepted superstition. He was the black Bishop who had lived with them in a black dress, and already they were frightening their children with tales of his devil's Order. All memory of the real man, in their hurt pride because of his desertion, they wiped from their minds. Only the black spirit was left, to frighten the children. The man was gone, good riddance, and another demon populated their long nights.

They were still glad to see Starns, though, when they were puzzled or disheartened about something. They did not forget him and his value, though they spoke warily when he came. They were still pleased when he played with their children and made them laugh, when he preached his quiet sermons to them, when he chatted about the weather and their health, gave a child a carved toy or a root he found that looked like a bird or a fish.

But his authority was gone, and he knew it.

When they were sick, and it came to real pain, they called for him, but now they were angry if he did not come as soon as they thought he should. Once, when he told one family that a woman's crushed hand had to be cut from her body along with most of the arm, the family told him quickly they would shoot him if he touched her. He fed her herbs and watched her die. The family would not let him bury her. And that night, in the chapel, when Starns held a solitary service for the woman and prayed for her soul, they heard about it and came the next day to make him revoke his spell. In the excitement one of them called him murderer and pointed his rifle.

Go on and shoot, then, Starns told them and gave them his wide chest to aim at. Only then did they remember what he had been to them, and, ashamed of themselves and faintly disgusted with him for his present position, they walked away.

I hope you may feel different tomorrow, was all he said.

Starns watched them fall back into their slovenly ways with the speed of weeds. Their farming became again the impoverished business of thin and neglected fields, half harvested. When he asked them what they thought they were doing, planting and pulling up in haste and indifference and selling to Jimmy Rode for half value, changing completely all that the fruitful years had taught them, they presented to him the face of his own mountain childhood and shrugged, told him to mind his own business.

Where are your crops now, Starns, that you should talk so big to us?

Once two men in uniforms with polished buttons rode into the valley and called a meeting and told the people there was going to be a war, that those who were men were needed to fight. Starns stood with the rest and listened to the flaring words as long as he could. Then he got up before everyone, forgetting how things had changed, and told them flatly nobody was going nowhere in no war. They yelled him down, what did he know about it, about fighting, man's work? He had to watch a few young men, haughty as roosters, go off to war for no better reasons than flaring words, many of them boys he had taught in the church school. He watched them ride, guns asling under their arms, and did not sleep for weeks.

But still, when he rang the bell on the post in the chapel yard, a few came down the slopes to him. He preached to them as best he could and prayed with them. They took their time about coming, the service never started when it should or held enough of everybody's attention to be called a divine service, but every Sunday morning there was one. They sat before him and remembered, the few who came, the singing and the crowds, so recent, so quick to forget, and they left the chapel feeling bad about coming and worse about Starns, trying to keep on with no Billy Cobb for the chants and the smooth sermons, with almost no ritual to follow lest someone remember the black Bishop and get mad.

Most of all, though they did not reason closely upon it, they missed the passion and authority of the deposed Bishop Ames. For his presence, either physical or spiritual, had given the rude church a power and meaning now revoked, annulled, forever past and gone, and for it there was no substitute.

But still, when their pains ran deep enough, they called for him and he went to them, gathering his medicine bottles and pasteboard-covered books with pages yellowing and torn. He rode the circuits and held his awkward prayer meetings for his people, who no longer believed what he said.

But still in their pain they called him and became frightened and then angry when he was too exhausted to come.

He turned over on his back, rested. Squinting, he saw Jacob sitting within a ring of pine cones Cora had playfully placed around him, and he smiled.

Cora. And that Jacob. Look at that.

Then the ease of his nap went away and his stomach ached again. He remembered what he had to do. The bag was not yet a third full and he had to pack it by nightfall. The sun, when he looked, had slipped past noon.

"Cora, just how long have I been a-laying here?"

"For some time, Starns, why not? Good for you. Here, Jacob."

She put another cone within her boy's reach and left him to consider it. She came over and sat by Starns.

"Listen. What am I going to do now about Harlan?"

Starns shook his head. He didn't know.

Of all the mountain people, Harlan reacted first when they were told that Bishop Ames had left them and gone to this place they could not remotely conceive. He said out loud, "Yes, I was waiting for that. I am not surprised. Jean, Cora, come on." He took his family back up to his cabin and told Starns if he came by again, he would not stop at the mission. He was through with it, he said.

"Cora, I don't know. What's happened now?"

"Well, you know how him and Jean have always been. I have never minded it, Starns. It was something between my girl Jean and me, his great feeling for her, and hers, too, for him, and we let it be that way. Jean is a good girl, and a smart one."

She gazed at Jacob, encircled by the cones, kicking at one of them now with his foot.

"Just this morning, Starns, he told me Jean wasn't mine."

"What?"

"Oh, Starns, he tells Jean I'm not her momma, that Margaret was. He hates Jacob. Oh, Starns, everthing was so fine, what happened?"

Oh, Starns, the Bishop, can't you understand it, he has quit us, said Billy Cobb's voice to Starns's memory, and he remembered Harlan that first day in the mountain store, when Bishop Ames told him what Christian burial was and said to him, Charms? Spells? Is that all you think it is, what I offer you?

He sat up quickly.

"Cora, listen. I don't know what to tell Harlan. Only the Bishop knows that. And he is gone now, but he will be back one day. He will know what to say and he will make it right, you wait and see if he don't. That's all I can say to ye, Cora."

He stood up.

"Now we got to move on. You want me to tote Jacob some?"

She shook her head sadly, picked Jacob from his ring of pine-cone playthings and followed him.

Starns swung the bag, thinking, He will come back, he will. And I will be here when he does. He will come back. He will.

By late afternoon the bag was half full, most of it ginger and bloodroot. Starns was disappointed. It don't come to my hand like it used to, he thought.

He was slogging along, sweating and mopping, when Cora stopped him. "Starns, listen."

They stood by a laurel thicket and listened to the series of shuffling noises, coming louder and closer. In a moment they could hear the puffing and grunting.

Then they saw the stooping figures top the slope above them.

They slipped into the laurel thicket and watched the shuffling, strung-out line of men and women go by them, not thirty yards off.

"Sang pickers?" asked Cora.

Starns nodded. "Yes, it's bad. Once they find that thing and get paid for it, they won't do nothing else. Just root for it all day, and run to mischief. It's the hardest thing in these woods to come by, but they won't hear that. It is bad. Hush, let them go on by."

They withdrew further into the tangled droop of the laurel and watched. A dozen people went by, puffing and grunting and muttering to themselves, their eyes fixed on the dirt. They pawed through the brush, bent over, touching the weeds and plants as animals absently paw the bars of cages, humping along like bedraggled bears they went, kicking, stooping, digging, cursing, humping on and digging again. Their clothes were trailing rags and their hair hung lank and matted to their shoulders.

"Why, Cardell!" said Cora.

Starns had already seen him. And behind him, backs bent and their eyes glazed, Ellen and Cief. As he passed, they heard Cief's tongueless voice moaning to himself.

Starns held Cora's arm. "No, let them go on," he said.

"I didn't know they had fallen to that," she said. "There just ain't enough for them at home, I reckon."

"I reckon," said Starns. "Maybe they'll get some, who knows? Come on, let's cut through this way."

Not far from the laurel thicket was the spring they had stopped by that morning. Starns refilled the canteen and Cora gave some to Jacob while Starns knelt and drank from his hands. When he got up, he was dizzy and almost stumbled.

"You're played out," said Cora. "This here is enough, Starns."

He hefted the bag, only two-thirds full, and nodded. She took the bag from him and he followed her a little way above the spring into some shade, and they sat down. Jacob was hungry and petulant and did not want to crawl away from her, but she made him.

She set her back against a side of rock covered with earth and took Starns by the shoulders, rested his head in her lap.

"Ah me, Cora," he said.

I will have to ask him, she thought. I have always had to ask.

"Can me and Jacob stay with you?"

"Huh?"

"You heard. I'm asking you again after all these years. I don't want to go back to him, Starns. I am scared of the man now. Let me and Jacob stay with you."

"Why, Cora, you scared? You have never been scared of nothing, that I know of."

She shook her head. How could the man know some things so deep, be such a baby about others?

"You didn't know Harlan the way he was with Margaret. It is that way again. And I have this one to think about now." She nodded her head at Jacob, who was sulking, wanting his mother's lap.

Now, what am I going to do about this? he wondered. Harlan and Cora. Harlan and his yellow-haired Jean, who rode the slopes with him once. Harlan, whom he married to Cora, the only woman Starns ever got along with, because Cora wanted Harlan and he wanted her, and Starns loved them both. Their family had been his pleasure and, when Jacob came, his unvaunted pride.

He sat up away from her and did not know what to say. He thought of Cora and Cief in the empty fields with him when he first came, thought of Cief and Ellen now, humping along behind the crazed sang pickers.

He will come back, he will. But what can I do now?

He rubbed his eyes. A warbler scolded him, mocked at him, and he looked up just in time to catch its stripes passing over the branches of a balsam.

When he looked down from that, he saw them.

"Hey! Hey!"

He scrambled on hands and knees to a tiny grove set under a shady overhang of rock above the spring. There he sat back on his knees and, grinning, he pointed. "Cora, look at that!"

They stood motionless in the deep shade of the overhang, reaching to their tiny height from the rich ground moist from an underground spurt of the spring. Their long tan stems drooped slightly, demurely. They looked like a standing pack of tiny, delicate giraffes cooling themselves in the shade.

Cora ran over. "Is it sang for sure?"

"It is." He took the largest stem before him and followed it down, dug and then lifted it up. It came out easily, and he rubbed the dirt off the root and measured it with his thumb. He quickly counted the rest and looked about with sharp, searching, counting eyes. There were perhaps fifty-odd plants growing around his knees, and three other colonies stood nearby.

"Cora, this here solves some things, damned if it don't!"

Quickly he gathered the sang, cut them to the roots and popped them into his bag. In half an hour he had them all and the bag bulged. Then he took two roots from the top, carried them to the spring and washed them off. With one of his knives he scraped them carefully and sat down with Cora again.

"Here, have some."

Together they bit the root. The pungent taste smarted in their mouths, but then, soon, they felt a gentle warmth and vigor in their bodies, as if the magic of youth was returned to their blood. Cora gave Jacob some, but he spat it out.

"He don't need it," both Cora and Starns said at the same time, and they laughed and gnawed the sang.

Now, then, Starns thought. If I take it to the Watauga and don't let Jimmy Rode know I got it, let's see. Twelve dollars a pound last I heard, maybe more now. That will be a lot of money. One, Cief and Ellen won't have to go with them hunchers no more. Two, I can get glass windows for the chapel. And, three, I'll pay off Jimmy Rode for what Harlan owes him, get Harlan clear, then things will be better for Cora and Jacob.

I can still take care of my own, thought Starns, eating the Emperor's root of life.

2

CIRCLE FOUR

Harlan

Wrong oh wrong. Yes, Margaret, I know I have done wrong.

Weave and click your shuttle and loom, my Margaret, keep your back toward my eyes and do not look at me. My cabin is dark, and I have fired no light for your coming tonight. Do not turn and look at me because I could not stand it, because now I know how you was always right, and me wrong, always, and them wrong, always.

But it was so pleasant. You was always fair with me, you will allow me that much. Pleasant to ride with them and sing with them and tolerate their spells and charms, thinking them just somehow not the same as the ones you and me scorned, different somehow from Ma's. And the crops, they growed so great and fine, and Jean, she growed so strong and straight, things went so well. And Cora. Yes, I have loved her more than you, I will not lie now. My snarly bitch, her legs my cradle, she give me pleasant, sunny days and soft nights I never had with you. I am bound to say it was pleasant, rattle your loom or not, it was.

I am so bound, Margaret, to tell you that I loved it, thinking it good and right, and, yes, blessing whatever spells and charms made it so.

Fool, fool, fool, Harlan, to believe such things. Yes, you are right and I am wrong.

Slow and sure goes your loom, you the only one to handle it, just as you was always the only one to know what was right and what wrong.

And slow, so slow Harlan to come into his true senses and see this, but now he has. It is clear enough now. I see that of all things, there is only one that don't fright me to death now. And that one thing is the thought of you, Margaret, saying there will be no spells. When you said it, lying here on this bed, when you said, Harlan, hush, I want no trouble now, and held to it, and had done, it was the right thing. It was fine and right, and I have done bad and wrong ever since, because they fooled me so.

His powers was all lies, Margaret. It was me seen him begin to lose them, down below the Fall with his black dress all flowing about without the rope to hold it. His face then, it was the very face of our ma when Pa died, and you and me had to conjur over him a-dying, and suffer all them hexing fools, and suffer her beating us when he was gone, and she seen he was gone and could do nothing but beat us, saying we faulted the charms and the spells.

In his black dress, he was just like her.

Soon after I seen him there he run from us and betrayed us and tore loose all, yes. Everthing come undone then, all the sayings and fine songs and prayers they put into us, that we loved. And all the other things, the ones I fear, they come again as they always have to me, but for these past six years me thinking that for each one there was a hex, a spell against or a charm for. So that when it would come time for me and Cora to join you and Orlean and little Joseph, it would be all right and good. So that when it come time even for my Jean to come to the dark ground and find us there, she would be all right, and it would be good. That is what the spells say, and the charms, that it is all right and good, and I have believed it until now, denying you, but you have come to me and I see you are right, as always, and no, it is not right, and no, it is not fine, and spells and charms are terrible things to make a man think different.

Slow, slow Harlan to come to see it after all this, but he has, and now he will come to you, Margaret, and have done like you.

But it is so hard to leave. I promised Cora I would work hard this month. Cora, yes, I must tell you I favor her still, even though this day she took her Jacob and run off to Starns. I ought to get ahold of both of them and prove her wrong to have done that to me. I don't want to leave it all the way it is now.

And the others. Like Juba and Tate, still charmed by them men. It was me, Margaret, wasn't it, who said, Yes, the mission can come on into the valley. It was me said so when that Bishop was at me about burying you, and when Jacob Larman was saying, Well, Harlan, well? I have got to go see them all. I can't leave them the way they are now.

Or leave Jean. Not my girl. No.

Margaret, when we was babies, you must have stole all my strength and kept it, for I have none. But wait. Just a little while longer click and weave, wait till I see what to do. Weave and click and wait.

Jean, you are in the yard now, standing there frighted, scared of your poor miserable daddy. But if I call, you will come to me, like you always have come to me, taking my knotted-up, dirty hands in yours and never minding my smell and sweat and black looks, but laughing and tossing your yellow hair, Jean, how can I leave you?

Jean, would you come to plow a field one day without me, with one of them charmers?

Jean, come in the cabin. Come in, honey, to me.

Juba

Since both my boys went off to see about the war there has been silence here. I have nothing to say now. Tate neither. I counted on Starns keeping them from it, and he tried but failed me, they paid him no mind and rode off, guns fierce, to win whatever war this is all by theirselves.

I said, Juba, it is time, let them go, but Juba would have none of that this time, and since they left it has been silent here.

So tonight, when the moon fulled and bats flew out of it and the things of the night commenced to crawl and hoot, there was nobody here but me and Tate again, after all this time. I had not enough for my hand, I had little to put my hand to, and so I started this walk in the night, and just when I left I passed Tate drunk, making a hair bullet.

I couldn't put up with that. I looked and left. He paid me no mind, and I couldn't raise a care about it.

I have come down to the cornfield and stood here. The corn is just now a-rising, and I did not know why it was here I come to stand. I said, oh, Tate, Tate, over a few times, but knowed he wasn't about to come to me like he did all them years ago when we walked out here together.

I recalled the time when I was this little girl and had a play sister I called and talked to, her to look and sound different ever time, and be different people I wanted to treat a certain way, and all that. I called her again, and she come, with a black ribbon about her neck and a new bonnet on her that I wanted, and a smile with two teeth out of her mouth. She had not growed old like me. She come, and we talked about everthing. We talked about my boys, and Starns who has failed me, and the black Bishop who has disallowed us all here, and she did not seem to mind it all so much. We talked then, in the place right here where me and Tate come years ago.

I heard some ruckus up the slope, near Harlan's cabin it seemed, one gunshot and then another, and it scared my play sister plumb away. I stood in the corn just rising out of the ground and wished for tassels to hit and a stalk to slap, just that aimless and empty-handed I was.

I was deep in regrets, yes, that sour I was. But the wind over the shoots and the shiny moon so near and soft, it took ahold of me and I was able, of a sudden, to forget my boys and to remember Tate and me when we come here, when we was young.

When at nights he would say, Juba? and I would say, Yessir? and he would take me out and lay me down young here where we wanted the thick stalks and soft tassels, and here, with a moon in a yellow night, we would make the corn grow. Both boys that lived, both Lafe and little Tate, they come into me in this field, in this place, both of them, and the corn them years rose like weeds from where Tate laid me down, young.

Young or old, I thought, what does it matter now? My boys are gone and Tate is crazy as a witch, making a hair bullet. The Bishop disallowed us and Starns cannot undo it, and me, I am just a dried-up old stalk myself from thinking on it, a wrinkly old woman, the kind I laughed at and giggled at, but dreaded, too, when I was a girl and made their sop for them.

In these black thoughts I heard him cough. It was Tate. He had no hair bullet neither, and his eyes was clear. The moon was on his face and it was calm and he come and touched my arm.

He is here now and I remember them old women and the sop I made for them, made so quick and fast, to get out and meet Tate. And later, when we come here, cooking fast then, too, to get it over soon and come here and do together for our field what the moon meant us to, soberly sharing what love we had with the yellow night and soft dirt and the deep seeds commencing to move, to come open and grow us corn and children.

Oh. There is somebody with us in this field. Moving to us through the shoots. Scared us for a minute.

It is only Harlan.

Cora

Hush, Jacob. Hush. It is not for me I am running with you, not for me. It is for you. I would not run from him else it was for you, my baby. Your pa will not get you, Jacob, I will see to that, but if it was only me I would turn and wait and let him find me. And I would tell him what is in me, I would hold out my arms and say, I am still the same woman, I do not care, and I would let him do what he wants with me. I would but for you turn and hold and tell him that chanty that only now do I remember aright from the years I run wild and only now know what it means, I would turn and hold, say, What does it matter, let me be told, where the body goes when the heart is cold.

Hush, Jacob. It is not for me I am running now.

Jimmy Rode

It was a long time I had been after Starns to come down and admit his Bishop was a fool and done badly by us, but he never would. I waited for the day I knowed would come, the day he would cuss that man. Then it did come, and then I felt worse about it than anything ever.

I was setting in my store talking with John Barco. It was not so cold, but we had a fire anyways and John put hisself down for a drink or two of my choice best, and I felt so good that night I give him some extra and took a little myself. That won't happen unless I am feeling fine, and I was. We was in there carrying on when they come to the door, and we both sat up looking at each other, because we could tell there was a lot of people out there.

I opened up the door. They was all in a bunch, talking to each other, a-quacking like the duck, and they asked me where was Starns. I said, He's not in the gristmill? and they said, no, they'd gone there first, and John Barco said, Well, what's wrong now?

I seen Cora then. She was standing in the middle of them with her shoulders all scrooched up, and they was bunched and gathered around her so she would stay there in the middle. She held little Jacob right up against her, gripping that child like a builder's vice. Her hair was all wild, like when she was young and wild and tore up and down these slopes a-rutting, but now she was in the middle of them, looking all around for something wasn't there but she was sure would be.

Then they told us what Harlan done, hadn't we heard him shooting?

Me and John had been carrying on so we hadn't heard Harlan with his rifle gun shoot his little Jean, go after Cora, and then end up slaying both Juba and Tate Benson where they stood in their field.

Such powerful torment, they said, to do that. But is it still in him? they wondered, bunching in around Cora, and where is he now? Cora said, Somewhere, he won't stop now, and they held their rifle guns like the man who waits on the bear and knows it will be one shot or none.

Well, come in, come in, I told them, and they gathered in the store, sending Cora in first and leaving Cardell and Earl there at the door to watch, and then asking me, Tell us, Mr. Rode, what do we do? How do we get Harlan and stop him? What do we do, James Rode?

I said, Well, well, we got enough guns here. Just wait till he comes and then shoot the madman down.

Cora made a noise at that, and they all looked at me sour and nodded, as if to say, well, we know that, that's plain to anybody, shoot him
down. But we don't want to do that. How can we stop him without
killing him? How, Mr. James Rode?

I wished for Jacob Larman then, or Bishop Ames, or somebody,
because I didn't know. I wanted them to stop calling me James Rode,
just say Jimmy, and let be, because I didn't know what to do.

Starns, I thought. Where are you? Why don't you get here?

Chips flew at the door, and Cardell and Earl flung theirselves in.
They hit the floor and lay listening.

Then we all heard him out there a-yelling, and John Barco put his
head up to the window quick and took it away quick, and said, He's
about thirty yards off, ye can see him plain in the moonlight. He looked
again, said, And he's hauling something, can't tell what.

It's Jean, said Cora. Oh, Harlan, she said, and clamped that baby boy
to her in them arms until it choked, and some of the others took him
from her and held him and her both.

I was scared but mad at myself, too. Big Mister James Rode, wanting
to be Jacob Larman or Bishop Ames, and now that trouble had come
for sure, was so tiny and shaking he couldn't even look at it. I went to
the window.

The moon was out, fulled, shining down all over Harlan where he
stood a ways out. Couldn't see his face, just him standing in the silver
light, one hand waving his rifle gun and the other holding something.
He moved and I seen it was Jean, her body on his hip.

He slung gunstock to his shoulder with that one arm and fired.
Splinters and chips flew on the door again. When I looked again he let
her little body loose and I seen her fall down in the dirt at his feet and
the moon strike that yellow hair all tangled over her head.

Harlan was ramrodding his gun, yelling and cussing, when Starns
come running from around back of the chapel. He was moving fast and
couldn't stop when he seen Harlan, not all at once, and so he sort of
staggered to a stop there and the two of them looked at each other in
the silver night, and it was bad, bad.

Starns's mouth fell open and he pointed there at Jean and Harlan said something to him and ramrodded. Starns said something back and moved toward him, and at the window we yelled.

"Get away from him!" we yelled. "He's killed three already! Run, Starns! Get in here! Over here!"

That made Harlan mad, I reckon, because he turned and flipped the gun up and fired. The ball hit the window and busted it, and down we slid.

When we looked again, Starns was on him, had the gun. He made his mistake right there, because he was so mad at that gun that while he was slamming the barrel on a rock, Harlan run. Starns drove in the sides of the barrel, and Harlan, like some thief with a precious poke, took up Jean and run all doubled up to the big barn and got in, carrying her, and then swung the doors shut.

We run out and told Starns what had happened.

I said, "Starns, you say what to do. I don't know. You say and Jimmy Rode will do what you tell him to."

He didn't even look at me, but that was all right.

Cora was on the steps of the store then, holding Jacob again, and he said, "Cora, are you all right?"

"Yes, I am. Don't let nobody hurt him, Starns," she said.

"No, Cora, I won't," he said, and looked at the barn. The man was just then having it all sink it, what Harlan had done, and he stood looking at the barn door like a man will look at his house burned down to ashes and rocks.

We all waited on Starns.

He went to the barn. We went after him.

He jerked open them doors and let them hang open wide. It was dark in there. Harlan didn't answer when he called.

"He's in there," Starns said. "I can hear him. Send somebody for a lantern."

I did, and while we waited I heard Harlan, too, heard him breathing and moving about in the hay. He was back near the toolroom, I figured, and Starns said, yes, he thought so too.

The lantern come and Starns took it. He told everbody to get plumb away, said it in this loud voice so Harlan would hear. They went, but I stayed at the door. It was the least a man like me could do now, acting so big all this time and remaining so little. I waited, and so I seen it happen. Seen it all fall out the way it did.

When Starns held up the lantern and walked in the barn, the light showed where Harlan was easy enough. He was on the straw piled up against the toolroom, his hand over Jean's face, looking to her there where he had set up her against the straw. He was talking to her.

Starns waited some. Then he went a few steps more, said, "Harlan."

Harlan turned away from Jean then. Looked at Starns blazing hate and fury. "Conjur this," he said. "Hex this." And then he jumped up and run at Starns with a barlow knife.

Harlan chased him around the barn. Starns, he was moving like a fast little boy chased by a bigger one; he would duck and dodge and stop and, most crying, say, "Now, Harlan, wait. Now, Harlan, wait," and then jump and duck and dodge again until finally he slipped on the straw and went to his knees, banging the lantern down. Harlan flung hisself at Starns and cut at him, almost missing but scraping his arm with the blade. Starns got him off, but he was a-bleeding when he come up.

Now, I had always wondered about William Starns, how he would move mad, like other men get mad. I never seen it until that night, when he come up bleeding. He looked around him and seen the pitchfork standing there by the toolshed. He had it and turned and gripped that thing.

Harlan come yelling and swinging, and Starns ripped into him, hit Harlan full in the stomach with that fork, drove it through him so hard the stained tips of the thing come out of Harlan's back.

Harlan went all loose then and finished. The knife fell and then Harlan fell, but still could not go down because Starns's grip on the pitchfork was so mighty it held Harlan up, hanging.

Then the anger went away from Starns, though he would still grip that fork. I seen it so plain. At the pitchfork he stared, up and down the handle in his hands, for the longest time. A man could see it meant something awful to him, the way he had killed Harlan.

He stood there and would not take his hands or eyes from the fork.

Everbody come in with me then, and somebody said, "Starns, let him loose, let him loose."

Then it was he looked from the handle of the fork to where it went in, and to Harlan's face.

That was when he cursed Bishop Ames. He said something about a little girl and some dead dogs and cursed Bishop Ames.

John Barco and some others then, with me, moved finally, and we got to Starns and took Harlan from him. Earl Larman, it was, held Harlan, and John Barco started to pull away the fork and then left it, while Starns watched.

We slid Harlan down on the straw, and he set there, alive for a minute until from his mouth the blood come and spilled onto the straw, staining it there next to his Jean's little hand where it lay.

Cora come in then and said, "Oh, Starns," and then she sat down with Harlan in the straw.

That was when he moved again, did Starns, and I know that on the cold slopes and in the dark woods that night the brutes and beasts and all creatures was froze in their tracks, as we was, when he throwed back his bald head and howled like a great dog.

3

NESTOR'S DEATH

THROUGH THE NARROW, treacherous ruts of a road in the flatlands of eastern Carolina a wagon bounced and jolted recklessly, traveling in a cold winter afternoon of the year 1865. Above the wagon, scudding clouds revolved in the wind, and before it a faint greenish tinge spread out on the white-sand soil of the road.

An old woman turned her dark, frightened face toward the sky, peering apprehensively upward from the wagon bed. One horizon was luminous, and the air was thick. There was a muttering of distant thunder.

"Stom fo sho," said the old woman.

With one hand, cramped and twisted as seawood, she clutched a black cotton shawl's corners to the hollow of her dark throat, and with the other held hopelessly to the side of the wagon. The shuddering blows of the wagon wheels slamming into rocks and rain-washed holes jolted her, shook her heavy, pendant flesh through to the bone. Each impact lifted and smacked her down again against the hard boards of the wagon bed. It happened any moment she forgot to anticipate it.

"Whoo. Shoo. Praise God."

With her, sitting close down in the wagon bed, were two other Negroes, a young man and his wife. From time to time they looked timidly out at the country going past them in the green dusk, at board-flat, sandy scrub country bastioned by clumps of tough, tattered, wind-thin brushwood and pine. Every time they looked, she said the same thing.

"Yes, I tol you he would take us to hell."

The wagon jumped, a rock spun from under a wheel, and the wagon slammed down once again onto the hard, whitish sand.

"To hell. I was agin it, Lord."

"Hush," said the young man, but both he and his wife looked with the old woman, fearfully, at the driver. They could not see much of him. His head was bent into the wind, above his shoulders all they could see was the back rim of his hat. His coat, unbuttoned, flapped against one side of his seat like a wing.

The wagon was pulled by one tired and mouth-aching horse that floundered often and needed the whip. Sometimes the wagon wheels sank into the soft, sandy ground on each side of the two thin ruts of the road and slowed almost to a halt until the driver cracked his whip or hit with it. Then the horse would strain, lunge against his slippery, sweat-soaked harnessing, and they would move on.

The old woman kept up her indignant muttering. "I didn't git in this wagon, Lord. I was put in. Shoo. Ain't no sense in it nohow. Everbody knows the war's most over. Why can't we be free where we is?"

The young man leaned out and looked ahead, then reached quickly for the edge of a canvas sheet.

He said, "Lights up yonder." The three Negroes quickly pulled up the canvas and slipped under it, squirming down between sacks of sand, clumsily moving them about until they filled out the swell of the canvas.

The old woman chewed her yellowed lips and tried to rest the side of her head on the palm of one stiff hand. She coughed and kept up her muttering until the young man shushed her again.

With the creak and squeal of straining wood and rusting iron the wagon came to a halt. The three Negroes heard the wheel brake rip down and felt the wagon tip and bend to the right as the driver got off. He walked around and whispered to them through a crack in the siding.

"I won't be long. Don't worry."

His boots stepped off into silence. Faintly they heard voices and then a door shutting. Under the wagon a frog spoke, scaring them. They waited for a long time, lying cramped on their sides between the sacks, listening to crickets and wind.

"Done gone off and left us. Best go back to home."

"Hush up," whispered the young man wearily. "Git out of this wagon and thas all. You gonna have us heard if you don't stop."

"Praise God. Whoo."

They waited.

When the door opened again and slammed shut, they heard several voices, getting louder, the driver's among them. He was talking to two other men.

"You're sure that's his name, then?" He was excited about something. "You're certain?"

"Yes, that's it," came an answer. "And he looks just like you said, or used to, anyhow. It is most likely your man, all right."

"And you believe he's alive now?"

"Well, he was when we seen him day before yesterday, when we took food and things out there."

"Maybe not, though," said another voice. "He looked low to me. Had a lot of trouble breathing, I seen that."

"You say the house is right off this road?"

"That's right. Big house, but way back. Hedge goes up the road to it. Great big porch and all, you'll see it."

"You'll have to watch for it, though."

"I will."

"He was a funny-looking redneck, I'll tell you that, in that rich man's bed. He work for you or something, Mister?"

"Yes. Thank you, gentlemen."

"Shore. Yes, sir. So long."

The wagon tipped and bent and came level. The whip slit the air and the tired horse lunged into his harnessing. They rode for a mile and stopped. The Negroes came out from under their canvas. Without looking at them, the driver handed down over the seatback a sack of chicken and some parched corn. The young man took it and began to thank him.

"All right. Now, I am going to stop up ahead a little ways and see someone. Don't worry. If anybody asks, you are mine."

"Yessuh. Best we git under agin?"

"Until we're there. I'm sorry."

"Yessuh. Thas all right. Yessuh."

"Just say yes!"

"Yess, yess."

Under the canvas again, they ate their food lying down. The wagon rattled dangerously on down the road. The old woman, toothless, kneaded her chicken with hard, practiced fingers and sucked on it.

"Right to hell," she whispered.

The driver clasped and unclasped his hands several times before he raised the brass knocker. Then he knocked, with heavy, jerky raps. He waited, heard a bustling about inside the house. He knocked again. In the wagon the Negroes muttered to each other.

A woman, elderly, with gray hair and a delicate face, cracked the door one inch.

"Who is it?" she said. "Who are you?"

The driver clasped and unclasped his hands.

"They told me . . . a man named Starns . . . here in your house. Yes, that's right, William Starns."

"Do you know him? Are you his friend?"

"Yes," said the driver.

The woman opened the door a little wider and studied his face. She was thin and spinster gray, but her eyes were alert and steady. She decided to let him in. As she opened the door, he saw two other women standing with her, in their frail hands a rifle and a heavy pistol. As the door came open, they lowered their weapons. The woman with the pistol set it down on a table and picked up a kerosene lamp. The woman at the door spoke to her.

"Sarah, hold the lamp up. Now, what is your name, sir?"

"Jones. Mr. Jones. It doesn't matter."

"I see. Well, come in, Mr. Jones. I am sorry if we are rude, but we can't always tell who is going to be out there."

The driver nodded, took off his hat and went into the house.

"Git down. Somebody."

A lantern was held up to the side of the wagon by a young girl wearing a large man's faded overcoat. She had a freckled, tomboyish face, and her voice was sharp and pert. She spoke to the Negroes.

"You can come on in the house and get warm." She got no response. "It's all right, your master said you could."

"No," whispered the young Negro, under the canvas. "Git out of this wagon, and thas all."

The old woman snorted and threw aside her edge of the canvas sheet. Her gnarled hands gripped the side of the wagon and she pulled herself to her feet. "Stay in it, then," she said. "I needs the comfort. The Lord knows that." She climbed painfully over the backboard and down.

The girl held the lantern up higher for her, and then waved it at the wagon. "Aren't there two more?" she asked. "Yessum, but they all right. They loves that wagon." The girl shrugged, turned and headed toward the house. The old woman hobbled after her, but when she came up onto the broad, spacious porch, she stopped and straightened herself, arranging her cotton shawl meticulously. Except for that one long sea journey when she was a child, her life had been lived in the sight of a big house like this one. Its sudden presence was a comfort to her. She entered it eagerly.

In the parlor the driver sat talking with the three ladies. They sat straight in their chairs, as if entertaining him on a Sunday afternoon, though the night wind sliding through the large room was very cold. The old Negro shuffled up to a small wood fire in the large brick fireplace and rubbed her hands together and worked her stiff fingers. In a moment the girl brought her some hot coffee in a mug. She blew on it, sniffed its steam and looked about her at the large parlor room. It should look better, she thought. Fine place like this shouldn't be left to dust and dirt.

The women were talking to the driver, talking busily, with interest about someone. The old Negro watched them. They spoke gently and quietly but very deftly, picking up where the other left off, as if at Sunday gossip. They spoke one after the other, telling their story.

"No, sir, he told us very little about himself, and we have never asked."

"Oh, we saw right away that he was not a well man, but the Colonel couldn't find anyone else we could trust."

"We had to have some kind of man here."

"I beg your pardon, sir? Oh, yes. Why, he was working in some store in Fayetteville, cleaning it out and so on. The Colonel was in there one day during his last furlough. The owner told him he had to get rid of this man he had, because the man was getting too weak to carry anything heavy, and maybe he would do for the Colonel, you see. The Colonel talked to him and hired him on the spot. The Colonel was my husband, Mr. Jones. He was a good judge of men."

All three ladies paused for a moment, as if to salute the vanquished Colonel. Then the story continued.

"Well, he frightened us at first. Yes. He was such a lonely man. Just like he didn't have a tongue. Frances Jane, that's my daughter, sir, standing over there, she made friends with him first. I forget just how."

"I remember how. She got after him about something. That's what did it. Frances Jane, what did you get after him for?"

At the fireplace, standing by the old Negro, Frances Jane was staring at the ceiling. On her pert young face was a hurt, puzzled expression. She looked at the ladies, then the driver. When she spoke, there was defiance in her voice, but mingled with such weakness and huskiness that she did not trust herself to long phrases. She pretended indifference.

"Oh, nothing much. There was a stray bitch got under the back porch. Had her some puppies there. That's all."

"Frances Jane, finish your story, please. Do not speak in incomplete statements."

The girl bit her lip. "He was going to put them in a sack and drown them. The puppies. I said he was mean. I got mad at him."

She looked up at the ceiling again. He was in the room just over their heads.

"And what did he say then, Frances Jane? Tell this gentleman."

"He said he was sorry. He thanked me for showing him he was wrong. Said if I'd help him, he'd try to take care of them. I did. They're almost grown now."

"Yes, and after that, Mr. Jones, why he was suddenly warm and friendly to all of us. Frances Jane has just adored him."

The girl spat into the fire and crossed her arms like a man. Standing by her, the old Negro became aware of her youthful anguish. She put a cramped hand on the girl's shoulder and whispered, "Don't you take on so. It'll be all right, honey." She knew where she was now. She was in a house where the master was dying. Frances Jane shook her young head, but did not move away.

The ladies resumed their tale.

"I just don't know what we'd have done without him. Why, we've never had any trouble with soldiers or anyone like that. He would just go out and talk to them and they would leave us alone."

"Yes, nothing bad has happened here since he came. It isn't that he has really done anything much to speak about, except, well, ordinary things, food and cloth and all that, you know, things we couldn't get by ourselves, and he has worked on this house a good deal."

"Sarah, wait a minute, once there were some soldiers, too."

"Oh, yes, but that wasn't the same."

"Mr. Jones, they came up to the house—our own soldiers, mind—shooting off their guns and using the foulest language. We were frightened out of our wits, but he, well, he said that they were, too, and he took Frances Jane by the hand, took her right with him, and went out and talked to those men very quietly and then brought them in the house. We fed them what we could, and they were decent men, most of them just boys. He got one of them to sing a song for Frances Jane. Then they all sang, and she did a dance and flirted with them like a scamp, and when they left, they were very nice."

"What? Oh, yes. Well, it is his stomach. It's in his stomach."

"He got more and more feeble all the time. He would eat just two bites and then say he was full and couldn't eat any more, and then, finally, we had to put him to bed."

"Now, we have tried, we certainly have, to do our best for him, Mr. Jones. But we are not trained nurses, sir. He is such a big man, it is hard for us to move him, and all. We have caused him more pain than anything else, I'm afraid."

"Yes. And all he will say is that he is sorry to cause us such trouble."

"All by herself, at night and without a saddle even, Frances Jane rode to Fayetteville to get a doctor. How she found one, much less got him to come, we still don't know. She won't talk about it. Sarah, what was it the doctor said?"

"He said the disease was an internal cancerous affection, brought on by a life of exposure and hardship."

"Yes. Evidently he has led a life of great hardship and exposure."

"The doctor said he could even feel the thing. Right there at the opening of his stomach. No wonder he couldn't eat. The doctor said it is like he is dying of starvation, Mr. Jones."

"That's right. Just like he is starving to death."

The driver got up suddenly. "I want to see him now," he said.

"Well. Let's see. Frances Jane."

The girl nodded and slipped quietly up the stairs. In a moment she came halfway down again.

"He's awake."

The women rose and led the way up to his room, and the driver followed them. The old Negro put down her coffee and followed them soberly, taking the steps one foot at a time.

They had put him in their best front bedroom, in a bed with a white canopy hanging over him. When they entered, he did not seem to notice them. The girl went quickly to the bedroom fireplace, stooped and bellowed up the small flames, and laid on another log. The women gathered around the bed, and one of them spoke to him.

"Mr. Starns, you have a visitor."

On a white pillow his face turned slowly toward them. Out of a hurricane of crow's-feet and deep lines his rheumy eyes blinked until his sight came clear. Starns wet his lips and gazed at the tall driver standing by his bed in the dark frock coat, hat in his hand, the handsome, ascetic face still haggard from doubts and torments unconquered in Europe.

"Some men told me you were here," he said.

"Well."

"I wasn't sure it was you."

"Well, yes, it's me. How are you, Bishop?"

"I'm not your bishop anymore, Starns."

"Oh, yes, I reckon you are."

The ladies looked at each other, confused. The one who had opened the door to the driver spoke gently.

"We will leave you gentlemen to converse alone."

Decorously they filed out of the room, passing the old Negro, who stepped aside into the shadow cast by the open door. Frances Jane, before she followed them, spoke fiercely to the driver.

"Don't you dare bother him."

In the hallway the ladies looked at each other. Their voices floated into the sickroom.

"Bishop? A bishop?"

"Well, why not? If anybody deserves one, he does. Anyway, it is not our business."

"But why did he say Bishop?"

"Maybe that's his name instead of Jones. Or maybe he is a bishop, he looks like one. Anyway, I certainly don't intend to ask. Sarah, now, that's all. Hold the lamp up higher, please."

Their voices faded away.

"How's Rachael?"

"I don't know. Well, the last I heard."

"Oh. How was Rome, Italy?"

"I didn't stay there long."

"I didn't think you would."

There was a long silence. The driver laid his hat on the bed and stood clasping and unclasping his hands. From the shadow of the door, slowly as if hunting, the old Negro emerged. She moved forward until she felt she was within the circle of this master's suffering, and then stopped, and felt at peace with herself. His sunken cheeks and tired, filmy eyes, like the big house, comforted her. She was where she belonged, she felt.

Slowly Starns managed a grin. "Well, Bishop, it is like you see. Some old bitches got ahold of me, after all."

"Ha. Yes, they think a lot of you, Starns."

"Well, they are good people. And I can't do nothing about it, noways."

The driver's hands were clasped tight. "I am glad God gave me this chance to see you again," he said.

"Are you?"

"Shall I pray with you, Starns?"

"Nossir."

"That is what I came here to do."

"Yes, I reckon it is. But you ain't going to do it."

"Because I am not your Bishop anymore?"

"No, no. You are still that to me."

"Why, then?"

"Where you been all this time?"

"What?"

"I say, where you been all this time? Why did you go? Harlan is dead, and his Jean by his own hand, and Juba and Tate."

"Starns, I am sorry."

"You killed them."

"Starns."

The old Negro stepped closer to the bed. Her eyes brooded on the sick man's face, on the agony that was twisting his features. She welcomed it without wondering about it or listening to what was being said. She took it as her own. "Praise God," she whispered, and stole yet closer. She did not think it would be very long now.

"Yes," Starns said. "Yes, you killed them. And Harlan with my hands." *Yes, you come to me and to them, and you give us something wonderful to do in this life and then left and it all left with you, went away when you did.* "Oh, I tried to keep it going, but I failed. You wasn't there. I could not do it by myself." *Why did you? Why bring us to that place so fine and warm and then leave?* "What happened to you, Bishop?"

"Starns, I had to do what I thought right."

"Then, all that, it was right? Harlan killing his Jean, his own child, and then me him, that was right?"

"Starns, I did not do that. That was not my doing."

"Whose, then?" *I'll never forgive you for it neither, not if I was to live on a thousand years. Bitty Cobb was right. You quit.* "You quit."

"No, no. I had been wrong. Full of pride. I had to make peace with the one and only God. I had to seek Him out."

"Well, did you find Him?"

The driver sighed. "I did the best I could," he said.

"No, I won't listen to that. You might have done the best you could, but it was for you and nobody else. So when poor folks with poor ways wasn't of no more use, didn't make you feel good and holy no more, then it was good-by to them."

"Don't say that to me. I have spent my life loving God and all His creatures."

"What for? So he could say to you, Go on lay down your load and praise my name whilst them that followed you fall in the river? Love me and be happy whilst they suffer and die?"

"Starns, you are all confused. Starns, God is love."

"Oh, no he ain't. Nossir, whatever he is, that he ain't. You can't fool me." *I know what that is. That is square scored-off beams set so flush an ant can't get between. It is sweating and ringing a bell, it is fine wood floors where the dust is light and rests easy to clean, it is the smell of that smoky candlewax a-running. It is Harlan's hand on my shoulder, and Cora and Ellen singing in the bright morning.* "You can't fool me about that. God and his love, that is up in the thunder and the rain somewheres." *It ain't my brother's hand it ain't my sister's song.* "And it has always been too much for me. It has been too damn much for you too, Bishop."

"Starns, I must tell you that you are dying."

"Is that so?"

"You must let God love you, Starns."

"Let him love Harlan first."

In the fireplace a log popped and sizzled, and a new side of it sprouted flames. The flare of light caught the hem of the old woman's long skirt as she moved slowly past it. Now she stood just behind the driver, looking from him to the bed and back again. Her wrinkled face was a dark, angry knot. Her yellow lips gaped.

Why do he torment this man? she wondered. She inched forward once again, drawn by a deep desire. Starns did not see her. His eyes were on the tall driver.

Oh, Bishop, don't you see? It is you was God to me. You come to me and raised me up and we raised them up and then you just went off and left us. What kind of a creature are you, to do that? To make us love you, poor fools, and then leave us to ruin? "I cursed you when I lost you. But not until I killed, not until I hit Harlan with that fork the way my little girl's dogs was throwed about. Then I damned your soul, yes, I did."

The driver did not speak.

"I would have done anything for you. But you left me, and I ended up killing."

"Starns," said the driver. "Do you curse me now?"

In the bed Starns shifted his body weakly, and the driver saw that he was no longer a big man. Under the covers his form was wasted down to thinness. Half of him had been pared away.

Starns thought for a minute. "Well," he said, "I want to." *But no, I can't. It is just that way. No, how can ground cuss wind that freezes it and thaws it out and freezes it up again? What would I have been if you hadn't never come?* "No, I don't curse you none, not now. I am glad you come here tonight. Makes me think, what would my sorry life ever have been if I hadn't met you that day, Bishop, by that burning church?"

They looked at each other for a moment, then Starns turned slowly onto his side and said, "But I just wonder, would Harlan still be alive."

The old Negro saw that her moment had come. She moved quickly. "Watch out!" she said. "Lemme by!"

She grabbed Starns by the shoulders and sat her heavy bulk on the edge of the bed. He was in a sudden spasm, blind. She held him hard, gripping him so that his head was free of the bed. He vomited into a bowl on the night table.

She wiped his mouth with her hand and peered into the bowl. It looked like red coffee grounds.

"The mastuh has got blood running inside him. You git down and git them women."

The driver stared at her.

"Well, git!"

Starns retched again. The driver fled from the room.

She gripped Starns hard, holding him that way until they all came back into the room. His spasm had passed, but still she held him and talked softly, sending rich whispers into his ear.

He became quiet, and his sight returned. He gazed into the face of the slave wiping his mouth, holding him in her practiced arms.

"I am sorry to cause you so much trouble," he said. "Thanks."

"Sho."

Reluctantly, because one of the ladies told her to, she eased him back against the pillows. She stood up from the bed and let her old hands fall to her sides, empty and aching. The ladies came closer to the bed. Behind them stood the young girl, biting her lip, behind her the driver, staring at the dying man with brilliant black eyes.

Starns coughed twice, quietly, without blood. Then he began to open and close his mouth. One of the ladies bent over him to hear, but drew back quickly when she realized he was not trying to say anything.

The old slave snorted at her. "Hush. No call fo that. This mastuh be all right. He just got to learn to walk to his glory. Like a baby, he got to learn."

She hovered over the bed, drawn to him by the authority they both alone possessed, a life of bondage. In the large bedroom, firelit, under the ghostly white canopy hanging above their heads, to Bishop Nahum Ames they seemed suddenly two mute priests, one ministering to the other, at this passing of a life lived for others. His brilliant eyes reflected their devotion. His betrayal of William Starns, the price he had paid for his shaky peace with God, sank into his heart. He stepped back, away from their overpowering sanctity, shattered by it, the holiness and dignity given to them, two slaves of the world.

She peered at his straining eyes, now turned back up into his head. She laid a hard black hand softly to his temple, then touched the dry and failing flesh of his forehead with a yellow palm.

Starns jerked, arched his back in spasm.

"Walk, Mastuh. Walk, baby, to yo glory."

The driver left the room and the house.

"Yes," said one of the ladies. "I think so. Sarah, take Frances Jane out now."

Later he regained consciousness for the last time. His burning fever, which had dried him out like a wool shirt in the sun, left him dazed, and he could not see very well. But the pain was gone from his stomach. He felt much better, and realized that he was hungry. There seemed to be a light in front of his eyes, but he could not tell where it came from. Then he heard some people talking, as if from a great distance.

Madam, have you ever heard of Jesus Christ?
Shore. He passed through here about a month ago.

With a ghastly smile Starns remembered a sardonic mountain woman in a wagging bonnet, and he thought of the shadowed slopes of Valle Sanctus. His crops, the big meals. He remembered dimly the vision of Jesus he'd had years ago, sitting on a split-rail fence and smiling and waving, and he thought of people dancing, and he was very hungry.

He turned his face on the pillow. The light about his eyes increased. He blinked. His sight came suddenly very clear and he saw the fireplace.

A stick, back in one sooty corner, was sitting up against the stone, its top end smoldering. The fire had melted a piece of chinked clay, which flowed down and hung in a swelling ball over the edge of the stone. Starns remembered his speechless father and his wan mother in the cabin far back in the high mountains. He was so hungry.

He tried to reach out and touch the clay with his finger and put it into his mouth.

When Starns was dead, three elderly ladies mourned him with delicate composure, a stricken girl sat on the stone floor of the kitchen sobbing out the pure grief of her youth, comforted by an old Negro woman who had already taken up his duties and his place, and a deranged man in a flapping black frock coat drove two terrified slaves to freedom, lashing his staggering horse.

Epilogue

PROMENADE HOME

THE SWEEPING RAINS, hard on the land, did not come this year, and what fell today was soft and straight down. It will be a good season for the crops, my ghosts and specters, and if your pale hands could take up again the sickle and the threshers, you would do well. I have done what I could to keep it up, from the day I stopped being a soldier and learned what happened here and said to myself, well, there is no other place I can live.

So all these long years Billy Cobb has been here, walking where you walked, farming where you farmed, and preaching, too, sometimes, when he could stand it. And from my porch tonight I can look down through you, ghosts, and see the broken stones and dirt piles where the mission was, where nobody would go live from the day Starns left it. The moon shines down on the blackdirt valley, and it is something, but who would live there? Not me.

Yet on these slopes the land is good, and the crops will be good, though I have had to give up today on Starns's cabbages, they will have to round theirselves out without me. They will. Cora's Jacob, whose legs growed out longer than hers even, and whose thighs have been rich with children, he will see to them, or one of Cardell's black-eyed grandsons with the quick hands like his, they will do it. I am not leaving anything that will not make out without me, I know that.

Except the cedar chest. That nobody knows but me, and I don't mean for nobody to, neither. The coverlid, Cora, that you and Harlan brought me when I was sick, the uniform, and the Bishop's long Christ-like lists, nobody will know what they are when I am gone.

Or the big cigar box, neither, that I brought away from that tall house in the eastern flatlands when I went there after the war where Starns died. Them ladies give it to me, and in it the silver buckle with a piece of leather belt on it, and a pair of steel-rimmed spectacles, one eyeglass cracked. It was all that was left of him, they said, all that he owned when he died.

Or the letters lying under them. To me, from that artist and traveling man I wrote after reading a story in one of his books about his travels in the 1880's. He thought maybe I was right, that it was him, but in the change and slow reply of letters we could never be sure, because he, the artist, had never known him like I had. The story I happened to read was the one about his sunset man, a man he come across sitting by a riverbank at sunset, smoking a long clay pipe, with a face like a saint in the desert and a mind calm and placid. He had a wooden box beside him that he carried everywhere, in it old books and piles of papers and all kinds of Bibles, their margins scrawled with his ink script, histories and philosophies and poems and the gospel itself, rewritten, corrected. He was living with a tribe of ragged, store-sneaking Indians near the Croatan Sound of this same state, who prized him highly, living with them as their priest who made the sun go down at night and come up in the morning. While the artist stood beside him, he put it down, he let the sun slip down, with his bare feet in the river, smoking the clay pipe. The sun, this artist wrote, set that afternoon over the Sound, and when its tip seemed to touch the waters a great red shadow streaked across the smooth expanse, and the crazy man got up and waved his pipe at it in a certain formal way while both the sun and its red shadow went down together. He talked then about how he would bring it back up again the next morning and what a burden it was to have to do that twice a day, and the artist wrote his story about that, called him the sunset man. I read it and wondered, and wrote. Still, we never found out for sure.

Bishop, it is the first thing I mean to ask you about when I am a ghost, believe me.

Now, what is it? You are restless, all, moving about in the mist, looking to the brush beyond my hickories. I see that it, too, is moving now, and I will guess that the spirit you wait for is coming back and you are grateful for that.

And I remember now, when I was first ordained and commenced my preaching days, how he fixed me about the blessings, how he fixed me about that. We had a feast of some kind and I stood up to say the grace, a fine ordained minister now who could say just as long and pretty a blessing as he seen fit. The big pans was brought out and put on the table and I got up all full of thankfulness and invention and give a long, long blessing. Then you took away the tops and there wasn't nothing there at all but two peas and one bean.

And you all giggled like young'uns at hide-and-seek, and laughed at me and my long-winded thankfulness, and Starns, he peered over into the pans there very carefully and said with a straight face, Must have got tired a-waiting on ye, Billy. And then he laughed, and I did, too, and got the point, all right. Then the steaming food was brought in and we couldn't eat it for laughing. I remember that now, how that struck us all so funny in that good day of our lives, how we carried on and slapped the table and then later danced and I sung for you with Ellen and then later knelt and prayed and the next day fell to work and squabbling again.

I remember it so clear, it seems to me that you would, too, and laugh again like I am doing now, but no, you don't laugh, you look with your eyes that are streaming mist, you look to the moving brush, and now I see him, too, stepping out of it, coming back out of the laurel thickets and walking up through my hickories, the bald and smiling ghost of William Starns.

"Well, did you find who you was looking for?"

"Why, Billy, it's you. You are one of mine. Why do you think we have gathered? I just didn't know you, you have got so old. Come on."

"Starns, I will be with you in just a minute."

And I suspect that's right, too, because the throat that sang your dances and your songs is old and it has blood in it. I'm ready, there is nobody living I care for now, but, still, I do wonder just where it is I will go when I rise from this chair and step down to you from my porch. The preacher I have been says one thing, the soldier another. A man should feel positive at a time like this, but I am not. Maybe I will go to you in heaven, you with your hands all joined waiting for me to sing your dancing again with some angel playing on an ivory fiddle, or maybe I will go to you deep and tangled around the rich roots of this blackdirt valley and lie there with you forever, who knows?

Either way, because it is you I seek. In your smiles was my hope, and from your pain came my understanding, and either way I will never come loose from you again, my mountain people, ghosts, my own.

NOTE

Many major events of this book are based upon stories of the Valle Crucis mission, which the author heard, read, and wondered about during summers in western North Carolina. The true history of Valle Crucis, the actual struggle of the bishop who conceived it and the deacon who ran it, lies in bits and pieces in century-old books of church history. Out of some of these fragments, with little regard for historical accuracy of dates or attending circumstances, the author has tried to make a story with its own life and people and place.